SWORDBANE

SWORDBANE

Paul Joseph Santoro Emerick

To order additional copies of this book, contact:
Xlibris
844-714-8691
www.Xlibris.com
Orders@Xlibris.com
844931

CONTENTS

Chapter 1   A Duel Among Legends 1

Chapter 2   A Near War's End Dilemma 5

Chapter 3   Painful Memories on King's Road 10

Chapter 4   Reconciliation from Past and Present..............17

Chapter 5   Till Death Do Upon Rescue 21

Chapter 6   Unfinished Revenge 29

Chapter 7   A Father's Love for His Daughter 38

Chapter 8   The Oath to Make War and Death One 44

Chapter 9   Vanity with Knighthood 51

Chapter 10 To Bring a New Era 61

Chapter 11 The Plot Unleashed..66

Chapter 12 Reminiscing and Intimacy 77

Chapter 13 A New War Unleashed 84

Chapter 14 Unforgiven Memories.....................................97

Chapter 15 Love in Dark Places 109

Chapter 16 Finding Hope While in Despair....................112

Chapter 17 Good and Bad Intentions to Pave the Road....116

Chapter 18 A Father's Honor and Dignity 124

Chapter 19 The Road to Forgiveness................................129

Chapter 20 Winning Hearts and Minds............................142

Chapter 21 Tragic Timing of Triumphs and Plagues 148

Chapter 22 Sowing the Seeds of War and Death 160

Chapter 23 Sowing and Reaping War and Death............168

Chapter 24 The Dark Lord's Arrival 173

Chapter 25 Raising Hell on Dire-Wolfback.....................179

Chapter 26 Honor Among Raiders and Looters...............188

Chapter 27 Continuing to Pave the Road of Hell............ 200

Chapter 28 Discord, Division, and the Pursuit of Unity.... 206

Chapter 29 Tournament and Coming Full Circle............211

Chapter 30 To Finally Attain Divine Appeasement.........222

Chapter 31   Chosen Vessel of War and Death.....................................228
Chapter 32   Following the Tracks of Darkness..............................234
Chapter 33   Hoisted by His Own Lust for Loot.............................238
Chapter 34   Into the Wilderness of War...245
Chapter 35   Fortune Favors the Persistent 260
Chapter 36   A Love the Famous Will Never Receive 264
Chapter 37   Bride of the Dark Lord 271
Chapter 38   Birth of a New Omen...277
Chapter 39   New Revelation/Mark of the Dark Lord 281
Chapter 40   The Promised Reckoning..287
Chapter 41   Bracing the Reckoning..291
Chapter 42   Dark Passage to Hope 299
Chapter 43   To Lose a City or Not Fight Another Day....................304
Chapter 44   Dark Victory...314
Chapter 45   Finding Ascendancy and Divine Blessings 319
Chapter 46   Divine Abode 324
Chapter 47   The Trial of Freedom and Nonattachment...................329
Chapter 48   The Trial of Pursuit and Passion.................................332
Chapter 49   The Trial for Justice and Sacrifice...............................336
Chapter 50   Returning Home 348
Chapter 51   Breaking the Covenant..354
Chapter 52   Battle of the Chosen Vessels...374
Chapter 53   Dark Lord's Second Coming 391
Chapter 54   A Widow's Revenge 403
Chapter 55   To Mourn a Broken Victory..411
Chapter 56   Farewell to War and New Welcome to Peace 421
Chapter 57   Forging New Beginnings 431

Closing Epigraphs..445

CHAPTER ONE

A Duel Among Legends

Throngs of chants and loud shouts drown out any simple ambient noise that could be heard at the seaport capital city amphitheater of Citadella Neapola. The amphitheater was as impressive and massive as the cosmopolitan city itself, not to mention nearly as old, over 1,500 years. Both the city and amphitheater were heavily built using innovative ingenuity and concrete dating prior to the establishment of the United Kingdom of Swordbane, and during the epic age of the once great and fabled Lupercalian Empire. It was during that time the founders of that city, the werewolf species or race (also known as Lupercalians), used the amphitheater as both an entertainment spectacle and a means to dispense justice for violent offenders.

Though their empire mysteriously had withered and eventually disappeared along with the ruling Lupercalian species itself during the waves of barbarian invasions from the Nordlands north of their empire, much of their edifices including those of Citadella Neapola remained in use, and many of their former subjects also still remained in the very unchanged cosmopolitan environment while adding additional buildings in the city, reflecting their diverse backgrounds, including humans from both the Nordland immigrant descendants and the local indigenous humans, Citadellans (who still adopted their Lupercalian predecessors' architecture), dwarves, elves, and the occasional other small folk consisting of gnomes and halflings.

Despite the fall of the Lupercalian Empire, the city and much of the former empire's domain was a testament unto itself of withstanding the test of time after the Lupercalians' presence had faded from their former controlled lands while bringing various peoples together, led by an enthusiastic and inspiring Nordling king of the constitutional-monarchy successor state, which became known as the United Kingdom of Swordbane.

It was a kingdom that not only brought together the different aforementioned races into the original Lupercalian and human Citadellan built cities but also possessed over a thousand square miles with hundreds of settlements bearing separate distinction of human Nordland, elvish, dwarven, and other small-folk architecture in various terrains including temperate coasts and valleys, grass plains, heavy forests, snow-covered mountain ranges, and hot deserts including those bordering the Eastern Marjawan Kingdom.

Despite the golden age of the Lupercalian Empire passing, many of the kingdom's inhabitants considered the time they lived in, while not perfect, as still acceptable, with moderate satisfaction.

If there was ever a sign to exemplify that mood of content or even surpass it, it was to be found in the United Kingdom's capital arena or amphitheater. Thousands of spectators stood from their seats, excited and cheering on what would become the epic ensuing fight and one that could be considered the most legendary of spectacles in the both city and kingdom's history. Within the center of the arena stood at four ends, four combatants ready to duel. An elf from the woodlands, of moderate height though slender in stature, had raven-black hair short with the exception of the upper portion, which was tied back in the form of a topknot. This elf had sharp brown eyes and was wearing a combination of brown leather armor cuirass that came in the form of the elven linothorax design. He also had gloves along with decorative elven-mail boots and pauldrons. He was armed with an exotic elven composite bow in hand and a quiver full of exotic silver-tipped arrows. He also carried a scabbard hanging and slung to his back, carrying an exotic elven-made long sword that had a slight curve and it could be wielded with either one or two hands. Additionally, he also had a useful utility belt with a side holster holding a grapple throwing hook with detachable magnetic prongs, and an additional side-waist holster that was empty but able to hold additional objects. This wood elf named Linitus was a ranger who had just been distinguished three months prior for saving the very same person he would be fighting.

Opposite to the elven ranger was a knight clad in combination of segments of half-plate mail in vital areas including the cuirass, faulds, pauldrons, vambraces, and greaves, all overlapping an underlayer of hauberk chain mail. Her armor stood out with a transition violet-azure dye tint and bore an emblem on the center of the breastplate with a silver sigil of a dragon, the same sigil that matched her small round shield also made of plate mail tinted with a violet dye. This knight and her armor were both unique symbols of royalty. She was Princess Marin, also known informally as the Princess Knight for being the only female knight in the kingdom of Swordbane, not to mention being one of royalty. She was of near-equal stature as the elven ranger though slightly taller and noticeably more muscular though also of somewhat slender build. She had golden-brown hair that some might consider bronze hair, light warm white skin, blue eyes with a gaze of determination and sheer conviction of the chivalric sort.

Her posture, though different from her dueling adversary Linitus's, still showed a readiness of anticipation and versatility to let the opponent decide to strike first or for her to unleash a quick and powerful lash with a long sword that she wielded in her right hand opposite to her left hand bearing her dragon-sigil shield. Her long sword was unique in that it possessed an unnatural ability to ignite with a light burning glow of flame surrounding the blade. This blade, though not unique like her armor, was the same as that possessed by several hundred knights. She along with her fellow knights who possessed those same flame-wielding blades belonged to the Knighthood Order of the Eternal Flame. It was their personal vow upon being knighted to protect the capital (Citadella Neapola), their appointed king (who currently was Princess Marin's father, King Ascentius IV), and all the domains that belonged to the United Kingdom of Swordbane including human, elven, dwarven, and other small folk.

Facing diagonally opposite on both sides to both elven ranger and princess knight were two other figures. One was a small adolescent who was in fact a halfling bearing a black cloak covering a long blue robed tunic. He bore a small silver wand that sparkled at the tip, and throughout Swordbane, he was known as Wyatt the Spell-Slinger. He carried that name with distinction in his school of magic for being able to cast various spells with the tip of his wand in a sudden moment.

The other opponent facing directly at the Spell-Slinger was another fairly small-stature figure though slightly taller and built much more muscular. He was a dwarf with a full gray beard and a haughty disposition that could easily change depending on his mood. He carried a heavy two-handed war hammer made of dwarven steel and sported dwarven forged armor in segments including pauldrons, gauntlets, and boots that were distinguished also with the same azure color iconically associated with the kingdom's standard colors and as both the Princess Knight and the Spell-Slinger, except the dwarf's armor color had a gold embroidered color offset. He was known as Smokey Peat, captain of the king's guard who earned that position while saving the royal family during an orc-and-goblin raid in one of the dwarven fortress settlements while the king incidentally was there to tour and survey his kingdom. Prior to his appointment as captain of the king's guard, Peat was also a member of a rare elite dwarf order known as the Sacred Stone Clan Guard. As such, he was considered a dwarf guardian of the Sacred Stone of Karaz-Barazbad, from where he was initially initiated into the order in being tasked to personally oversee, advise on, and manage the defenses of the dwarven fortifications throughout the kingdom. Despite being appointed as captain of the king's guard, he was still permitted to carry and maintain the same title of membership as a dwarf guardian. This dwarf guardian in particular also carried a large barrel nearly his size surprisingly in a somewhat awkward position, being slung around his back. It was not just any barrel however, but one that had oil inside and would easily be set off by a flame when it reached the end of a rope fuse after being sparked.

After moments of staring and sizing up each other, the four combatants simultaneously reacted at the same time and charged at each other, unleashing their own forms of shouts or war cries as they braced for combat.

CHAPTER TWO

A Near War's End Dilemma

It was only three months prior to the duel at the amphitheater that the Siege of Marjawan was near its end. It was exactly ninety sunsets in which Linitus the elven ranger, wearing the same clothes and armament, encountered Marin the Princess Knight, who also bore the same armor and armament, in a perilous yet destined epic encounter. It was at that siege that the two figures would cement a monumental relationship unlike any other in the history of Swordbane.

The siege itself was a six-month siege and was the climax of a lengthy drawn-out war that lasted roughly twenty years. It was a war between the United Kingdom of Swordbane and the eastern Kingdom of Marjawan, which had sparked from a series of brutal territorial raids by Marjawan against the border settlements and fortifications of humans and dwarves that were on the outer periphery of Swordbane kingdom territory.

After the Great Massacre in which the Marjawani spies bribed a treacherous dwarf to gain access to a secret pathway, to plant oil barrel bombs under the desert dwarven border fortress of Grimaz-Kadrinbad and set them off nearly simultaneously with a decoy caravan that concealed flaming explosive oil barrels at the fortress gates. Immediately afterward, a somewhat small but deadly raiding party of twenty Marjawani Kalashi assassins flooded the inner gateway to initiate a killing spree against any and all subjects of Swordbane including dwarven, human, and even a few elves that were present.

It was not a random attack but one that was well planned as it was on the night that the king of Swordbane, Ascentius IV himself, was present and residing at a way-stop on his royal tour and survey of his kingdom. The Swordbane monarch would never forget that night as he lost a few people close to him including his wife Gretchen, mother of Marin. Gretchen, a queen but also distinguished as Nordling warrior maiden, stood by Ascentius's side and sacrificed her own body to shield Ascentius from a hail of arrows let loose by several Kalashi assassins.

Marin, five years old at that time, also remembered that night ingrained in her mind, watching her mother flip a table and instruct her daughter to take cover while being assertive and insistent to not let Ascentius fight alone. Though her husband would have preferred to not let his wife risk sacrificing herself to fight in his stead, he knew that he would have to compromise as he had done before between the values of his Citadellan culture, which was patriarchal and more reserved from having women fight, and his wife's Nordling culture in which it was common and even expected for women to share the same roles as the men, including in warfare.

It was that mixture of backgrounds in which Marin, while outwardly showing some aspects of what was considered higher Citadellan culture including in dress attire would also exhibit the same streak and penchant as her mother's Nordling culture in being assertive and being headstrong, not wanting to back out of a fight that was seen as righteous to be in. While her mother had fallen and her father initially reacted in mournful despair for the loss of the one he loved dearly, it was Marin at that moment who while also feeling the same pain simultaneously felt an urge to direct her sense of impassioned anger toward the same perpetrators that caused the death of her mother, not knowing that her father, lost in thought from the loss of his wife, had let his guard down and she would not risk letting these assassins fell another parent. Picking up a cutting knife from the floor that fell along with the table that she used for cover, Marin charged frantically in a craze toward the nearest Kalashi assassin and punctured his throat with the knife. The assassin fell quickly in his own pool of blood before Marin went quickly after the next assassin.

By that point, Ascentius realized the gravity of the situation in which he needed to recompose himself for the sake of not losing his daughter as he had lost his beloved wife. He quickly picked up his sword and shouted in anger with the same sense of frantic adrenaline toward the other assassin, who was facing the back of Marin and poised to strike her.

Marin quickly heard Ascentius shout her name and ducked just in time as the assassin behind her swung and struck the empty air instead as the second assassin still was ascertaining what was going on. Ascentius struck the third assassin, while Marin flanked and struck the second assassin by the time he turned again to direct his attention to Marin, only to find the sharp dinner knife piercing one of his eyes and screaming in agony. Marin then pulled out the knife and threatened to pierce the other eye of the assassin if he would not reveal who sent him.

Ascentius, much to his surprise, was lost at not only how deadly and hell-bent his daughter was for revenge but also at how learned she was to speak first in the Citadellan common language and then attempting in Marjawani tongue. The assassin could not hold back his expressions despite being in pain, to show that he did understand her on her second attempt, from the way he turned his head, and while he uttered nothing other than curses in Marjawani at them, both Marin and her father knew it was an attack from Marjawan. Her father, still enraged by the loss of his wife, decided he knew enough to no longer spare the life of his wife's killer and used his blade to strike and sever the assassin's head. The severed head packed in a vintage chest (a Nordling custom) would be used later as a symbolic message to declare war which would be sent along with a spear (a Citadellan custom) by one of Swordbane's emissaries to deliver to the Sharj, ruler of Marjawan. It was that fateful night that started a long drawn-out war between Swordbane and Marjawan. While the Sharj did send his assassins to strike and attempt to deliver a crucial (but failed) blow to Swordbane and its monarchy, it was done so in dubious circumstances.

No one truly knew why outside the Sharj's inner circle when they saw the Sharj held an audience with a mysterious dark-robed figure who spoke in an unrecognizable tongue that apparently only the Sharj seemed to comprehend. Some suspected the Sharj ordered the attempted assassination because he was possessed by the dark-robed figure, while others thought he was persuaded by sheer greed and jealousy to safeguard any attempted trade expeditions by Swordbane to find a trade route and seize advantage by cutting off Marjawan as intermediate source of trade for lucrative commodities from exotic kingdoms lying much farther to the east. Whatever the Sharj's reasons for attacking, little did either kingdom know that it was a war well planned and orchestrated as a distraction from a much larger insidious plot.

Now twenty years later from the start of war, one which was declared by the king himself as a crusade to exact justice, Ascentius stared at the jeweled exotic enemy capital, Marjawan, from which the adversarial eastern kingdom derived its name, finding himself full circle ready to bring the long war to an end.

The city was in a sense imprisoned from the various siege works that Ascentius's royal army had erected to weaken and cause the city to be given by capitulation. He knew it would fall eventually and that by waiting it out he would save lives, especially among his own forces. However, that would all change when the Swordbane monarch received word of news by one of his scouts that a contingent of his forces was being led by a battlefield commander to take the fight to Marjawan from within.

The king, as tradition would allow it, would consider executing any battlefield officer for insubordination, for waging war in this manner against his explicit orders to withhold the siege; however, he would relent and could not bear to do so when he found out it was being led by his own daughter, Marin. She was twenty years older, at the age of twenty-five, and had been knighted as the first female among the order of the Eternal Flame at the age of twenty. She distinguished herself in battle to be entrusted by her own father eventually with command of a small retinue of elite dwarven guardian warriors whom she was fondly attached to, admiring their similar, shared traits of impulsiveness and being headstrong.

While the royal scout continued to inform the king of the Princess Knight's last known whereabouts, she and her contingent advanced deeply near the inner city walls of Marjawan that separated the royal palace complex of the Sharj from the rest of the city. The scout had let the king know that his daughter was safe but her contingent's advance had slowed and was being surrounded and overwhelmed by Marjawani forces.

Angered at first, the king changed to a disposition of grave concern, for despite being insubordinate as a battlefield officer, Marin was still his beloved daughter first and foremost. He knew why she had done it, why she had elected to disobey his standing orders to maintain the siege and to infiltrate deep into the enemy territory of the city. She wanted revenge as much as he did, but she did not temper herself in the way he had to reason and be pragmatic in approaching war cautiously and with methodical calculation as was considered the proper Citadellan way to conduct war. To him, she took after and embraced much of the aspects of her maternal Nordling side, pursuing revenge with impulsiveness and without hesitancy. To be fair, he thought to himself, she did wait to strike once the siege was firmly established rather than rashly attack much earlier, possibly even before the army marched steadily toward the city of Marjawan itself. Regardless, he knew that while he had to find some way to rescue his daughter, there had to be some way to do so without risking high casualties among his besieging army. But how? It seemed as if it was a near war's end dilemma with no clear answer in sight.

Why not send another small retinue force with the best abilities and chance to locate and bring back the Princess Knight and her contingent? It was that sudden and verbally blurted-out thought that came into speech from an overhearing elven ranger scout belonging to the same small company as the leading reconnaissance scout that reported to the king of the princess's whereabouts and dire situation. The king at first might have resolved to reprimand the serving elven ranger that it was not his place to give battlefield and strategic advice; however, it was the substance of the advice itself that the monarch quickly knew was relevant and worth pursuing.

The king, astonished in agreement, inquired about the identity of this elven wood ranger, who revealed himself as Linitus, from a village hamlet near the urbanized elven settlement of Salvinia Parf Edhellen. It was the largest elven settlement within the Kingdom of Swordbane and only less than one hundred miles from the kingdom's capital and coastal metropolis, Citadella Neapola.

Ascentius, recalling that name from long ago, only became further astonished when Linitus explained further that he was only a boy, age seven, when the king first met him and his family while the king returned on his way from Grimaz-Kadrinbad after the Great Massacre to bury his late wife and former queen at Citadella Neapola.

CHAPTER THREE

Painful Memories on King's Road

As Linitus explained, it was twenty years ago and only a few weeks after the Great Massacre that Ascentius by royal escort marched back from Grimaz-Kadrinbad, taking the Royal Road, or simply known as the King's Road. After several weeks of traversing through desert, temperate grasslands, low mountain passes, the king and his royal caravan were only less than 100 miles or about five to ten days' march from the capital, Citadella Neapola, to hold a royal burial with full honors and lay his wife to rest.

The king throughout much of that return trip was in a constant state of caring for his daughter Marin both emotionally as well as tending to some of her basic needs, as she struggled in mourning the death of her mother the queen. Perhaps equally, Marin the princess was mutually aware of how this loss took a toll on her king father, and she in turn also embraced him to provide the same comfort in mourning as best as she knew for a five-year-old. As they sat in their royal carriage, outside the view and environment was somewhat also a reflection of the mood, with steady pour of rain and a gloom that hovered around the caravan as it traversed through an open field path surrounded on each side by thick forests while staying on the King's Road.

Normally through the distance, the caravan would be within sight of the large elven urbanized settlement of Salvinia Parf Edhellen. However, the dense fog and gloom prevented that from being visible. It was only through confirmation by sending a scout to navigate ahead and relay back that the king would find out how far their caravan was from the elven settlement. As the hoofbeats of the horse galloping could be heard and almost felt before a frantic noise of despair was unleashed, Ascentius as well as the rest of the caravan could tell immediately that something was not right.

They saw when the horse and rider both became visible that the rider was impaled with several arrows through his abdomen, dangling and barely staying mounted on the horse then eventually falling completely off. The captain of the guard immediately yelled with a loud voice both in Citadellan tongue and in dwarven to bear arms and prepare for combat in defending the king. This guard captain stood out among the rest of the guard, bearing a large two-handed war hammer crafted in dwarven steel while wearing elaborate blue-and-golden pieces of splint-mail armor in addition to a very noticeable two-horned helmet with a protruding center head spike. Fancifully smoking a pipe of exotic plant, this dwarven guard captain, was known by both humans and dwarves as Smokey Peat. He was intimidating and a stubborn force to be reckoned with despite his short stature in comparison to humans and elves. He had only earned his reputation after being promoted as King's Guard captain after holding back and fighting his way through the royal banquet room to find and protect the king during the night of the Great Massacre. Though Smokey Peat was relieved to see both King Ascentius and Princess Marin alive and physically well, he quickly realized they were both mourning and holding in their arms Queen Gretchen. As fierce as the dwarf was in fighting his way to them, he was equally intimidating in unleashing without holding back a loud dwarven war cry of mourning. To him, it was still a failure to lose one royal family member despite the other two being safe.

The dwarf immediately went before the king and swore that night that because he felt he had failed them as his people were hosting their family, he would indebt himself and serve as the king's own personal bodyguard to stay as close to the king as possible. Ascentius, still somewhat in shock, recomposed himself, and after looking at the great bloodshed in both the royal banquet hall as well as the hallway leading up to it, realized not only how fortunate he and his daughter were in surviving but also took note of how much carnage this dwarven guardian dealt and would endure to come to their rescue. Various corpses of Kalashi assassins lay scattered in the hallway as well as both dwarven warriors and members of the king's guard. The king's own guard captain, a Citadellan by the name of Marius, who temporarily sealed the royal banquet door and fought to the death, lay lifeless next to the broken banquet door on the hallway.

After having enough sense to assess the situation, Ascentius accepted Smokey Peat's offer and charged him from that night to be not only the captain of the king's guard but also the personal protector of the king, and more importantly, Ascentius made the dwarven guardian swear a second vow to personally protect his only child, Marin. Now several weeks later, it would be the first true test in which the king's new guard captain would be measured to see how well he would be able to keep those vows.

The king, sliding a carriage screen door after the immediate call to arms, realized quickly without even asking after spotting the fallen scout and the horse frantically dashing about. Ascentius immediately directed his royal guard army to maintain formation while calling upon spear infantry to advance forward, with archers staying to their rear and having both spears and bows drawn. Quietly, Ascentius gave his guard captain a personal command to switch places and stay inside the royal carriage to protect and watch over his princess daughter. Smokey Peat, understanding the king's wishes, nodded without hesitancy. Marin, somewhat in a state of anxiety yet also feeling the same alertness and urgency, quickly drew from her own dress a concealed knife. It was the same one she used on the night of the Great Massacre. The dwarven guard captain, somewhat shocked but also equally impressed, praised the princess for battle heartiness and determination to defend herself. While Smokey Peat would never have thought a human royal princess would human react the same way Marin did, he did mention as a verbal afterthought the praise that she must have taken after her mother, knowing that the late queen was a Nordling and one that followed the associated attributes of women in her culture to be aggressive to the point of fighting alongside males of their clan.

Marin, while nodding slightly to acknowledge the dwarf's astonishment and praise, had only thought of two things: to survive whatever came her way and to fight by her father's side to ensure she would not lose him as they did with her mother the queen. The princess did question why the dwarf had chosen to look after her as captain of the guard and not the king. Smokey Peat responded truthfully about carrying out the king's order to look after her personally. Marin, ever so clever, decided to compel the dwarf to watch over the king by simply opening the carriage door and quickly proceeding to the other side of the carriage to fight alongside her king father. The dwarf, still quickly amazed but concerned, followed closely behind her, though not as quickly as the princess. Upon catching the princess on the other side, Smokey Peat quickly saw a visibly upset but somewhat relieved Ascentius.

The king sighed and consented, knowing that despite the good intentions of the dwarf guard captain to fulfill his duties, he was set back by the sheer determination and headstrong will of his daughter to get her way, to force the dwarf to protect her father as much as her. The king in front of his daughter turned to the dwarf guard captain to order explicitly that when they did return to Citadella Neapola, the dwarf would be in charge of not only the safety of his daughter but also teaching her how to better fight and defend herself, knowing that it seemed to both of them that Marin was determined to make a habit in the future of being in situations like this, where she would need to know how best to fight in order to better survive. This would be especially true for any future attack attempts made against the king and by extension Marin herself. The dwarf nodded in a modest though somewhat cautious manner, knowing and pointing out that he would have to instruct the princess not only in how to defend herself in a fight, but also in how to follow the orders of the king. Marin, in her own cute five-year-old demeanor, both grunted and shifted in smiling, knowing that she would get her way to some extent in wanting to know how to fight even in the dwarven form of martial combat.

When the conversation concluded only moments later did the loud sound of scrambling and desperation of alertness from various officers of the king's army give way to a louder throng of voices. War chants in the distance sounded like screams and shrieks in very unfamiliar or vaguely familiar tongues, scary and frightening but the voices were discernible enough for both Ascentius and Smokey Peat to look at each other and see in each other's eyes the same validation of who their attackers were, with the king first verbally stating it was goblins.

Though the forests along the Royal Road had many creatures, it was rare for goblins to be there, not to mention a war band of them so large that it could be discerned from the many screeching war cries and tongues of cursing that could be made out to be in the hundreds. The king himself had wondered, with the timing from his return after several weeks from the horrible night in which he lost many close to him including his own wife, if this sudden event was not part of the same plot to get rid of him and his daughter. The timing and circumstances seemed most evident to indicate that.

As the screeching and war cries continued, the volume and intensity appeared to get louder as figures of goblins emerged from dense foliage of the flanking forestland surrounding both sides of the King's Road. The goblins were armed in various forms of scavenged worn-out armor while bearing various crude forms of jagged weapons varying from bows and arrows to short swords, and some even had crude blackened, burnt wood shields. They were terrifying to see despite being small in stature like the dwarves that made up a portion of the king's army. The goblins were distinct also from the dwarves in having various tones of green skin, a slender frame of body that was more jagged and chiseled in their features while having also high cheekbones, sharp jawlines, narrow protruding beaky or hooked noses, pointed ears similar to the elves', and various hairstyles (usually bound in a ponytail or shaved bald). Their eyes appeared very feline with a yellow iris and black pupils.

The king's army, including the royal guard, stood their ground and held their formation despite the frantic and terrifying goblin charge that came in full force. The ensuing battle became one of steady attrition with the king's forces being able to hold their ground despite taking some casualties and delivering far heavier amounts upon the goblins.

Marin, ever so eager, who saw that one of the king's guards had fallen, quickly picked up the slain guard's sword and charged into the fray where the fighting seemed heaviest. Again, being quick on foot, both Ascentius and Smokey Peat called out for her and went after her to ensure her safety. The princess, much to their surprise as well as that of the king's army and the goblins, had a strong presence of command and morale, inspiring many of the king's own men to break ranks and chase after the goblins, who quickly shifted in full retreat into the dense forest. Both the king and Smokey Peat, however, realized that this was a dangerous feigned retreat that could end in disaster with many goblins being armed with bow and arrow poised to let loose a hail of arrows upon their enemy pursuers, which they eventually did.

Marin and many of the king's forces that broke ranks to pursue the retreating goblins realized they were falling into a trap with many of the arrows picking off various Swordbane troops. Marin was fortunate to be shielded by one of the king's guards who sacrificed himself and his body to protect her. After only moments with many of the Swordbane troops lying in agony on the field yards away from the forest tree line, a second wave of goblins emerged, poised to pick off the fallen soldiers, some of whom fought back despite being wounded and having only limited success. Marin herself emerged from the fallen soldier that had protected her, only to find herself surrounded by a trio of goblins armed with small sharp, jagged swords. She pulled out her small knife and dared them to attack. As they were about to, however, a small stream of whistling arrows flew by and struck one by one each of the goblins.

Marin, in disbelief, turned and looked in the direction from which the arrows came, the forest. She raised her hands in shock, only to see two ominous and strange figures. They were cloaked in blue and were definitely not goblins. They were elves, forest elves, to be exact, with both having pointed ears, snow-white skin somewhat similar to hers, dark-brown hair, and very slender chiseled features. One was close to the height of an average Citadellan human adult, while another was noticeably shorter but still about a half foot taller than her. He was an elven male child, visibly and probably a few years older than Marin.

As the pair of elves, father and son, came forward, they stared at Marin. The oldest, the father elf, addressed her and let her know that he and his band of forest elves had beaten off the last of the goblins. Marin, relieved, stood and gave them her gratitude while still somewhat awed and staring at the boy elf, who could not help but stare back while holding his bow in and much like his father. She asked who they were while still staring back at the elven boy with curiosity. The father responded, letting her know that he was called Valentius Sidarn and that his son was Linitus of the forest-elf Sidarn family. They belonged to a small collection of elven hamlets outside the walls of the main city, Salvinia Parf Edhellen.

Marin, still somewhat lost for words while still ever so curious and fond of the young wood elf Linitus, was barely able to compose herself and thank them again before overhearing from the distance a loud and concerned shout from her father Ascentius, who called out to her while noticing along with Smokey Peat following closely behind that Marin was within visible distance from the cloud of fog to be spotted. The king ran faster and faster to embrace her, thanking the great divine forces that he had not lost her, while crying tears of both joy and anger and scolding her (out of fear of losing her) to never to be so brash to risk her own life as she had. Marin, recognizably seeing how shaken her father was, also was in tears, feeling remorseful of his fear, and promised to be more careful.

As the king stood up again after kneeling to embrace his daughter, he regained himself to the situation at hand and realized that these two elves had likely been the source of salvation for his daughter's life. The two elves recognized the royal emblems that the king had and kneeled immediately. The king commanded them to rise and again thanked them while telling them that it was he who should kneel in gratitude for saving him from losing another loved one.

Linitus and more so Valentius could tell from the king's face and expression that he had endured much pain and was internally in a state of tormented grief. Valentius placed his hand upon the king's shoulder in a modest manner and pleaded with the king that they were honored to be of service. Valentius went further to invite the king to stay with his army camped outside as guests to the hamlet and the forest-elf house of Sidarn while Valentius's wife, Efsuna, would feed him and his closest while providing the king with an elven herbal remedy to soothe him of his pain as well as let him sleep well. Ascentius agreed, and it was during that brief stay, while still never forgetting the loss of his wife, he could find some manner of comfort to try to feel at peace at least temporarily and find some sense of security to sleep for a time.

During that night and the next morning, when the king stayed and had meals in Valentius's house, he came to feel as if he truly knew in a more intimate way about his royal subjects and who they were as caring individuals who, as helpless as the king had initially perceived them in fulfilling his accepted notion of rationale to provide security and governance throughout his kingdom, could be depended on perhaps equally as much in his time of need. He pointed out that recognition as humbly as he could to Valentius and his family before departing and thanked them again not only for their hospitality, but also for showing him one of the greatest lessons he could learn outside his royal castles and tents. He vowed to never forget that day, or them. If only he remembered Linitus had become an adult instead of the boy he once knew briefly from so long ago . . . This would come as a reminder nearly twenty years later.

CHAPTER FOUR

Reconciliation from Past and Present

Twenty years later inside the Swordbane Kingdom encampment on the field surrounding the besieged city of Marjawan, Ascentius faced his own conviction from his past. He had realized that despite one of the most humbling lessons he had learned that he had in some part forgotten or left behind as a footnote in his life, the ones whom he was most indebted to.

He instructed Linitus, now an adult elven ranger and twenty-seven years of age, to follow him inside his personal royal tent to speak in private. Linitus did as commanded, and when the two were alone, the king suddenly kneeled down and pleaded for forgiveness.

Linitus, shocked and in awe, asked the king to rise and also asked what he had done to offend one of his subjects. The king, despite the many years tending to his duties, realized that he failed in doing one of the utmost in importance: he neglected his own subjects that he was most indebted to, Linitus's own family, in not seeing them ever since that day he left their hamlet on his way to bury his departed wife. He felt guilty of recognizing the very same one who had once saved his daughter.

Linitus, drawing from his own heart and sense of compassion where the king was coming from, accepted his remorse but told him that neither the elf ranger himself nor his family ever expected the king to see them since that fateful day nearly twenty years ago. He consoled the king that in Linitus's own belief, the king was a good man with a good heart who had his own path to follow separately with his own duties and obligations to attend to. He let the king know that the relative safety that his family enjoyed being part of the Kingdom of Swordbane was in itself the greatest gift, so they did not feel neglected, as well as the reputation Ascentius had of fostering better cooperation and harmony among the different races in his kingdom: human, elven, dwarven, and various small folks including halflings and gnomes.

The king, feeling somewhat consoled, thanked the elven ranger while rising to his feet. Seeming somewhat reconciled to the past that came to him once again including his daughter being once again in peril, Ascentius now was ready to move forward in the present. He set up various figures and a map depicting Marjawan to explain the present situation to Linitus and the other senior officers that he had brought later into his royal tent, including his own guard captain, Smokey Peat.

Smokey Peat was also somewhat in shock upon realizing that Linitus, now an adult elven ranger, was once the same small elven boy that the dwarf guard captain encountered with the king nearly twenty years ago upon that fateful raid with the goblins. The dwarven guard captain could not keep his composure and went to embrace the slender elven ranger while pointing out in reminiscence that this would be just like the old days, when the elf would rescue the princess as he once did when he was a boy and she was a girl.

Linitus returned a cautious but positive facial expression of acknowledgement, but the elf (as the king knew and could share the same visual expression) knew that it was an entirely different situation and possibly more challenging to rescue the Princess Knight than in those many years before.

As Ascentius laid out the present battle positions and strategies to maintain the siege in the hopes of getting Marjawani forces to capitulate, the king (ever so renowned in his repertoire of strategy and calculation to minimize casualties) had shared that Linitus's plan to send a small contingent possibly of equal numbers as Marin's when she charged into the besieged city would still need a creative means to insert into the city with the best success and least amount of failure. The king introduced that the wizards from the settlement of Colonia Aldion would be able to provide such support by using their magical services and contraptions to transport the contingent through the city to the location where Marin and her remaining forces were last known to be at, from the elven ranger scout group's last sighting.

Ascentius signaled with one of his hands to introduce the war council to the specific wizard who would be spearheading the transportation and insertion of that contingent. Near the tent entrance proceeded a dark hooded figure of small stature who gradually made his way to face the king and the small war council consisting of Peat, Linitus, and several of the king's high-ranking battlefield officers as well as the lead elven ranger scouting officer. The king informed the council that this mage was the newly renowned Wyatt the Spell-Slinger, who had a reputation from his ability to cast multiple spells in a sudden moment. The hooded figure stood at a low and similar height as Smokey Peat, perhaps a few inches shorter than the dwarf guardian.

Wyatt lowered his hood while gently bending his head in recognition of the king. The war council stood somewhat amazed to realize that this important and recently renowned figure was in fact a halfling who appeared to be no more than the age of ten. They, including Linitus himself, were dumbfounded, almost wondering or questioning if this was not a mistake, and the king could tell from their realization that more explanation was perhaps needed. The king let them know that despite his young age, Wyatt was the top of his school of wizardry and advanced in his learning, not only studying magic as early as he did but also graduating earlier than most other student peers to be commissioned to the service of the crown only a year ago. Smokey Peat, while taking a puff from his smoke pipe, still pondered with respect to the king's judgment, asking if he was that capable given the direness in which the life of his daughter the Princess Knight was at stake.

Much to the dwarven guard captain's surprise, Wyatt revealed the next step of their plan by using his wand and a few small voice utterances to shape the smoke coming from Smokey Peat's pipe to resemble a floating ship being attached to some round contraption above. Everyone stood somewhat amazed while the king mentioned that as the next step in their war plan while Wyatt cleverly cast another spell to make Peat's smoke pipe disappear from the dwarf's own hand only to emerge from the Wyatt's other hand not carrying the wand. Peat grumbled in a heap of feeling insulted, while being somewhat appeased when the halfling wizard handed back to the dwarf his smoke pipe.

Peat meanwhile directed his attention to the next matter at hand, what to do once the wizard had transported him to Marin's location, not to mention who would be in charge of this rescue overall, expecting it to be him as the king's guard. Much to the surprise of Peat as well as the rest of the ones in the assembled council, the king announced that it would be Linitus.

Linitus, shocked and somewhat surprised, objected humbly and initially raised the question of whether someone else more experienced and better for the task, including the dwarven guard captain, should be given command. While the king acknowledged the elven ranger's concern, he pointed out that Linitus had already demonstrated what the king considered the best needed skills to be the fittest, by demonstrating both a tactical mind to carry out the rescue plan as well as a past record in both combat and experience from rescuing Marin before. Respecting the authority of the sovereign monarch, Linitus along with the rest of the council accepted the king's decision.

CHAPTER FIVE

Till Death Do Upon Rescue

Along the ramparts of the exotic mud mortar and red sandstone walls of Marjawan and its sparkling blue glazed gate of monumental proportions, made of lapis lazuli stone, stood a long narrow column of Marjawani archers at the ready with bows and arrows in hand. From their vantage point, they could see the Swordbane army's siege works of crude palisade walls surrounding Marjawan as well as all siege weaponry that Swordbane had assembled, including large scorpion, ballista, and catapult platforms.

Marjawan also was equipped with its own siege platforms, including more-advanced trebuchets that hurled large boulder projectiles more than twice the distance of Swordbane's catapults. However, the Marjawani mounted trebuchets were still out of range from the nearest dugout barricades erected and surrounding the desert city.

Among all the various figures that Swordbane had commanded from a distance, one stood out and became clearer. It was small and rising high in the air while gradually moving forward in the sky, edging ever so close toward the walls of Marjawan. The city's defending forces, upon noticing the awkward-looking object, began to call to arms and its various commanders began preparing the archers for them to launch a volley toward this awkward flying contraption that came from their enemy's siege camp.

It was a unique object that Marjawan had never seen from Swordbane. A flying wooden vessel was strapped to a floating buoyant object with an intricate set of machinery like movable parts compacted together in an assembly above the frame of the flying vessel but attached also below the buoyant-looking inflatable piece that resembled a balloon. The Marjawani forces were both astonished and shocked in an alerted manner. The Marjawani archers held back until given the order by their garrisoned cohort commanders to let loose their volley of arrows.

As menacing as they might have perceived the view looking above, the same could also be said from the vantage point of the occupants on board the flying vessel platform while looking below and approaching high above the city walls. Various reactions were shared from these rare and surreal experiences. Linitus, taking in the view with a degree of awe and amazement, tried to balance out that feeling with being internally reminded by his sense of purpose to scout and survey visually below for the presence of Marin the Princess Knight and her Swordbane forces. The elven ranger was looking for anything and everything that would indicate the whereabouts of Marin and her contingent, whether it was exotic transition-hue violet-azure-like tinted armor the Princess Knight was renowned for donning while in combat, a Swordbane banner, an Eternal Flame Order banner, or even simply a makeshift fire or other signs to indicate possible wakes of destruction from the path Marin and her contingent would have made while advancing through the vast jeweled desert city.

Meanwhile, toward the port side of the floating vessel, two other figures had very different reactions from their surreal experience of flying over the enemy Marjawani army. Peat the dwarven guardian captain, ever known to enjoy the view and have a good smoke, was far removed from having such an experience. Instead, being intimidated by the height above and the view and what he saw from the floating vessel, he could not help but react from feeling nauseated, and he vomited over the side of the floating ship. As he was doing so, the flying ship's navigator and captain on hand, Wyatt the young halfling dark-robed wizard, could not help but laugh from what he was seeing, finding the dwarf's reaction humorous. The dwarf, taking notice, pointed his war hammer at the halfling and warned him that he wouldn't be laughing for long once the vessel went down and the wizard would depend on the dwarven guardian to save him. However, this only caused the preadolescent to laugh further.

The short-lived commotion, however, was interrupted as Linitus took note of the arrow volley that Marjawan's forces had fired upon them. The elf ranger told the crew on board, being a contingent mixture of mainly thirty or so human infantry, a handful of dwarven guardians like Peat, and a small detachment of the elven ranger scouting party to which Linitus belonged. It was a contingent of no more than fifty personnel. Regardless, these were considered perhaps the best that the Swordbane army had for reconnaissance and elite units to rescue the Princess Knight while taking the lowest risk for the king to risk more of his forces from being diverted in maintaining the siege outside the desert city.

While the Marjawani arrows soared ever so high in the air, they gradually came to a slow descent before landing back down helplessly on the ground of the open field outside the city walls. Even the closest arrow was still no more than a dozen feet or so from striking the ventral hull of the floating ship. To his credit, Linitus openly complimented Wyatt for his execution of placing the ship high enough to be out of range from the arrows of the enemy. Wyatt nodded in proud satisfaction while walking toward Linitus to assist the elven ranger in monitoring the desert urban landscape below to survey and locate the Princess Knight's forces. They could not help but notice also that the Marjawani forces, despite their failed efforts to down the floating vessel by arrow fire, still sounded large trumpets as alarms to notify various forces in the city of the intrusion.

Many of the Marjawani forces were revealed from various buildings and streets below, gazing at the floating Swordbane vessel from high above. Many of the forces were garbed in typical Marjawani military clothing, which were violet colors (representing their faction's national colors) in conjunction with various assortments of armor that their soldiers had donned depending on their rank and type of unit varying from archer, sword and spear infantry, cavalry, and (a few) elite exotic Kalashi assassins who covered their faces except for their eyes with black- and purple-dyed cloth. This army however, regardless of appearance, was unified in their understanding and reaction of perceiving the floating Swordbane vessel as a threat while pointing at it and trying to follow its path from below.

Not surprisingly, Marjawan's forces were not the only ones below to have noticed the odd floating spectacle. In one of the urban quarters of the desert city near an alleyway outside, intense heavy close-quarters combat was taking place between Marin and several of her surviving company of knights from the Order of the Eternal Flame. There were no more than a dozen of them left that survived out of an original company of seventy-five knights. Marin had lost roughly half of her company alone from scaling along the weakest and most easy-to-traverse part of the city's desert walls and lost the rest of her remaining company gradually through attrition as they left a bloody trail in pursuit of gaining access to the inner wall and to the city's royal palace in the hopes of capturing its ruler, the Sharj. They were in fact perhaps a few hundred yards away from the city's inner wall that separated the royal palace complex and the city nobility's estates from the rest of the urban quarters. However, their view from below made it difficult to tell how close and where the inner walls were as the small narrow streets had multiple storied buildings obscuring their intended route of destination.

As Marin was fighting and slaying one Marjawani warrior after another, one of her knights quickly called and addressed her by her title while telling her to look above and notice the awe-inspiring vessel that flew and hovered above them. Marin was not sure how to make sense of what was happening or who the ones in the vessel above were, but she did not care as long as she was able to gain access to the royal palace and take the Marjawani Sharj either dead or alive, though she hoped it would be dead, as personal revenge for the loss of her mother. One of the knights pleaded with her to consider signaling to the floating vessel above in the hopes that it was an ally. Perhaps they could alleviate the outnumbering opposition that the Princess Knight and her forces faced as well as use the flying contraption as a means to find safety and possibly finish their remaining pathway to reach the royal complex.

Marin, despite her initial reluctance, saw the reasoning of her concerned fellow knight and relented. She knew if there was any chance to grab their attention that a noticeable signal would be needed. She called for one of her knights to prepare to let loose an arrow with a bow, and prior to giving the order to fire, she used her exotic flaming sword, called Sol's Fury, to light the arrow. Upon the lighting of the arrow, the knight holding it drew back the string of the bow and let loose to fire the arrow high above in the air in the direction of the bow of the flying Swordbane vessel. At that point, Marin and her knights could only hope that it was indeed their possible means of salvation and that the occupants on board the floating vessel above did notice the signal that the knights of the Eternal Flame tried to send them.

As the floating vessel continued to traverse high above the Marjawan cityscape, the crew, though mainly Linitus and Wyatt, continued surveying various signs of the urban landscape and life below. Only for a brief moment did both of them notice a flaming flicker, a lone stray arrow rising slowly in the air, with Linitus verbally indicating while also pointing out the direction where it was and from where it came. It was on the starboard half of the ship looking toward the city below though still well ahead of reaching. Wyatt, using his magical wand with the wave of his hand as a substitute for steering, directed the ship to make a thirty-degree turn to starboard.

Only moments later did Linitus notice and point out again, seeing a few figures shining below in their armor, fighting off dozens of dark black-and-purple-clothed Marjawani warriors below. It was clear that this was Marin's contingent, with Marin herself standing out in her bright azure-purple transitioned armor, slaying ever so elegantly various approaching foes from different directions. However, Linitus soon realized from turning his head that he wasn't the only one aboard who lost their gaze in amazement at the Princess Knight's fighting prowess below. It had caught the attention also of the rest of the crew, including Peat, who showed expressions of pride and eagerness as if he had made a bet with Wyatt in bragging about how well the dwarf guard captain had trained the Princess Knight, as well as possibly wagering on how many enemies she felled, which evidently Peat actually did against the halfling wizard.

Linitus, however, regaining his composure and keeping in mind the mission at hand, used a loud and commanding voice to direct the warriors on board the floating vessel to prepare for combat. He then gave a nod and verbal gesture to Wyatt, indicating that they were ready to be transported below via the wizard's teleportation spell-casting. The young halfling wizard, with a childish smile of slight mischief, nodded back and waved his hands, holding his magical silver wand while calling upon some enchanted words. In an instant, everyone on board flashed before their own eyes, only to teleport and reappear in the narrow alleys of Marjawan below, a few dozen feet away from Marin and her now six remaining knights that strove to stay alive and fight off the ongoing waves of Marjawani infantry.

When Linitus assessed the situation and noticed the Eternal Flame knights in their vicinity, he called while pointing the direction with one of his hands for the rescuing forces to make their way to join the Princess Knight's remaining contingent and fight off the Marjawani forces. Marin, hearing such a loud and commanding voice, could not help but turn her attention toward her would-be rescuer.

She was awestruck in setting eyes upon the source of the voice. It was an elf dressed in a leather cuirass covering a white-and-brown tunic and brown leggings in addition to exotic elvish light-mail armor including shoulder pauldrons and exquisite angelic-looking wing extensions protruding from the outer sides of the elven-mail greaves that covered his leather boots. He had black raven-like hair tied in a ponytail or bun, and his facial expression exuded genuine confidence along with a sense of heroic chivalry. He was not a knight, but from looking at him, he was as close to being one as an elven ranger could get, from Marin's first impression.

Her look on him was still fixed and had made her lost as if time had slowed. He looked just as fixated on her, though aware of the surroundings and fighting that transpired. He drew his elven gold-like bow while taking a silver-tipped arrow from his quiver and quickly drawing back while still facing her. She was in shock, wondering still who he was and if he was not a friend but in fact a foe in deception.

As the elf let loose one of his silver-tipped arrows, it seemed to Marin that her life would flash before her eyes and she instinctively closed her eyes as if she knew her time had come to an end. However, she still felt her heart beat and slowly opened her eyes, only to notice that a Marjawani warrior had fallen from behind her with the same silver arrow now deep inside that enemy warrior's chest. She looked back and gave an expression that Linitus could read all too well from her face: Who are you?

It only took another moment before she realized she needed to regain her composure and finish the fighting while gradually moving toward the elven ranger as much as he made his way fighting toward her. The fighting continued to intensify, though gradually the Marjawani forces were waning and starting to pull back to regroup out of recognition that despite being smaller in number, the reinforcements were taking too much of a toll on the city defenders that would be better spared for use elsewhere while the city was under siege.

The combined forces under both the commands of Princess Marin and Linitus began to merge and combine into one cohesive group. As the few remaining Marjawani warriors dwindled, only four of the Swordbane warriors stood out in capturing the attention of the rest of their company. Peat charged furiously after any retreating Marjawani warriors he could smack his war hammer at close range while hurling a large explosive and flammable wooden barrel filled with burning oil toward several retreating foes. The barrel exploded immediately onto the two retreating Marjawani soldiers. Meanwhile, Wyatt, still being renowned and distinguished with his ascribed title Spell Slinger, furiously cast spell after spell, alternating between zapping Marjawani archers with bolts of lightning and hurling fireballs that emanated from the halfling wizard's wand.

However, both Wyatt and Peat along with the rest of the Swordbane company could not help but eventually watch and stare at the sight that impressed all of them, adopting elaborate and impromptu choreographed fighting by Linitus and Marin in unison against a half dozen or so Marjawani Kalashi assassins. The elven ranger and Princess Knight had quite literally danced around in combat, striking with bow and arrow as well as flaming sword and shield in vivid motion against what seemed at first fiercely opposing warriors who went down one by one like quick-melting snow. It was perhaps the last strike against the last remaining assassin in which the two impressed not only their fellowship but also themselves when Linitus quickly unsheathed his elven long blade to draw in a sudden unsuspected swift strike severing the head of the assassin at the same time that Marin blocked the foe's curved scimitar strike with her elaborate small round shield while turning to lunge quickly and pierce the assassin's abdomen with her flaming sword. Her face looked instantly at the same time noticing that Linitus had faced her also as he turned in the same motion as the direction in which he struck his foe. Their eyes locked on to each other at once again with both a sense of mutual anxiety and relief that they seemed to have worked well in instinctively trusting each other to fight at each other's side. They now sighed and nodded at each other while taking several breaths of relief.

Marin eventually broke the same staring gaze and asked the same question that she pondered from when she first stared at this attractive yet mysterious elven ranger: Who are you? The elven ranger's response was inquisitive and deflective, letting her know that whether she realized it or not, they knew each other from another time in life. It caught her off guard, but unlike her father, she was quicker to recognize and draw back all the possibilities of who this elf could be that she would know, while taking into account his youthfulness and that they had met before, likely much earlier in life.

To her astonishment and full realization that took away the last of her knightly composure while forcing her to drop her sword and shield lightly immediately, the elf removed from under his tunic a small but exquisite necklace that had a founding symbol of Swordbane, Draco Argenti Invictus, the legendary invincible silver dragon considered a messenger of the deity spirit Sol Invictus that helped the first king of Swordbane forge an alliance among the different peoples into one kingdom following the Nordling migration invasion and the demise of the Lupercalian Empire. There was only one elf Marin ever knew who had such a necklace. He was the elven boy that had once saved her during her childhood nearly twenty years ago near the King's Road outside Salvinia Parf Edhellen. Marin, grateful in return at the time, had once gifted that necklace to that young elven boy as a reminder of her gratitude and as a symbol of their eternal bond of friendship.

CHAPTER SIX

Unfinished Revenge

Returning to Wyatt's flying contraption were the original company along with the Princess Knight and her few remaining fellow knights. The floating vessel continued to sail majestically high above the urban backdrop of Marjawan. The crew originally planned to return the princess safely to her father King Ascentius, only they were not headed back the same direction that they came, but rather the opposite. They were on a new course to the Sharj's royal palace. While on board the vessel, Marin persuaded Linitus as acting commander of the mission that as important as it was to return her safely alive, she would fight to her dying breath against anyone that stood in her way, including Linitus and his company until she exacted revenge against the Sharj of Marjawan for the death of her mother as well as the other ones who had fallen during the night of the Great Massacre.

Rather than risk such an unnecessary confrontation while sensing her determination, Linitus reluctantly agreed and ordered his company regiment to make preparations to attack the Sharj's royal palace. Marin, taking a moment to consider her actions and the circumstances that her elf rescuer was compelled to deal with, tried to offer consolation by reminding him that as much as it was important for one in the elven ranger's position to follow the orders of his lord king, it was also important in his demonstration of leadership to recognize and seize initiative, including to deal an unsurprising blow to the enemy that could very well end the war sooner than later. Linitus shook his head in acknowledgement and, in a somewhat limited sense, agreed with the Princess Knight's reason in that regard. It was risky, he knew, but she had a point. If they could capture or possibly slay the Sharj, it would deal a big enough blow to the morale of the Marjawani to surrender and thus end the war without further bloodshed.

Meanwhile, Wyatt, using his magic and the motion of his hand holding his magical wand, maintained the floating vessel's course in that direction. As the floating vessel sailed deeper above enemy territory, the resistance from the Marjawani forces became fiercer. Between the royal palace complex and the rest of the many urban small dwellings stood a majestic moat filled with water that obstructed the normal path an invading force would seek to attack the palace, along with another thick layer of exotic mud mortar and red sandstone wall with a swarm of Marjawani archers and infantry occupying the top wall ramparts.

Volley after volley was emitted from this swarm of enemy archers, and much to Wyatt's surprise, the enemy this time was actually within range in part because of higher elevation of the inner palace-complex walls, to be able to strike with a small handful of arrows at the bottom hull of the floating ship. However, it was not enough to take down the ship as it still sailed along with its inflatable balloon-like apparatus unharmed while being securely attached above the frame and mast of the flying vessel. Within minutes, the vessel was within visible range for Wyatt to teleport from the vessel down to the high rising garden terrace of the palace. The palace itself was unique compared to the rest of the city as it had a distinct almost a step-pyramid-like series of platforms, or what the Marjawani called a ziggurat, along with a central ramp-like stairway that could access the patio roof from where the garden terrace was located, with a central stone edifice being presumably the royal palace throne.

Linitus, finding an open spot on the terrace patio located on the highest platform of the edifice, quickly gave the order for Wyatt to teleport him alongside Marin and Peat, who had insisted to follow along to ensure the Princess Knight's safety as the dwarf felt compelled to atone for his earlier failure as well as to still uphold his personal vow for her safety that he made to the king.

In an instant Linitus, Peat, and Marin found themselves disappearing and reappearing before a flick of motion from Wyatt's wand. It was still very surreal to all three of them, with Peat commenting that he would have to take note of getting used to that and quickly finding the nearest exotic garden shrub to vomit from his sense of teleportation sickness. Linitus and

Marin could not help but look at each other to shrug and laugh somewhat modestly.

However, within an instant loud footsteps and shadows emerged from different directions of the garden. Dark shrouded figures clothed in the Marjawani black and purple surrounded the three companions. These shadowy figures had covered their heads and faces, giving cold deathly stares at the Swordbane intruders who dared to attack on the Sharj's own royal palace grounds. They were the Sharj's elites, the Kalashi assassins, and the best presumably among them, for being so close in guarding the Sharj. Some of them brought to bear small iron-tipped spears as well as wicker-like shields, and others brandished curved scimitar swords that were both sharp and shiny. These warriors within thirty feet from the heroes circled them.

Both sides were eager and ready to anticipate how the other side would strike. However, surprisingly with only the loud howl of a whistle that Linitus gave, a sudden spread volley of arrows encircled the elven ranger and his companions. These arrows were launched by the elven rangers on board the skyship still looming above the palace complex. One by one, these elven rangers from above quickly felled many of the original three dozen or so elite Marjawani warriors. The few that did survive quickly shouted in anger and charged toward the three Swordbane companions. Anticipating the movement of the enemy, Linitus and Marin both used their respective swords in an elegant choreographed series of movements consisting of parries, strafes, strikes, and dodges to repel and vanquish the remaining Marjawani assassins. Peat, the small burly dwarven guardian on the other hand, chose a more direct and blunt approach of charging at a few Marjawani assassins while frantically spinning his war hammer in a chaotic whirl. He knocked several of the assassins down while making follow-up blows to their skulls.

Within moments, the three Swordbane companions prevailed in slaying the remaining palace guard assassins and took a brief pause to not only catch their breaths but also revel in the moment that they had triumphed with the assistance of their Swordbane company from the flying vessel above against one of the most fearsome foes they had met. Now all that stood in their way while they looked from less than two hundred feet were the sealed iron doors to the throne room of the Sharj himself.

The three companions took their strides and paced toward the throne room doors. Upon reaching the doors and noticing they were sealed,

Linitus and Marin both looked at each other with a somewhat visible sigh of annoyance and slight despair, wondering how they would overcome their next challenge in order to confront and take down the Sharj. Peat, however, gave a startled but loud chuckle followed by a short laugh while snapping his fingers to indicate that he had just the right thing or object to remedy that obstacle. He quickly took from behind his back (after unstrapping) a large barrel filled with explosive oil). The dwarf placed it on the stone ground next to the bottom of the sealed door. He quickly let Linitus know to spark one of his arrows to set it on fire and shoot it at the barrel. Linitus, with a bright face of both curiosity and excitement, did exactly as his dwarven companion instructed and drawing his bow, let loose one of the elf ranger's flaming arrows. Instantly, the flame-lit arrow struck the oil-filled barrel and produced a sudden tumultuous explosion. Meanwhile, the three companions took cover as best as they could, given the short moment.

Immediately, the explosion shook the floor of the patio while also causing a heavy impact that broke apart the iron doors, which had become nearly detached from the building. Peat, with a few strokes of his war hammer, quickly tore down the barely attached iron doors so that the Princess Knight and elven ranger could enter inside and deal with the enemy monarch, the Sharj, once and for all.

The throne room was dim inside, with only a few lit candles and oil lamps, but bright enough to be seen in the light now emanating from the outside opening where the sealed doors would have covered, in addition to several lit oil lamps placed about the throne room. At the far end stood four Marjawani Kalashi elite assassins who were exquisitely covered in exotic metal armor. Additionally, a single figure sat on the jeweled decorated stone throne. This figure was covered in heavy coated chain-mail and plate-mail armor including his face covered with a chain-link metal veil secured by a helm-like ornate crown covered with several jewels. He held a jeweled shiny spear with an exquisite metal tip point at the ground.

It was evident that this particular figure was none other than the Sharj of Marjawan himself. Upon anticipating after the explosion a follow-up attack, the Sharj quickly signaled, pointed with his spear for his elite assassin bodyguards to attack the company of heroes. The Marjawani assassin bodyguards, four present in total, quickly acknowledged with the nod of their heads. They quickly shouted while charging at Linitus and Marin. Much to their surprise, they were caught off guard. Out of nowhere, a war hammer was flung through the air and struck one of the guards. The three remaining guards looked and wondered what had transpired. Equally surprised, Linitus and Marin turned to find Peat, smiling and giving a short burst of laughter and taunts toward the remaining unsuspecting foes.

By the time the Marjawani assassin bodyguards regained their composure to charge again at the Swordbane heroes, they quickly found themselves attacked by surprise once again when a fireball hurled through the air struck another elite bodyguard. Even Peat this time was surprised, wondering who could have done it. He turned his head to realize it was none other than Wyatt the wizard Spell-Slinger, who smiled and could not help but blow the tip of his wand that produced a small waft of smoke.

Meanwhile before the other two guards could gain full composure, Linitus and Marin both attacked with equal ferocity, catching their remaining opponents off guard. Marin threw her shield in the air to strike one of the elite Marjawani guards in the head before it ricocheted back to her and she held it in front of her while charging and smacking the same guard with it. Before the other guard could turn and bring his scimitar to a halfway position to strike down the Princess Knight, an arrow quickly struck the unsuspecting Marjawani elite guard. Marin had turned, wondering who potentially saved her life. She realized it was Linitus, who lowered his bow while giving a gesture of pride, pointing his thumb near his eye and bending it down to let Marin know he had a greater sense of combat surroundings. Marin, through a mixture of reactions, felt somewhat slighted but also relieved and impressed at the same time. She gave a slight grin and nodded to acknowledge her gratitude for the elf watching her back. Clearly in her mind, her father had chosen well to have this elf, this former childhood friend who had once saved her before, during those distant years from her young-adult life, to be the instrument of her safety and well-being. For a quick sudden moment, she wondered (as prideful and martial as she exhibited herself to be) that perhaps this one elf had shown her a sense of her own strength being a potential vulnerability where they complemented each other well as a team, with him not overly exposing her weaknesses but having a sense of caring and cheerfulness about them while letting her also be able to reflect upon them. He was equally experienced in combat as her, if not more so, and that moment had become ever more evident even to her.

Returning quickly to the matter at hand and disrupting her from her quick mental thought, Linitus with a loud but clear voice of imposing authority instructed the last remaining figure, the Sharj, to stand down and surrender. The Sharj laughed a brief moment before rising before his throne to assume a combat posture to fight what seemed to him a ragtag upstart set of intruders who happened to be fighting behind the name of his enemy foe. The Sharj mocked them openly and told them that it was they who should surrender lest he feed them to his scorpion-beast mount. He quickly summoned behind his throne a large scorpion the size of a horse, which the Sharj mounted. The four on the other side: an elven ranger, a female knight of the Order of the Eternal Flame, a dwarven guardian, and a young halfling wizard, all stood with their own weapons at the ready to engage this deadly mounted-foe combination.

Frantically, the dwarf, elf, and Princess Knight parried, struck, and evaded the sudden deadly strikes that the Sharj's mount gave with its large clawlike pincers and its venomous stinger tail. It was a fight for survival. Meanwhile, Wyatt, being armed with only a magical wand, kept his distance and pondered how he could be of much use. With a quick moment in realizing and snapping his fingers to show his eagerness at finding a possible solution, the halfling wizard quickly used his wand in a heavy tug-like motion while chanting words unfamiliar in the common tongue. Immediately as this happened, the scorpion beast suddenly found itself levitating in the air while the Sharj himself shouted in surprise and utter disbelief of what was happening. Within a moment, the scorpion was erratically shaking to the point where Sharj fell off his beast mount, and in another moment with a heavily violent smack of Wyatt's wand against one of the throne-room walls, a similar effect had carried over in which the scorpion was violently smacked and hurled to the opposite throne-room wall until the beast was splattered in an ugly mess with venom leaking over the wall and throne-room floor.

The Sharj meanwhile picked himself up and, seeing no retreat, realized that he had underestimated this unlikely group of companions. Regardless, the Marjawani monarch had no intention to surrender. He quickly shouted and started whirling his bright exotic scimitar across the air toward his foes. The four Swordbane companions in return brought their weapons ready to strike at this foreign adversary. However, much to the surprise of Linitus, Peat, and Wyatt, they saw the Princess Knight, Marin, strike first. She slapped back the Sharj's scimitar with her own shield while lifting up the shield to slap back and then slap forward or strike toward the Sharj's face. She then lifted her right knee to strike the Sharj near the groin, at which point the Marjawani sovereign fell to his knees not withholding his facial and verbal expression of pain while holding his hands over his groin area.

The Sharj was down, and everyone knew that Marin was now in a position to deal the finishing blow and slay him. She intended to do so while raising up her flame-lit sword and uttering a few words of proclamation that this would be the moment in which she would fulfill her personal vow of avenging the many deaths the Sharj had caused, including that of Marin's own mother.

Before she could deal the final blow as her blade was about to descend, Linitus interjected, much to her displeasure. She was furious and turned her fiery gaze toward the elven ranger, ready to strike him instead, until he reminded her that if she struck the Sharj a mortal blow instead of taking him prisoner, the repercussions could be worse as the Marjawani might perceive the Sharj's death as that of a martyr warrior from which would draw inspiration for further resistance and warfare being prolonged that much more. Instead, the elf proposed to the Princess Knight to personally deliver the Sharj as a prisoner of war to King Ascentius in order for the king to decide. Linitus, who would imagine it would be beneficial for Ascentius to choose to spare the Sharj's life while making an example of him as a prisoner in order to lower the morale of his Marjawani subjects to surrender. The Marjawani were not ones known for being inspired when their great leaders, warriors, priests, and prophets were captured, chained, and shown in public as humiliated prisoners. This would be, however, exactly what Linitus proposed to both Marin and later the king.

Marin, though wanting revenge, gripped her sword as hard as she could. She could not hold back her anger and thirst for revenge while unleashing a somewhat exotic war cry that echoed in tone both her Citadellan and Nordling upbringing. She then quickly dropped her sword while cursing toward the defeated Sharj. Knowing Linitus was right, including for the higher and more virtuous cause of ending the war rather than prolonging it, while saving potentially more lives, Marin conceded to the elf ranger's suggestion while looking at him and nodding. She ordered Wyatt to use his magic and create a set of magical bond chains to bind the Sharj. Peat walked over to pull the now-deposed Marjawani ruler to his feet and forced-march the Sharj (or ex-Sharj) to the patio from whence the companions came.

From the sky above with great eagerness and anticipation, the skyship's mixed field-crew retinue of Citadellan knights, dwarven guardians, and elven rangers erupted in cheers upon sighting several figures emerge from the throne-room edifice doorway next to the patio garden. They were shocked and amazed to know that their efforts and sacrifices had paid off and that the ones who led them to battle did so personally on their behalf to seize what they presumed correctly to be the now-deposed Sharj.

Teleporting aboard, Linitus took command jointly with Marin once again. The elf directed Wyatt to change the floating vessel's course back to King Ascentius's encampment, while the Princess Knight directed the halfling wizard to use his magic to amplify her voice and let her speak loud enough for the whole Marjawani capital as well as within the vicinity where the Swordbane forces were besieging the city.

Marin loudly proclaimed before the city that the forces of Swordbane had captured the city's once-great sovereign and he stood in chains. The Princess Knight repeated herself several times, and within moments, the crew on board the ship, including the deposed Sharj himself with his head down in humiliation could hear the many voices from the city's military guard as well as its inhabitants shouting in disbelief, wailing and bemoaning what they heard from Marin.

As much as Marin wanted the deposed Sharj dead for revenge, she consoled herself internally by admitting that her childhood elf friend who had come to her rescue now as he had once done those many years ago during their youth, that same Linitus, now an adult, was ultimately right, and with that new sense of relief and invigoration, her thirst for revenge was substituted for the greater satisfaction of knowing that she had dealt a worse blow than death upon the Sharj and Marjawan. She had dealt them the inescapable fate of eternal humiliation that they could never undo, knowing that their greatest foe, Swordbane, had humiliated their jeweled capital city by not only besieging the city but also capturing their own ruler, the Sharj, from within his own palace and chaining him before his foe, displaying him as a prisoner before his own people while floating high above the air, where his own subjects were helpless to rescue their ruler from being taken to the other side and delivered to their enemy king Ascentius. It was truly the greatest gift of revenge that satisfied Marin. For whatever it was worth in hindsight, she took a moment to reflect while gazing both at the defeated enemy capital, and her comrades in arms, in particular Linitus.

Had this elven ranger, no, this now legend, at least in her mind, had he not come on her father's behalf, who knew what fate would have been in store for her different from the outcome she now found herself in. She was grateful eternally while still feeling a sense of remorse for this one elven childhood friend that both she and her father had neglected to see in all those younger years had come back to her to not only save her again (which she would not easily admit), but also teach her profoundly in ways that she would not have felt as fulfilled before. Now for the first time in many years, she felt as if a huge burden had been lifted and she found some sense of justice and atonement for her kingdom, for her father, for her mother's memory, and even for herself. She felt as if a part of her was whole again and she could rest. Truly, she was indebted to this young heroic elven ranger, yet feeling the unconditional compassion and presence of unlimited sense of freedom, she seemingly had no debt that needed to be paid. Her father and she were blessed, more than Marin thought before. She wanted to extend that same feeling back to others but especially to Linitus, though she knew he already seemed to be in a state of pure bliss, absent of any wants and desires while exuding the highest form of contentment. She saw his face looking toward the clouds and the sunset from the sky west toward Swordbane, west toward home, toward Salvinia Parf Edhellen. She was ready to go back also, to go back home to the kingdom capital of Citadella Neapola. This time, however, she would make sure that she would not neglect the one who rescued them (as she and her father had done before), the one who befriended her as a child, the one who had now brought to her a sense of eternal joy and grace.

Chapter Seven

A Father's Love for His Daughter

Gazing above with the sun setting from behind, Ascentius in awe and in pure eagerness awaited the return of Linitus along with his most prized and beloved daughter, Marin. As the flying vessel came closer to nearly hovering above him and his guards, the king's anxiety became direr, and he gripped his hand in a fist and hoped. Within a moment, he saw a sudden flash. It startled him even more as the king, for all his posture of being stoic and seemingly mighty beyond emotion, could not hold back from saying his daughter's name, Marin, with a sudden burst of fear of losing her. For that moment, he felt as if he gave in to his greatest fear ever to be experienced from living a mortal life: the loss of his only child, his daughter, his beloved Princess Marin.

In another sudden moment, a voice from behind called out to him, addressing him as Father. It was a voice that the king instantly recognized. In that very moment, he turned around, and his tears of sadness became tears of joy. It was in that moment that Ascentius stood frozen yet relieved seeing his daughter rush to him, dropping her sword and shield to embrace her father. In the background stood as witnesses the three other unlikely companions: the young halfling wizard who operated this flying magical contraption as the instrument for this reunion, the dwarf bodyguard captain seeking to uphold his vow of returning the princess to his king, and perhaps most of all, the elf ranger who led this rescue to make sure the reunion would happen. All three of these companions stood content in the moment of what had transpired. They were each delighted to play their part while sharing the same looks with each other in affirmation of what they had done.

Moments later after embracing his daughter for a time, Ascentius's emotions were a flurry of joy, relief, sadness at what could have been, and anger. In his mind, he knew that while he was happy and thankful of the outcome, it came at a great and possibly unnecessary risk. Tears still came down his face, yet the king of Swordbane composed himself as best as he could, putting the personal moment aside and remembering to keep the matters at hand in perspective. Marin knew this from his expression and initiated the conversation by letting him know that as possible recompense for her insubordination, she and the leading companions that stood behind her as well as both their contingents had achieved what seemed impossible: they had taken the war to the palace complex of Marjawan itself and brought back as prisoner the enemy's very own leader, the Sharj.

The king acknowledged what she said, but his face was stern and with a slight tone of anger. He chastised his daughter by asking her one question: At what cost?

In her thoughts to seek an answer, Marin could not find one. She knew he was right. She had lost most of her own contingent of Eternal Flame knights that she led and even the mixed fielded contingent that was dispatched to rescue her took some casualties. She felt remorse and a sense of self-disappointment, which her face could not hide. She acknowledged before her father while struggling through all her stubbornness to admit that it was too great and that she had made a rash decision without consideration for her father, her king's standing orders.

The three other hero companions stood like stone statues each thinking to himself, being grateful for not receiving the chastisement Marin was being dealt and not wanting to be in the same position as Marin. Yet Linitus, for all his apprehension, felt compelled deep within to intercede in case the king would be harder and stricter in punishing Marin. For the elf, she was still his close friend and perhaps much more. He could not bear for her to be made an example of the king's punishment for insubordination. The elf stood a few paces forward, and with a sense of challenging himself in not withholding, he pleaded to Ascentius to consider showing mercy toward his own daughter whatever the punishment might be while reminding the same thing as Marin had, that they had essentially ended the war by capturing the Sharj. Additionally, the elf ranger reminded the king that though there was a cost of lives that Marin had risked perhaps unnecessarily from her brash preemptive assault, this cost perhaps weighed far less than the lives of the king's army as a whole from prolonging the siege beyond this day and now the war was essentially over.

Pondering in amazement, Ascentius could not hold back and nodded heavily while admitting with a heavy heart that the elf ranger was right. Despite the danger that Marin had initially taken, the follow-up response that she, Linitus, and their company took was immensely favorable. Swordbane was now in a position to compel Marjawan and its other desert settlements to capitulate and acknowledge that the war was over. Even more from a personal view, Ascentius now had the moment he wanted to exact justice upon the Sharj, the one he held ultimately accountable all those years for the assassins directed to massacre those closest to the king, including his own wife, his own beloved queen, Gretchen.

In all the waves of emotion while being consoled by rationalism and pragmatism, Ascentius came to realize that Linitus was ultimately right and even more valuable for his clarity in making sense of the bigger context of what had resulted, not to mention the invaluable role the elf ranger himself had taken in both rescue of his daughter and consequently the capture of his most despised adversary.

The Swordbane king made in a moment a series of proclamations starting with a declaration in front of the elf ranger as well those present, including Marin, Peat, and Wyatt, that as a reward for his valor and achievement, Linitus would be given the honorary title Legend, the highest honor of distinction Swordbane would give, and the elf would be given any desired reward of his choosing that the king would grant. It was so astonishing for all to witness that no one's face could hold back the awe that struck them. No one else during this lifetime had been bestowed such an esteemed title of recognition save for Dux Decius, who was awarded the title in recognition of being the lone survivor and leading commander of the king's raiding party against a large settlement belonging to a hostile group of Nordling barbarians in the northern mountainous western lands. Ascentius also promoted Linitus to any post of command he wanted, while suggesting to be general commander of the Swordbane legion assigned outside Linitus's own home region of Salvinia Parf Edhellen.

The next proclamation of Ascentius in relation to his daughter was when he was about to discipline her by effectively removing her from the knighthood order of the Eternal Flame while pardoning her insubordination from his full punishment, which in Swordbane would have been death, which he could not bear to do as her father. He justified this dictate by acknowledging the same things Linitus had pointed out as well as Marin herself in that they had both delivered the deposed ruler of Marjawan, whom Ascentius held responsible for the war that started in the first place, and that Marin along with her companions had consequently and effectively ended the war.

However, as Ascentius finished his proclamation, Linitus thought about Marin and knew how the proclamation of her soon-to-be expulsion from her knightly order dealt a painful blow to her heart; the elf ranger could not let the proclamation pass for this fellow warrior whom he still called and considered (even after all those years) a friend from bearing what seemed to be the unbearable punishment. The elf ranger instead interceded and pleaded again for further clemency by openly announcing to the king in wishing to use his desired reward to spare Marin, the king's own daughter, from being removed as a knight in the Eternal Flame Order.

As soon as he made his reward known, everyone in the king's vicinity, including the king himself, was as awestruck if not more than when the king had first bestowed Linitus the unconditional reward. The king in fact was nearly as speechless as Marin herself. The elf could have asked for anything as his reward, but the one thing he wished, which had no direct material benefit to him, made a deep sense of both indebtedness and gratitude fill the heart of the Princess Knight. Marin knew in her heart maybe earlier than at this critical point that her father was right to proclaim her elf companion and rescuer a Legend, for he had shown that in multiple ways just in the span of less than a day.

The king recognized the elf's fervent wish to use it as his reward granted by the wish, knowing that the king of Swordbane was honor bound to grant it. He could have instructed his daughter to take a moment to render her gratitude for such an act, but he did not have to. Marin, of her own free will and gratefulness, kneeled before Linitus and thanked him. She also asked why. The elf, recognizing her appreciation as well as sense of understanding, replied that he had everything he wanted, essentially a life without desires for wealth, status, or even a title such as Legend. He told her that he only served and desired out of the love he had for others, including her as a friend.

Marin, heart-stricken, saw that in all her years and in all her pursuits, including the status of knighthood, she had much to learn from this one that she once called and would call again friend. She could not let him go again. For her, this day was an omen. It was a sign of things to come and to not let go, to not let him go from her life. Once there was a part of her that felt numb and missing, but now it felt completed and made whole. Her inward tears of joy had filled a pool of both internal and external happiness.

She rose up after the elf had consoled her and placed his hand on her shoulder. Her face changed from remorse, gratitude, and joy to one of determination and a sense of fate that had to be fulfilled. She turned to Ascentius and said loudly enough for those close to them to hear as a plea to her father, her king, a request. It was not a request that she had expected her father to grant simply because she as his beloved and only daughter, his princess, wanted it. Rather, it was a request from a tone and sense of maturity and aspiration to learn and develop as a better person, as a better commander. She had asked the king to assign Linitus a new station in his army, to serve as personal protector and mentor for her. She admitted in perhaps her humblest state in all her life why she had made such a request: that despite her abilities with a degree of taking command and leadership, she had still much to learn from this elf ranger while he stood by her side and there was no one better in all the kingdom that she felt could benefit in learning from.

Though Peat was already Marin's personal protector and former mentor, the dwarf understood where she was coming from in her reasoning, and the dwarven guardian could not object. Despite teaching Marin how to fight prior to her ascension as a knight to the order of the Eternal Flame as well as instilling a basic level of command and leadership, Linitus had far surpassed even the dwarf's estimate in serving as both a mentor and protector to his princess. The elf ranger seemed to possess the qualities of a natural-born leader.

Ascentius, looking from the array of faces in front of him, could tell that this admission and request from his own daughter, one of his own officers of a knightly order, came from a place of humility and admission of seeking betterment. The king himself could tell that this was a request that was genuine and could not be refused. It was hard enough to believe in some sense all that had transpired from the arrival of this one elf ranger, a person whom he and his daughter once knew so many years ago, and now he had come to them again by what seemed like a divine portent that had to be adhered to.

Now this elf had been (as much in Marin's mind as Ascentius's) a sign from the divine looking down upon them. He could not refuse, nor did any hesitation enter his mind from his own daughter's request. It had to be granted for his daughter's sake and, by extension, for his sake in having peace of mind as well as for the well-being of Swordbane. Never that he knew about in the many years of Swordbane's existence as a united kingdom had a hero not only saved the king's daughter but also brought an end to a drawn-out war on the very same day. The king nodded and granted his daughter's request. All of the company present kneeled before the king, acknowledging his final and perhaps most prominent bestowment. This was a special moment that they had witnessed in not only Ascentius granting perhaps the humblest and most selfless request from his daughter coming from a position of seeking self-betterment, but also in witnessing a father's love for his daughter.

CHAPTER EIGHT

The Oath to Make War and Death One

As the siege of Marjawan came to an end, far to the northwest in a valley with meadows and semi-arid landscape just east of the great mountain range that separated the coastal heartland of Swordbane from the rest of the interior lay a mixed orc-and-goblin camp known as Orcum Tribus Uruk Kazaht. It was given such a name using both the Lupercalian-Citadellan language and the orcish language. It was the largest orc-and-goblin settlement in the region, cluttered in vast acres of pitched-up hide tents and wooden structures surrounded by a thick wooden palisade. It was also known to have a few trolls residing in the settlement.

Few humans, elves, dwarves, and other small folks of the non-beastly nature would venture to such a seemingly terrifying and dangerous settlement. However, from a distance across the horizon as the sun was setting, two shadowy figures emerged, drawing closer to the orcish-goblin settlement. The figures approached fast while riding on horseback. As they came closer to one of the wooden gated entrances, they suddenly stopped when several orc sentinel gate guards spoke in their orcish language to command the two figures to identify themselves. Ordinarily, the orcs would have killed them on sight; however, these figures with their dark cloaks exuded a sense of darkness that made the orc guards give them a chance to make their case for being admitted rather than being slain outside the wooden gates.

The two figures slowly withdrew from their horse mounts, and one of them, the leading one speaking in Citadellan tongue with authority told the sentinels that they knew who he was. He went on to say that it is he the chosen vessel and dark lord who would make war and death become one. The other figure, moving his hands and casting a spell, made the words spoken decipherable by the sentinels to comprehend audibly what the first ominous figure was stating. The sentinels went into utter amazement. These orc guards were expecting the figures to falter or say anything that might be more expected such as that these two figures wished to join them in their typical evil schemes of raiding and looting. They never expected to hear such words and knew that this was beyond their scope to ascertain what to do with the figures other than to direct them to their leader, a goblin shaman who co-led the settlement along with the most fearsome and dominating orc in the settlement capable to lead as the settlement's war captain.

The orc guards themselves were distinguishable from their shorter goblin counterparts and, like the other orcs, were tall of stature, usually at least a height of six feet and possibly as tall as eight feet, though some of the slender ones were as short as five and a half feet and were usually lightweight to be mounted on dire wolves. These orc guards also had dark blue-grayish skin tone and, like the goblins, had pointed ears, though slightly less pronounced than their goblin counterparts'. Their hairstyles were much the same as the goblins, usually either shaved bald or tied in some form of knot or ponytail. Their teeth were jagged like the goblins', but they also had a pair of protruding tusklike fangs extending from their bottom-teeth line. Perhaps the most notable distinction between them and their goblin counterparts were also their noses as the orcs had broad and somewhat flat-looking noses in contrast to the goblins' narrow protruding noses. Much of their features they attribute to their original patron deity, Orcus, the bestial demon lord that reigns over the underworld damnation of hell.

Within moments, the wooden palisade, making a sharp cracking noise, began to open. An orc guard captain walked out to present himself and identify himself before the mysterious and dark-cloaked figures while telling them that they would follow him to the settlement's war tent, the main tent housing the supreme orc leader of the settlement and a nearby tent housing its chief goblin shaman. The two figures shook their heads to acknowledge the orc guard captain's directions while following him.

Within moments, many of the settlement's orc and goblin residents began to emerge, surrounding the two figures being escorted by the guard captain, while the other settlement guards made a path to prevent the settlement's denizens from overcrowding the mysterious visitors in reaching their destination. Some of the goblins and orcs were curious enough to not withstand howling, shrieking, and uttering war cries of fear and damnation to see how the guests would react. Unsurprisingly, the cloaked guests kept straight faces without reaction, which amazed many of the settlement's occupants.

Only a few more moments went by in which the two shadowy visitors reached the central part of the settlement with a large wooden and hide-covered war tent adjacent to a small circular tent covered in various totems of animal bones mounted and impaled. The guard captain, in orcish tongue, called out to announce to the settlement's war captain and leading chief goblin shaman that they had mysterious guests who needed an audience to discern their fates.

Within moments, a heavy couple of thuds could be heard in which a large orc figure wearing ornamental animal bones for armor emerged from the opening tent cover. He was no doubt the orcish war captain. Both imposing and intimidating, he came out angered from being disturbed, while calling out in orcish tongue on what grounds the two figures had the right to command such an audience.

Meanwhile in another moment, a goblin figure suddenly emerged from his tent covering. This goblin had an ornament head dress and also wore various animal bones for dress attire in addition to some worn cloth and jewelry surrounding the goblin's tattooed arms. The goblin, speaking in his own tongue, also demanded by what authority he and his orcish war captain were disturbed. In a matter of moments, a small cadre of goblin and lightweight orcs mounted on huge wolf beasts known as dire wolves began to encircle and surround the two figures, trying to get a reaction out of them and wanting to sense and taste their fear. However, the two figures maintained their composure and stood still despite the attempts by the settlement to provoke them into fear.

Then suddenly, both figures looked at each other and agreed to lower their hoods simultaneously to reveal themselves. One of them, who had cast the spell earlier to instantly translate their words from their Citadellan tongue to orcish as well as goblin, began to speak to the settlement's leaders and those present to witness the spectacle. This figure repeated what the first figure had said, pointing to the first figure and letting the settlement be aware that they knew who this other Citadellan was.

At the next moment, the other Citadellan unleashed a loud war cry that sounded half human and close to a wolflike howl. Immediately, the wolves that the orc and goblins were mounted on began to throw forward their mount riders and break their stance to huddle near the Citadellan that called unto them, while unleashing a chorus of brief howls. This act alone drew great amazement among not only the common orc and goblin folks of the settlement but also their leaders, one of whom (the goblin chief shaman) seemed to be familiar with the Citadellan who had gained the attention and obedience of the settlement's dire wolves.

The Citadellan that had called and summoned the wolves to heed him, next spoke before the settlement while looking at both the war captain and chief shaman, stating what he had said earlier: that he had come to make war and death become one as the chosen vessel and dark lord. The other dark, shadowy Citadellan, who was slender and bald-headed, confirmed what the former, his leader, had said. This bald Citadellan announced who they were clearly before the settlement, stating that he was Agaroman, chief wizard and advisor to his leader, Decius Maximus Invictus (though previously known by his first name Decius as an orphan). Agaroman went on to say that the settlement had borne witness to the tales being true and not of hearsay or false rumors. He had announced before the settlement's various inhabitants that Decius was indeed as he claimed, the destined dark lord and chosen vessel of the deity spirits of war and death, as well as the Child of the Wolf, and heir to the once-great Lupercalian wolfling race, for whom he would reclaim their legacy by making a new empire out of their inspiration. Agaroman went further to state that Decius was indeed the very same one from the stories to be marked for death from conflict since infanthood, only to be saved and raised by a pack of wolves until he was later picked up by a reconnaissance group of Citadellans to ascertain and rescue the survivors of a rare but vicious raid by a small war band of Nordling barbarians near the surrounding hills of the once-fabled ruined city of Imperia Capitolina, the once-great capital of the Lupercalian Empire that preceded the era of the reign of humans.

The goblin shaman, in awe despite being somehow familiar with Decius, still felt obligated to challenge the authority of what was declared. He asked one question before he would concede what he had witnessed as a possible omen from a higher divine authority calling to the settlement inhabited by beasts: how did they or even this man who testified about his companion in arms and leader know this was true?

Agaroman, still bold and straight faced, pronounced before them that he was there as witness to this event while acting as a reconnaissance and rescue member of that party. He was the one who saw the pack of wolves embracing Decius as one of their own twenty-five or so years ago when he was just an infant barely able to crawl, and Agaroman, while startling the wolves, was able to pick up the infant Decius to bring back to Citadella Neapola to be raised in one of the Swordbane kingdom's orders of knighthood, the Order of the Black Wolf.

Decius, meanwhile, stood still and confident, waiting for Agaroman to finish before restating to the settlement that he came as chosen vessel and dark lord to make war and death become one. It was a saying that the goblin shaman had heard before but not for many years; his screeching became more excited, and he cheered, realizing what those words meant. Immediately, the goblin shaman lowered his head and bowed before Decius. Without much hesitation, the orc war captain followed the shaman's lead while signaling with a staring gesture of command before the leading orc raiding captains to do the same, which they did. Subsequently, the whole settlement bowed down in prostration and acknowledgment of Decius.

Decius and even more so Agaroman stood in some awe yet also held a disposition expecting the outcome they had witnessed in the recognition and submission to authority by such a large beastly settlement. The two figures did not expect any less than what had transpired, and they believed in a fatalistic yet prophetic way in everything that they had stated before this settlement. Their words carried a great sound in command for not only had the various orcs and goblins bowed before this dark-clothed Citadellan, but other smaller groups of species did the same, including large trolls and even some human raiders who had joined the settlement and were accepted in, though with a mostly lower degree of status and standing.

The trolls themselves were tall hairy-looking primate beasts that soared up to heights of ten to twelve feet on average and were very muscular, walking either on four limbs or in a bipedal stance. They had sharp jagged teeth with two fangs protruding from the top teeth line. They had broad noses, sunken eyes with slightly protruding eyebrow ridges, and broad foreheads. Only their front faces exposed their pitch-black skin, with the rest of their heads and bodies being covered with black furry hair. Though known to have a very aggressive temperament that was quick to anger, many of the trolls were accustomed to coexisting and living with their smaller goblin and orc counterparts, while all of them considered one another as part of the common mutual bond of fellow bestial races.

Suddenly, Decius discarded his black robe and cloak to reveal his warlike posture and figure clad in black Citadellan plate-mail armor, and he drew his long sword from his scabbard to lift high in the air. Additionally, despite his appearance standing out in being of average height, with chiseled facial features, olive skin, dark brown eyes, short black straight hair, and a clean-shaven face, his facial appearance nonetheless revealed an ambitious demeanor in which he seemed both confident and intimidating. He commanded loudly to all those present to rise and remember this day for he had come to fulfill the prophecy to become the vessel and merge the deity spirit of Calu, known for his role in presiding over death, with that of Laran, the deity spirit associated with presiding over war. Decius told the settlement that they would follow him and help fulfill this prophecy in order to usher in a new era. It would be an era in which a new empire inspired by the likeness of the Lupercalian Empire would rise to topple Swordbane, the human-heir kingdom that had filled the void of the old Lupercalian Empire that had disappeared with the Lupercalian wolfling race itself.

Upon ending his proclamation, a loud and resounding wave of chants and war cries emerged from the various inhabitants of the settlement. They were filled with utter satisfaction and bliss in their own sadistic minds at what they had understood and heard. In their minds, it was finally what they had waited for: a leader with seemingly abundant ambition and a vision for unending domination had come before them to take command and lead on the path of war, death, and destruction. They embraced him and his prophetic words along with the words of Agaroman.

That night, many howls, chants, and war cries of celebration filled the orc-goblin camp as they saw that this was a new era for them. It would be one in which their relative remoteness and lack of political standing would change with the tidings that this one, Decius Maximus Invictus, would bring. For them, as many goblin shamans had passed down in their various tribes, it was a prophecy that came long ago, which foretold that there would be one who would command the wolves, symbols of both Calu (deity spirit of death) and Laran (deity spirit of war), to acknowledge his authority as an omen prior to being chosen and made a vessel in merging the power from both spirits into one.

As the settlement continued to celebrate until the end of night, Decius along with Agaroman met privately with the chief goblin shaman leader along with the orc war captain to make plans of executing the prophecy that they intended to make into a reality. The next morning by sunlight, the same two Citadellans (Decius and Agaroman) that rode into the orc-goblin camp rode out, heading south. The nearest settlement and intended destination from that direction would be Imperia Sanctum Novus, an isolated Citadellan oasis and metropolitan sanctuary settlement lying in the high desert and outer boundaries of the Kingdom of Swordbane.

CHAPTER NINE

Vanity with Knighthood

The sun rose bright outside the gates of Marjawan, with the Swordbane kingdom's siege encampment preparing to receive an envoy from a group of high-ranking Marjawani officials the day after their miraculous victory against the Sharj. Hundreds of military tents still remained erected, with the Swordbane monarch's royal tent standing out most prominently with a shiny dragon statue emblem at the pinnacle of the tent. The Marjawani dignitaries dressed in their colorful loose-cloth robes along with their decorative and exquisite turbans waited patiently to be received formally by King Ascentius and his council.

Ascentius stood discussing with Peat, his close dwarf bodyguard who also served on the king's council of advisors. The two stood near the entrance of the tent, discussing plans for outlining terms for Marjawan to concede in order to end the war with the Kingdom of Swordbane, the latter of which visibly emerged as the clear victor. They also discussed making the preparations for the Swordbane army's long march back home, while considering which route to take. The two representative sides both considered marching back to Grimaz-Kadrinbad since it was both the closest route and a symbolically meaningful way-stop to pay tribute to the dwarven fortress settlement that opened the wound in their twenty-year-long war.

However, both agreed when Ascentius weighed the merits in stopping by to pay such tribute to the site that their army was too large to be sufficiently provisioned by that dwarven fortification alone. Peat (though wanting to pay tribute to this site of his dwarven heritage) agreed, seeing that a greater matter needed to be addressed, as Ascentius pointed out. The two searched for the next closest location that could be used to provision the forces of Swordbane in their route back to the capital while referring to a map of the continent Hesperion, which included the many rivers, mountains, and settlements listed among the lands of Swordbane to the west, Marjawan to the east, the barbarian Nordling lands to the north, as well as some of the known major orc and goblin settlements near the center going eastward that separated as a buffer barrier between the previous three factions except along the forest coast that was shared between Swordbane and the Nordlings while being in frequent contention.

Ascentius, in a moment with an expression of delighted resolve, pointed out and indicated a lone, fairly isolated but very sizable urban settlement in the high desert belonging to Swordbane that connected to the low desert of Marjawan and the borders of Swordbane kingdom's holdings. It was a way-stop pilgrimage site known as Imperium Sanctum Novus, or simply known as Sanctum Novus. It was believed to be the last settlement that the ancient feral man-wolf race of Lupercalians founded as well as the last known one they occupied before their mysterious departure from the western lands when their empire fell apart and the Nordlings made their first successful invasion against the various settlements of the Lupercalian Empire, including most notably the ancient former capital Imperia Capitolina and the seaport city of Citadella Neapola, which would become the seat of the then newly established Swordbane kingdom.

Swordbane became essentially the middle ages' cultural synthesis between the local human Citadellan culture, which adopted many of their former ruling man-wolf Lupercalian cultural traits, including what they considered higher civilized ways of living and observing customs, and certain aspects of the Nordling barbarian conquerors' customs that would make up the Kingdom of Swordbane. The kingdom itself had inherited many of the settlements of the prior Lupercalian Empire that were already brought together through its reign of domination, the various other races consisting again of Citadellan humans that resided along the western coastline in scattered settlements, elven settlements along the redwood and other forests' coastal interior, dwarves of the deeper inland mountains as well as deserts, and other hamlets of small folk including halflings and gnomes. During the Lupercalians' reign as a dominant ruling minority, they had instituted something of a caste system, in which the

Lupercalians were at the top in various government and military positions while employing the nonhuman races to serve in auxiliary roles to facilitate trade, lumber milling, exquisite product manufacturing while relegating the Citadellan humans to serve as the bulk of unskilled and, to some degree, skilled labor, including construction, agriculture, and the lower ranks of the Lupercalian imperial legions. It was truly a watershed once under mysterious circumstances, the Lupercalian Empire had fallen over time, until several major tribes of the Nordlings who fought various battles with them saw the opportunity to immigrate en masse and take over the empire's settlements that would become Swordbane when the first Nordling barbarian chieftain formally adopted Citadellan customs at the expense of discarding some of his own native ones in order to be seen and accepted as a legitimate ruler while intermarrying with a local Citadellan woman of higher economic and noble standing. This trend would continue in many succeeding generations as a gesture to uphold some degree of harmony and cultural synthesis between the native Citadellans and the migrant conquering Nordling descendants until the point where King Ascentius himself visibly looked closer (in traits of overall appearance) to resembling his Citadellan subjects than his Nordling assimilated-settler subjects. He would be the first king in this long dynasty line to break tradition and instead marry a Nordling, Gretchen, as his wife.

Lost in thought, Ascentius reflected heavily upon those historic settlement names on the map about the history that his dynasty had come from, with its deeply rooted history. However, composing himself again to the subject at hand, Ascentius indicated to his dwarven bodyguard and companion that while Imperium Sanctum Novus would be an ideal place to resupply his forces en route back to the kingdom's capital, they had to be careful and send advance scouting parties to make sure there were no remaining Marjawani forces separated from their settlements that would lie waiting to ambush the kingdom's main force after the war was over, in case those remaining forces of opposition had not found out that the war was over and they still considered assaulting Swordbane's army as a legitimate target. Most likely this would not happen, as Peat pointed out, and Ascentius agreed that the leading general and regional representative of the garrison was effective in securing the outlying area around Imperium Sanctum Novus from attacking raids by Marjawani forces, not to mention any goblin-orc combined forces that would dare to venture into those parts of the high desert.

Upon agreeing that Imperium Sanctum Novus would be the main replenishment location for Swordbane's army and to send a reconnaissance scouting party ahead, the next matter that Ascentius brought up was who would lead it. The two both considered Linitus as an ideal candidate in light of his leadership abilities, including bringing the war to an end as well as the elf's proficiency as a ranger to be effective in scouting. Upon discussing further however, Ascentius did weigh in that he had appointed Linitus as essentially the new bodyguard and personal instructor in arms to his daughter the day prior, after the victory and capture of the Sharj while Ascentius made a series of royal decrees.

Ascentius was apprehensive to relegate Linitus to this possible new role with his daughter being left alone. Peat attempted to assuage the king's concern by mentioning that he could reinstate the dwarf guardian even on a temporary basis to serve as Marin's chief bodyguard. Upon considering, Ascentius asked the dwarf about the current whereabouts of his daughter. Peat, caught off guard and disappointed to admit he did not know, had proven the king's point inadvertently in why the monarch would be hesitant to go with the dwarf's suggestion. It was not out of a lack of trust in the dwarf's genuineness to fulfill his vows of protecting both Ascentius and his daughter Marin, but as Ascentius indicated, his daughter from her headstrong nature and, to an extent, her own sense of vanity in being a knight, did not see the need to be watched over by those with good intentions, including Ascentius himself as well as Peat.

Marin had a tendency to go wherever the action was, unless there was someone else to keep her well-grounded from seeking danger elsewhere and perhaps draw her to a more secure place of familiarity. That was what the king pointed out about Linitus, and that wherever the elf ranger was, more than likely his daughter would also be close by. Peat, though unhappy with what the king admitted, saw that the dwarf's own ability to safeguard the princess was perhaps diminished over the years by her headstrong defiance against being watched over by someone else. The dwarf, as such, consented with a sigh while admitting that the king was most likely correct. Ascentius, sensing the point he brought as wounding the dwarf from his vows and perhaps standing among being close to the royal family, consoled the dwarf and told Peat to know that he did well to make sure Marin was as capable as she could be to take care of herself all these years in staying alive and learning to fight, in part from what the dwarf himself had taught her in addition to her martial training under the Order of the Eternal Flame. Peat nodded again, accepting as much consolation. He was somewhat relieved to know that the king acknowledged the dwarf doing what he could to ensure Marin was still alive as well as the woman she was in the present.

However, Ascentius admitted that his daughter's recent actions were still on his mind. To him she had acquired a taste of what he would consider knights' vanity in placing their status and what they had achieved in passing the initiations of knighthood as a badge of inherent merit to overcome any obstacle that stood in their way to complete their own quests and maintain their personal vows.

However, it would not take long for the Swordbane king and his dwarven-guardian chief of guards to find the Princess Knight. As Ascentius surmised, he was correct and found out that his daughter was under the close but watchful eye of her new appointed mentor in arms and close bodyguard.

Loud sounds of clanging between swords as well as the intermittent sounds of exertion of the wielders striking those swords and parrying could be heard in the Swordbane siege camp within the camp's sparring training area. There was a sizable crowd of enlisted soldiers as well as knights spectating and cheering aloud at what would become perhaps the best sparring practice fight they had ever seen between two sword wielders. Marin and Linitus could be seen strafing, sidestepping, evading through dodges, as well as parrying between sword strikes. Marin, adorned in her transition azure-violet combination of plate-mail and chain-mail armor, struck from high above and swung heavily with the full force of her flaming blade while blocking with her small circular embellished dragon-sigil shield blows that Linitus had exchanged in faster but less heavily exerted strikes. The two were nearly on par with each other while seemingly able to choreograph their moves naturally. It would only be a moment when eventually, as skilled and powerful Marin had seemed with her imposing armor, weapons, and stance, she made a misstep and miscalculated her movement and direction of force from striking her blade while being off balance. It was an opportunity that Linitus took advantage of; he both dodged and tripped her toward the ground and pinned her down with one of his knees and placed his long slightly curved elven blade next to the Princess Knight's neck where it was not thoroughly covered by her combination of plate mail and chain mail, to expose the vulnerability where she would have received a mortal strike had it been a fight to the death.

Marin, smacking one fist against the ground while showing an expression of frustration but also acceptance, stated loud enough to be heard that she yielded. Linitus, meanwhile, offered her his hand to help get her up on her feet. Her pride still somewhat wounded by her loss to the elf ranger, she thanked him but declined, stating she could get herself up, which the elf acknowledged.

Watching the outcome of the elf ranger prevailing over his daughter, the king had asserted again to his dwarf companion and chief bodyguard that her stance and behavior exposed his upheld views about the vanity of knights like his daughter might exert in combat as well as in defeat. Ascentius also stated again this sparring demonstration between the two was validation in the king's mind that he had done well to grant Marin's request (the one part where he saw her maturity seeking to grow and improve) to appoint Linitus as the mentor in training Marin, and perhaps in due time, the elf could actually reform Marin's headstrong character and sense of knightly vanity to be tempered with the discipline, patience, concentration, and leadership that Linitus seemed to exert. The king confided to Peat that he could tell as much as Marin by this point that Linitus was a good influence upon his daughter and, even more so, a divinely sent gift, in the king's mind, to watch over his beloved Marin.

Peat reluctantly agreed, though again still not pleased with how this upstart elf, as he saw it, in some sense had demoted the dwarf as the personal protector of the king's daughter when he had appeared the second time in their lives just yesterday of all days, in a most fortuitous moment. Peat again agreed and conceded that this in some part had to be, as the king stated, a sign or portent from the divine spirits that this elf ranger had a purpose to be in their presence regardless of the circumstances, including the impact on the dwarf's positional rank and standing. Peat again at least was content to know that in some manner perhaps, he had set the moment as a transition in which he passed on his formative influence, training, and protection of the king's daughter to someone else who at least had a genuine nature as well as qualities that perhaps no one better besides the king himself could impart to Marin in not only becoming better able to protect herself, but also in developing into a person with a more balanced and better way of living her own life.

In a sudden moment, Ascentius noted while watching how Marin, despite her pride being wounded and refusing Linitus's hand to get herself up, had quickly and somewhat humbly pursued the elf ranger to teach her what she did wrong during her last move and to show or demonstrate to her how to correct her stance to be more balanced including in her movements. The king admitted that before Linitus appeared the second time in their lives, though he would not expect this to happen as it was generally considered a taboo between humans and elves, he could actually envision and admire the prospect of a future in which his daughter and Linitus shared a more intimate life together. Perhaps not in this lifetime of the two becoming soul mates, as he admitted the stigma and taboo being so strong against elves and humans to intermarry, despite the harmony that existed between humans and elves as well as the other races in the kingdom. However, he saw from how they interacted, they tended to naturally gravitate toward each other in sparring with such elegance in their choreographed movements despite their fighting styles being so different. It was as if they complemented each other to form a perfect union to admire their differences but also their disposition to engage each other in understanding.

Peat, the dwarf guardian, was of a much different and adverse opinion than the king; the former was more accustomed to accepting the stigmas and taboos that existed against intermarriage. Peat was shocked to hear the king say these things and could not hold back asking the king how the subjects of the kingdom would be able to handle it. The king shrugged lightly and understood the dwarf's concern from a standpoint of actuality as this had not happened before, but in the king's mind, balance should be sought between ideals of pragmatism and progress of reform over time. He reminded the dwarf that changes, even good ones, happen over time and that people of all races can be ready for them and should be open to their views being challenged while considering how other changes have already happened before.

Ascentius mentioned an example by asking the dwarf if it was not a bad thing for the first of his male bloodline, a Nordling chieftain who became a king from establishing the Kingdom of Swordbane in the western coastlands, to decide to form both a political and symbolic union in ruling by intermarrying with a local Citadellan. Despite both being human, they had distinguishable differences in both custom and physical traits, with the Citadellans typically being more swarthy, olive-skinned, darker-haired as well as eye color, short to medium in stature in contrast to the Nordlings, who in general were much taller, more muscular, and larger in stature as well as lighter in complexion, hair, and eye color. Ascentius himself embodied the physical features of those two cultures coming together from ancestral intermarriage (though more dominant from his Citadellan ancestry) with himself having light olive skin, dark brown and gray hair, a short beard, hazel eyes, and a slightly muscular, above average height build. The king also brought up another point that despite those differences, the two human cultures (at least for the descendants of the Nordlings that had settled along the southern western coastline) had formed such a close harmony that there was seldom distinction of obstacles between the two despite the awareness of the physical differences. The dwarf admitted that the king was in some respects correct and there was harmony between the Nordling descendants that had settled down and assimilated to a large extent in the warmer southern Hesperion western coastlands inhabited by the existing Citadellan locals, and perhaps change, including intermarriage, was possible between humans and other races as much as between the different races of humans themselves. The dwarf went on to agree that perhaps the king was right: in due time, society would change and be ready for when another step of change would happen between humans intermarrying with other races as much as within their own different groups of humans.

Taking another moment to think back on what Ascentius had stated, Peat could not help but ask what it was like with how Ascentius's subjects received him when he broke with tradition to marry a Nordling from their native lands up north as opposed to marrying a local noble Citadellan woman. Ascentius reflected back, thinking about his fondest moments with Gretchen as well as the question itself, and he told his chief of guard that if he had to do it all over again, he would. Despite some of the criticism even from the local nobility, Gretchen had a personality along with a fierce sense of loyalty, ambition and a carefree determined spirit that he felt naturally bonded to. She was his soul mate, and regardless of how different they were in both appearance and lifestyle, they had no barriers in seeing each other as who they were as individual persons. He took some solace in knowing that while admitting to Peat that perhaps that same spark of love that attracted him to Gretchen he saw also resonating in a way between Marin and Linitus. He could not help but recognize and appreciate it, for it reminded him of his past with the love of his life.

Only a short time later, the two heard a loud charging noise approaching the martial training grounds of the camp. In a moment, an armored human figure came riding on a white steed. He was a tall Nordling knight that quickly dismounted while proclaiming that he, the Dreadful Knight, had come to challenge the new contender who had beaten the Princess Knight from a sparring duel. This knight wore red scale-mail armor along with a red helmet covering around the head except for the front that exposed the face. As the Dreadful Knight declared seeking this victor who bested the Princess Knight to test his might, he quickly drew from his scabbard a sword that lit aflame just as Marin's had done. It was clear that he was from the same knighthood as Marin, the Order of the Eternal Flame.

The crowd of other knights as well as enlisted soldiers stood silent, watching in awe and wondering in their own minds who would win in the possible duel between Linitus and the Dreadful Knight. The Dreadful Knight, again sounding haughty and prideful in his tone, called out the challenger who had bested Marin. Still no reply.

Linitus was next to Marin at this point, conversing while overhearing and observing what was going on. The elf consoled Marin that he had no intention to spar again. He told her that he was content to spar with her to improve her training as well as perhaps for him to learn even a few things from her. He did not want to give in to this newly appeared and prideful knight's challenge for the sake of a victory of vanity and prestige.

However, the Dreadful Knight could tell from his own assumption (which happened to be correct) that the one next to Marin, a pointy-eared elf bearing a topknot, dressed in a combination of leather and elven mail armor, was probably the one who had bested her since none of the other soldiers or knights in Swordbane had bested Marin in duel combat before, except for one who led Imperium Sanctum Novus as its acting general and the Dreadful Knight himself, who was able to match Marin in combat though neither of the two had yet bested each other.

The Dreadful Knight slowly approached Marin and Linitus while calling out the elf and asking who he was. The challenging knight pointed his flaming blade toward the elf, making insulting gestures and stating that he was willing to bet that he could not only match Marin in combat, but also easily lop the elf's pointy ears in two strokes. Linitus was angered by both the behavior and words of the haughty knight, and Marin could sense as well as empathize with the same anger while admonishing the Dreadful Knight, more properly known as Edwin Baldwin, to be mindful of what he was doing and keep his behavior in line with the expectations of their mutual order, the Eternal Flame.

Edwin the Dreadful Knight scoffed at the warning by his fellow knight and still hurled insults while pointing his blade at Linitus. Linitus kept his composure through a stern angry look. He was determined to teach this knight a lesson on his own vanity. The elf quietly and calmly told the knight that he would accept his challenge. The two walked over toward the central makeshift fighting-grounds arena to duel. The knight again approached the elf ranger to exchange more insulting words while pointing his blade at the elf. This time while the Dreadful Knight was in midsentence, hurling cursory insults at the elf, Linitus caught him off guard and suddenly kicked him in the groin, causing Edwin to kneel in pain. Linitus then got his blade and drew it near the knight's neck while pointing out that he took down the prideful knight in a single stroke despite all the words that Edwin was spouting. The crowd that watched stood in amazement as well as amusement. Some would consider the elf's fighting style as unknightly or a lack of chivalric display. For Linitus, it did not matter as much. For him, what his challenger had said was less honorable than what he had done to best his challenger in the surprising manner that he had.

As the Dreadful Knight still on his knees, groaning from pain, slowly began to get up, Linitus walked away with the crowd mostly cheering and Marin approaching to congratulate him on his cunning though not-so-knightly approach to victory. Even the king and Peat could not hold back their whirl of changing expressions of surprise, amusement, and being impressed by the swift resolve of the elf ranger. They both looked at each other and knew he was gifted in many ways, even in combat.

Ascentius decidedly admitted to Peat that Linitus would certainly be the best candidate to be in charge of leading the scouting party for the Swordbane army even if it meant Marin being sent along with the elf as part of the reconnaissance. The king admitted perhaps not only she would be safer in being embedded with this reconnaissance party but she would also learn more from her elf mentor about losing the vanity that came with knighthood, by learning his ways despite her still being a knight.

CHAPTER TEN

To Bring a New Era

The road closest from Orcus Tribus Uruk Kazaht was less than a half day away at full gallop by horse. The two dark-clothed riders, Decius and Agaroman, knew the route well enough to reach the dirt road that connected Imperia Sanctum Novus in the south from the semi-sedentary settlement to the north, Barbarum Hulliz-Colonia Collis. This settlement in the north was on a hilly and grassy plain in the hinterlands that would eventually become the forest and mountain domain of the Nordlings. Barbarum Hulliz was the first trade route deep inland that had a mixed influence both physically and culturally between Nordling and Citadellan. Its main lifeline to the south, from which it received many trade wares from the Citadellans of Swordbane was its southern neighbor in the northern desert, Imperium Sanctum Novus. Sanctum Novus was unique in not only being the furthest inland settlement of Swordbane as well as its predecessor Lupercalian Empire, but it was also the only settlement that never fell during the Nordling invasion that toppled the empire a millennium ago. The Lupercalian species and the Citadellans that lived in Sanctum Novus came to rely more on each other for survival before, during, and even after the Nordling invasions. Eventually when the Lupercalians disappeared in mysterious circumstances, the Citadellans became the only people in the lone desert settlement, which had found itself trading from a distance with many races including the Marjawani, Nordlings who eventually gave up any ambition to conquer such a lone fortified settlement from what was to them unbearable desert heat, and even the orcs and goblins from the far hinterlands, including Orcum Tribus Uruk Kazaht as well as farther northeast such as Regnum Goblinum Tohiish-Skiir and Regnum Goblinum Iheshat near swampy plains and the foothills adjacent to the Great Easterly Mountains.

It was, however, on this dirt road that Decius and his advisor sorcerer Agaroman would travel south to the source of this far-flung trade. At full gallop, they would reach Sanctum Novus in less than a week. On the morning of their arrival, on the outskirts outside the desert city, the two dark-clothed figures would remove their hoods while pacing toward the desert city gates. Near the city, within the first ten miles the dirt road became paved with concrete and stone. On either side of the road was a series of lotted palm-date groves belonging to several local aristocratic families of farmers of the settlement city. The dates were practically the only locally grown crop that the settlement could produce, though it was also known to produce rare desert dyes and incense harvested from local exotic plants including desert sage, gold blood, and Lupercalian ambrosia. These resources, though common in the settlement, were valued delicacies throughout Swordbane, so it was able to resist trading for the same commodities at exorbitant prices with its neighboring rival Marjawan. Marjawan had considered raiding the lone Swordbane settlement and attempted once, ending in dismal failure. It was a settlement very difficult to take over, with its lone position making logistics extremely difficult for campaigning across the desert expanse, even for a desert kingdom like Marjawan. The settlement itself was designed to be well provisioned in holding out while having sturdy stone desert walls made in the time of the Lupercalian Empire. These walls were strong enough to be considered a defender's dream to bar any invaders or anyone else, for that matter. Only two people would have access to the city, and they were fast approaching.

Within yards from the city gates, the settlement's gate guards immediately recognized the dark-clothed figures to let them in. They called out loudly to sound the trumpets and informed the guard's captain of the two figures' return. Immediately the settlement which was largely a mixture of military as well as some degree of religious clergy and civilian laity came out and cheered in huge throngs. To Decius and Agaroman, it was a return home with a much informal delighted hero's welcome, though not quite as grandiose as a military victory triumph parade.

As the two mounted figures continued to pace along deep into the city's interior, more people gathered, throwing red roses and palm fronds on the paved road, street, or avenue, which became flanked in the city's interior by the Great Colonnade of Sanctum Novus, made of desert stone columns. Upon reaching the heart of the city at the main plaza, Decius and Agaroman passed through the Triumphal Arch of the Order of the Black Wolf, named after the legendary knightly order that was originally a fraternal cult that had famously led the defense of Sanctum Novus during the barbarian Nordling invasions and when Marjawan decided it was an opportune time to strike the settlement while the rest of the then Lupercalian Empire was in disarray. This calculated decision by Marjawan at the time, however, again proved unsuccessful, and the Black Wolf Order became recognized in receiving a monumental arch to commemorate their victory in defense of the ancient city.

Decius and Agaroman proceeded steadily after passing through the city's triumphal arch, and eventually made their way to the plaza's interior or government-religious precinct. In front of the two figures stood a temple complex with the exterior being walled, with added columns along with a portico-like entranceway that led to the interior courtyard precinct and contained the main temple compound of the city's titular patron deity Laran, the deity of war. The Order of the Black Wolf dedicated and erected the temple during the ancient city's original founding by the Lupercalian ruling species, considered the patriarch class of the city, along with their human Citadellan servants and lower class of Citadellan colonist citizens, who were considered plebes. The city, Sanctum Novus, as a whole was a jewel in the desert, very much like the city of Marjawan though the former was on a somewhat smaller yet still urbanized scale.

Before approaching the portico portal entrance to the main city temple, Decius and Agaroman abruptly dismounted and turned around while being surrounded by the elite guards of the city, the knights of the Order of the Black Wolf. These knights though Citadellan human in form wore elaborate military armor made in the Citadellan legionary manner of segmented plate mail that covered their bodies, while wearing black garments under the armor and bearing fierce-looking helmets shaped like the head of a Lupercalian man-wolf. The average person, even a Citadellan from the more urbanized western coastal parts of the Swordbane kingdom, did not wear such attire as it would possibly be seen as frightening and intimidating from the armor itself. These elite Black Wolf knights' very long swords were wielded in two hands instead of the typical Citadellan short sword and rectangular shield that the Swordbane military had adopted from its Lupercalian imperial predecessor.

While standing before the plaza and turning toward the crowd, Decius would be introduced by Agaroman in a ceremonial way of Decius himself making an important announcement before the city's inhabitants. Agaroman made a proclamation to the crowd that Decius Maximus Invictus, appointed dux (a title of joint civilian- and military-held governorship of Imperium Sanctum Novus), had returned bearing great gifts before the city.

Then Decius restating his full name and title, dux of Imperium Sanctum Novus, brought word of a treaty that he and his advisor Agaroman had made with the orcs and goblins in which the latter would end their raids toward all Citadellan merchants coming to and from Sanctum Novus. Knowing that this was a great announcement that needed more backing beyond words or status, Decius withdrew from his mounted travel bag a long jagged but ornate goblin totem staff along with a Citadellan spear. Decius had asserted that he had no need to present the spear as a symbolic declaration of war to the orcs and goblins since they had reached for an understanding of peace while the totem Decius brought back was explained by the dux as a symbolic gesture of submission of the beastly creatures before the dux and the city of Sanctum Novus.

Immediately the city's crowd erupted into more cheers, chanting Dux Invicta, a way of bestowing the recognition of seemingly invincible power Decius had to lead and defend the city and its surrounding region. In another moment, Decius announced before the city that his time had come and now its merchants would soon not have to worry about raids by the Nordling barbarians as well, which were diminishing over time as Decius campaigned not against goblin and orc raiders during his earlier years of military service in Sanctum Novus but rather he headed farther north to exact retribution toward Nordling settlements that also engaged in raids against Citadellan merchants on their way toward the friendly semi-barbarian settlement of Barbarum Hulliz, the settlement Citadellans preferred to call Colonia Collis. The latter name was ascribed by the few Citadellan merchants that had partially settled there among the Nordlings to engage in trade on a daily basis.

The goblins and orcs had heard of Decius's accolades in warfare against Nordling raids in large part from one reputable goblin shaman witness. Consequently, the beast races respected and feared his reputed harshness toward the Nordling survivors in making them march, some to their death, through the high desert to Sanctum Novus, only to be forced to fight in the city's gladiator pits, which was one of the few remnant customs passed down from the Lupercalian species even after their empire fell, which the surviving Citadellans preserved and still enjoyed in seeing vanquished prisoners of war including raiders be forced to fight each other to the death. For the Citadellans, this was a means to exact their interpretation of justice and possibly to fill their primal lust for revenge against the Nordling barbarians that they saw as a recurring threat to their perceived orderly and higher form of civilized society while having their caravans frequently raided upon.

Now that the city was utterly under the sway of Decius from not only earning status in war but also in showing his statesmanship and prudence in making alliances with former foes such as goblins, orcs, and trolls, he was now in a position to bring about a new era, one in which the customs of the Lupercalians and their empire would be restored even without their direct presence. Both Decius and Agaroman would make this new empire an imitation and a modern emulation of the old empire. They would upend what they saw as the corrupt status quo of the Kingdom of Swordbane and bring its settlements back into the reenvisioned glory of the empire that it once was. The two figures stared at each other, smiling and nodding in a way that seemed they could read each others' minds in the next phase of their plan.

CHAPTER ELEVEN

The Plot Unleashed

After making his declaration before the city, Decius, the dux of Sanctum Novus, made his way through the interior grounds of the Temple of Laran. He entered slowly and ceremoniously into the temple sanctuary, approaching an altar with a miniature-model-like portico shrine. On top of the altar table stood a mounted miniature sword pointed upward, representing Laran, the deity spirit of war, and in front of it was a miniature model of a wolf made of cast bronze that was erected in a howling posture, representing Calu, the deity spirit of death and presider of the underworld including its realm of condemnation.

While Laran was a somewhat accepted remnant of the ancient Lupercalian religion, which the Citadellans had adopted, Calu was one that was controversial and dangerous to transgress when rendering worship and libation offerings of wine, incense, and even animal blood sacrifices. After the establishment of Swordbane, the first Nordling king banned the worship of Calu, with that first king seeing the deity spirit as evil, and that king was suspicious though at best he tolerated Laran. Additionally, the Nordlings had an aversion toward wolves, or cautious appreciation at best. Even the ancient Lupercalian species bearing a man-wolf resemblance was very much held with deep xenophobia and animosity by many of the Nordlings since their years of back-and-forth warfare and invasions with the Lupercalians.

Now, in defiance of this tradition banning the worship of Calu, nobody stood more defiant than both Decius and Agaroman, the latter of whom taught the former during his youth about the history and worship of this controversial deity spirit of the underworld. To Decius, it seemed a destined omen from both Laran and Calu that since childbirth he was literally raised by wolves after being one of the few survivors of a rare raid near the hilly outskirts surrounding the ancient former Lupercalian capital city of Imperia Capitolina that lay inland about fifty miles east of Citadella Neapola and about fifty miles south of Salvinia Parf Edhellen.

Agaroman thought as much of Decius, seeing the dux's life being destined, and the wizard advisor reinforced that notion over the years. Both of them saw over the years the city endure economic hardship, stagnation, social disenfranchisement, as well as political neglect of the city they led, Sanctum Novus. Now it had to come to an end, and Decius, surviving all the battles he had against overwhelming numbers at times when patrolling and making incursions deep into Nordling territorial settlements, had learned to grow as both a military leader and a statesman.

It was now, however, Decius's time to begin a new era. But first, he and Agaroman both thought, knew in their minds, and had planned for this day among their first pivotal days to unleash the plot that they had constructed in the past several years. It was time for the parties of individuals that they both considered as the obvious visible sign of corruption to be held accountable and dealt with. The clergy members from the various religious orders were known for corruption, including selling indulgences for the remission of sins that the citizens had committed while getting the very same followers of their temple orders addicted to committing further sins, to exploit these citizens for their wealth. All the more, while many of the same corrupt clergy that had used (or for a lack of better words, abused) their position for wealth also preyed upon the citizens' youth in sexual behavior secretly despite taking vows of celibacy. The dux and his sorcerer advisor were aware of this but knew prior to this moment whatever leverage they had among the city's folk was not enough even to upset and replace the status quo, the religious order. If anything was done as punishment toward the corrupt clergy without clear and evident proof, then the perpetrator even in the name of justice would have to answer before King Ascentius. Though Decius had a lot of power and authority as regional governor and as military leader of the legion assigned to him while also leading the Order of the Black Wolf, his authority did not have any hold on the clergy who, like him, had to answer to ultimately just the king.

Though Ascentius was aware of the cases levied against many of the clergy, he would only hear the ones who were brought forth to present their accusation as well as evidence for the supposed crimes of the accused priest. Often however, this would not happen as many of the clergy would elude justice when a possible petitioner who had been waiting to present his or her case died under mysterious circumstances, usually from the pocketknife of a local thug that would intimidate even if it meant death for the petitioner to recant his or her accusation.

For Decius, as much evil as he had planned to bring in order to bring about this new era, his new era, his moral compass, if one could say that, had certain unacceptable points that he would not cross, especially in the name of religion. Devotion and piety were among his most prized characteristics, where corruption, as he saw it, had no place to infiltrate the holiest temples for worshiping that which was worthy of praise and veneration. In his mind, using enemy prisoners of war to kill each other was legitimate as a means to exact justice while, by chance, people could enjoy it for pleasure. Bribing or persuading former enemies, like orcs and goblins, to become new allies to be used as a part of a new army, a new empire to defend against common foes such as the Nordlings, was fair and necessary. Even things that Decius and his closest advisor Agaroman had not yet done but would do to unleash this new era were necessary and right in their minds, however cruel and harsh it would be upon his foes and, to some extent, the common citizenry of Sanctum Novus. If his mentor had to stage another war just like he did in Decius's youth for the sake of pleasing both Calu and Laran, their respective deities of death (along with the underworld) and war, in order to bring this new era, then so be it, he would. If they had to incubate and spread a plague in order to bring a civilization like the Kingdom of Swordbane further to its knees and bring this new era for ending the corruption and status quo that kept them and their city, Sanctum Novus, weak and deterred from becoming like the Lupercalian Empire, then they both would do it without hesitation. They would pursue it further if more deaths were needed than what was rendered in the twenty-year war between Swordbane and Marjawan in order to appease both Calu and Laran. They would do whatever it took to execute the final part of their plan and make both deity spirits, death and war, become one, with their powers jointly infused into Decius upon receiving their acknowledgment and approval for him to be their chosen vessel.

After burning his incense offering quietly and humbly before the altar dedicated to both Calu and Laran, Decius next took from the hands of

Agaroman standing next to him the goblet filled with red wine. Decius chanted several words of the ancient Lupercalian prayer of invocation before transferring a portion of the red wine from the goblet over the incense, offering a form of libation. Smoke immediately seared out from the contact made between the wine and the burning incense. Decius finished the last few words of his prayer invocation before lifting the goblet up before the altar and then proceeded to consume the rest of the liquid content. For him, it was the beginning of symbolic completion, of his dedication to the prophecy that both he and Agaroman would do everything to ensure would unfold while staying pious and devoted toward both Calu and Laran.

The two figures next walked out of the temple sanctuary, exited through a secret back way, and made their way to another walled-portico complex that had an inner garden courtyard and a main building surrounded by the outer walls. This building also had a portico entrance and was three stories tall. It was the estate residence of the city's dux, Decius. Many referred to it also as the Ducal Palace. Through the first gate door, Decius had walked sternly with a purpose, with his advisor Agaroman doing the same also while remaining a few steps behind the dux.

This palace complex was well guarded without any common citizens being able to see what happened inside. In the main vestibule stood an open ceiling-free perimeter, or atrium, as it is called, surrounded by the rest of the living-room hallway with ceiling enclosures. In front of Decius and Agaroman stood various tunic- and toga-robed figures bearing an array of symbolic religious necklaces. They were clergy from various religious temple orders, including Sol Invictus (the god of the sun and mythological dragons), Aritimi (the goddess spirit of love and hunting), Silvanus (the god of the woodlands, forces of nature, and sacred boundaries), and even Laran, whose priests Decius despised for being the most corrupt since he himself as the dux identified heavily and personally with that particular deity in addition to Calu. These various clergy figures were being watched and surrounded by a larger combined force of Black Wolf knights as well as a handful of city guards. The present clergy were eager, frightened, and surprised. They did not know what fate was in store for them but knew it was not very promising when the dux and leader of the Black Wolf knighthood had summoned them under heavily guarded watch. Their intuition would prove to be correct.

Upon Agaroman announcing loudly and formally Decius's title, the dux stood back, waiting for the various clergy to give their full attention and possibly show a gesture of recognition to hierarchical respect such as kneeling. None of the clergy did, however. They despised Decius and couldn't care less what the dux thought of them though they were still intimidated by his presence. Regardless, they knew whatever their misdeeds were, there was nothing in their minds that this regional titleholder of office could do to punish them without the king's approval. If there was any other day they thought the same beforehand as they had now, then they would have been correct. Tragically on this day, they would find out otherwise.

Decius stood and delivered a speech using a tone of authority and sternness. He knew these priests he had summoned, accused of various corrupt actions, would object and not accept his authority. He would be ready for the first one to challenge in only the first few moments that he addressed them. When that happened, the dux stated their various crimes including corruption of indulgences for personal wealth, violation of celibacy vows while preying upon the youth, and even paying others to intimidate or outright murder anyone that leveled a request of audience to present their case before the king against these clergy. Then, a male priest from the temple order of Laran, openly interrupted and rebuked Decius by stating he was not the king but only a pretender and an upstart bastard. The dux quickly walked up the defiant clergyman and pulled not his sword from his scabbard by his waist, but instead a hidden knife under one of his black metal gauntlets, and the dux slit in a quick fell swoop the throat of the Laran priest. The defiant and now-stricken clergyman quickly lay in a pool of his own blood while the other priests stood shocked and speechless.

Decius would have none of it if anyone else was to defy him. He went to say that if any one of them did, he would personally slit all their throats as punishment in advance. As soon as he could tell he had their attention as well as respect, though now out of fear, Decius informed the accused clergy that he himself would be the new divine appointed instrument or chosen vessel to bring his form of justice in a new era and Imperium Sanctum Novus would no longer be under the banner of Swordbane, relegated to a second class-city with the majority of its treasury being spent and wasted at the benefit and leisure of the king. The dux would introduce what would be a remnant to usher in a new era, bringing back the Lupercalian Empire, at least in spirit.

As such, the dux's first act as sovereign ruler in his own city no longer under the king's authority would be to bring accountability toward the corrupt priesthood, at least the ones in his own city that he personally summoned. He would act as such by giving these summoned clergy a punishment, a form of trial by ordeal that he would even subject himself to. The accused priests, not surprisingly, stood shocked, even more so than before and wondered with further anxiety what went through this mad regional leader's head. Decius and Agaroman could both tell that from seeing the priests' reaction, not that it mattered, nor did the two care. They had other plans including the priests. They knew that the king would have to take them in if they sought refuge as clergy if even to be heard for a future trial by the king himself. It was for this conclusion that both the now-ascended warlord dux and his sorcerer advisor planned to unleash the next phase of their plot.

Decius told the clergy that they would go with him to an afflicted colony quarantined outside the city, to be exposed to the same affliction that the inhabitants of the colony had. They would stay there for three days, and whoever prevailed unscathed would clearly be seen in the eyes of the divine spirits as innocent. The clergy's faces became deeper in utter despair. They knew if they did not go along, Decius would slay them just as quickly and without hesitancy. Their only choice was to comply and hope that they would emerge without being afflicted themselves after exposure for three days.

Prior to entering the afflicted quarantined colony, Agaroman administered a vaccine injection to Decius's arm, using a syringe with a sharp needlelike object. The sorcerer offered the same injection to any of the sentenced priests, but all of them rejected the offer with the view that this could be a deadlier curse of affliction and possibly more potent than the one they would face. The sorcerer shrugged and said that they would only have themselves to blame should they not emerge unscathed without accepting his offering.

Only a short time later, Decius and the priests arrived at the afflicted colony and remained there for three long days. At the end of the third day and the start of dawn of the fourth day, Decius and the priests emerged from the locked colony. All of them had signs of affliction, including severe coughing, except for Decius. The settlement's general and regional ruler had now become victor of the symbolic trial by ordeal. Decius had declared that the divine had granted him to be chosen, not only for his course of action condemning the priests secularly by his authority but also now divine condemnation as shown by their incurment of inflictions. The priests, being present to observe while coughing hard, each gave cold and hateful stares but said nothing, knowing that they could suffer a worse fate. Much to their surprise after being afflicted, they were not sent back to the colony from which they emerged. Decius instead told them that should they survive their affliction, they would remain banished from Sanctum Novus. However, he did offer them escort to the next nearest human settlement, still quite far, which would be either Colonia Mons Salvina (barely on the other side, the western side, of the Swordbane coastal mountain range) or Barbarum Hulliz-Colonia Collis, a region of plains and grasslands that followed along the northern end of the great basin and northeast of the Swordbane coastal mountain range. With little choice, the priests agreed to accept the offer. Much to their surprise and regret, their escort that showed up later that day was little more than a small band of orcs, goblins, and a human bandit leader known throughout both the western and eastern sides of the Swordbane coastal mountain range as Dirty Dale.

Dale was a former sheep shanker bearing a sharp hook on a pole and dressed in an unkempt fur attire and cotton-like armor. Many had come up with rumors and insulting names and stories, including that this Dale was allegedly a sheep shagger. If anyone dared to mention this to the bandit leader's face, such a person would earn Dale's ire and be lucky to survive his sharp hook pole.

The priests remained under close watch by Decius's elite city praetorian guard who were also members of the Knighthood Order of the Black Wolf. Meanwhile, Decius had changed his attire from a black robe like those worn by penitents to his full military general and Black Wolf order regalia. He had donned a short black tunic along with black breeches going down to just under his kneecaps. He wore over his short tunic black breastplate armor engraved with his symbol bearing the face of a wolf howling, with sword and shield behind the wolf-face sigil. Additionally, Decius being general and commander of the Black Wolf knights also had leg-guard greaves and arm guards also made of steel and tinted in black like his breastplate. Finally for his military attire and ensemble, the dux had also had a customized artisan-made enclosed helmet in the shape of a wolf head that was truly intimidating.

Upon donning his gear from a distance in front of the priests, Decius awaited for both the arrival of his close advisor Agaroman, who appeared using his sorcery spell of teleporting, upon the sorcerer hearing news that the trial was over. Agaroman inspected Decius as well as the condemned priests. The sorcerer affirmed Decius's emergence as victor and innocent in the eyes of the deity spirits because of punishing the priests for their crimes, and the sorcerer ruled that the clergy's displayed and exhibited afflictions were truly a divine ordained condemnation.

Decius awaited outside the city gates with Agaroman for a short time before a message was sent to them from one of the city guards surveying the horizon that a large group of orcs, goblins, even a troll, not to mention what appeared to be some fur-covered human bandits appeared, marching steadily toward the city, with some of them mounted on dire wolves. Decius and Agaroman both smiled with the loud announcement, while Decius told the priests that their escort had arrived. The priests were, not surprisingly, speechless as well as in utter fear. Never before had a settlement in Swordbane allowed such an arrangement where they would have their own subjects escorted to another settlement of the kingdom by such villainous denizens. While having bouts of coughing, the still-surviving clergy wondered and whispered to each other in speculation of what this dux of Nova Sanctum was planning. What was he up to as to be involved with beastly races such as orcs, goblins, and possibly trolls? They were not beyond speculation.

A short time later, the orc-and-goblin delegation had arrived. At the front of this large war band stood a large troll carrying on its back the orc war captain himself from the settlement of Orcum Tribus Uruk Kazaht along with the goblin chief shaman of the settlement who was being carried in a litter-like sled chariot that six dire wolves pulled. This orc war captain and the goblin chief shaman were incidentally the same ones that Decius and Agaroman had negotiated a treaty with as well as started what many in Swordbane would consider an unholy alliance between the dux (representing his regional settlement) and the multitude of scattered settlements of orcs, goblins, and other beastly creatures that would unite under this dux who had promised them he would fulfill the prophecy of making the deities of war and death become one with him as their chosen vessel to lead the beastly creatures on a bloodthirsty war against Swordbane. Among the city guard, the settlement's farmers who labored in the palm-tree groves on either side of the settlement's paved roads, and even again the condemned priests, this beastly contingent was truly a sight to see, marching toward the dux without either side provoking each other into possible combat.

Only a moment later, the dismounted goblin shaman and orc war captain approached, walking up to Decius and Agaroman to tell them that what seemed to be the impossible had been finally done. The various goblin and orc scout messengers from Uruk Kazaht had delivered word of the dux's prophecy and call to allegiance. All the surrounding goblin, orc, and other beastly settlements had accepted this offer to unite under the banner of this dux, or as they knew him from the many rumors of his prophetic arrival at Uruk Kazaht, the Wolf King and the Dark Lord of War and Death. Decius had truly earned a reputation in not only being respected by the goblins, orcs, and other beastly races but also being feared, and in a twisted sense, he was their salvation, to fulfill the prophecy of bringing a new era of darkness and order. For Decius and Agaroman, it was justifiable to make such an alliance in order to bring order to a world they both saw as flawed and corrupt despite portraying what they considered an idealistic facade of pursuits that were considered divinely just and good.

For the dux and his advisor, the only proper order to assert against forces that threatened was to eliminate those forces or bring them under the yoke of domination as they had come to understand from reading the ancient histories of Swordbane's predecessor of power, the Lupercalian Empire. For Decius and Agaroman, it was up to them to garner support to bring about a contemporary version of the Lupercalian Empire, or what they considered the remnants of it. They would do it by using this new alliance of Citadellans who supported them along with the various orc-goblin forces and those in league with them to bring down the Kingdom of Swordbane once and for all in a series of painful strikes, some more overt while others more clandestine.

There were still other parts to this plot besides outright war and domination that Decius would use. He had a group of afflicted priests, not to mention a colony of others that he would use and weaponize to slowly overwhelm and decimate Swordbane in the hopes of inciting a pandemic that would further strain the kingdom and its resources while Sanctum Novus would break away and fight for its autonomy.

Decius also had plans to deal with the Nordling barbarians to the north. He would appease both Laran and Calu for bringing war and death to the barbarians that still opposed him, but he and Agaroman planned to bring various barbarian settlements to the point of submitting before his combined forces and he would conscript these barbarian settlements' war bands into his army to use against Swordbane later on. It would be a further and perpetual series of fighting and death, enough that when it was time, the dark-lord dux and his sorcerer would be ready to enact their final phase of the plot: to cause enough death and destruction in war and call upon the deities of war and death to become as one with him infused by the deity spirits' powers. It was a difficult process for them to get this far, but now it seemed all the necessary pieces were in place to make this seemingly unimagined prophecy a reality.

Throughout the day, a settlement-wide announcement was proclaimed with a triumphant ceremonial procession in which Decius and Agaroman led their goblin-orc guests through the main city street avenue to be watched and amazed by the settlements' predominantly Citadellan population, some of whom were just as shocked as the priests condemned outside the walls, though many of the local subject civilians saw this procession as a similar sign or omen of prophetic triumph of their dux as the goblins and orcs had. The settlement's people en masse cheered on the procession, believing that their leader had ended the longstanding feuds and frequent series of skirmishes between the orc and goblin forces that raided their caravans. In their minds, they were happy knowing that their general, their hero, their dux had fought so hard to earn his reputation to be feared and respected enough to have the orcs and goblins submit before them. It became more symbolic as well to see many of the dire wolves come into the city that hosted the knightly order that represented the very same creature.

After declaring that this delegation of orcs and goblins indeed had come as a follow-up to affirm from the dux's earlier proclamation that they had established a treaty as well as a common alliance between Sanctum Novus and the various orc-goblin settlements west of the Great Easterly Mountains. By the end of the dux's proclamation, in another symbolic gesture to convince the settlement's population of his declaration of a new era in which he had been chosen to lead them and their new allies, the Citadellan general gave a sudden wolflike howl that prompted the dire wolves mounted by their goblin riders to reply in the same manner as deference before Decius's authority in commanding not only the forces of humans, goblins, and orcs, but also the leading predators of nature. The large crowds replied also in cheers hailing their local ruler no longer as a proxy of authority to Swordbane's monarch, but instead elevating the dux as now their new supreme leader to lead and represent them. As sunset approached, Decius, Agaroman, and the leaders of this goblin-orc delegation retired into the dux's government residence to discuss and decide how to further carry out their future plans.

A small guarded convoy on both horseback and wolf mount escorted the afflicted priests as well as the others from the settlement's afflicted colony north and eventually westward to Colonia Mons Salvinia and other Swordbane settlements. Under the dux's orders, these afflicted were to be returned to Swordbane's western settlements to be examined further and treated by the other clergy of the settlements.

The dux had also given a written symbolic message for the priests to deliver to the various settlements of Swordbane in witness to the omen or trial of the dux emerging unscathed: follow under his banner or suffer the same fate as the corrupt priests who had committed sin. Failing to do so and receiving the same affliction was considered by the dux and his advisor as tantamount to being guilty in still staying in allegiance as accomplices to the corruption that Swordbane had tolerated. This would be the first act of several in which the dux was no longer under allegiance to the king of Swordbane and the dux would bring back a remnant of the Lupercalian Empire under his command. The dux made sure this message would be delivered, for he had ordered it to be inked painfully as a tattoo into the backs of the priests.

CHAPTER TWELVE

Reminiscing and Intimacy

Several hundred miles away from Sanctum Novus, the Swordbane king's army would march en route to that destined lone urbanized Citadellan settlement in the high desert. The army had just left the settlement of Marjawan Oztuz on the eastern bank of the Great Desert River to stop only briefly to acquire temporary provisions from the dwarven stronghold of Grimaz-Kadrinbad a few miles on the other side of the riverbank. The majority of the army still marched en route to Sanctum Novus after camping only briefly overnight in pitched tents outside Kadrinbad. It would take at least about two weeks' march at the earliest for them to arrive outside the walls of Sanctum Novus to receive further provisions before marching still further westward toward the main coastal heartland of the kingdom.

Many of the soldiers and knights of Swordbane were quite jovial, and understandably so in seeing the end of a two-decade-long war between their kingdom and their eastern rival, Marjawan. The soldiers and knights traded stories about their experiences in war as well as their future aspirations and endeavors when they arrived back at their home settlement garrisons, many of those being Citadellan coastal strongholds, while others were the more mountainous interior dwarven strongholds in addition to Kadrinbad (some of the dwarf veterans had disbanded after being formally discharged from the war to return to their usual mining operations and other crafts of trade, including metal parts manufacturing and weapon smithing). Meanwhile, the elves that served in various capacities, including scouting and acting as skirmishers, would later disband and return to their former lives in the various settlements in and around the elven city stronghold of Salvinia Parf Edhellen, which was in the redwood forest region just inland and less than a hundred miles east from the kingdom capital.

The rest of the army, being humans of both Citadellan and assimilated Nordling heritage or a mixture of both, again would retire back to their assigned stronghold settlements that dotted the kingdom's western coast, forming the core of the kingdom itself. The outlook was truly optimistic and would be that way until an unexpected turn of events soon came to pass.

The king's army eventually marched through a great pass of mesas and other elevated areas that separated the high desert from the low desert to enter the former, where it would be somewhat colder especially at night, though still relatively hot during the daytime, especially in the summer season as it was.

After making the transition, the royal army was only a few days' march away from Sanctum Novus, which was located toward the southwestern part of the Great High Desert. The king had decided to send Linitus along with his new company of distinguished veterans, which included Wyatt, the king's close guard chieftain Peat, and his daughter Marin, whom he had entrusted to Linitus's watch, all to serve as scouts. The king was somewhat hesitant in doing this as it did put his daughter in potential harm's way, but the war was already over and there were no foreseeable dangers that the king would expect en route only a few days from Sanctum Novus. Besides, Ascentius knew that Decius, the appointed dux of the region, whom he had commissioned, was highly distinguished in battle as well as highly capable of leading the city to ensure there were no threats within his region of command. Decius had after all impressed the king while rising in the ranks as both a knight and soldier on the field, serving alongside Ascentius in quelling a large barbarian Nordling incursion that swept southward a few years ago, with the Nordling tribes being rallied by their last king who saw the opportunity to strike Swordbane's territorial holdings in the Collis Vallem region north of both Sanctum Novus and, to a lesser extent, Uruk Kazaht. This Nordling king, Ulfner, was powerful and deadly in battle. However, upon challenging Decius in single combat to represent the king, Decius slew the great barbarian chieftain swiftly in only one blow shortly after their duel commenced. Decius immediately set an impression to Ascentius that he would be reliable and deadly enough while having sufficient troops and resources at his command to keep the Nordling barbarians at bay as well as any potential threats the goblins and orcs might consider posing against this then newly appointed regional leader, or dux, of the king.

The king thought, while en route to Sanctum Novus, more and more about the appointed dux. Ascentius had known Decius prior, while seeing him briefly train over the years in both Citadella Neapola and also in the order that Decius later joined, the Knighthood of the Black Wolf, based in Sanctum Novus. The memories and flashbacks swirled, with the king also recalling the annual arena tournament of champions in the amphitheater of Citadella Neapola, how this particular Citadellan knight was formidable enough to best his own daughter Marin, who herself though barely a knight less than five years ago had bested or matched everyone else in combat except Edwin Baldwin (aka the Dreadful Knight), who was able to match Marin but not surpass her, and recently Linitus the elf ranger. Ascentius was impressed in not only seeing Decius in combat firsthand but also in hearing from one of the royal advisors and wizards, Agaroman, firsthand about Decius's miraculous infancy story: being raised briefly by wolves after being left for dead when his biological parents were murdered along with much of a religious caravan headed on a pilgrimage to the ancient ruins of Imperia Capitolina, the seat of power of the then Lupercalian Empire. That thought, however, troubled Ascentius, who had been a witness to the aftermath of death and destruction of the caravan, including a memory of Decius as an infant being picked up personally by Agaroman when the nurturing wolf pack apparently trusted the wizard and permitted him to do so.

It truly was a miracle for Decius to have emerged so successfully in station and rank over the years, so the king did not hold back in rewarding the Citadellan for what Ascentius would consider Decius's rightful merit in demonstrating command, leadership, and martial prowess. Until recently from the arrival and presence of Linitus, the king had even considered his appointed general and dux as a suitable candidate to wed his daughter and pass succession to the throne. Decius had attained over time the reputation and love of the general public of the kingdom's subjects, though perhaps too much, and the king wondered if such fame acquired by the dux would come at his expense. He shrugged off the thought of it while keeping in mind the sound judgment to rely on gauging and measuring his appointed dux's loyalty by his past deeds and the reputation that had been shown thus far as any indication.

Though Decius would be a deadly rival, the king was content in his mind to not seriously consider that, ultimately knowing there was no cause that would lead him to believe it. They both shared common interests in the kingdom, wanting stability and order, and addressing acts of corruption while providing stronger integrity of the kingdom as a whole with its military bulwark. The king knew that despite showing some tone of displeasure for the delay in obtaining the king's audience to make rulings on certain cases involving corruption allegations and scandals, the dux still was willing to wait for the king to make his own judgment on such matters that Ascentius considered important enough for him in his position to handle directly, especially when the allegations of corruption involved clergy. The king respected Decius for that and knew that there was probably no greater general to depend on to watch the kingdom's frontier while seeking provisions for the royal army en route to returning to the western coastal heartlands.

As the king reminisced in the pitched tent camp, Wyatt's magical skyship floated high above the desert. Looking down from above, the view was surreal among the floating vessel's occupants save Wyatt, the conductor and builder of the flying contraption who was very adjusted to spectacular views from high above. Linitus looked down at the dots of the royal encampment of tents while sitting alongside Marin near the edge of the ship's port side. Over the days, the Princess Knight and her new mentor in combat had grown fairly attached. The two had talked about various topics, from reminiscing about their childhood when they briefly met each other, to their own separate upbringings in growing up to become who they were, their personal interests, and even fighting strategies and topics, which was expected since Linitus, being in charge of Marin, was responsible for instructing the Princess Knight in his knowledge of how to fight and survive. Marin was impressed not only by the elf's humble upbringing and serene outlook in life, but also by his uncanny imagination for devising the ideas he had into practical and effective strategies that he drew upon from his upbringing of hunting and scouting. He found ways to translate what he learned and apply into actual matters of warfare.

The princess, for her part, had mutually impressed the elf somewhat from her vivid descriptions about living in the royal cosmopolitan capital of Citadella Neapola to make anyone see it as a truly magical place. He was also drawn to and amused by her recollections of regimented and martial upbringing despite being of royalty in which Peat the annoying, stubborn, and somewhat haughty veteran dwarf guardian had a softer and caring side that no one saw, except Marin and her father, the king.

Additionally, the elf was impressed by Marin's stubbornness (which he pointed out to Marin, seeing how the dwarf might have imparted that to her) and determination to overcome all obstacles, including being the first female knight of Swordbane, which she had to endure the same training and discipline as all other knights despite the perceived social outlier qualities that were held against her, being a woman and of royalty. She was much more than that, so she wanted to prove herself to society and challenge that notion. It was that sense of understanding she appreciated, and she became fonder of Linitus for recognizing that, for recognizing her as a person and having an open mind to empathize with her in imagining her perspective while not discounting her simply because of her status as a woman and as royalty.

In a way, they both saw and acknowledged a mutual, shared commonality of determination and self-identity that may have converged in how they were able to relate, with Linitus being from a relatively humble background and rising to his station from his own skill in a similar but somewhat reverse manner. Meanwhile, Marin from the opposite end of the spectrum, being in a higher inherited position of royalty, endured lessons of humility in her life, including undergoing the training to be a knight and serve a higher purpose as well as serve others in need, much as Linitus did in his own capacity as an elf ranger who learned what was passed on to him from his father and previous generations of ancestors. The two stared at each other deeply while still sharing a common and deep sense of respect and understanding.

Marin admitted that she could see herself in some way wanting to experience what she considered the utter bliss and freedom that she so wanted and felt Linitus as her companion and mentor had. She finally opened up to him, admitting that she was grateful that despite all these years being apart, she was able to reunite with him and perhaps being separated so long made the sharing of their experiences more meaningful, to appreciate what they had and aspired to attain in their station in life. Perhaps more so for her, since she admitted to Linitus her slight envy that he had everything he wanted and was content despite being so far away from home and family in a war fought bitterly between humans that really had nothing to do with elves apart from his people being subjects of Swordbane and, as such, called to serve along with the dwarves and other small folk.

Linitus acknowledged and shrugged while indicating that despite him experiencing such bliss and content, which he did, he too had experienced the same things she had and perhaps was more scared than she knew, which made Marin feel even guiltier about her own status and privilege in being royal. He had shared with her that despite her losing many of her fellow knights under and by her own command, which she had to bear the burden and ownership in doing, the elf ranger lost several personal friends that he knew and grew up with, from the neighboring elven hamlets outside Salvinia Parf Edhellen. Some of these losses were in consequence of saving Marin's own life and the lives of her few surviving knights. Linitus knew he would have to live with his own convicted conscience as he took it upon himself to explain to the families of his departed elf ranger comrades that they gave their lives to save a member of the royal throne, but he would never tell them what he considered the full truth. The full truth, to some extent, haunted him more. He would never tell their surviving kin that it was a sacrifice that could have been avoided; despite that, it did end the war and perhaps saved more lives in the long run, after rescuing the princess, when they took the fortunate chance to capture the ruler of Marjawan and end the war. It was Linitus's own initiative out of a desire to save a longtime former friend, Marin, that he risked the lives of many of his elven companions, not all of whom survived the rescue attempt. Some of them did perish from the fight on the streets and alleys of Marjawan's capital city to rescue Marin.

The admission and confession that Linitus gave made Marin's heart sink with a heavy burden of guilt. It was one that Linitus planted not out of anger or intention to make her feel such guilt, but he truthfully felt himself to blame in leading some of his own ranger company to their deaths by his own initiative and he trusted her enough to admit his feelings openly to her. Marin, seeing how he felt, knew that but still felt compelled by her own guilt regardless to ask forgiveness for her rash command decision-making. She held out her hand to clasp Linitus's hand, telling him that he would not have to worry about not admitting that part to his fallen comrades' kin. She personally would be there by his side to let the surviving elven families know that the fallen elven rangers had sacrificed their lives for her and she would seek their forgiveness in telling them the full story.

Linitus, touched by Marin's gesture, placed his other hand on top of her hand also.

It was an intimate moment for both of them, in which time seemed to have no meaning. They looked intimately at each other and stared intently until they both felt the same urge from each other's instinctive body language to finally share a mutual, deep, and intimate kiss. No one was looking as Peat was inside the captain's cabin of the flying ship and Wyatt was not within their immediate sight while standing far away from them on the other end of the deck at the prow of the flying ship, looking down and scanning ahead. It was their own private and discreet moment, which they impulsively acted upon and kept to themselves as such, at least for now.

CHAPTER THIRTEEN

A New War Unleashed

The next day during early sunrise, as planned, Ascentius dispatched the Dreadful Knight, Edwin Baldwin, along with his company of horse-mounted Eternal Flame knights to send notice to Sanctum Novus and its dux that the royal army would arrive soon for provisions and to be formally hosted. The Dreadful Knight with his company of about three dozen Eternal Flame knights rode at full haste toward the desert settlement.

The Swordbane army under Ascentius's command marched at its steady pace while maintaining a tight and organized maniple checkered formation. Infantry marched in grouped cohorts at the front while archers marched right behind, with the third rank being cavalry at the rear. Elf-ranger skirmishers and dwarf-guardian auxiliaries marched at opposite flanks along with a small dwarf-guardian contingent that acted as chief bodyguard near the center rear of the formation embedded with Ascentius's mounted contingent of Citadellan and Nordling Eternal Flame knights. This was not the typical marching formation that Ascentius would have his soldiers utilize, compared to being organized in a line array of a long column-like formation, but the king made the decision that it was best to have his army assume a ready standard combat formation in the event that they would be caught off guard and attacked by a possible raiding Marjawan party that might be unaware that the war was over or possibly a goblin-orc raiding party that might be daring enough to attack the king's formidable army for any possible spoils of war to loot.

Looking from a bird's-eye view above, the occupants of Wyatt's floating skyship saw a truly magnificent sight below. Upon waking up in each other's arms while still near the port-side skyline end of the ship, Linitus and Marin became captivated at seeing such a large and beautiful side of the kingdom's army while looking further ahead to see into the distance just above the horizon the approaching view of Sanctum Novus. Marin asked her newfound lover if the view was not the most majestic he had ever seen, to which Linitus nodded his head in affirmation.

However, the moments of bliss would last for only so long. Only a few hours later, Linitus with his eagle-like sight noticed something unusual that caught his attention upon scouting and surveilling from high above, something hidden among the mountain thistle trees on the nearest mountains above the high desert plain about a dozen or so miles from Sanctum Novus in the distance. He spotted what appeared to be embedded among the mountain foliage scattered waves of figures. He looked intently, with as much concentration as possible, verifying until he reacted with a face of utter concern and alertness.

Everything was not well, and even Marin could tell. After only a moment, Linitus shouted out, sighting orcs and goblins. He immediately stated that there was an army of them, at least ten thousand strong. They were poised and ready to march. Immediately, the elf ranger had Wyatt use a teleportation spell to transport the two of them along with Marin to Ascentius, to warn the king of the impending danger. It was most likely a full mounted assault against the settlement and possibly a large planned raid against the Swordbane kingdom's army. When Linitus reported it to the king, Ascentius immediately ordered for a small half dozen of his mounted knights to send word to Sanctum Novus of the foreseen, impending threat. It was a threat; however, the king and everyone else in his army was completely oblivious to what had recently transpired, in the form of an alliance made between his appointed dux and the combined forces of orcs and goblins as well as to the dux's recent declaration of insurrection and rebellion against the kingdom and its sovereign ruler.

The half dozen of dispatched mounted knights rode at full haste with orders to send word to Sanctum Novus as well as to notify the dux to make last-minute preparations bracing for war against the invading orc-goblin army. Again however, the dispatched knights were unaware of Decius's mutual pact and collaboration with the goblins and orcs against the king.

Linitus had offered to send direct word to Sanctum Novus instead, but the king rejected his offer, letting the elf ranger know that his services were best needed to do as he had done, to remain high above on board Wyatt's skyship with his daughter to both protect her and continue to survey and report on further impending threats that were equally dire. The elf ranger and the Princess Knight both complied with his order by saluting the king and teleporting with their wizard companion Wyatt back to the skyship to further scout and survey any other major threats from high above.

Only another hour later, the king had ordered a change in formation upon marching toward the walls of Sanctum Novus, with the army directed to face outward and outboard from the western section of the desert city's walls, which faced directly toward the position of the goblin-orc army along the western red rock and tree-covered mountains. The mountain landscape itself was a notable geographical feature being a few miles away but surrounding much of the western and northern periphery of what was mostly desertlike landscape.

The army's formation still remained the same as it had before. Though the king looked behind and above at the walls of the settlement. He wondered why it had taken so long for the settlement to respond and mount a quick alarm call to quarters with archers and soldiers from the settlement itself to man the ramparts of the walls as well as for the dux to sally some sizeable force outside the city walls to further augment the overall force of the king's army to repel the anticipated invading goblin-orc army.

Unsurprisingly, the goblin-orc army marched eastward in a somewhat awkward and less-refined formation down from the red mountains covered with trees toward the open desert plain that lay west of Sanctum Novus. This goblin-orc army began to eventually march at full pace, planning to charge at maximum force toward the Swordbane army.

The king, still nervous, could not hold his frustration in, cursing about what was taking so long for his best capable general to assist his forces. Suddenly from the wall ramparts above and unexpectedly, the Dreadful Knight appeared. Edwin Baldwin spoke loudly, addressing both the king and his army. He informed Ascentius that the dux had received word, including the latest developments, and he would respond in kind. Then Edwin cryptically followed up to announce loudly enough for his words to be heard that his new lord Decius had issued a message to the king and one that only Ascentius would understand personally as he once said to his dux, "Remember the eve of victory, for its tree must bleed to enjoy the fruits of labor." It was a painful, sudden, and surprising response that the king could translate very well despite the confusion of faces among his own men when Edwin reiterated the message that Decius had ordered the Dreadful Knight to reply when Ascentius had earlier requested for Sanctum Novus to help mount its defenses to supplement and fight in unison with the Swordbane army outside the city walls against the goblin-orc army.

Within another moment of Edwin's cryptic and ominous message, a full contingent of the desert settlement's Citadellan archers as well as shockingly multiple bands of orc and goblin warriors mounted the wall ramparts also with bows and arrows in hand. It was a sight that was unbelievable to not only Ascentius and his forces on the ground that saw what was going on, but also from high above in the skyship with its occupants including Linitus, Marin, Wyatt, and Peat looking down in horror and utter shock.

Immediately, the Dreadful Knight himself, raising his flaming blade up high, gave the command for the combined local Citadellan garrison, goblin warriors, and orc archers aligned along the rampart battlements and arrow slits of the settlement's western walls to let loose a volley of arrows toward the king's army that originally and ironically intended to defend its now-fortified attacker against what was perceived to be the threat of a large-scale attacking goblin-orc army. Now, in that very moment of heartbreaking betrayal, it all made sense, at least to an extent it did for Ascentius and only him at that very moment. It was an ambush and slaughter waiting to happen and poised to cause confusion and immediate loss of morale to an army that was sworn to defend one of its own settlements against an outside force, which the latter had now made a deadly alliance with the dux and his garrisoned forces in the settlement against the kingdom and the crown that the former was expected to keep fealty toward the latter at all times.

The king, though still lost in words and thought, managed to compose himself to yell loudly and authoritatively for his forces to hold steady as they would soon be encroached on and attacked from nearly all directions, with the goblin-orc forces going head-on and hard against the front ranks of the kingdom's army while the now-apparent garrison of Sanctum Novus had turned against them with its embedded archers combined with goblins and orcs that had already arrived at the settlement, attacking from the walls behind. Meanwhile several moments later, the southern gates of the desert city's walls were opened, with more of the newly combined forces of local Citadellan infantry, including members of the Black Wolf knights, along with multiple bands of goblins and orcs streaming outside the walls and making their way to attack the left flank of the king's royal army.

What surprised the betrayed forces of the king even more, which Linitus and his skyship company could see at first hand with a deeper sense of shock and awe, was a teleportation field had flashed toward the rear force of the goblin-orc army that engaged the Swordbane forces from the west end of the city walls. Emerging from that teleportation field was a dark-robed and hooded figure who had a magical staff and seemed to be the wizard. He came along with a dozen Black Wolf knights led by a figure who was prominently dressed in full knight armor bearing a pitch-black color along with a helmet that resembled the head of a wolf. This leading figure was positioned between a goblin shaman and a large orc-looking chieftain who held a chain leash to a large dire wolf, the type of animal that normally goblins and lightweight orcs would mount during raids and conventional attacks. This leading Black Wolf knight figure was immediately recognized from the distance by Marin. She looked utterly terrified and furthermore alarmed, if not outright horrified, from her expression in giving a loud abrupt shout, saying this leading figure's name: Decius.

Linitus could tell he was an important and familiar name that he had heard of and quickly recalled that this was the same one bearing that name who happened to be the dux of the settlement. Still he asked Marin out of natural surprise and curiosity in case he happened to be wrong. Marin confirmed with a slight painful nod. They could see that not only the orc-looking chieftain held a large dire wolf upon a leash but other orcs and goblins came in with other large dire wolves of their own. Decius promptly mounted the one being held by the orc chieftain after taking custody of the leash while raising his large long pitch-black sword in the air as a command to rally the goblins and orcs that were mounted on their own respective dire wolves. The dux, without hesitancy, gave the order to charge. In a sudden moment, the wolves howled in tandem with an eerie howl that Decius, this dark-clad knight figure had led in chant while charging suddenly and ferociously around the flank of the large and less organized though still deadly mass of goblins and orcs that fought the Swordbane army head-on.

Even at that realization, from below rising high in the sky toward them, a trailing ball of fire came forth unceasing toward the skyship. Linitus noticed and called quickly within moments to Wyatt's attention. The young halfling wizard responded by quickly spell-casting a fireball from the opposite direction. The flaming projectile was hurled on a course to intercept the other fireball aimed at the skyship. Just in time with a loud blast and boom of collision in the sky, the two fireballs collided and exploded. The elf ranger and halfling wizard both realized at the same time, with Linitus pointing to the source of the first oncoming fireball. It was the Citadellan human wizard covered in dark robes who hurled from his flaming hands another flaming ball of fire toward the skyship. Marin called out his name, though less surprised than before, indicating that it was Agaroman, the wizard and advisor to Decius. The second flaming fireball Agaroman launched was hurled furiously toward the skyship, but once again, Wyatt would be ready to fire another fireball back to intercept the one cast by his fellow spell-casting nemesis. The two battling wizards would continue this back-and-forth battling of magic abilities.

As the exchange of fireball spell-casting continued along with the battle below showing a vicious slaughter like none seen before, Marin and Linitus thought instinctively the exact same thing: they had to go down to save Ascentius and what forces they could. This last-minute defense ploy by Decius was all but a ruse between the desert settlement and the goblin-orc forces to lure the king's army to a state of utter annihilation.

Linitus devised immediately on the spot a plan to have Wyatt teleport both him and Marin down to the ground to rescue Ascentius and any loyal forces that could be saved. Linitus, knowing that Wyatt had to stay on board the ship to counter the fireballs cast by Agaroman, asked the halfling wizard to teleport him and Marin to the surface below while the wizard would still stay on board with Peat to assist him. Wyatt nodded his head and pointed to the nearest location where he could teleport his two companions to, an opening behind the flanks of the encircling orc-goblin army. It would be too difficult, especially without a clear opening for the halfling wizard to teleport his companions directly to the immediate vicinity of the king, with his focus on staying on the ship to counteract the spell-casting attacks from Agaroman. Linitus knew this or could at least tell and, before being ready to depart through teleportation, told the wizard to look for his signal, which would be a large colorful flare that the elf ranger would shoot high into the sky.

Peat had another idea in mind, which Marin agreed with by having the dwarf guardian blow his horn intermittently, three times in quick succession to indicate that Wyatt should look out for the three of them, provided the dwarf guardian was to accompany Linitus and Marin. Still, Linitus knew that the dwarf guardian, not being one to abandon a battle, would be of greater use remaining on board instead. Linitus decided to alter the proposed immediate plan, suggesting for Peat to instead stay with the skyship and keep sight of where the elf ranger and Princess Knight were on the ground in order to better assist Wyatt in locating them on the ground, while the halfling wizard could better maintain his focus on dueling magical fireballs from afar against Agaroman. Peat initially protested while indicating the pride of dwarves to not cower away from direct battle, while also personally giving an oath to ensure the king's survival. Looking about the deck of the skyship and noticing several barrels lying about, Linitus came up with an alternate plan and a creative way to appease the dwarf at least with a sense of doing something purposeful for fighting while the skyship was high above the army of goblin-orcs below. The elf ranger asked the dwarf guardian if he had brought on board any explosive barrels of fire, to which the dwarf nodded. The elf looked down and immediately drew a large smiling laugh and grin from Peat, who chuckled and gave a sudden pinch to the elf's cheek for suggesting such a novel idea. Linitus thought to himself while looking at Marin with consolation that at least their dwarf-guardian companion was content with that reason to still stay on board even if it meant causing mayhem from above while dangerously large explosive barrels plummeted to the masses of orcs and goblins below. With the preparations made, Linitus commanded Wyatt to transport the elf ranger and the Princess Knight to the field of battle, or what would eventually be a field of slaughter.

Linitus and Marin looked at each other passionately and purposefully, knowing that while it might be their last time together fighting through a horde of goblins, orcs, and even fearsome disloyal Citadellan Black Wolf knights, at least they had their meaningful moments together, both intimately and on the field of battle.

Quickly with the wave of his silver wand, Wyatt teleported the elf ranger and the Princess Knight down to the surface near the site where there was an opening between the king, his forces, and that of their attackers. It was still a distance away, so Linitus and Marin would have to fight through the mayhem in order to reach Ascentius before it was too late.

Having adjusted enough to this form of instant teleportation, Linitus and Marin quickly looked around and spotted the king a far distance away by several hundred yards, separated by barren desert and the corpses that littered the field of battle. The two companions and lovers sped furiously, dashing toward Ascentius while preparing to fight through throngs of enemy forces.

As they charged head-on, Linitus drew his bow along with not one, but three arrows, shooting them quickly toward three orc warriors that became aware of the new arrivals and charged at the elf ranger and the Princess Knight, but only a few steps later, they were slain by the arrows. Marin was surprised and gave a quick look, being impressed by the seemingly uncanny abilities of Linitus. Quickly, she regained her attention soon after while parrying with her flaming long sword and shield at a group of small green goblin warriors that charged toward her and Linitus. She furiously struck them using her sword and even her shield as a weapon. The elf ranger stared at her a brief moment before giving a small compliment. It felt as if the two were challenging each other in their prowess for fighting, in the form of a contest for slaying their foes in the most audacious ways to see which one of them could outperform the other.

Immediately, the elf pulled from behind his quiver a large cylinder-like receptacle or canister holding many arrows in a compartmented container almost like a beehive housing many honeycombs of arrows. It was twenty, to be exact. Linitus took a latch attached to the cylinder container and drew that latch back with the string of his bow. He unleashed the string with the latch that hurled this honeycomb-like receptacle of arrows, which quickly dispersed and scattered a few meters apart from each other, though still traveling the same direction. Immediately, the dispersed arrows struck multiple goblins and orcs as well as even two Citadellan infantry from the desert city that were now considered rebel enemies to the kingdom.

Marin was dumbfounded as well as further impressed beyond belief. She admitted that Linitus needed to teach her someday how to do that and asked what that was called. The elf grinned mildly and told her that he had a feeling that if he did something like that, it would cause her to be more open in wanting to learn from him. Marin blushed and hated to admit that he was probably right, being as headstrong as she was to not want to learn unless the topic at hand had caught her interest enough to make an impression, which the elf's special weapon contraption clearly did. Linitus told her he would later teach her about the device he used, which had several names but was commonly called an arrow sabot barrage assembly.

Once more continuing the battle at hand, Linitus and Marin fought their way through the right front flank of the enemy forces, with the intensity picking up as they got closer to reaching ranks or what was left of their own loyalist Swordbane forces. The fighting was fierce where, again to Marin's surprise, Linitus came up with another fighting tactic or improvisation as the elf ranger took from his waist satchel a small but still noticeable glass bottle that smelled of fuel, much like the explosive barrels that Peat regularly used, including in the current battle. Marin's surprise quickly became further amazement when Linitus took the pointed end of the capped glass bottle, pulled back the string of his bow, and let loose the bottle quickly, hurling it dauntlessly toward a small crowd of goblins and orcs, some of whom had their attention on them while others were focused on the front ranks of the dwindling forces of Swordbane soldiers. The hurled bottle of flaming fuel quickly erupted into a fairly large enveloping circle of flames that lit the goblins and orcs on fire, making them screech in agony while falling down in pain, with some running before succumbing to the burning pain. None of the forces still loyal to Swordbane, however, suffered the effects as Linitus made sure to still aim and shoot the explosive bottle deep enough in the ranks of the enemy to not be at risk of his own allies catching alight. That daring move itself quickly melted away the morale of at least the immediate goblin-orc ranks in that part of the battlefield to fall back toward the rear of the army.

So impressive was the fighting of Linitus and Marin that even as Decius, mounted on his dire wolf with his contingent of dire-wolf-mounted goblins and orcs, charged and slaughtered elements of Swordbane loyalist forces, the two lone combatants caught the attention of the now-traitor dux from a distance. He could tell that they were a noticeable morale distraction, if not a possible outright obstruction to his objective of winning the battle, slaughtering the Swordbane army, and either capturing or killing the king himself. He began to unleash a howl as a signal to alarm his dire wolf cavalry contingent to attack them as well as to catch the attention of and possibly put fear into these two upstart combatants. Decius was unfamiliar with the elf ranger, and he was more alarmed at what he could do from what little he saw of wreaking havoc in such a short time toward his forces, but he recognized Marin and knew she, although somewhat challenging, was no match against Decius himself even in one-on-one melee combat.

Upon hearing the chant of howls, Linitus looked and knew that the situation now was not very optimistic. Fast approaching from somewhat of a distance was a dozen or so of the dire-wolf-mounted company led by this treacherous dux. Deciding quickly, Linitus instructed Marin to advance to find her father and he would hold back this advancing cavalry contingent. Marin, seeing that his life was at risk, objected, especially knowing how deadly Decius was in combat even if Linitus was able to best her in fighting. She did not want to contemplate the possible consequence that this elf ranger, whom she now saw not only as a mentor and friend, but also one that she developed feelings for as a lover could fall by the blade of the deadliest and most formidable warrior she knew. She could not take that chance and thought their odds were better together.

Linitus, feeling the same way in not wanting to risk losing her, reminded her about the more important focus at hand: the king, her father, who needed to be rescued. There was no time to argue over this, so he reminded her that every passing and fleeting moment counted. Marin quickly placed her lips to his and gave him a sudden kiss and then quickly broke away while nodding and agreeing reluctantly. She turned and charged forward toward her father, advancing through the already dissipating ranks of goblin-orc forces that largely fled after Linitus's last great gesture for attacking.

Meanwhile, the elf ranger drew quickly and fired one arrow volley after another toward the approaching dire-wolf cavalry contingent led by Decius. By the time that Decius and his contingent were within close range to pass and strike the elf ranger by blade, the dux had lost half of his dire-wolf company that followed him into combat. This elf ranger would be a formidable challenge, which the dux was looking forward to.

Not wanting to lose the opportunity to kill the elf ranger from being outnumbered, while seeing an opportunity to both duel his new adversary in combat and to distract him from what was originally intended for him to do the same to Decius, the dux ordered his remaining cavalry to go after the Princess Knight and the king to bring back either dead or alive. Linitus, easily overhearing the dux's loud command, knew what was going on and fired a volley of three arrows at once, striking at least three of the six remaining dire-wolf riders before Decius had fully dismounted and charged toward the elf ranger to try to strike him down. As the dux charged and swung, the elf ranger dodged and tumbled to the side. Linitus quickly gained his footing while attaching his bow to his special bow strap as quickly as he could unsheathe his elegant slightly curved elven long blade to parry the next ferocious strike that Decius made toward the elf. The two parried back and forth nonstop in a fierce duel while the larger battle that loomed would become more and more of a slaughter as it unfolded around them.

As Linitus held off Decius, Marin still charged and fought on to find her father. Eventually she caught up with the small, dwindling cadre of dwarf guardians and Eternal Flame knights that encircled the king to act as his closest bodyguards. One by one they slowly fell, giving their lives for Ascentius in order to hold out and protect the king as long as possible. Marin spotted her father and quickly approached him.

The king, though initially in somewhat a state of shock in which one can tell his mind was partially in the moment able to fight the opposition at hand, still seemed occupied in his thoughts about not only what was happening around him, but also in still processing that his own best appointed general and dux along with the settlement's local forces had betrayed him and his kingdom. It was a blow to his heart internally, and he tried to compose himself to still remember that he and his forces were fighting for survival if there was a chance.

When Marin approached the king, she besought him to go with her and be teleported to the skyship. The king, still partially confined to his thoughts including those of past cryptic words and at the present seeing so many of his men die before him, he was utterly and visibly lost for words on what to do. The slaughter before him had taken a toll both physically and psychologically in seeing so many of his soldiers fall before him.

Meanwhile, from high above on board the skyship, Wyatt though somewhat strained in focus and concentration, held off the fireballs that Agaroman cast from below. The only reprieve and rest the halfling wizard and his skyship would find came when a group of orcs and goblins fleeing from the devastating attack caused by Linitus earlier had alerted the dark-robed wizard about the attack and the pressing threat that the elf ranger posed. Agaroman broke off his steady attack of fireballs and teleported toward the distance that the goblin and orc survivors pointed as the location from where they fled.

Wyatt, though wondering about the sudden cessation of his wizard opponent's attacks, looked about the death-stricken battlefield. He surveyed the unfolding actions below while taking note and being amazed at how quickly and precisely Agaroman had teleported to be at a vicinity only a dozen or so yards away from the fighting that had taken place between Linitus and the enemy leader, Dux Decius. To Wyatt's surprise, Marin was not in sight anywhere near Linitus. Peat took note of that and told the halfling wizard not to worry. The dwarf had spotted the princess and the king just a moment ago.

With the halfling wizard being relieved that both his newfound companions on the ground below were okay, Wyatt hurried and began to cast a spell to teleport Linitus back to the skyship. Linitus appeared shocked and poised to strike and parry before realizing that he was no longer fighting what at this point he would consider as being his deadliest adversary. The elf ranger thanked his halfling wizard friend and wondered how long he might be able to hold off Decius, admitting that Marin was right about how ferocious and deadly this leader of Sanctum Novus was. He then thought of Marin and asked both Peat and Wyatt her whereabouts. The dwarf gave a calm laugh, telling the elf to relax and that Peat had sighted where the princess was and that she had been able to reach the king.

Without hesitation, Linitus quickly pointed and told Wyatt to teleport both of them back to the skyship along with any survivors. Wyatt nodded and did so, but he was only able to teleport a few at a time. Linitus wondered how many more Swordbane soldiers and knights were still alive, fighting the ensuing battle. He did not know if he could rescue them all, and he knew there was no way that he, or more specifically Wyatt, could rescue all of them, especially while dealing with a wizard that this newly declared enemy had that was as powerful as Wyatt. It was not a risk Linitus could afford to take at the expense of saving as many soldiers as the skyship could hold, as much as he wished he could.

In a short moment, a flickering bright flash emerged on the deck of the skyship as Marin and Ascentius appeared. Marin was calm, but her father was still somewhat visibly shaken and distraught. Marin approached Linitus and embraced him. She counted her blessings, feeling that it was fortunate for her not only to be alive with her father and within relative safety, but that her personal guardian, mentor, companion, and newfound lover that had been willing to give his life was also safe.

When Ascentius looked about, he realized he was no longer on the battlefield, or what the rest of the survivors on board would consider a field of slaughter. Ascentius, sounding almost desperate as if pleading or begging, ordered the wizard to send him back to be with his men even if it meant dying alongside them. He did not feel right to be spared from the same fate of death that had fallen upon or would soon fall upon so many of his soldiers. Marin and Linitus both objected. From their vantage point, it was more important not only in the closeness that they had as Ascentius was Marin's father, but also to protect his position as king. There were no appointed male heirs, and Marin would have an uphill struggle to claim the throne without marrying a suitable heir among the kingdom's nobility, which was by tradition expected to happen prior to the current king passing away or abdicating. If Ascentius fell, the kingdom would be in utter disarray and more vulnerable to fall under control of Decius and his new alliance with the goblins and orcs. To them, keeping Ascentius on board and escaping was not only nonnegotiable but also necessary, not to mention they did not think the king after what unfolded was currently in the right state of mind, given the trauma he witnessed in seeing nearly all his soldiers and knights dying in masses before him. Linitus, with an aura and natural sense of leadership, took authority upon himself in deciding what to do next. Marin, recognizing his strong leadership abilities and sense of judgment, would accept whatever Linitus would decide next. Even Peat, as much as the dwarf was stubborn and resistant toward being told by this young adult elf what to do, recognized the peril of the situation and did the same as Marin. The dwarf relented to Linitus's leadership and command. Linitus told Marin to take her father into the skyship's main cabin and tend to him. The elf ranger also continued to instruct Wyatt to teleport as many of the loyalist survivors from the battle below as could be saved and carried on board the floating vessel while changing course to retreat toward the coastal Swordbane mountains and their nearest settlement. Peat knew right away the geographical lay of the kingdom and indicated for the halfling to change course slightly to the southwest toward the dwarven chief stronghold of Mestthos-Inethbad. The halfling wizard nodded and started teleporting a few of the king's soldiers at a time. Though Marin held and comforted her father, he was still shocked and in disbelief. Eventually, Marin called loudly for Peat. The dwarf came to help her calm her father down and collect himself.

Meanwhile, Linitus used sharp attention to detail to assist Wyatt in surveilling and pointing the location on the ground below where to teleport the few still-surviving Swordbane army soldiers and knights as the skyship drifted southwestward in retreat. Internally, the elf ranger knew that this was perhaps the most painful and sorrowful day he had ever experienced. Never had he seen so much death at such a large scale so viciously as had taken place outside Sanctum Novus. A previous war that ended only after twenty years, even before the elf ranger came to be old enough to fight in, now gave way for a new unleashed and perhaps more catastrophic war that had only started today. It was a day he wished he could forget. It was a day that he would always come to remember and would never go away. It was a day that would forever be ingrained in his mind no matter how hard he would try to overcome that memory.

CHAPTER FOURTEEN

Unforgiven Memories

As the slaughter from the battlefield outside the walls of Sanctum Novus came to an end, the anguish from Dux Decius could be heard from a great distance. He was angered that his newfound adversary, the elf ranger, suddenly teleported from the fight. Decius knew instinctively that the elf had made it to the safety of the skyship and would later assume the same for Marin as well as her father, the king. The dux unleashed a loud, deafening howl of anger that could be heard everywhere. All his soldiers that were alive could hear him (a great many in his army still were alive despite the token number of casualties that were sustained in the dux's attempt to wipe out the king and his army). Only a short moment later, the surviving dire wolves of Sanctum Novus's army responded in cadence with a follow-up series of howls. The orcs, goblins, and the Citadellan forces loyal to Sanctum Novus over the Swordbane crown looked on. In unison, seeing it more as a cause for victory as well as anger, these forces unleashed a loud series of war cries together while proclaiming victory on a desert battlefield heavily filled with fallen corpses, many of which were fallen soldiers of the kingdom. It was in many respects a less honorable victory, but still a victory nonetheless that became a symbolic reminder that one settlement as prepared as Sanctum Novus could start a new era with new allegiances between orcs, goblins, and even humans.

Immediately after unleashing their war cries, the victorious combined forces of this diverse army rallied around their leader. They chanted the dux's title. It became a wave of "long live the dux," or from some goblins and orcs "long live the dark lord," instead of the previous homage that the city was expected to give for its former ruler, the king of Swordbane.

Decius, taking a moment to catch his breath while turning all about, realized that he had usurped his former lord's place despite not capturing or killing the king of Swordbane. The dux's forces were fiercely loyal to him as their commander. It was another symbolic omen to them among the several they had heard about their commander's lifespan in this prophetic quest to make "war and death become one" as a chosen vessel of the deity spirits.

Another moment, the dux mounted his new personal dire wolf and called out again to his army to announce their victory. Preparations were hastily made in which the fallen on both sides would be given mass funeral pyres while separating the fallen on both sides of the battle. Though the dux despised the king and was eager for bloodshed, he had a personal code to honor the soldiers on both sides of the fallen and not just his own, including in rendering final funeral rites. A portion of his army was delegated the responsibility to gather the fallen and make the preparations for the mass pyre funerals. Meanwhile, Decius, those close to him in his circle, and a large majority of his army marched back into the city gates of Sanctum Novus.

As the dux's victorious army marched back inside the city gates, Decius sent several of his soldiers as heralds to announce the city's victory over the crown's loyalist army and that Imperia Sanctum Novus would be the first independent Citadellan settlement to fulfill the establishment of a new remnant Lupercalian Empire, granted ironically without the leadership of the original founding Lupercalian race, though that would change in the dux's future plans. Over time, the people of the desert urban settlement as well as in other locales conquered or that joined into this new reenvisioned successor state would call it the Remnant, seeing that this government newly founded by the dux was in truth a remnant of what once was the Lupercalian Empire long ago.

As the heralds finished making the dux's declaration of victory, the masses of the civilian population came out from their homes and while still seeing the dux as more attuned to their own needs than the Swordbane crown, they quickly and without hesitation formed crowds by the street walk to cheer on their local ruler once again, though this time for throwing off the yoke of what they saw as an inept and corrupt monarchy that lacked sufficient resolve to address their needs as the dux was able to provide. By the time Decius, his close company, and the greater bulk of the now Remnant army consisted of the rough unlikely-match contingent of Citadellan soldiers native to the region by many generations, the orcs, goblins, and even some dire wolves. For the city, the sight of the dire wolves, not to mention their dux riding a large one was, a symbolic reminder and omen in their eyes of the city's long, ancient history in being the symbol of their patron totem, the wolf, which derived from its history as the last holdout never to truly fall to Nordling barbarians over a thousand years ago while being the last refuge of the wolf-man-like Lupercalian species, before they ultimately disappeared in what were considered unknown and mysterious circumstances.

Just as before, an extravagant makeshift and impromptu parade and ceremony played out in the city's main avenue as the dux's army contingent made their processional way to the heart of the desert city, again residing next to the main city's temple of Laran. This would be the same temple in which Decius gave his new proclamation establishing his new Remnant of the once-great Lupercalian empire before the masses.

The dux made his way to the temple sanctuary with not only Agaroman following behind him, but also the orc war captain and the goblin shaman of Uruk Kazaht, as well as Decius's newfound dire-wolf companion that he had mounted earlier in battle. Decius had once again made a ceremonial offering of incense and wine libation at the makeshift dual shrine of Laran and Calu in the presence of his three closest advisors. He also stood with several prominent families and their patriarchal heads of the desert city. Those witnessing were in awe of not only the dux's direct approach in making his way to the temple altar and shrine, but they also took notice of Decius's stern appearance of utter devout intent when making his offerings. He was truly pious in what he believed and thought for where no one could dispute it.

From a distance, one prominent Citadellan family's patriarchal head, Lucius Cornelius Diem, was a local city senator who held in high esteem the religious devotion of the dux. The senator's eldest daughter, Lucia, in particular gazed intently upon Decius and was immediately attracted to his seemingly known characteristics of ambition and piety on display. After making his offerings, the dux turned back to look at those present while declaring that the city's victory was satisfying and glorious in following the path that both Laran and Calu had set for both his destiny and the city. The dux, however, when receiving elation and clapping from the few among the pews of the temple, took note while gazing back among the various persons present that Diem's daughter in particular was in a deep trancelike stare looking back at him. He could tell she was attracted to him, though Decius maintained his subtleness to still look and smile about the general audience while thinking, wondering what else was going through the senator's daughter's mind. Was she really awestruck by the dux, or something else? Her piety might be as intent in her attention in communicating to the deity spirits as much as his.

Regardless, Decius mentally noted that she, being youthful though clearly an adult, had attractive features similar to his own, being also of Citadellan descent for a human. She had an olive complexion, a slender but chiseled young appearance especially around her face, dark-brown eyes, and black raven-like hair that was wavy.

Agaroman even took notice of the lost-in-trance stare she had for Decius and secretly whispered to his lord that perhaps in due time this woman who stared at him would be the one for him to choose as his wife in establishing a new dynasty for the Remnant. Decius nodded and agreed.

Only later in the evening did more celebration commence, with a festive banquet being held at the dux's urban palace estate. Several prominent local families, including senators, were in attendance. When seated in assigned chairs at the various banquet tables inside the main hallway and atrium of the dux's estate, many of the new senators chatted side by side with Citadellan soldiers and knights of the Black Wolf order. It seemed somewhat odd, though less so as time went on throughout the evening. At the center rectangular table, seated next to the dux and his advisor Agaroman, were the leaders of this new Remnant coalition, including the goblin shaman and the orc war captain of Uruk Kazaht. Next to them also was seated the Dreadful Knight himself, Edwin Baldwin, and the few knights of the Eternal Flame that joined Edwin to betray their former king in return for allotments of estates that they felt the king should have given them long ago and their new dux or dark lord had promised them to receive in Collis Vallem, far north of Sanctum Novus but south of the forest and mountain interior of the Nordling barbarian domain. These now-sellsword knights would receive their new estates once this new coalition of the Remnant conquered the region, which itself was fairly lawless and subject to multiple raids with only a few pockets of orderly townships. Edwin himself, being the leading envoy knight among his cavalry company dispatched by Ascentius prior to the battle, ironically was the first in his company to join the dux after being swayed. Edwin himself managed to convince the few knights that ultimately decided to switch sides of fealty to the dux. The other ones that were horrified by the betrayal to the king and had refused the offer were swiftly and unceremoniously killed on the spot even while putting up token resistance in the dux's halls upon being earlier received by the dux.

The tables had both the common and luxury fare of Citadellan food, including bacon-wrapped dates, sautéed pine nuts, white Citadellan bread and olive oil dip, farrumo (a sautéed wheat grain), various spice-rubbed meats, grapes, olives, cured meats, and various dry cheeses as well as red wine diluted with some water and date juice for beverages. The mood was quite cheerful among each of the high-ranking dignitaries, military officers, and other local government officials. Several of them gave toasts and verbal praise of Decius's rapid series of changes to undo the corruption in the city and chart it on a new course of prosperity.

However, as Edwin the Dreadful Knight gave his toast, he asked out of curiosity about the meaning of those cryptic words in the message the dux gave earlier to his betrayed former king. No one in the hall knew except for Dux Decius himself, his closest advisor and confidant Agaroman, and ironically the goblin shaman.

The raising of the question in those cryptic words immediately stirred deep memories in Decius's mind. For him, as much as anyone could levy a moral charge that the dux had betrayed his now former king, Decius knew those words would be ingrained in both his mind and now Ascentius's, especially in returning the favor of what the dux considered a mutual personal betrayal nearly five years ago. It was an event that Decius instantly reflected upon his thoughts through a flash in time.

He was a moderate ranking officer in the king's army and fairly recently knighted into the Order of the Black Wolf. He wore the same attire in military armor as he did in the present except for the red cape and several pendants that he received later as lord regent and commander of Sanctum Novus. During this time nearly five years ago, however, he was simply Sir Decius or young Lord Decius fighting along with his contingent of Citadellan Black Wolf knights in the north deep between the borders of the Nordling barbarians' mountainous woodland territory and the buffer high-basin plains on the northern reaches of Collis Vallem. This knightly order along with a token-size regiment of other Citadellan forces were dispatched to carry out a reprisal attack to a series of raids conducted by the violent neighboring tribal bands of Nordling barbarians toward the scattered villages of Citadellan and assimilated Nordling inhabitants that were adjacent and outside the woodlands along the northern plains and hills of Collis Vallem.

Ultimately, the assigned regiment that Decius served in was ordered by the king himself to send the ultimate message and attack the main barbarian settlement itself in that part of the woodland and mountainous region, Barbarum Aries, the Nordling tribe of the ruling Ram clan. To most, this was suicidal as this Nordling settlement in particular was more fortified than the other Nordling settlements and it was deep in the high woodlands in the mountainous regions of the barbarians' domain. Regardless, Decius being a subcommander and second in command eventually took charge of the operation once his commanding officer was killed in combat. Decius was promising in leadership even during that time and used his abilities to maintain effective unit cohesion while carrying out their daring raid on the capital barbarian settlement, efficiently as well as brutally slaughtering many of the unsuspecting Nordlings unprepared in the dead cold of night.

However, knowing his forces were outnumbered and in peril of being overwhelmed after initially infiltrating the barbarian settlement, Decius took a gamble and decided that they had to retreat as their actions stirred many of the lesser neighboring barbarian settlements of their whereabouts. Ironically while ordering the company of Citadellan Black Wolf knights and infantry regulars to fall back, Decius saw a goblin held prisoner in a locked cage high in one of the Nordling woodland trees. This was the goblin shaman of Uruk Kazaht.

Decius decided to free the goblin while making a pact of mutual survival with the short green pointy-eared creature to help them find the best path to retreat out of the woods and return to the prairie land and hills of Collis Vallem that bordered it. The goblin agreed and taught Decius, who already had a natural affinity with wolves, how to summon dark beast creatures, including dire wolves, for aid. The Citadellan commander agreed, and as his small company or what was left of it continued to traverse out of the forest, both he and the goblin shaman summoned multiple creatures of the forest to provide aid and attack the Nordling barbarian war bands that were pursuing them. Although they appeared to be in the clear, making their way out of the forest to see the open plains, their barbarian nemesis pursuers still followed closely behind and forced Decius to make the hasty order to come to a halt and form ranks with the surviving soldiers and knights in his regiment to fight the Nordlings as soon as they stepped out of the woods and into the open plains.

Unfortunately, rain had also settled in earlier, and the field was muddy along with the timing in which they fought at night. The king's army with Ascentius present was at camp outside the woods; he took notice and ordered his larger force of contingents to march in rank to engage the Nordlings. Decius spotted the allied forces of the king at the same time. The commander wanted to send word of his knights and soldiers needing aid and fighting off the ensuing battle with the Nordlings. The goblin shaman, being gifted in teleporting, assisted and teleported both Decius and him to the king's center army mass. Knowing that goblins and orcs were traditionally considered hostile by Swordbane's forces, Decius ordered the king's guard not to attack on sight while asking for an audience with the king, expecting Ascentius to reinforce his soldiers and knights.

Much to Decius's surprise and dismay, however, while he pleaded for aid, Ascentius pulled back in doing so at the last minute, seeing an ever-increasing swarm of barbarians pulling out from the woods to overwhelm Decius's men that were several hundred yards into the open plain. Instead, Ascentius ordered for his infantry archers to form and shoot indiscriminate volleys high into the air, risking to take out many of the Nordlings at the expense of friendly fire also striking Decius's men in close-combat vicinity that engaged the Nordlings. The high-pitched hail of arrows let loose in a barrage by Ascentius's column of archers indiscriminately struck down whatever target they fell upon. Decius, feeling helpless at the time, could do nothing but watch as both his immediate comrades and the enemy they fought fell together by the order of the king.

Ascentius could tell that Decius did not take this lightly and explained to the then-young junior knight and commander that the king's action was one born out of necessity, by saying to Decius the same words that the dux would return to his former king as his vengeful cryptic reply: Remember the eve of victory, for its tree must bleed to enjoy the fruits of labor.

For Ascentius, the risk of losing several forces of Swordbane was necessary in certain maneuvers like he had done to inflict much damage to the enemy in order to prevent sending more of his soldiers and knights to possibly die in combat. Decius, however, never felt that it was justified to leave his own men behind. These were the same men that he knew personally and would trust his life with as much as they trusted theirs with Decius and ultimately with their king, Ascentius.

Though Ascentius had attained the intended result by sunrise in counting the many dead belonging to the Nordlings, who far outnumbered the fallen of his forces, of the ones that Decius served with, only Decius along with the goblin shaman managed to stay alive. None of the other soldiers and Black Wolf knights that served along with Decius during the mountain forest settlement raids survived. For Decius, this was a personal deep loathing and secretive betrayal for which he would never forgive Ascentius. It was a seed of resentfulness and hate for serving under Ascentius despite certain aspects of the king that the dux had respect for.

Ironically, after the battle Decius would part ways with the goblin shaman, ensuring safety while establishing a future bond of kinship that would play out in the coalition now between the Citadellans of the high desert basin and the beast races of goblins, orcs, and trolls. In the aftermath of surviving, Decius had immediately received full commendations and honors from Ascentius as well as earned the king's trust in his ability to command, including being promoted to dux, a title that was essentially lord, governor, acting regent, and general while being assigned command to Sanctum Novus, the desert powerhouse settlement of Swordbane east of the southern coastal mountains and closest to deliver future responses in force to any enemies of Swordbane along the eastern frontier of the kingdom's boundaries.

Afterward, Decius would continue to hone his skill as not only a leader and now statesmanlike regent, but he would make a rare triumph of bestowment by the king for his daring raids against the Nordlings. Upon receiving the bestowed laurel of victor by the king at the capital, Citadella Neapola, Decius made a rare appearance at the annual arena tournament of champions to compete, where he had earned his motto "Invictus Maximus," meaning the greatest in never being defeated, for he had defeated all the tournament competitors in the public spectacle of gladiator dueling, including the Dreadful Knight Edwin Baldwin and the king's own daughter, Marin, who was ferocious in her own right, being known as the Princess Knight. On his return to Sanctum Novus, Decius would appoint Agaroman, his mentor and confidant during his orphaned youth, to serve as his regional advisor and the only one in whom Decius had confided what happened during the eve of his victory as the lone Swordbane military survivor during the reprisal raids.

Knowing the pain and torment that haunted the mind of Decius as he descended into a brief but long enough pause when Decius was asked the meaning of the cryptic message that Edwin had delivered to Ascentius, Agaroman interrupted and told the Dreadful Knight as well as the rest of the dining guests that it was a tale that would best be told and shared by Decius himself for another night, in an effort to divert attention from the topic and put it to the side, even if temporarily. It had worked as Edwin could tell that it could wait and he conceded.

Meanwhile from a distance at the other end of the dining hall, on a traditional Citadellan triclinium with a table for dining opposite to the main table of the dux, Senator Diem's daughter Lucia could tell that the brief question being raised by the new ally and ex-knight of the Eternal Flame order had taken a toll on her newfound love interest. In a way, it attracted her even more to see a very human and vulnerable side of the dux that she felt compelled to comfort and soothe. Lucia excused herself from the immediate presence of her father while providing a justification stating that her lord was in need and she would tend to him in a somewhat subservient manner. The senator, her father, initially perplexed and showing some hesitancy by his reaction, was about to object but hesitated, seeing that his daughter was determined to do something that might be meaningful and perhaps best left to her own designs. So he acquiesced and watched.

Approaching gracefully with an attitude of concern and servitude as well as compassion, Lucia holding a pitcher of wine asked Decius in a tone respectful of title if he was okay, while placing her hand gently on his shoulder. Decius felt it immediately, and though breaking out of his own brief state of thought, he turned around and quickly diverted his attention to the one that abruptly tended to him. Looking up, he saw a sharp, well-dressed young-adult Citadellan woman with beautiful wavy black hair, wearing ornate jewelry, who happened to be holding a pitcher of wine to offer to him. Though she wore different clothing from earlier and now much more exquisite, her beauty exemplified the aura that she carried in expressing a genuine concern and care for him. Their eyes locked in a deep mutual stare of attraction, though Decius was able to still maintain a sense of statesman leader-like composure to respond while raising his empty glass toward her to indicate he would have another glass of red wine. Lucia poured him a glass and handed it to him while noticing also that he happened to already have one chalice next to him already filled with wine. The dux could read her facial expression of surprise while verbally telling her that the glass was not for him, but rather for her, and he made a counter-gesture of chivalry in handing the chalice back to her.

Lucia blushed and was not able to restrain her further attraction to this dux and now a new factional leader of an emerging rival to Swordbane. She nodded while doing a simple curtsy gesture to express that she was honored. The dux rose up to excuse himself before his table and took the senator's daughter by her hand while telling her to walk with him toward one of his private office chambers.

His personal invitation shocked all the faces around him, not to mention Lucia's father, Senator Diem, who from a distance looked intently at what had transpired. The senator and all the high-ranking figures at the dux's banquet table were in awe, even Agaroman, who shared a mild concern. The most powerful person in the dining hall, in all of Sanctum Novus and east of Swordbane's western holdings was swayed by the simple servitude and gesture of compassion by a young-adult woman, granted of nobility status, to leave his moment of personal celebration and spend it with someone that he barely knew. Yet for all it was worth, Senator Diem, able to tell the concern from the dux's advisor, walked gently toward the dux's banquet table to explain to Agaroman that his daughter, while having an attraction to the dux and obviously a mutual attraction at that, had also the best qualities a woman of high Citadellan political status and upbringing could embody, including being protective of her family, which in that case would include Decius if it was meant to be that they would one day be married. The wizard advisor responded that was precisely his concern, which surprised the senator, who wanted to know why it would be a bad thing for a concern. The wizard responded again, stating that the dux had a larger purpose to focus on, especially since Ascentius was neither captured nor slain on the field of battle and consequently the Kingdom of Swordbane had not fallen. He also went on to say that additionally, the dux was believed by many, including Agaroman, to be the intended prophetic vessel for making the deity spirits Laran and Calu, war and death, become one.

While Agaroman respected the senator and the daughter's genuine though also ambitious intentions that she would make a great potential wife and political consort, it was important for the dux to not be overly invested in a possible newfound matter of love from his ascribed destiny. The senator understood, but also assured the wizard advisor that his daughter would support the dux to pursue all those important endeavors while the senator himself would monitor from a certain distance to ensure his daughter would not become a distraction for the dux. Agaroman subtly contemplated and nodded his head in acquiescence to the senator's approach, advising him to make sure to do so and tread carefully. He too would ensure that no one, no matter how close they were, even by mutual affection to the dux, would get in the way of fulfilling his ambitions. The senator nodded slowly and gave a bowing gesture while returning to his table.

Senator Diem, though he would like to see his family elevate in station, was not expecting his daughter to do it so abruptly, especially in the simple yet direct manner of how she approached Dux Decius, but he recognized they both had many compatible qualities and characteristics, including moving up in station, or as the Citadellans called it in their language, pursuing cursus honorum, while they both had a genuine sense of ambition and loyalty as personal values.

As the evening banquet came to a close a few hours later well past midnight and the various guests of honor left, the senator patiently sat at his triclinium table area, waiting somewhat eagerly for his eldest daughter to return. Eventually, Agaroman walked up to him and told the senator that it was time to retire, while acknowledging the senator's concern for his daughter and assuring him that the dux would return her to the senator the next day. As the senator reluctantly nodded, he rose from his table and was poised to take the first step in walking out. The wizard interrupted him again to let him know that this was one of the few moments that he was as puzzled as the senator and both of them could only speculate what the dux and the senator's daughter were talking about or doing in the other chamber. He went further to tell Senator Diem that no woman in all the years that Agaroman knew Decius came close to attracting the dux as the senator's daughter, except maybe briefly the Princess Knight, Marin.

The wizard then thought about comparing the two women and asked the senator impromptu to ascertain further to what extent his daughter was ambitious and that she would care for the dux if their love was meant to be. The senator responded without hesitation that his daughter was fiercely ambitious and loyal to the dux from the qualities she seemed to admire about him, granted they really did not know each other that well yet. Agaroman smiled and nodded while declaring his joyous relief and letting Senator Diem know that it was a good-enough sign for him to know that and time would tell if the two would be good together.

The wizard had reenvisioned how his dux's destiny, though still on track for what they set out for Decius to do, could be further supported by a woman as devout as the senator's daughter. Perhaps it would be in this new Remnant government that a new future dynasty of duxes or dark-lord successors to lead Sanctum Novus while Decius, after becoming the vessel in making war and death, would possibly occupy another plane to claim as his own. Perhaps it would be wise to establish a connection with both the primordial plane of the world of Sanctum Novus and whichever station Decius would occupy in the future. The wizard would tread carefully but seemed to agree even internally that Lady Lucia Diem would perhaps be acceptable as the mother for his dark lord's offspring to lead Sanctum Novus and all its future territories under a mortal form of leadership as divinely ascended. Still, the wizard and the senator took another moment looking at a narrow hallway with a closed door in the distance (that would be the dux's office chamber and personal living quarters adjacent to it), both wondering still what their concerning interests were doing, while Senator Diem asked, had any woman ever made the dux happy or genuinely cared for him? Agaroman replied no while still holding a mild tone of concern and intrigue.

CHAPTER FIFTEEN

Love in Dark Places

As the voices from the hallway gradually became less loud over time, the dux and the senator's daughter became gradually more intrigued and attracted to each other. Sitting on the intersecting ends of reclined cushioned bicliniums while sharing a bowl of grapes, Decius told Lucia what was on his mind when Edwin Baldwin had raised the question at the banquet hall of the dux's estate. He had told her about why he had devised such a cryptic message to his former king as a form of tongue-in-cheek retaliation in which the dux ultimately rebelled and considered his act of betrayal as being reciprocal for those years in which he felt the king had abandoned and betrayed the dux's own soldiers.

Lucia, seeing the anger that manifested in Decius's face while recalling and sharing his past story, gently placed her hand on his cheek and moved her arm around his back. She had realized that despite being now in the highest position of office without further subjecting himself to fealty to the king, this person who outwardly carried an aura of invulnerability without weakness was inwardly still a man that carried pain and remorse. He could not prevent everyone that he cared for from dying, and he was in his own way genuine about who he was, or at least it was what she believed he thought of himself. She told him that regardless of the past, he could not change what happened, but he could still effect change in the present and future to have meaning, including to the memory of those he cared about.

Decius looked up and his face changed. He saw a woman who saw him differently than others had, and to some extent, he wondered if she saw or knew the extent of who he was and what he would become. He let her know plainly, out of concern that he did not want this woman to be misled into thinking he was flawless even in his own nature despite the conflicting aura that he showed in public contrasted with his internal being, both of which Lucia now saw and she admired him even that much more.

She assured him that she saw him as the right one to do what he had done, that both his piety and his ambition were justified. It shocked him to his core, but he asked again, could she really feel comfortable in knowing and caring for one like him who would not only do what he had done as revenge against his king, but also make alliances with beastly creatures, including ones that she saw at the banquet, to rise up in power even if it benefitted their home, Sanctum Novus? Could she feel comfortable knowing that he would not simply honor Laran, the city's titular deity of war, but publicly worship also Calu, the deity spirit of death that was previously banned until Decius's rise to power as dux? Would she be at peace or in a content-enough state knowing that her prospective lover Decius would commit the most destructive and horrifying acts to his enemies in order to attain a worthy status as dark lord in the name of both deity spirits to accept him as their mutual chosen vessel in which to merge their essence into him? To his surprise, she told him she would love him in the darkest places as long as he stayed true to who he was, even if it paved such a dark road as he had described. It scared him but also exhilarated him to know that there was a woman that perhaps did understand him, had the ability to love him, was devoted to both him and his pursuits, while also sharing a strong sense of mutual ambition. They looked into each other's eyes and face intently after he heard her words, and they embraced for a long deep, passionate kiss.

Following the kiss, the dux broke off abruptly and, thinking about this newfound love who would embark with him on his destined path, asked about what she had wanted and that he cared to meet the wants and needs of those who were genuine, who mutually cared for him. Lucia thought only of the concept of family. She told the dux she only wanted to ask from him two things: to provide and care for her family, including her senator father, and to let her have the honor of being his consort to give him the first of his offspring, a male heir to carry his line of rule whether before or after it was time for him to become the destined prophetic chosen vessel of Calu and Laran.

Decius looked at her intently and acknowledged her requests by telling her it would be so. Another moment of intense stares and the two newfound lovers embraced each other and, without cessation, kissed each other deeply while Decius carried his newfound love, Lucia, the senator's eldest daughter, to his bed. They would sleep that night forgetting about the politics and intrigue that the dux had so often become accommodated to, and he shared a commonality in relating to Lucia, who was attuned to the same politics and intrigue that became the common talk in the circles of her family with her father serving as senator.

For once, Decius found someone worthy to be with as companion and mutual lover to share his ambitions with. Lucia did not have the martial prowess or leadership disposition of command outwardly as Marin had, which had at one time mildly attracted the dux when looking for a woman in matching as a potential soul mate and prospective spouse. However, Senator Diem's daughter had the same raw ambition that the dux had. She had a skilled acumen to manage certain affairs, including governmental and financial matters, on the dux's behalf (she had acquired such related experience in serving the same capacity on behalf of her father as her mother did). Her mother and father had both taught her, at least in their own household away from the public eye, to manage the senator's mercantile business while acquiring the raw products of dates and even incense from the property holdings of her father's estate and to set up business arrangements for procuring commercial trade. She adopted and embraced the Citadellan virtue of being the caring mother and wife of the family that was extolled to her from her mother, though Lucia was yet to be either a mother or wife, at least for the time being. It was enough for Decius to know that he could sleep in some sense of bliss and peace despite the ironic role he would steadily embrace as no longer just the dux of Sanctum Novus, but also the dark lord of the Remnant that would reestablish the reenvisioned form of a new Lupercalian Empire, or at least one that emulated it. For now, Decius was at peace to be with someone who finally understood him and accepted him on a more personal level. He finally found a woman he could accept and care for in return while they would build their futures together.

CHAPTER SIXTEEN

Finding Hope While in Despair

Hundreds of miles away from Sanctum Novus in standstill twilight of a sky full of stars flew what seemed a moving shadow from above, while looking from the ground save only one brightly lit flame. From the opposite vantage point above, on board the skyship, darkness seemed everywhere except for the leeward side of the snow-capped Great Coastal Mountains in the distance. Wyatt's skyship soared ever so gently like a bird of passage migrating patiently and unceasingly through the night until it reached its destination near midnight.

Standing patiently and every so often looking behind when not scanning the landscape from the deck of the ship, Linitus stared at the captain's cabin, wondering if King Ascentius's state of being, his condition, had improved. When he was not standing, the elf ranger sat down once or twice with his legs folded, to meditate and clear his thoughts even for a moment before returning to the situation at hand and reflecting on what had unfolded earlier.

During his meditation, as hard as it was, Linitus would let go of what had happened to think of a quiet and peaceful place, a forest with bright lighting and animals that lived in harmony. It was a place and state of mind absent of all evil and sheltered from sadness. When it rained, only the tears of joy and happiness filled a pond teeming with utter tranquility. It was a state of thought that the elf had used throughout the years to help deal with great trials of adversity.

As time went on, for several hours Marin had tended to her father, to calm him from his state of utter shock and devastation. It was a rare moment for those close to the king to see a vulnerable side of their lord and his grief, which none had known except perhaps Peat and Marin during the Great Massacre of Kadrinbad.

Eventually and suddenly, a door opened, with the sound of hinges being the most audible sound in the quiet, serene air of the sky that only felt the otherwise occasional sound of a gusty wind breeze. Everyone turned to see, but especially Linitus. Marin crept out, head down and with a clear expression of sadness before closing the door. She issued a message that no one save her was to disturb the king, which everyone acknowledged and solemnly nodded.

Linitus walked up to her and instinctively knew that although she tended to her father, she too had a nature of feeling alone and wounded by what had transpired. She had little time to process the massive loss that had been inflicted upon the king's army and those she served. The elf ranger could tell and slowly reached toward her; they embraced each other while she shed tears. She had confided to him both great pleasure for helping her to save her father and remorse in knowing how close she was to losing him. She could not bear the thought of losing another parent. Linitus, having empathy, thought of being in her position and placed his hand on the Princess Knight's cheek while acknowledging that he knew. The princess never questioned her newfound lover's place of empathy nor did she put herself in his place to know yet, only that it was enough for her to have someone else to be there for her, to listen to her and acknowledge her feelings while hearing those words.

As much as she felt the pain and the swirl of emotions from high to low in the earlier battle, which Linitus acknowledged and shared, he kept hidden from her any personal feelings of loss that he felt, away from his newfound lover's periphery. The elf had lost all those of his elven race who served as rangers for the reconnaissance scout battalion of the king's army. It was only at this point that Linitus was the lone surviving elf from the onslaught outside the walls of Sanctum Novus. Nobody thought of or realized the circumstance initially, with only a few dozen survivors that Wyatt had picked up who were mostly human Swordbane soldiers and knights as well as three dwarf guardians.

The elf in his mind knew that at some point, he would have to take it upon himself to find the surviving kin of each of his fellow elf rangers that he personally knew who had all died in the field of combat and let their next of kin know at least that his fallen elven comrades gave their lives not only for the well-being of Swordbane after defeating Marjawan, but also in saving the king and the kingdom from a new threat within. In his mind, he had as much obligation to not let the memories of his fellow elf warriors in service to the crown be in vain as Marin had invested in the well-being of her father, both emotionally and physically.

After embracing each other another moment longer, Linitus broke off and told Marin to ask the king upon sunrise to walk out from his cabin quarters and look down from the ship to remind him that his role as king and his kingdom still had meaning. The princess nodded her head while still shedding tears.

Another hour later, still late at night, the skyship came to an abrupt stop, floating high above an elevated and mountainous landscape in transition between high desert and temperate grassland plain. Below flashed a series of lights dotted about the landscape. The floating vessel had reached its destination at Mestthos-Inethbad, the legendary dwarven mountain fortress city along the southern leeward end of the Great Coastal Mountains.

Peat had called the crew on board upon catching sight of the fortress city below to identify their point of arrival, for the dwarf was familiar with it and had been there on several occasions. Upon identifying the main dwarven fortress below, Linitus called upon Peat and asked Wyatt to transport below via teleportation and to be ready to teleport them back upon the elf's signal of first light. The halfling wizard quietly obliged, wondering what the elf ranger had in mind, though having full trust that his companion had uncanny leadership and wise judgment to handle the affairs below with the dwarven settlement that was part of the Kingdom of Swordbane.

Hours went by quietly and suddenly, when sunlight began to pierce the eastern horizon. Looking below just as Linitus had commanded, Marin had walked out of the cabin with her father, both wondering yet trusting the elf's intentions in requesting the king to come out. Meanwhile, Wyatt was mesmerized to see dotted all around the fortress city's wall ramparts, paved streets, and atop some of the flat roofs countless dwarves clad in dwarven steel armor bearing a wide assortment of weapons, chanting in unison loudly with one voice that would make the mountains around the city tremble. They all chanted the same words loudly with pride: "All hail Swordbane. All hail the king." In another moment, from the very same spot where Wyatt had earlier teleported Linitus and Smokey Peat, now stood the same two companions, with the elf signaling to be teleported after firing a cylindrical object that quickly dispersed into a stream of flashing lights that dispersed again and again while emitting a loud thunderous series of majestic crackles.

Marin and her father in their previous moment of grief had now been encouraged with a renewed sense of purpose. The crown now came as a reminder to them, especially the king, that as much as it was a burden to carry, it had a meaningful purpose. There were still lives in the kingdom that Ascentius had a purpose to lead, serve, and protect even when coming from one of his deepest and darkest moments in life.

In another moment, a bright flash could be heard, felt, and even seen flickering behind the Swordbane monarch. The king and the princess, in their tears, turned to see both the elf ranger and the king's most trusted dwarf bodyguard. Linitus and Peat saluted while kneeling and offering their respective sword and war hammer before the king to show their fealty. Linitus then rose and told the king and the princess that despite losing an army from betrayal, they had plenty who were still loyal in giving their lives to the crown and they had many more lives of subjects in the kingdom that were in need of the crown's protection.

Linitus went on further to say that despite what happened and what they could not control beyond their status and position, they could still control how they would react and respond with that which was within their means.

The king nodded his head to acknowledge what the elf ranger had said, while standing still in tears next to his daughter Marin. Ascentius then out of surprise, with humility and further gratitude, knelt on both knees while taking Linitus's hand and kissing it ceremoniously. The king thanked him.

Linitus, accepting the king's gesture while also surprised, helped Ascentius from his knees to stand and replied that it was time for His Highness and the princess to let the tears they shed of joy fill the pool of happiness from which their subjects would be nourished.

Marin, in her heart still touched, also could not help holding on to what the elf ranger, her lover, had said and done. Without caring about status, office, position, what her subjects thought nor her father if negatively at all, Marin went over to the arms of Linitus and embraced him once more while kissing and thanking him once more. She told him finally how she felt after knowing him. She took one tear from her finger and placed it upon his face while telling him she had finally found her own nourishment from his pool of happiness.

CHAPTER SEVENTEEN

Good and Bad Intentions to Pave the Road

Over two hundred miles away, east of Mestthos-Inethbad during the same sunrise that also came upon Sanctum Novus, the dux awoke in his bed, lying next to Senator Diem's daughter Lucia. If he could stay longer by her, he would have, but his internal nature called upon him to do as he felt was obligatory in tending to his duties as the dux of not only the city and surrounding region, but also in what would be his ever-growing new empire, including his acquisitions of orc- and goblin-held territory as both beastly races had freely joined the Remnant. The dux quickly took a bath in a special chamber with a bathtub-size pool adjacent to his main bedroom.

By the time he was entering the waters of his bath, Lucia had also awoken, feeling the relatively cool morning air and emptiness from which she had earlier felt the warmth of her newfound lover. She walked over to the dux's tub quietly, and surprising the dux from behind, she gently placed her arms to rub his back. At first reaction internally, the dux would normally have been startled and he knew even as silent as Lucia had been, he could still barely hear her footsteps to know it was her. Without even turning while feeling in his mind her aura, he invited her to join him and for him to return the favor and wash her back as well. He stretched his arm to take her hand. Lucia accepted the offer and gently took his hand while gradually submerging partially in the pool. For a few minutes, they had another moment of intimacy and the dux told her that while he felt saddened to leave her presence momentarily, given his position and responsibilities, he still had to tend to those callings. Lucia placed her arm on his shoulder in a moment of understanding while letting him know that she understood his role and the importance of sharing the valuable and personal time they would have together when he was not assuming his duties. As soon as he got out of the bath, Lucia did the same and took a towel from one of the tending servants of the dux to dry him as well as help one of his other attendants to have his dress military attire and regalia prepared for when Decius would go into one of the halls of his palace estate to have a formal council meeting with his ranking cabinet that included the dux's personal advisor and master wizard Agaroman, the orc war captain of Uruk Kazaht as well as the goblin chief shaman of also Uruk Kazaht, several senators including Lucia's father Senator Diem, and now recently the Dreadful Knight, Edwin Baldwin.

Upon entering the dux's main wardroom and council chamber after hearing his name formally called by one of his lieutenant Black Wolf knights, Decius walked in at a steady and confident pace that showed a strong presence of his leadership and command. All the council attendees had risen out of respect for the dux, and Decius commanded them to return to being seated. The dux then called for the matters of the day, including updated reports for a count of the losses on both sides from the previous day's battle. The orc war captain reported, with Agaroman translating that the Ascentius's army lost over 9,500 men (or nearly his entire accompanying army), while the coalition of the Remnant had lost about 3,000 men mainly from the combined goblin-orc army that mustered and charged headlong into the Swordbane crown's army as well as a few casualties of the Citadellan local forces of both regular infantry along with some knights of the Black Wolf order. The dux was pleased and acknowledged that the battle was overall decisively successful despite the fairly noticeable losses on their side.

Decius also asked any of the military staff on the council for any developments of Ascentius's whereabouts, either dead or alive. The various figures on the military council shook their heads, not being able to confirm the Swordbane monarch's whereabouts. The dux admitted that he was not surprised, given that this former king most likely was teleported with the skyship that had fled after the battle, while calling the king a coward who would run rather than fight and die with his men.

Following up on this conjecture, Decius called upon one of his scouts to muster several couriers to let the entire settlement know that the now-deposed King Ascentius had abandoned his settlement and that the Remnant's victory was an omen from the divine spirits in their blessing, in consequence of the neglect and social disenfranchisement by the kingdom's former sovereign. Decius also informed the council that he had dispatched several packs of well-trained goblin dire-wolf rider scouts to survey the path and direction that the skyship had taken to flee.

The dux told the council that while he had to still await the confirmation from his scouts, it was likely that the skyship would head for Mestthos-Inethbad and he explained in anticipation and clarification for those present who were not familiar that this site was a heavily fortified dwarf settlement. The dux would prepare to enhance Sanctum Novus's defenses if an attack came from that direction while setting up an organized network of minor fortified way-stop stations with signal fires in roughly six to eight directions around the city in a circumference where each way-stop station would serve as resting post for the dispatched scouts while patrolling the newfound borders that would be from the first two mountain chains west of Sanctum Novus, which were still east of the leeward side of the great Swordbane mountains. Inethbad again lay in the southern half of the leeward side of the Great Coastal Mountains (also referred to as the Swordbane Mountains) at a junction pass between the leeward and windward sides of the mountain chain.

All the council members were fairly impressed and content with the dux's shrewd mind and planning for operations and patrolling the western border of his holdings from the Swordbane kingdom if and when the latter decided to stage and execute an assault against the high desert city. The Dreadful Knight, still eager for a taste of knightly honor and glory from battle, asked the dux if and when they would besiege Inethbad since it was perhaps the closest settlement of opposition, with the local dwarves being still loyally allied to the Swordbane crown.

The dux stood quiet for a brief moment before replying that his forces would not immediately plan a siege on the dwarven settlement since it was both well-fortified and likely prepared to withstand a siege by the time the Swordbane crown would assemble a large relief force to sally the potential besieging attack. The dux instead informed the new turncoat knight that he and an assembled force of mounted knights as well as goblin and orc dire-wolf riders would stage organized expedition raiding parties to attack any and all caravans that were loyal to the Kingdom of Swordbane as well to charge a new toll to help fill the coffers for expenditures to fund over time the Remnant's many project developments and its rapidly expanding army.

The dux also addressed another military member of the council who stood in the back, behind the main council meeting table. This other member was introduced as none other than the infamous human north-plain highlands raider, Dirty Dale, who had joined the goblin-orc settlement of Uruk Kazaht several years ago. Dirty Dale acknowledged in a somewhat unceremonious gesture of hand signs toward some of the nonmilitary members of the councils his disdain and unkempt reputation that lacked etiquette to his peers if they had not earned his respect in the field of combat like Decius had. The dux grinned and replied in a sarcastic witty manner asking for the human raider to have some patience with the senators as they might find new respect for each other's skills over time. Dale quietly deferred and acknowledged the dux's subtle plea by nodding and leaning back toward the shadows near one of the pillars of the hallway council chamber. The dux continued by stating that while the Dreadful Knight would stage his area of operations initially on the trade routes around Sanctum Novus against Swordbane, the Dreadful Knight would make his way north eventually alongside Dirty Dale to stage against both the northern Citadellan and semi-barbarian settlements while eventually making incursions farther north into the barbarian Nordlings' holdings.

The dux, using a map on the table with various figures representing his forces and different opposition, showed that he would use gradually more aggressive hit-and-run attacks against the barbarians to force them to submit to his rule and be conscripted at swordpoint. He did not expect all the barbarian forces to join the Remnant, but rather thought that through conjunction of defeating their leadership and making a show of strength, he would make the barbarians gradually yield to the Remnant forces for self-preservation and seeking better prospects in living under the suzerainty of Sanctum Novus while having portions of their settlements conscripted or mustered in war bands to use in further building up the Remnant forces to use against Swordbane later on.

The room was briefly quiet while the council members paused before several claps issued and they increased steadily and then rapidly. The council members were quite pleased with the dux's approach to building up their forces while keeping the barbarians to the north loyal and subject to their overall control should the plan work. It would not be an easy task, but even the dux acknowledged this while pointing out that the northern barbarians had never faced a strong enough counterattack especially in the form of a coalition between Citadellans of the high desert basin along with the beast-race subjects the former presided over, including goblins, orcs, and even domesticated dire wolves and trolls used for war. It would likely and potentially turn the tables of power in Sanctum Novus's favor to not only subdue a potential rival foe, but also later on force that would-be rival to join and increase their numbers for their ultimate prize: the campaign and conquest of the western Citadellan coastal heartlands, not to mention finally getting rid of the Swordbane king.

Meanwhile, Decius asked his advisor Agaroman for any additional suggestions and advice on what to do going forward. The wizard initially shrugged, but when he looked at Senator Diem's face and recalled the senator's concern for his daughter's whereabouts, the wizard inquired about the dux's plans for not only fulfilling his role in the prophecy to become a vessel for the deity spirits of war and death, but also establish a potential dynasty with an heir to his throne. Though it was felt that the dux was put on the spot, Decius replied that he had looked into the matter and it was being addressed. While feeling somewhat embarrassed and awkward, Decius felt compelled to acknowledge that he would later announce in greater detail about that issue. Agaroman was fairly pleased and content. Senator Diem, on the other hand, still was concerned about his daughter's whereabouts not to mention her well-being, and he contemplated whether to ask the dux bluntly and directly about that matter in front of the council. However, he held back and realized from still more internal contemplation if what the dux had just said was in fact an admission that his daughter and the dux were in fact already intimate with each other since the prior evening.

It bit and shook Diem to the core, since he had hoped his daughter would be okay. Yet at the same time, he knew his daughter's nature in seeking someone that she saw pulling in and sharing a large degree of ambition with her and someone that she felt would elevate her own family's standing, in addition to wanting to be the exemplified model of the virtuous Citadellan wife and future mother who would care and provide for the internal matters of her family as well as being a patron to others outside the family circle. To an extent, Diem respected and wanted to allow latitude for his daughter to exercise that aspiration of elevating herself and, by extension, her own family to a higher status within their local Citadellan society. It was acceptable and, to an extent, admirable in his mind for their culture to have daughters seeking such goals, while it was not uncommon in Citadellan tradition for the women and men to cohabitate in a somewhat informal ritualized way, to live with their respective partners for a certain amount of time before they would be considered, by traditional common law, de facto husband and wife. That is, provided they had not been in a formal marriage ceremony to actually attain more immediately the civil status of marriage and the young-adult daughter had not retreated to her own family's home for more than two consecutive days during that time of cohabitation with her intended male partner.

Perhaps Lucia was cleverer than Diem had given her credit for, to orchestrate a means to be in that situation to charm the dux, though Diem did not doubt that his daughter was genuinely in love with the dux. There was no way to truly know. The dux, by his own reputation, was a great person in Sanctum Novus as well as throughout the western lands to have earned a reputation to be feared as much as respected, so the senator felt that sense of concern for his own daughter's well-being in seeing her potential newfound love as being dangerous.

Though Decius could not read the thoughts from the other side of the table, he could tell visually Senator Diem was occupied to an extent. The dux, with nothing else left to say, dismissed the council members to attend to their duties of office. Each member rose and walked away while saluting the dux by pounding one's fist against one's chest. Decius returned the same gesture. Senator Diem slowly stood up last among his colleagues, still lost in thought and wondering whether to inquire about his beloved Lucia. The dux interrupted Diem's thoughts while calling for him to come over in private. Decius informed the senator in private that his daughter was okay while staying overnight in his palace, and if she wished, the dux would allow her to return to Diem and her family at any time. Diem, hearing the news, was pleased to know this and was nodding his head but still pondering the ire of the dux if he actually asked whether his daughter had relations with the dux during the night. Diem wondered how intimate they had really become but decided to hold back, until he mustered enough confidence and resolution to rephrase by asking whether Decius intended to marry his daughter or engage in the less-formal marriage custom of cohabitation.

Decius was caught off guard somewhat by the question being introduced so suddenly. Agaroman, being close enough to overhear, objected to the senator's inquiry as being too personal for his knowledge and place. The senator bowed to the dux and asked forgiveness for the offense while stating that he had asked out of a sense of care for his daughter and her prospects in finding a suitable husband. Decius waved his hand in reply while telling the senator and potential father-in-law that he had understood the senator's concern while taking no offense and even went further to admit that his daughter was indeed the one he intended to be the mother of his future heir someday.

Diem was pleased, without holding back his expression though it did become somewhat less enthusiastic as Agaroman interrupted again to let the senator know that while his daughter would be privileged to be the mother of the dux's future heir, out of caution she would not get in the way of the dux's focus to fulfill the prophecy of being the chosen vessel in making the divine spirits of war and death become one from combining their essence with the dux's. The wizard went further to emphasize the importance of Dux Decius not being overly committed to any potential personal vows of matrimony that would seem to prioritize his lover over his obligation, devotion and service first and foremost to Laran and Calu.

The senator looked at first still somewhat disappointed, even hoping to show that sense of depression to the dux in the hopes it would cause Decius to reconsider, but Decius reluctantly agreed with his wizard advisor that his duties to the divine came first and foremost and it was a complementary role in which Lucia would be expected to relent and accept his duties to his would-be empire came before his love for her, as much as Decius would allow space for her role as the co-ruler consort of his future dynasty and empire. The dux even stated that he was proud to know the senator's daughter was able to acknowledge and exhibit this even when the dux had to depart her presence and hold council. Diem nodded his head to acknowledge while looking down.

In the senator's mind, the dux was correct in the Citadellan tradition and customs to point that out as it was expected for both the males and females to follow a system of different and complementary roles to support their family unit, or as they would call it (especially in the high desert basin), their wolf-pack hierarchy cultural value system that they had adopted from their Lupercalian forebears since the ancient times. To lift the senator's hopes and mood while being true to his assessment, Decius told Diem before departing that Diem and his family had raised Lucia well, being the first and only woman the dux had ever considered bonding with. The senator was pleased, and his internal feelings became exhibited externally in that sense of praise and acknowledgement from his own stately leader. Perhaps Decius was right; if what Decius said of his daughter, his beloved Lucia, was true, then Diem could feel his inward and outward attainment of peace and calm, knowing he and his wife had done well to receive such praise and admiration coming from a stately leader for their upbringing of their beloved daughter to be worthy of meriting that leader's attention and attraction to her and the values she exhibited in reflection, at least in part, of her parents.

CHAPTER EIGHTEEN

A Father's Honor and Dignity

A few days later, Diem came once again to the dux's estate. He was sent notice on behalf of the dux that he was invited. When he arrived at the front entrance portico made from marble, stucco, and concrete, the senator was escorted by one of the dux's servants to wait in the atrium of the main hallway.

A moment later, Diem was surprised and relieved when his daughter Lucia walked in. He quickly approached her, and they embraced each other while he asked his daughter how she was faring. Lucia assured her father that she was doing well and that she elected to stay at the dux's residence ever since the first night she had met Decius. She told her father that she missed him and, with Decius's permission, invited her father to the dux's government estate to visit with her father. The two sat on two bicliniums, or adjacent reclining couch-like beds, near a center table, where Lucia called upon two of the estate servants to bring out various small appetizers along with Citadellan red wine. Both Lucia and her father sat down now that they had reunited and were at ease, particularly Diem.

As the two slowly and almost ceremoniously partook of the food and wine, they began to converse. Diem asked his daughter about why she stayed and if she had truly fallen in love with the dux. Lucia let her father know that she was very much in love with Decius and that she and the dux both related so intimately in their ambitions and values that she had not wanted to depart from him ever since. She went on to say that while she knew that her father was worried about her, it was precisely the reason she had invited him to assure her well-being was being met and exceeded by the dux.

Diem was pleased and could not hold back his expression while continuing the conversation, inquiring from his daughter about her and Decius. Diem thought it best to consider a formal ceremony of marriage to solidify his daughter's love with Decius's. Diem as her father would have the honor to walk her down the temple sanctuary and transfer his ritual manus, or symbolic manumission of custody and authority of her to the dux, as it should be between husband and wife.

Lucia looked down intently and mildly frowned, knowing that her father would request that. She explained to him that she would want to do the same as he would, but the gesture of transferring manus in the ceremony itself by placing his hand on hers on the dux's, as she explained, would be seen possibly as a sign of the dux's submission to a higher authority for permission, as mild as the gesture might seem.

As she could see (and possibly expected) a mixture of sadness and slight anger on her father's face, Lucia placed his hand over hers and told him that she had difficulty at first in accepting this rationale, but she understood as a sign of piety and submission on her part that she had only one option to be the dux's wife without engaging in the more formal ceremony of marriage. She would enact and assert her right as Citadellan daughters, including nobility, would have to fulfill the other condition of marriage by cohabitation in the dux's house for one straight year in order to be recognized by de facto custom, or Citadellan common law, as his wife without the dux having to relent in attaining a gesture of permission from another authority.

Diem understood what she had explained except for why the simple and modest gesture to be briefly exhibited between him and the dux when symbolically transferring custody of his daughter to be wed would matter. Lucia responded that Decius as not only dux but also in his personal quest to fulfill the ancient prophecy of making the deity spirits of war and death become one, as a chosen vessel, had to ensure he was suitable and worthy for that role without taking any risks or compromises in appearing submissive even with the slightest symbolic, ceremonial gesture.

Diem understood again though he was somewhat perplexed that his daughter actually believed in such a prophecy, and he asked her if she truly did. Lucia nodded and affirmed that she did so indeed. She asked her father if there was anyone else he knew who had attained omens and favors from the divine as Decius being born and raised feral even briefly by wolves, being the single survivor from Ascentius's dispatched elite company of knights and infantry during the reprisal raids against the barbarians in the north, his victory against the Kingdom of Swordbane (granted, it was seen as a deceitful slaughter in declaring Sanctum Novus's secession), and even his ability to call upon and commune with the wolves, the symbolic animal of not only Sanctum Novus but also both Calu and Laran. Diem nodded and acknowledged that Decius had certainly achieved and distinguished himself in the annals of Citadellan culture but asked how anyone, even with those accolades, could achieve such a task.

Lucia, with a somewhat solemn and sad face, knew what both Decius and Agaroman had told her that Decius would have to do and asked whether she was prepared to still stand by him. She confided to her father that her future spouse would do unimaginable things, whether it was making an alliance with more beastly creatures like orcs and goblins, slaughtering the army of a former lord, or condemning corrupt temple clergy to be infected by a plague and later banished in order to spread a pandemic into the borders of an enemy. It was by such reasoning, as Lucia explained, necessary in order to appease both the deity spirits of war and death to warrant their attention and consider Decius as a worthy candidate host for them to transfer their conjoined essence into as their vessel to bring order and control in a new resurrected form of an empire, reminiscent of the one that their Citadellan ancestors had once been a part of under the ancient and indomitable Lupercalian Empire over a thousand years ago.

To Diem, it seemed in one aspect that his daughter had been fanaticized in the same cult that a small but growing minority of members within Sanctum Novus converted to during the span of Decius's reign as dux. Diem could understand and respect his daughter being ambitious as well as having many traits like that in common with Decius for the two to be considered an ideal match for setting up a line of heirs. Still, he was apprehensive about believing such a prophecy could be achieved by the dux. However, Diem also admitted to his daughter he would not exclude the possibility that Decius could achieve such a near-impossible task if anyone could at all. Diem admitted if there was anyone with that much ambition, leadership, and capability, Decius probably exemplified it in the flesh.

Diem also knew what she meant by unimaginable things, or to an extent, he thought he did. He knew how leaders like Decius, being in a state of war, especially more frequently in dealing with raids outside

Sanctum Novus, had to contemplate decisions that would potentially condemn one's soul and even one's own humanity in order to do what they thought was right. It was in this sense both good and possibly bad, if not outright evil intentions toward one's enemies, that a capable leader would have to pave the road of his domination. He told his daughter as such after she had explained this. He advised her that as Decius's wife, his other half, she needed to be there for him and to use her influence and affection toward him to bring the best out of him as well as to further his ambitions as long as they would benefit Sanctum Novus, regardless of the cost toward their enemies, as brutal as it might be.

Returning to the matter of marriage, Diem told his daughter that though he resented the decision by both his daughter and the dux to attain a status of recognized marriage by the common-law custom of cohabitation instead of the traditional wedding ceremony involving manumission of his daughter from his authority and house to be transferred to the dux, ultimately Diem accepted his daughter's wishes. He would do so even if it would come at the lesser expense of not receiving the dignity and status for both him personally and his family house to ritually and formally transfer custody of his daughter to the dux during the marriage ceremony.

Lucia, grateful and appreciative of her father's understanding and reluctant consent, suddenly embraced her father and thanked him while stating profusely that regardless of formalities and status, she would always be his daughter and telling him as others had that both he and his wife, Lucia's mother, had done well in raising her to be capable as the alpha female and household matriarch, second only to Decius, to raise their future house and raise under her care future heirs to be leaders of the dux's future empire. Diem nodded his head in consent while stating he knew as well.

Before her father departed with one final hug and kiss on the cheek, Lucia told him that anytime he, Lucia's mother, or her siblings wanted to come to her or reside in the dux's estate, a room would be set aside for them. Decius had many rooms in his estate, but he only used one room personally, his dux chamber, being fairly modest in his living except when inviting guests over for lavish parties. The only other person at his estate that occupied one of the main rooms aside from the estate's servants was his close advisor Agaroman.

Diem nodded for the gesture of openness from his daughter and bid her a farewell while promising as she had asked that he would send her regards to both her mother and siblings. It was a sad day for him but also somewhat joyous in seeing that his daughter had not only grown up but also moved on in her own way and, like her father, sought to be the best in attaining the highest status and position with a worthy match in whom she seemed to have found her soul mate. Wherever Decius was, she would be there, either by his side or tending to his affairs at his estate on his behalf while he was away. To Diem, that was always the expectation he and his wife had extolled to their daughter with that type of embodiment. Yet now it was immersed deeper in his mind with some sadness that he no longer would have his daughter permanently next to him to share their close family moments with his wife as they had before. Diem missed the days when he could carry his beloved little Lucia upon his back while walking about his own private estate and date plantation and teaching her about when the dates would be ripe to harvest or how to extract the materials from various exotic plants that would be used for incense. Compelled as he was, he had to tell her about those memories so she would cherish them not only as a daughter, but also when she and Decius would one day become parents of their own children. Lucia vowed to do so and kissed her father before he departed. She held back her tears in front of her father, but as soon as Diem had departed, she released those tears, knowing that she also cherished those memories and, in some part, wished she could relive them again. He was right though; in a different way, she would relive and cherish those memories again when she and Decius had children of their own to spend those special moments with.

CHAPTER NINETEEN

The Road to Forgiveness

Hundreds of miles away on the same day, the sun shone brightly above the forest canopy of redwood and sequoia trees covering the coastal interior of the Swordbane kingdom heartlands like a blanket that warms and cools the many inhabitants that call this region home. Only a few noticeable but still serene obstructions stood out, though they might appear as majestic ornaments in their own right. Between both ends of the serene forest lay a gap. It was a field of grass with a paved stone road, the Royal Road of Swordbane (also known as the King's Road) with several elegant elven wooden huts placed along the border between the grass on either side of the road and the outer border where the trees of the forest met the grass plain. Elven children ran and played about the fields while the older adolescents either supervised or learned the various trades of their adult parents: sewing clothes from the various plant materials that were used, plowing and sowing fields for some crops while rotating crops and harvesting other food crops that were ripe, watering the exotic fruit groves domesticated from the forest, and hunting. As the various elven hamlets peacefully went about their day, their attention was caught when the sun was partially obscured. The various elves of the hamlets looked up in amazement and curiosity while their children erupted in excitement, trying to keep up with the floating ship high in the sky. For some of the inhabitants, it was truly a sight to see that they had never seen before nor probably would see again, at least not for a very long time, if that.

The view on board Wyatt's skyship looking down was equally

mesmerizing. Even Linitus calling this region his home had never seen its beauty from so high above while looking down. As he gazed while standing side by side with his newly beloved companion, he pointed out the various famous landmarks to Marin and provided vivid details of the lore for each of the places. From a distance, the most enchanting and noticeable stood near the horizon but approached gradually. It was a sight that they both knew well, even when they encountered each other as children. That landmark in particular gleamed and glistened from the reflection of the sun's bright rays. It was the famous elven city of Salvinia Parf Edhellen, or Parf Edhellen for short. It was an ancient city founded during the time of at least the Lupercalian Empire or possibly predating it and combined a beautiful mix of Citadellan and elf architecture. Besides its sparkling stone walls, the city held mass populace amenities including its own amphitheater, circuit horse race track, and a majestic temple of dedicated to the deity spirit of Silvanus, protector and guardian of the forest, nature, and uncultivated land, which the elves in particular had a strong attachment to.

As the skyship drew ever closer to the city, so did the intimate conversations and emotions shared between the elf ranger and the Princess Knight. Without their knowing, from a high vantage point and corner on the aftercastle peered King Ascentius. The king could not help but watch intently at the close bonding and affection that the two shared for each other, which reminded him of his departed and beloved Gretchen. Despite the differences and objections general society might place between his daughter and the elf ranger, Ascentius was convinced morally and internally that the two perhaps at this point shared genuine fondness and feelings toward each other that could withstand and overcome any barrier that would oppose their bond of love. Ascentius decided at least in his mind for the moment that while it could wait, it might be a destined portent to see their love and be reminded of the love he once shared with Gretchen, so perhaps it would be best to arrange one day for the two to not only get married in a royal wedding but also pass on his reign to Linitus as a successor king along with his daughter Marin to rule as queen. Even if Linitus had no direct lineage to the crown and his family was, at best, of local nobility standing, Linitus had shown and demonstrated his ability to lead and command beyond expectation, while having talents that surpassed what would have been initially and ordinarily expected. He was a true, capable, and determined leader. Unlike Decius, Linitus had neither ulterior motives of his own, nor any noticeable vices in personality. If the subjects had any objection about his legitimacy to be a future king, Linitus could easily remove those doubts when a moment of opportunity presented itself as he had done several times so far.

Behind the king, Peat stood by, also peering and noticing what he could tell from the king's expression and possible thoughts. The dwarf guardian could not help but share aloud to his king about sharing the same feeling to some extent. The dwarf pointed out that they made a good potential pair including possibly as natural lovers and perhaps he was wrong to judge the elf too harshly, despite seeing Linitus as an upstart.

The king nodded while asking his dwarf guard and companion how close they thought they could get in rescuing Marin as well as capturing the Sharj in Marjawan without Linitus, about how their fate would be any different or the same in Decius's betrayal and alliance with the goblin-orc army against Ascentius himself and his forces. The dwarf shook his head slowly while sighing, admitting that he did not know, but admitted that their fates likely would have been different without the talents and abilities of the elf ranger.

Ascentius shook his head, and in one sweeping admission caught Peat by surprise, confiding that if their love did hold true, Ascentius would not only see to it that they had a royal wedding, but also would pass on his throne to the elf ranger. Peat was nearly dumbfounded and started to ask about how the king's subjects would react, until the king raised his hand to interrupt and acknowledged to the dwarf guardian that he thought the same, but just as Linitus had demonstrated, he would be capable of winning the hearts of the people as he had won not only the princess's personal admiration but also the king's, with respect to the elf ranger's character and qualities. It was time for a new change, and the people would adapt just as they had over the years since the fall of the Lupercalian Empire and the rise of the Swordbane kingdom, where a large portion of human barbarian Nordling invaders settled, intermingled, and adapted while starting a new blended society with the local human Citadellans of the western coast lands. Society would change but also adapt just as it had before.

As the king and dwarf turned their attention to the approaching city of Parf Edhellen, Ascentius knew that he had to take charge in alerting the elven inhabitants of his kingdom of the spark of war that had transpired from the betrayal of Sanctum Novus and the dux against his reign recently.

He would also have to deliver the news that only one, Linitus, out of all the dispatched elven irregular rangers, had emerged as a survivor from both the combined campaign against Marjawan and the betrayal massacre outside the walls of Sanctum Novus.

The only promising news was he could find some consolation in telling his elven subjects as well as human subjects that the long, drawn-out conflict with Marjawan was over and the king's forces, or what was left of them, had personally defeated and captured the Sharj. The king would see to it that the Sharj, who was, fortunately for Swordbane, recaptured by Wyatt during the onslaught outside the walls of Sanctum Novus, would be held accountable for his plot and deaths inflicted against the kingdom that led to the long bloody war. Ascentius would personally see to it and make an example of the Sharj by planning even under short notice a royal triumphal march and procession with the Sharj in chains. The few surviving dozens of warriors on board the skyship would serve as the representatives of his remaining army to march in procession along with the king himself and the small company of heroes he and the other surviving soldiers held in high regard for saving them: Peat, Wyatt, and especially Linitus and his daughter Marin from that final battle resulting in the Sharj's capture. These four heroes would ride in their own designated chariots to follow right behind the king's chariot at the front of the procession.

Though this was a show of prestige, extravagance, and to an extent, vanity, it was still considered a proud Western, or more specifically, Citadellan tradition for solidifying legitimacy that had been passed down from the times of the Lupercalian Empire to be carried over to the current ruling Kingdom of Swordbane. If the king had a better chance to uphold the stability of the kingdom and retain his own legitimacy as the sovereign of the western lands, he had to show his subjects tangible results that they could understand, including defeating and capturing a once-adversary foreign head of state. Doing so, the king thought more deeply, might stir the sense of pride and patriotism among his various subjects: human, elven, dwarves, and other small folk, including halflings and gnomes, that they still had a common and relevant bond of uncanny determination to overcome odds by working together, even when weary from one war against a foreign and distant foe to hopefully still be prepared for the next war against one close by and domestic.

Only after pondering such plans and sharing with Peat did the king decide on enacting the next plan to slowly and patiently orchestrate for

Linitus to become his eventual successor. Ascentius decided he had to no longer pretend and feign some degree of ignorance of the obvious and overt display that the elf ranger had fallen in love with his daughter. It was time to let them know he was aware, and perhaps for the better sake of the kingdom, the two of them should have a royal marriage to continue his line of succession through Marin, granted Linitus would take the place of the ruling head of state, keeping in line with a blended Citadellan and Nordling tradition that even Swordbane rulers were content to adopt since the kingdom's inception that the males would be the prime sovereign rulers, though female queens and princesses were still very well respected and able to project power in more discreet ways in their standing and position.

As Linitus and Marin still stood caught in the shared thoughts and dreams of what they would do together, they speculated about the future prospective adventures they would share during and after their stay in and around Parf Edhellen. As their embrace, emotions, and thoughts of their future aspirations coalesced and melded into a powerful convergence between two winds, an abrupt halt forced it to come to a stop. Suddenly, Ascentius interrupted his daughter and her newfound lover, Linitus. The king asked, though in some sense it was a command, for his daughter to leave and allow a moment between her king father and Linitus. Marin shook her head and complied.

Linitus, though externally composed, had internally some degree of anxiety in not knowing how much the king knew about the elf ranger's personal attachment to his daughter and how Ascentius would handle it. There was a possibility that it could be another matter more direct and pertinent to the king seeking counsel or wanting to task Linitus with a particular quest at hand. For his part, Ascentius could tell and wanted to be direct while putting Linitus at ease. The king raised his hand as the elf was about to give a bow and place his hand on his chest as a gesture of fealty. Ascentius told Linitus that he knew. He knew that the two had grown personally and romantically attached. Though he only wanted the talented elf ranger to watch over and mentor his daughter, he acknowledged that they did have a personal and affectionate bond that even reminded Ascentius to some extent of the one he shared with his beloved, the late Gretchen. Linitus felt, to some extent, disappointed in possibly letting down the king with his vow while becoming attached to the king's daughter Marin, the one he was supposed to mentor in leadership and martial combat. Falling in love with her was, he knew, certainly not among the charges that the elf ranger was commissioned by the king. The elf ranger informed the king that he understood and that he would be ready for the king's judgment for possibly not fulfilling the king's expectations to the explicit extent of his appointed post.

Again, Ascentius waved his hand in a calm and dismissive manner, stating that it was not needed and again he understood the attachment the two had even back in childhood. The king, peering more closely at Linitus, asked solemnly and calmly if Linitus had truly fallen in love with Marin and if Linitus would do everything possible to protect her and uphold their love while keeping his earlier vows to train and mentor Marin in fighting. Linitus responded in firm calmness and confidence that he indeed had fallen in love with Marin and he would do everything possible to protect her and uphold their love with all his heart while still keeping his earlier vows to the king. Linitus looked down and acknowledged the possible reality that the kingdom would have a hard time socially to accept such a union between elf and human, but he would do everything in his resolve to prove that his love for Marin and vice versa would overcome all obstacles set before them.

Ascentius, emotionally touched, held back any emotional display. Still, he felt pierced and convinced from his heart that this was a person who had a righteous and kind spirit very much deserving of his daughter, her love, and his royal consent and blessing as her father and king. He told Linitus that he knew and that if the kingdom since it was founded and even during Ascentius's reign had fostered a small but frequent union of love between different humans overcoming all the odds and differences between their cultures, between Citadellans and the later Nordlings who settled in the western coastlands, then truly such a devoted love could withstand the many prejudices stacked against it and could inspire others to be tolerant of the union between elf and human in general. Society would learn that love could transcend the confines that society earlier tried to impose on the very word itself.

After hearing all that was said, Linitus was equally touched to his inner core at the king's words and at his acceptance of the recent but also noticeable relationship that Linitus had with the king's daughter. The elf confided to the king that he knew and understood that if Ascentius was to allow their relationship to be public, they would face not only serious implications, but also high demands or expectations for the role he would fill in being married to Marin.

Ascentius shook his head and pointed out to Linitus he already met the demands or expectations several times by what he has done. The king believed Linitus would further the kingdom's future and prosperity if given such an opportunity to lead all of Swordbane. Taking a moment to pause, Ascentius told Linitus there would be several tasks at hand still to do, and that which the elf ranger might consider a public display of vanity he might not be looking forward to. Linitus knew and agreed with the king it would be detrimental regardless of gaining the affection and, more importantly, acceptance of the general society, though he wondered what tasks of public display would need to be performed. The king, anticipating and seeing the curiosity on the elf's face in wanting to ask, once again motioned with his hand to say that he would let Linitus know when the time came, after they had departed Salvinia Parf Edhellen. Linitus, trusting the orders of his liege, bowed slightly and nodded.

Looking intently at the majestic elven city, the king sharing the view with Linitus confided that if it was meant to be, he would be proud to call him son and hoped someday he would have him as a son-in-law, by marriage to his daughter Marin. The king continued further, wanting to let Linitus know that he was indebted to him beyond repaying. He was grateful to have a determined warrior like Linitus for a collective and methodical approach to saving not only his kingdom at this point, but also his life and the life of his only child.

Linitus acknowledged and nodded, stating that if the roles were reversed, he knew Ascentius would do the same. Ascentius nodded but, reflecting back on how the last battle came about, confided that he would but he did not think that the same predicament would have ever happened if Linitus had led the same life he had and been in his position of kingship. Ascentius could only wonder if the reason (or one of the reasons) that Decius had betrayed him was a prior feeling and perhaps a reasonable pretext for considering it reciprocal betrayal. Ascentius still recalled being there several years ago when he had ordered his troops to let loose an indiscriminate hail of arrows to rain down from above, striking both Decius's companion soldiers and the Nordling barbarians that emerged from the forest line to engage with what was left of Decius's men on the rainy and muddy hills on the northern plains of Collis Vallem. To Decius, the loss of his comrades in arms was personal, and Ascentius had fully understood it, even more so since that recent fateful day outside Sanctum Novus.

Ascentius wondered if it was truly a mistake to save so many of his men in taking the least amount of risk by allowing far smaller numbers that would be sacrificed on his side of the battle lines. It was not a decision taken lightly, but he did so in the hopes of having fewer men die under his command than if he had committed to a full-on relief-and-reinforcement engagement by deploying his infantry without using archers. He wondered, had Linitus been in his place, would the elf ranger make the same decision? It haunted the king to ponder that, and seeing Linitus as someone who could be trusted and could provide counsel even to him, Ascentius decided he had to share the meaning of that cryptic message the Dreadful Knight had delivered on behalf of Decius outside the walls of Sanctum Novus.

From a different vantage point, Linitus noticed the king was lost in thought, if only for a moment. The elf ranger expressed his concern for the king's well-being by asking if he was okay. Ascentius quickly regained his thoughts and composure to let Linitus know that before departing for the surface, to Parf Edhellen, he had to personally confide to both Linitus and his daughter Marin about that event from which Decius harbored his deep loathing, resentment, and feeling of betrayal by his former sovereign.

In another moment after taking time to confide about that event to both Marin and Linitus, Ascentius asked them both to forgive him and counsel him whenever an opportunity came to avoid making the same decisions that would potentially lead to the betrayal and slaughter that unfolded during their last battle at Sanctum Novus. Needless to say, both Linitus and Marin were both shocked at how cold and calculating Ascentius would be in his own mind, even toward soldiers that served him to be dispensed as potential sacrifices on the battlefield for the greater good (in the king's mind) of saving more lives from being lost. Both Marin and Linitus understood that despite the good intentions of the king for ultimately saving the greatest possible number of his men, it paved a road or divide where Decius had never forgiven nor forgotten what Ascentius had done that day at the expense of Decius's own fellow soldiers and knights.

Recollecting his thoughts and not withholding some tears while feeling responsible at least in part for paving that road of revenge for Decius, Ascentius asked both his daughter and Linitus to forgive him for the many people that in consequence died for him, as a result of his actions several years ago. Marin also shed some tears at hearing her father's genuine remorse and went up to embrace him in her arms. She knew he needed her, and at the same time, she told him that she was equally guilty, even under different circumstances, of being consumed by her personal revenge and anger to risk the lives of the knights that served under her command while fighting deep through the cosmopolitan streets of Marjawan's capital at the end of their prior war. The king nodded his head while returning his daughter's embrace.

Linitus, though he was blameless in a practical sense, still thought about the loss of his fellow elven rangers also. Though he had no initial guilt in assuming his position of command with the intention to save the lives of the king's army as much as he could, he could not help but reflect deeper and still have a sense of guilt, of his own accord. He waited a moment until Marin and the king were done having their moment to confide and share their remorse. When they were done, the elf confided to them both that though he did not feel the same burden from his choices to be able to relate to them, he too still felt a deep sense of guilt as they both did, only for being the only one to survive while his fellow comrade elf rangers had perished either at Marjawan by the time the war had ended or ultimately at Sanctum Novus when the king's forces were betrayed and slaughtered.

Marin turned her attention to Linitus while embracing him next. The Princess Knight told him that he might feel guilty for being alive, but she wanted him to know he played no part to share any blame for the loss of life of those he served with. She and the king both understood that sense of guilt also of being a survivor while losing those close to them, including her late mother, Queen Gretchen. Ascentius had also told Linitus that he would join both the elf ranger and his daughter the princess in paying their respects when notifying the next of kin of the fallen elf rangers after Ascentius himself had personally arranged state affairs as head of state, by notifying the leading city officials and local town elven guard militia about the recent events that unfolded in both the victory from the war with Marjawan and the betrayal at Sanctum Novus. As much as Ascentius felt guilty in not first paying his respects, he and the other two acknowledged while nodding that his role as ruling king took precedence, to ensure the preparedness and survival of his subjects and settlements against any foreign threat as well as internal threats, as was the case with Sanctum Novus under Dux Decius. Ascentius knew in his own conscience as king to ensure everything was in order. The elven settlement's defenses and logistics had to be prepared for the larger impending instability that Dux Decius was planning to cause through the majority remainder of the Kingdom of Swordbane's domain.

Only less than an hour later, after making final preparations before departing and teleporting to the central forum plaza of Parf Edhellen, King Ascentius gave the command for Wyatt to transport the king, Linitus, and Marin as well as several surviving soldiers to serve as acting security for the king.

Upon reaching the surface at the main forum plaza, the sights below were as majestic as they were from above. At opposite ends of the plaza stood two majestic structures: the Basilica (or interchangeably, Temple) of Silvanus and the circus-track Hippodrome of Salvinia Parf Edhellen, where horse riders and horse charioteers raced in separate competitions. Adjacent to the Basilica of Silvanus stood the government headquarters compound of the city, which had its own local senate and a governor that served as local executive administrator while still swearing fealty and allegiance to the king. Those offices were completely made up of the local wood elves as stipulated by respect to the tradition of having a given settlement's population representation correspond to those appointed to administer and legislate locally over themselves while still being under the greater overlordship of the Swordbane crown.

As Linitus gave a brief and less-formal tour to Marin and pointed out the landmarks from up close, Ascentius subtly prompted the two that it was time for them to depart and perform their duties separately until Ascentius would later rejoin the two of them after he had briefed the local elven regional government on the kingdom's latest predicament and ensured the city and its surrounding domain would make the necessary preparations for a possible full-scale invasion of the city or even hit-and-run raids along the Royal Road and the nearby local elven hamlets outside the main city settlement. Marin gave her father a quick embrace before bidding farewell even if briefly, while Linitus rendered his own form of respect by making a slight bow while clenching a fist and placing an arm on his chest. Ascentius returned the same gesture and reminded him to be vigilant and keep his daughter safe even in friendly controlled territory. Linitus nodded and replied he would with all his heart.

Though duty compelled the two to be on their way about the various residences of the city and outside the city walls to report to the surviving next of kin of the fallen rangers, Linitus still took it upon himself to point out and share every tangible landmark the city had along the way, even if they were minor ones. The elf had a vast knowledge of his home region, which impressed Marin as much as the city itself. She had not known of a city with as many captivating landmarks save her own beloved place of home, the kingdom capital and great port city of Citadella Neapola.

As Linitus referred to his list of all the fellow elven rangers he served with, which tallied to two hundred and thirty-nine (excluding him) that had given their lives, he referred to his personal knowledge of their homes and family names to locate the respective quarters in the city and eventual hamlets outside the main city walls. Many of the hamlets lay south, west, and north of the city walls, with the thick forest bordering the east of the walls. Toward the western hamlets, in the path between the city walls and the outside land of the Great Forest River (also known as the Swordbane River), the gap between both riverbanks was accessible to cross by a large bridge connecting the outer land to one of the main walled gates of the city.

For Marin, it was truly beautiful to see, and she confided to her lover, Linitus, that she wished she had taken the time to explore all those years ago when they had been younger and had encountered each other. She admitted that she was happy at least at this stage in their lives to now explore it with him.

From house to house in the city and from hamlet to hamlet outside the city walls, the day grew long but cherishable between the two, as much as they could make of it despite Linitus dreading to have to tell each next of kin how the serving ranger scouts of their families had fallen in combat. These were the fellow warriors he served with, fought with, and would have died with had he been not as fortunate in the circumstances he had been in and with his own abilities to survive and persevere.

Linitus still felt guilty, and Marin, despite her best efforts to cheer him up after he approached the first of many houses, could not initially find a way to uplift his spirits. Several of the elven household members that received the unfortunate news made it harder for Linitus to live with himself knowing he was the only that had survived among his race while now serving in the king's own personal army division. Many of them asked if there were any survivors that were relatives of their immediate fallen kin before asking if any had survived at all, and if so, how many? Linitus did what he could to compose himself and hoped that they would not blame him for being the only deployed ranger among his race to still be alive on returning. None of them did, though awkwardly some said that they could tell from Linitus's expressions in front of them that he wished in some sense he had shared the same fate as his elven comrades rather than live as the only returning elven survivor deployed from the last war as well as the new emerging one.

At some point stopping along the way between hamlets, the elf ranger pulled Marin aside by some trees. Perplexed, she wanted to know what was wrong, though she already had a clear indication to know. The elf dropped down to his knees and cried, confessing to her that those few next of kin were right. As much as he was determined to fight to survive, to ensure the survival of Marin and her father the king, he could not save any of his own fellow elven warriors that served alongside him. He contemplated openly to her that he had thoughts of taking his own life in the hopes of joining his fellow departed warriors in the paradise that awaited in the next life, the elysium that Silvanus had promised them for being good, faithful servants to both nature and their neighbors.

Marin, shocked and concerned, held her lover in her arms and told him that she knew, at least to some extent, how he felt. She told him that she knew why he did not yet go through with what he contemplated. She stared at him deeply and intently.

Linitus, looking up at her and returning the hug, told her that she was right. She was the only reason why he did not go through with his thoughts, as much as he wanted to. Marin, taking a moment of calmness and gathering resolve from Linitus's moment of vulnerability, held back her tears at first until no longer able, to let him know that he had two hundred and thirty-nine reasons to still live, to still fight for the cause of righteousness, and to still seek justice for the loss of his fallen elven comrades and their other fellow soldiers and knights that had fallen. She let him know that in addition to her life and her father's, millions of lives in the kingdom still depended on him to serve and protect in his gifted capacity of leading and fighting. Finally, she told him in her most passionate voice (while still in tears) that living for one's country and one's kingdom was just as important as dying for it. She told him to swear and make a pledge that if she asked him anything beyond sharing their unconditional love, it was to survive as long as possible.

Linitus, taken back and feeling both personally touched and inspired by Marin's words, looked at her directly face to face and swore to her that he would not only love her unconditionally as he did with nature and as he did in his devotion to his deity spirit of worship, Silvanus, but also fight and survive as long as Marin had compelled him to. The two shared a kiss, sat back in each other's embrace against one of the redwood tree trunks, and looked out to appreciate and feel one with nature and the objects, ambient noise, and smells around them. They were at peace for a time. It felt endless. If they could, they would have enjoyed it for an eternity.

Eventually, they got up, continued going to the next set of remaining elven hamlet houses before returning to the city and reuniting with Ascentius while he was still tending to his duties in preparing Parf Edhellen for the war to come against the king's former vassal, Dux Decius, and his coalition of Sanctum Novus forces along with the goblin-orc forces.

CHAPTER TWENTY

Winning Hearts and Minds

As nighttime ended and the sun rose again early in the morning of the next day, hundreds of miles away to the east, Sanctum Novus sparkled like a majestic gem. The dux had assembled the main leaders of the city as part of his executive council to discuss and continue addressing further matters of his new revisionist nation-state that would emulate the ancient Lupercalian Empire as he saw it to be the true heir. Upon convening the assembly, the dux informed the council that he made an important decision to select a new appointee who would advise him and help him financially manage the affairs of the Remnant state.

Walking elegantly and confidently down the hallway and into the council chamber of the dux's estate was a well-dressed, ornate, and attractive young Citadellan woman who had captured the eyes of the council as well as the ire of some members that were present in the council. As Decius introduced her, Lucia nodded and took a calm curtsy-like bow before the council. She proceeded to walk toward an empty seat that had purposely been set aside for her to be seated at his left side while Agaroman still had his seat at the right of the dux's throne.

Agaroman, close advisor and master wizard to the dux, could not help but give a straight yet scornful look at what he saw. He respectfully objected before Decius that it was unprecedented for a woman even of nobility such as Lady Lucia Diem to be appointed to the council. It was not established by Citadellan tradition, at least in the desert region, for women to formally assume civic responsibilities outside those who served in the temple. However, like the Citadellan women of the coastal lands, the desert Citadellan women still wielded much influence and unofficial power within the confines of the estate villas of their families if they were of nobility, second only to their husbands in household authority.

Decius acknowledged his wizard mentor and advisor's apprehension but reminded him that ways had to change even at a pragmatic level in order for Sanctum Novus's lead coalition to stand a chance of mustering and fighting against its former overlord, the Kingdom of Swordbane. Again, it was important just as it was in the homes of the faraway deployed soldiers and knights for women, by their Citadellan custom, to take charge of the matters of the home and all that lay inside. As a symbolic step reaching outward from that expression, Decius reasoned that it was time for him as a leader to appoint Lady Lucia as his alpha female concubine to not only take charge of the affairs of his estate, but also to be entrusted with managing much of the financial affairs of the nation-state.

The dux's response elicited more positive though somewhat reluctant degrees of acceptance. However, it was clear some of the council members, including Agaroman, were still not of the same opinion as the dux. Regardless, they accepted his decision. Although Senator Diem was somewhat conflicted in sharing the same concern as Agaroman ascribing to the common belief that the affairs of the political state were best addressed by its male citizens, the senator found it fairly easy to accept Decius's decision as Diem personally knew his daughter was very capable and prudent in watching over her father's business affairs and estate in supporting both her parents prior to her recent lifestyle change of cohabitating with the dux to pursue the less-accepted marriage status. The senator, invoking his turn to speak, affirmed before Decius and the council that though he shared the same reservations and understood a possible conflict of interest on his part, he would still attest that his daughter Lucia was capable of managing affairs of the state as a potential quaestor for the Remnant to serve alongside Agaroman, who had previously assumed that role informally.

Decius nodded, saying that he knew what Diem had attested firsthand when he saw even from such a short time how Lucia managed his estate as dux. The dux had decided that Lucia and Agaroman would share the role of treasurer by letting Lucia manage the civic government planning matters of Sanctum Novus using half of the imperial Remnant's treasury funds, while Agaroman would be in charge with the other half to be used for managing the military, including enlisted and officer pay, provisions, logistics, and fortifying locations to house and station the nation-state's military throughout its holdings.

Additionally, respecting the status quo of the coalition partners of goblins and orcs as well as subordinates like the Dreadful Knight who were allotted vassalship over lands under the Remnant's control, Decius assured that the respective ruling entities under his authority and overlordship would have their own form of regional control while providing taxes or supplying sufficient quotas of soldiers for conscription into the dux's army. When they sought consensus, no one in the council chamber objected, and all of them nodded; even the ones who still held some resentment yet acquiesced out of respect and, to an extent, out of fear of the authority that Decius wielded. Truly, some had no reservations about what he had done, including the orc war captain and the goblin chief shaman of Uruk Kazaht, both of whom devotedly saw the dux as their one true dark lord to not be challenged in either authority or decision-making.

The dux took the universal nods and silent acquiescence as consent and announced that it was agreed and settled while adjourning the council. The present members got up from their seats and departed, while Agaroman gave both Lucia and her father, Senator Diem, a firm stare. In a mild gesture of seeking common ground that surprised the bald-headed mage, Lucia told him briefly that she had not forgotten their dark lord's destiny of making war and death become one as the chosen vessel.

Agaroman, though initially skeptical, still took her words at face value while stating that he would know in due time and hold her to that vow. For the wizard, Decius's vow as dark lord apparent and as a future candidate for being the host vessel of Calu and Laran could not be compromised to any extent by the soft heart of a Citadellan noblewoman filled with love, on the off chance of the dux being less devoted to fulfilling his dark vow to bring back a social order that had not been seen since the days of the Lupercalian Empire. His purpose required his utmost and full devotion without any distractions in pursuing such a dark path. The time and careful planning since that prophetic day that Decius was found as an infant nearly left to die had it not been the intervention for a sympathetic pack of wolves, ascribed as his portent and symbolic totem, of which Agaroman had been personally convinced and he affirmed his belief of the dark prophecy being true that there could and would be a chosen vessel to bring back the reenvisioned glorious reign of the Lupercalian Empire. Along with the wizard sorcerer's careful but well-orchestrated execution in swaying the now-deposed Sharj to initiate a bloody protracted war against Swordbane, his role and plan of helping Decius to fulfill the dark prophecy of chosen vesselhood could not be jeopardized by a possibly mutually ambitious woman that had a love interest in the dux. For Agaroman, her influence must not weaken Decius to become softer than the reputation he had earned, even to be recognized by some, if not many, as the dark lord and chief orchestrating embodiment of war and death that would bring a new state of order. Time would tell, and Agaroman would be as close to his lordship's side as possible to ensure he would not deviate into a character of compassion because of a young woman who gave the expression of being sweet and charming and exuded an aura of charity.

However, only a week later at a council meeting, Lucia's impact had already taken shape in ways that no one had fully expected. Neither the dux nor Senator Diem and Agaroman had expected to see how much this noble concubine appointed as co-treasurer could shape and change the way society had been a few days ago. In several acts of what seemed like social-development miracles, Lucia had used the new nation-state funds to repurpose and reopen an abandoned building in the desert city as a food distribution bank as well as community feeding center to support the impoverished as well as any bystanders that simply wanted a free meal, including off-duty goblins and orcs who simply pitched their makeshift tents by the street side. The dux's new appointed treasurer had fostered through her funding and procurement of a feeding center a public place from which the Citadellans of the desert city would find a setting to encounter and converse in more open and comfortable conversations with orcs and goblins. Though they were different in many ways, they both shared an appetite as well as interest to know each other, with curiosity now that they coexisted in the same city. It brought them closer so they would shape together this new coalition to make the Remnant the new powerhouse faction in the west. They both engaged in discussion of political intrigue despite the differences of approach and thought, while sharing about their own personal lives and culture. It had broken some barriers between these groups, who finally started to open up and trust each other.

Additionally, Lucia used more of the allocated funds for civic development from the treasury to provide a makeshift open stable pen converted into a large wolf den for the dire wolves to roam more freely about when their goblin riders were not riding them. She repurposed another abandoned building that was surrounded by a grove of palm trees outside the city walls, with enough space to use the public funds to convert this into a more open roaming pen that was at least two acres in area. The wolves, when supervised by their orc and goblin riders, were given dates and apples by the various children of both the patrician upper class and the plebian lower class of the city's populace as well as from the orphanage for which Lucia had also used more funds to upgrade the existing facilities, including hiring a couple of scholars to provide education to the orphans.

Decius had seen and been impressed by the organization and the handling approach of his concubine and appointed treasurer while openly admitting to her his pleasure in what she had done to transform Sanctum Novus. Remembering her vow to Agaroman and gauging the dux's response in order to not influence him by being too aspirant toward ideals that Swordbane would consider morally good, Lucia reminded her lord and lover that she did this in order to bring more order and cohesion between the local Citadellans and the newcomers from this beastly coalition while reminding the dux that it was important to build this cohesion to be used and managed by her dark lord lover to wage war and bring both death and destruction to their enemies in pursuit of bringing about his new empire and being the deity spirits' eventual chosen vessel.

Decius nodded and agreed. He placed his hand over Lucia's shoulder while wrapping his other hand under her bosom to remind her that though he had his destiny and vows to fulfill while not losing focus, there was no woman as worthy as her for him to be with and have at his side. She was worthy to be his alpha female as well as consort duchess, and he would be proud for her to bear his future son someday when it was the right time.

Lucia, blushing while giving a slight bow of appreciation, pursed her lips up to the dux, and the two mutually kissed. Though he was a dark lord and his role would seem uncomfortable as well as unsettling for many that crossed his path, she was still comfortable seeing a different side of Decius. In her conception and understanding of his role even as a perceived dark lord, he was genuinely devoted and sincere to fulfill a prophecy to bring a new order of prosperity.

She was still able to convince herself of that and that his means in going about it would ultimately justify achieving the desired end. She felt compelled to help balance the reputation the dux had earned as being the fearsome and wrathful leader, by showing up as his de facto consort, giving this dux a reasonable capacity to garner fervent loyalty and devotion from the masses in his empire. She would help him do so by winning their hearts and minds while making contributions to help improve their subjects' lots in life, even in marginal though still meaningful and somewhat measurable ways. She was proud to be his future wife even at the expense of being perceived as a temporary concubine for the time being. She thought to herself at least she would eventually and formally be recognized as his wife one day even if it was by the lesser of the two traditional Citadellan forms of marriage. Even more so she thought about her aspirations of also having the honor and recognition of being the mother of the dux's future son. She would be known as his heir's mother, and more importantly, she would be considered the symbolic mother of the dux's new nation-state; through her most recent acts as co-treasurer, she had demonstrated and learned to recognize in a maternal sense of the importance in caring for one's subjects as she considered it her present duty and station in life.

CHAPTER TWENTY-ONE

Tragic Timing of Triumphs and Plagues

After nearly a week of arranging the defenses, giving briefs from the most recent scouting reports, and finishing the last of notices to inform next of kin of the loss of their respective family members that served as rangers, the king as well as Linitus and Marin were ready to depart Salvinia Parf Edhellen. Aside from attending to their important tasks, Linitus had reintroduced Marin and King Ascentius to his family, whom they had not seen in twenty years. They exchanged greetings while Linitus's family, who hosted the three of them as guests of honor to stay at their hamlet under their hospitality, which Linitus, the king, and Princess Marin accepted with delight to pass the time when they were not attending to pressing matters during the past several days. On the final day, when they had finished their business, the three of them stood near the forum plaza of the elven city, and Linitus shot a silver flashing-light type of arrow in the sky as a cue for being transported. Wyatt saw the signal and had teleported the three of them aboard their skyship at once.

Once all the crew were on board, the skyship changed course while floating high in the air, leaving the backdrop of the elven city below and the sparkling rising morning sun above faced the skyship's stern. Per the king's orders, the skyship was charting its course due west toward the kingdom's capital, Citadella Neapola. Though the floating ship could easily reach the capital in less than a day, the king had dispatched a small elven contingent of cavalry from Parf Edhellen to the capital to inform the city of the king's arrival the next day and to make haste to receive the king and his company with a formal triumph and having the necessary preparations for it to be made. Although it would be challenging, the king knew that the capital's administration and military would be able to orchestrate such an arrangement even on short notice, and it was one that Ascentius wanted to have, not for the vanity of displaying his power and influence in and of itself, but in order to rally and raise the morale of his subjects for the war that Dux Decius and his dark coalition had brought upon the kingdom after it literally concluded a twenty-year-long bloody conflict with Marjawan.

Ascentius shared his agenda and plans to Linitus (who had already earned his complete trust) along with his trusted bodyguard Peat and his daughter Marin. At one point, Peat would have objected as he had earlier that the elf ranger attained so much trust from the king in such short order, even given the severity of unfolding events. However, after seeing how devoted, loyal, and dependable Linitus truly was, even Peat rendered his full trust and respect to him. Ascentius briefed all three of them as well as Wyatt that along with them, the surviving company on board would use the skyship to teleport near the main roadway from the northern city gate, the main entry gate, and ride on chariots with the king at the lead in a celebratory procession toward the main city plaza and forum, with the surviving knights to mount horses and ride at the rear while guarding and escorting the deposed Sharj to be forced-marched bound in chains as part of the parade in a symbolic gesture for the kingdom's subjects to witness, celebrate, and have their morale reaffirmed by the king's army bringing victory against Marjawan.

Though Linitus was not in favor of the display he considered a prideful sign of vanity, the elf ranger put aside his reservations in coming to the same conclusion that this symbolic gesture was perhaps necessary as the king saw it in providing affirmation to the kingdom's subjects of Ascentius's legitimacy and proven ability to rule over the kingdom even in a time of war, while preparing for the next one against Sanctum Novus and its dark coalition. The king knew and could tell from Linitus's face that he was trying to hold back his initial thoughts of this symbolic ritual and gesture. Ascentius acknowledged Linitus's reservations and told him that his loyalty in putting that aside to do what was necessary for the kingdom was one of the reasons that Ascentius had respected him that much more.

Later in the evening after briefing and after having an earlier dinner on board the skyship, with the recent food provisions that were provided by

Parf Edhellen, Linitus and Marin made a makeshift couch on the deck of the ship near the aftercastle to sit in the embrace of each other's arms. They were at this point literally inseparable so everyone on board knew, and even Marin's own father, the king, was content to accept that they were openly in love, without objecting. He knew in his heart that not only did they love each other but also he could perhaps not find a better suitor for a formal and political marriage arrangement to win the heart of his stubborn and martial daughter, and Linitus had all the qualities Ascentius would want for one to be with his daughter. Being an elf did not matter to Ascentius in the prospect of Linitus being his potential son-in-law, especially when recognizing his genuine character and virtues. For the king, he and even his dwarf guardian Peat, viewing from the above aftercastle deck the display of affection that Linitus and Marin shared was endearing to them both to admire from their vantage point. Eventually, out of respect for how both Linitus and Marin would spend their time together in each other's arms and conversing, the king commanded Peat to follow him as his guard captain and retire in the skyship's main cabin for the night.

Resting in each other's arms, Linitus then Marin both awakened the next day to a tantalizing pink-orange mélange-painted sky offset by the sun slowly rising. From the distance on the western horizon, they could see the Bay of Swordbane as well as the awe-inspiring coastal metropolis of Citadella Neapola. The walls of the city were towering, over fifty feet tall, and insulated stood thousands of residential buildings including ones that were multiple stories tall with a white stucco-like color topped with red barrel tiles made from clay. Interrupting the large expanse of barrel-tiled buildings stood even taller and much more majestic landmark monuments and regal buildings that looked like decorations that stood out from a beautiful layered cake of the large coastal metropolis.

The most majestic monuments still at a distance were distinguishable for Marin to return the favor and give Linitus a bird's-eye-view tour of her home, including the Great Amphitheater of Swordbane, the Grand Circus, the Royal Crown Palace also known as the King's Estate, the Senate house building (also known as the Royal Curia, which stood adjacent to the city plaza and forum), and the multiple majestic temples, with the most prominent being the Basilica of Sol Invictus, the deity spirit of creation including the sun and all stars that life depends on. Sol Invictus was also considered the chief deity spirit that presided most prominently among the pantheon of deity spirits.

As the skyship changed course to hover and go around the periphery of the great bay area in a series of planned waypoints that Ascentius had directed Wyatt to chart and course, the beauty of the bay itself caught the attention equally for Linitus seeing it the first time, for he rarely traveled outside the forest area of his home region of Parf Edhellen. Approaching the north of the coastal metropolis over an hour later and nearing the outer walls of the northern city gate from high above, Citadella Neapola's beauty had truly captivated the shock and awe of Linitus as he could see the city skyline from above more clearly, with its endless buildings and multiple standing landmarks that rivaled in beauty the ones of his beloved Parf Edhellen but surpassed in quantity as Neapola was a far bigger city both by land size and by population. Still in amazement at what he saw, Marin continued to explain to Linitus from her knowledge more lore about the city's landmarks and the significance they each held. The awe of the city's lore even from her seemed as vast as the city itself to captivate his awe.

As the two lovers shared their moment together, looking down to the city, Ascentius, though wanting to hold back, interrupted them in a calm and solemn manner, telling both that it was time. Linitus, letting go of Marin's hand from looking about the city below, walked toward his bow and large satchel to pull out a large cylinder-like object holding several arrow projectiles. Pulling back on the bow while holding the cylinder sabot assembly, the elf ranger aimed at the sky, facing the city, and after taking one gentle breath, he let loose the drawn arrow string along with the sabot cylinder.

Drifting like a flock of soaring birds across the air, the multiple arrows in the cylinder assembly separated but flew gracefully in close proximity to each other. A moment after waiting from the utter silence, a loud series of thuds and pops sounded as the arrows exploded into multiple vibrant colors of light. From below, a wave of cheers and audible chants of joy could be heard from the city, even from the skyship. The king, witnessing this, turned to Linitus and told him that this was one of many good signs to come in making sure that the city knew that they would have a reason to celebrate victory and still have hope in the days to come. Linitus understood and nodded in agreement. Marin went to him again and held his hand to still look together at the city below one final time before teleporting.

Upon reaching the surface from teleporting via Wyatt's spell-casting, everything that was staged and ready to commence for the triumph was in order. The pace of the parade and its arrangement played out exactly as the king had given orders for it to be devised. The king was alongside Peat as chariot driver on the front chariot. Following closely behind in formation, Marin and Linitus shared the next chariot together, along with Wyatt acting as the second chariot driver. The surviving infantry regulars along with the surviving knights of the Eternal Flame order followed while forced-marching the deposed and enchained Sharj, who still out of pride in not giving in while resisting was basically dragged by one of the mounted knights. Only a few infantry soldiers under the supervision of one knight stayed on board the skyship to stand guard watch from above.

Marching in procession along the Royal Road that led into the city from the main north gate, large crowds could be seen on either side of the city road, cheering endlessly while clapping and making other motions of celebratory display of their kingdom's achievement in the victory against Marjawan. Though Linitus preferred not to be in the public eye nor to be depicted as larger than life in such a celebration, his views in some aspect had changed, recognizing that perhaps such local human traditions did have a degree of worthwhile purpose as he felt this triumphal, or celebratory, parade was indeed giving hope as well as happiness to the people, beyond which he had not seen to such great measures.

Indeed, looking at all the multitudes in crowds, most were human and a mixed conglomerate of Citadellan, Nordling, or a combination of the two. There were, however, other nonhuman races that were present and presumably lived in the city, including elves, dwarves, and even some halflings as well as gnomes. It was truly a cosmopolitan place of gathering unlike any other, which tangibly showed to the elf ranger despite the many differences between the races, there was a place for them to call home and a kingdom with both a banner and crown to unite under. He understood in a larger context than he thought before that the role Ascentius had assumed was not only being king and serving the interests of his subjects, but it meant serving the interests of all his subjects from different races and Ascentius strove to do that faithfully without any bias as much as possible toward any race, including his own mixed-human though predominantly Citadellan background. The elf, after reflecting on all this internally, had found a deeper respect for Ascentius as king and considered his interests as being genuine and caring for his subjects, more than he had considered before.

However, as the triumph participants made their way closer toward the city plaza and forum, Linitus and Marin both noticed from a distance that in certain sections of the crowd, there were several people coughing who seemed unaware they had contracted a rapidly spreading plague. It was that which had been widely dispersed from the lone caravan company of priests that Dux Decius had exiled as punishment for their sins of corruption and abuse of their clerical office, after they were exposed to an afflicted outcast colony outside Sanctum Novus.

As the original caravan of afflicted exiled clergy headed northwest, it first exposed the northern basin plain and highland regions of human settlements, including Collis Vallem, followed by Barbarum Hulliz (also known in Citadellan tongue as Colonia Collis) due west, and ultimately the first major Swordbane settlement of Colonia Mons Salvinia, which was just a day and a half to two days of travel by horse, northeast of Parf Edhellen. The king's scout reports apparently and unfortunately for Swordbane were true. An emerging plague had indeed made its way west toward the coastal heartlands of Swordbane.

As the triumph still unfolded despite them taking notice of scattered individual signs of the plague's infliction in the crowd, Marin and Linitus did their best to maintain their composure without giving in to alert the crowd of the pandemic that was unfolding. It was crucial, as Ascentius explained to them, to follow through with carrying out the triumph while knowing that nothing could stop the emerging pandemic. Ascentius still instructed Marin, Linitus, and the rest of his participating parade army to keep their distance from the crowd in order to limit their exposure to the affliction.

The king, however, also assured them that prior to and even during their arrival, the royal crown's army in the city would be made aware of the emerging pandemic and would take action to isolate and quarantine any individuals that showed signs of being afflicted, including coughing profusely and visibly having difficulty in breathing. Sure enough, some of the city guards watching from the rear of the crowd did spot and isolate those afflicted, but it paled in comparison to the ones who were still present and not detained. Linitus and his comrades knew that it was too late. Lives would be lost in the city, at least even by a measurable token amount. It was only a matter of how long they could stave off losing more, if possible.

Linitus stated this observation loud enough for Marin and Wyatt to hear despite the still-persistent cheers and roars of celebration from the crowds. The elf ranger had informed his halfling wizard companion that as soon as the parade came to an end, they needed to talk about finding a cure or remedy to address this ongoing affliction and pandemic before it overwhelmed the kingdom where the Remnant would be better poised to exploit the situation and take over. Wyatt shook his head in acknowledgement of the shared mutual concern and planned to come up with some remedy to the plague at hand.

Finally, at the main plaza and forum, Ascentius stepped down from his chariot and scaled the steps to the central concrete-and-marble platform to give his speech. This platform was known as the legendary Rostra Di Spada Mortis, from where the first Swordbane king had put his sword to rest after conquering the city from the Lupercalians and instituting a new diverse society built on coexistence between the local Citadellans, Nordling invaders, and nonhuman races that called this coastal city their home.

As a symbolic gesture of marking where the first Swordbane king buried his sword, a marker stone base made of granite was placed on top of the Rostra at the very spot of the buried sword along with a ten-foot-tall cast-bronze, blue-hued statue of a dragon bearing a shield with a cross-and-sword insignia mounted on the granite stone base. The statue of the dragon was adopted as a symbolic homage to Sol Invictus, whose animal totem was often represented in the form of a dragon.

On the steps of the Rostra, Ascentius informed his subjects at large that the kingdom had indeed defeated Marjawan and captured its now-deposed Sharj, while the king pointed toward the Sharj, who stood humiliated while being forced-marched by the remaining army of the king's soldiers and knights. The crowd erupted in loud cheers as well as praises of the command and position of Ascentius as their king.

Additionally, Ascentius called forth both his daughter Marin and Linitus to stand next to him. As they did so, with Linitus somewhat in shock and feeling out of place, Marin held his hand subtly while quietly whispering for him not to worry about the large crowd, knowing that the elf ranger was not accustomed to being in front of so many people.

Ascentius announced to the crowd of the city's subjects that he was awarding laurels of recognition to both his daughter and Linitus for not only bringing an end to the war with Marjawan but also decisively saving the king's own life along with the soldiers and knights present in the triumph procession. Both Marin and Linitus bowed down in a kneeling posture with their heads facing down toward the king to receive the token laurels of recognition bestowed upon them while the king announced that they would be known by titles of distinction as Heroes of the Crown. Once again, the multitude of the king's subjects erupted in cheers and applause. Linitus and Marin assumed an at-attention stance a few paces behind the king. Marin once again whispered to assure her elf lover that despite the apprehension he felt in receiving this impromptu recognition, he should be at ease and know with peace of mind that he had rightfully earned it. Linitus nodded though he still felt internally somewhat still out of place again, not being accustomed to this type of war celebration pageantry.

A few moments later, Ascentius called forth and bestowed the same recognitions to Wyatt and Peat while proclaiming them along with Linitus and Marin as the newly created Crusader Order of Comradery of the Crown (or simply known as the Order of Comradery or the Comradery). The king had decided to create such an order not made exclusively of knights but of those from the crusade war against Marjawan in which Linitus, Marin, Wyatt, and Peat were of various fighting professions, yet all of them had demonstrated their ability to go above and beyond the call of duty in not only bringing an end to the last war but saving the king's life in the new one that just started.

Once again the crowd erupted into cheers. Linitus looked once again toward Marin, wondering in a facial expression if this display of recognition would end soon. Marin, though somewhat annoyed, understood that this triumph display, while necessary, was also becoming a drawn-out display of gestures with which she could understand her lover's frustration. She assured him that they were getting closer to being done with the elaborate pageantry.

Though they had only known each other for several weeks, Marin could tell so far that Linitus was fairly humble and not one to want to garner too much attention from large crowds. If there was perhaps anything that she could best him in and possibly teach him in return, it would be perhaps being acquainted with large audiences and possibly giving large public speeches to them. If they were to be ceremoniously wedded, then her elf lover would be expected to be capable of the various leadership roles he would perhaps assume as future king in succession to her father one day. Public speaking and being before a large crowd were certainly counted among the primary role functions of a sovereign monarch. Thinking of such a possibility, she nudged Linitus in the arm while looking toward her father and whispering that someday it would be his turn. The elf gulped in hesitation of thinking about that while Marin could not help but smile about getting a reaction that she would normally not expect in catching her lover off guard.

Meanwhile, toward the second half of his speech, while breaking the news and using it as a segue from what he had just announced, Ascentius went on to thank the surviving troops that had served under him to end their twenty-year-long conflict with Marjawan and mentioned to the crowd that the situation had become more dire with the recent development of the dux's betrayal and the secession of Sanctum Novus, which had aligned itself with the beastly creatures including goblins and orcs as well as even trolls. Ascentius went on to let the crowd know that while one war had ended, a new one had started with the importance for Swordbane to be prepared for the impending onslaught that the Remnant was expected to unleash against the kingdom. The crowds booed upon learning of Sanctum Novus's betrayal and its effort to secede.

Clearly, the king's gamble had paid off. While Ascentius knew he could not control the plague from reaching Citadella Neapola, he could still control his policies and actions to prepare the capital city for a possible attack by the dux.

Though the parade lasted over an hour, after the king had finished giving his speech of address to the various subjects attending, who had now started to disperse back to their daily business at hand, Ascentius went immediately toward Linitus and Marin. The king had told them that the triumph was over and now they had more pressing matters to attend to. Linitus and Marin nodded their heads, expressing concern that this parade type of event had likely exposed those present to the plague itself. The king again acknowledged their concern. He informed them that in the long run, this would be a necessary trade-off in order to instill and boost public morale in the new war to come with Sanctum Novus. Linitus and Marin both agreed and once again nodded their heads.

After the triumph came to an end, the king allowed various festivities to take place while making a quick transition departure with the newly bestowed Order of Comradery. Wyatt teleported the company along with the king to the Royal Crown Palace.

The next morning, the king summoned Linitus and Marin to the castle throne room at the Royal Crown Palace along with Wyatt and Peat. Upon entering the throne room with a rectangular table and chairs to be seated, both Linitus and Marin took a bow signaling their fealty to the king. Ascentius acknowledged and replied by telling them to rise, while the king clenched a fist to put against his chest in return for the same form of salute.

The throne room in full display was a spectacle to behold for those viewing it the first time. Linitus was no exception, not holding back to some degree and showing a slight expression of amazement through his eyes noticing and admiring the ornate furniture and marble veneer architecture in the throne room. As Linitus admired briefly, the king let the elf ranger know that because of all his heroic acts, natural ability to lead and command, and his genuine, trustworthy nature, the elf ranger would be included from now on in the king's royal council which had significantly dwindled from the loss of lords and knights that had fallen in both the concluding war against Marjawan and the recent betrayal and massacre of the king's forces by Decius at Sanctum Novus.

Linitus subtly nodded while telling the king that he was honored. Ascentius, being confident and firm, responded that he knew going forward he would have the elf ranger to serve as the primary advisor to the king as well as the king's appointed general to help lead the forces of Swordbane against Decius's formidable coalition. Linitus showed some feeling of reservation on his face but, Ascentius being aware of that, tried to dispel it, letting the elf ranger know that he had shown before and could do so again in surviving and overcoming various obstacles even in close life-and-death situations and reminding him that he had just done that in saving both the princess's life in Marjawan and the king's own life on the high desert plain outside the walls of Sanctum Novus. Linitus nodded again, stating he would do his best to lead. The king responded again that he knew Linitus would do so.

In opening the royal council meeting, Linitus and Marin were briefed by the king about the current state of affairs and the Kingdom of Swordbane. As they all knew the first matter at hand, they discussed the emerging plague pandemic that had already made its way into the city. Linitus suggested for the king to allocate any necessary resources to Wyatt so that the young halfling wizard could devise a potential remedy for the rapidly escalating plague. Wyatt was also present, along with the king's trusted chief bodyguard, Peat, as part of the small council meeting. The halfling wizard nodded in reaction to Linitus's suggestion for Wyatt to use his abilities and any of the kingdom's resources that could be spared. Wyatt had in mind several relatively harmless ideas for experimenting that could produce the cure for the kingdom's affliction that had started to spread among the major northern settlements of Swordbane.

Meanwhile, the king inquired, while looking toward Peat, about any reports of sightings and/or acts of hostility being done by the dux's coalition since its open rebellion against the kingdom. The dwarf chief guardian shook his head and indicated not yet as far as anywhere west of the Great Coastal Mountains, though he did mention that no word had been heard back from the outposts that lay along east of the north-south mountain chain, including east of Mestthos-Inethbad. Peat informed the king that it was possible the station outposts, which were used as caravan way-stops between Sanctum Novus and Inethbad, likely fell in preplanned attacks or raids by Decius's forces. The king, fearing as much, was led to the same conclusion and ordered Peat to send a courier with a message to Inethbad to maintain active vigilance against a possible future assault that Sanctum Novus might launch against that dwarven stronghold city fortress. Peat acknowledged and went off to summon a courier.

It was at this point Ascentius confided that while he would prepare the capital's defenses against invasion, it seemed likely that Decius had planned all along, possibly being directly responsible (which in fact he was), to introduce the plague to the kingdom's coastal heartland. Linitus interjected by admitting that if he had the same type of evil nature as Decius, he would do the same thing, seeking to weaken and demoralize Swordbane and its various large coastal cities before making a final invasion to take over.

The king, while agreeing, pondered what else could be done for the time being aside from Wyatt utilizing the time to uncover a potential cure for the unfolding calamity. In a moment, after dispatching a courier per the king's command, Peat returned with news from a messenger from Colonia Mons Salvinia, a major human settlement of Swordbane that was inland in the woods and low mountains just north of Parf Edhellen, which had recently received refugees from outlying small human villages. Apparently, the refugees reported to the local settlement militia that they had recently been displaced while their homes were razed and looted by a large but somewhat disorganized war band of goblin raiders. Marin, being the first to react from hearing this said, allowed instinctively that this had to be the work of goblins that had sided with Decius. Ascentius nodded while pondering.

After a short moment, Linitus had devised an idea, asking the king to let the elf ranger himself and his fellow comrades from the king's newly bestowed order go there personally and investigate the claim of goblin raiders. Ascentius, seeing the elf ranger having a prudent and decisive take addressing the situation directly, gave permission for Linitus to proceed and take his other three comrades, including the king's own daughter. While no one in the room present took notice, Marin had recognized that what her father was doing was still no small offer on his part, granting Linitus to not only let his daughter travel and adventure by the elf's side and extending that trust while not going with them and staying behind to assume his duties in leading the kingdom from its capital. It was a gesture that Marin both appreciated and did not take for granted.

Before departing the throne room after the council meeting had concluded and adjourned, Ascentius called to Linitus and Marin to stay behind. The two of them did so, and Ascentius speaking in private wanted to let them both know that while they were clearly in love, they had to make sure they followed carefully with caution in performing their duties and responsibilities with priority for the sake and well-being of the kingdom. Ascentius, placing his hand on Linitus's shoulder, told him that as much as the ranger loved his daughter the Princess Knight, he still had a responsibility to focus intently and clearly for her security and well-being. Additionally, Ascentius reminded Linitus that the king too loved his daughter as her father and pleaded for Linitus to watch her carefully in her actions while not engaging in reckless adventure warrior behavior, as the king would call it.

Linitus, being intent and having his mind open for empathy, let the king know that he understood and would guard Marin with his life. The king intently believed Linitus stating that and nodded before looking at his daughter, who was not pleased that the king having concern for her gave the impression she was overly vulnerable and required supervision. Still, she nodded toward her father and abruptly let him know that she understood his concern and would make sure to be more careful after Marjawan. She let her father know in consolation that at least she was in good hands with Linitus and her efforts along with Linitus's to help save her father the king and the few remaining survivors outside Sanctum Novus was a sign she had demonstrated her ability to be more responsible and reliable since the siege of Marjawan. Ascentius nodded and agreed.

After Ascentius talked to them in private, both Linitus and Marin bowed one more time in fealty to Ascentius before walking out of the throne room to rejoin Peat and Wyatt, who were waiting outside the royal castle of the king. Within moments, a flash was emitted outside the royal castle complex, and another flash was emitted on board Wyatt's skyship. Admiring the view of the majestic and cosmopolitan cityscape of Neapola, the Comradery bid their farewell while charting a course to their next destination.

CHAPTER TWENTY-TWO

Sowing the Seeds of War and Death

As the skyship made its way from the Swordbane capital to Colonia Mons Salvinia (or Mons Salvinia for short), hundreds of miles away on the same morning on the high desert plateau, Sanctum Novus would nearly at the same time make its preparations for further war. At the dux's estate in his council chamber, another morning meeting was held between Dux Decius and those closest to him for advice in his council.

There was much commotion on this particular morning as the Dreadful Knight and Dirty Dale with their respective contingents of raiding parties returned from their swift but destructive raids north of Uruk Kazaht, in the lands of Collis Vallem as well as Colonia Collis (also known as Barbarum Hulliz, in recognition of the Nordling barbarians that had settled along the hills of this prairie plains and forest region). Upon a sudden entrance being made just as the dux commenced with the council's agenda and briefings, the dux, though not one for tolerating unplanned interruptions, had no qualms about two of his leading henchmen interrupting and reporting on their recent progress.

The Dreadful Knight, still observing the conduct code and chivalry as a knight of the West, kneeled before his dark lord and reported that both he and Dirty Dale had achieved the first of many waves in sowing the seeds of war and death by razing various settlements in the northern plains basin and hilly region that had not surrendered or changed their fealty from Swordbane to the Remnant.

Decius was pleased and congratulated his still fairly new vassal knight.

Meanwhile, the dux turned his attention to Dirty Dale and asked if he had anything additional to report. The unkempt bandit spoke while alternately chewing food that was presented at the council table to confirm that he and his unique raiding party consisting mainly of a few goblins and a very large troll had succeeded in multiple raids against many trade caravans that would not pay new tolls when trading between the upper-basin plains of the Collis regions and their return destination of Colonia Mons Salvinia. Some, however, did pay this new toll in order to be on their way without any further disruption. The ones that did not were raided promptly and had their assets taken. Additionally, those refusing traveling merchants were either imprisoned summarily or were simply killed by Dale's raiding party. In sum, Dale reported that his raiding party had seized dozens of merchant wagons and at least half of them were en route to be transferred to Sanctum Novus for confiscation to support this new faction's expenses. The other half was divided in Uruk Kazaht among the many orcs and goblins in the settlement, with Dale being a rare human of some authority in that settlement allowed to keep a portion of the seized loot along with the rest of his raiding party.

Decius, not withholding, expressed a prominent yet chilling expression of joy while commending Dale on his progress. The dux being pleased as such additionally directed Dale to have the imprisoned merchants transferred to toil as slave labor in the various gold, silver, and copper mines located mainly north and one just east of Sanctum Novus until the next of kin or any representative from the kingdom wished to pay a ransom of 100 silver coins or 50 gold coins.

For the dux to take such delight and dole out such harsh punishment based from these reports was a rare sight and aspect that Senator Diem and his daughter Lucia were able to notice more prominently than before that perhaps Decius's reputation as dark lord preceded him among the beastly and human individuals that had a penchant for vicious behavior and took a borderline sadistic sense of gratitude for doing the destructive deeds in order to receive such welcome praise to be encouraged and reinforced in perpetuating only further torment, warfare, and infliction of death.

For Diem, it was some cautious form of concern to be aware of. Lucia, who was both Diem's daughter and still the dux's somewhat recent love interest, she perhaps surprised even her own father by not feeling the slightest bit shocked but her face seemed to exude a visible sense of content with her lover's role and what plots they had done and would do.

For herself, Lucia felt very comfortable accepting that the father of their future son would set out with the same amount of ambition she had to be indomitable, respected, and feared if necessary. He would not have any reservation about being called the dark lord, but rather embrace that less-formal title and make both those serving on his side or against him know that he truly would be worthy of such a title of distinction and notoriety, at least among his enemies.

After further expressing his pleasure from the reports, Decius had told the two men that their progress was pleasing and that each would be given a territory or some notable geographical demarcation to have direct and local lordship in the Collis upper basin plains. Both the Dreadful Knight and Dirty Dale were pleased while vowing to continue to sow war and death in the lands they tread upon in order to serve their dark lord. The dux nodded and told them that they would be tasked to return and continue to oversee rule in those regions while still expanding their incursions against defiant settlements and trade caravans going westward to the coastal mountains, inland, and the coastal valley region of Swordbane.

Dale and the Dreadful Knight nodded in confirmation. Before departing to continue their work, the two of them waited for the council meeting to adjourn for the day. Some members of the council voiced concern about the dux's two subordinates leaving the Collis regions they conquered vulnerable to further barbarian raids should the barbarians decide to make their way south unchecked against a severely weakened and noncentralized remote frontier society and government. The dux, holding once again that same wicked grin of a devious mind, told the council that he would expect such a possibility. He mentioned that should it happen, it would only make it easier for him to fast-track his plans to conquer the Nordlings once and for all.

Revealing a new diagram board of the dux's assault plan, the dux revealed his intention to overwhelm the barbarians in a daring attack against them deep in the mountainous woods in their home territory of Barbarum Aries. He would later offer for the ones that survived to join the dux and his quest to pacify the rest of the major Nordling tribes as well as all of Swordbane's western holdings. The dux did not expect the Nordlings to surrender easily, but planned to make an example of them and demoralize them with their loss to convince them that they would not survive unless they accepted to become part of the dux's new coalition.

As the council seemed pleased with the dux's plan for attacking the

Nordlings, Lucia paused for a moment and thought about the risk of exposure to the plague pandemic that Sanctum Novus had spread into the Collis high-basin plains as well as west toward the coastal heartland of Swordbane. She posed the matter to the council and asked how the combined forces of the Remnant would prevent (if it had not already from the recent raids it adopted) contracting the very same plague that it unleashed by using the banished afflicted priests to spread it. Decius turned and smiled slightly more while nodding to commend his concubine and future wife for pointing out that observation, while indicating his advisor Agaroman to take credit for already addressing that.

Even Agaroman was impressed by Lucia's insight and pragmatic concern, though he and Decius had taken that into account beforehand. Agaroman informed the rest of the high-ranking members of the dux's informal council that he had developed a vaccine with a mild form of the affliction and had the forces from the raiding party given doses of it prior to carrying out their raids and that even as the council was holding meeting, the wizard advisor had already produced and instructed several goblin shamans, including the chief goblin shaman, on how to replicate the vaccine to administer to Sanctum Novus's combined army, including the Citadellan soldiers and knights, orcs, goblins, and even a select few trolls, though the later was certainly the most difficult and intimidating to control when they received a jab to the limb in getting vaccinated. Eventually, Agaroman would enlist Lucia's help in setting up clinics to administer the same vaccines for the general city populace, and Lucia earnestly nodded.

The wizard went further to explain that they not only had the advantage in assembling a larger army to invade the high-basin lands as well as the barbarian lands to the north, but also were protected from the same spread of affliction they caused. They would still have the element of surprise and would retain any afflicted individuals of populations resisting the dux's authority to be released for spreading the plague to those resistant enemy settlements to further demoralize and weaken them.

While it was diabolical to the eyes of some of the council members, they agreed with the dux's reasoning that no quarter could be shown toward those that would oppose them and Sanctum Novus in their efforts to secede permanently from Swordbane while absorbing as much of the kingdom as possible to create their reenvisioned new Lupercalian empire. Still others in the council, while not fully content in the ethics of Agaroman and Decius's plan, still acquiesced, seeing that such means would be worth it to potentially save more lives in the long run, including the Citadellan soldiers and knights that could return to their families.

Meanwhile, both the goblin shaman and the orc war chief captain were able to understand what the wizard had said and could not help sharing different feelings of eagerness and war lust, applauding with shouts and banging the council table with their fists in their exceeding contentment with the plan. Truly in their minds, both Decius and Agaroman were worthy even as humans to lead them to a new age of war, death, and destruction. They had wanted a dark lord, regardless of his origin and upbringing, to lead them to a new age of fear and power. It would be one that would also command prestige and respect which had not been seen since the age of the Lupercalian Empire, the original predecessor to their now reforming imperial Remnant. After the battle outside Sanctum Novus, or as the beastly races were now starting to call it, the Great Slaughter, Decius had earned by that point the absolute trust and devotion of the orcs and goblins in addition to the dux's own Citadellan army of his city. His victory and execution of it became a visual symbol of what the orcs and goblins wanted to finally see from one worthy to proudly be called their dark lord. Only now, by this point the dux's combined army felt a large sense of seeming invincibility as long they were led by the dux.

For Decius's part, he gradually embraced his role as dark lord over time, and by this point, he not only saw himself as a political leader and military commander, but also had realized over time that he was seen as a popular patron and defender of his own subjects or citizens. He became grateful to see Lucia as a subtle teacher in reminding him that there was an acceptable and perhaps ideal balance between acting out the persona of a fearful dark sovereign among his enemies while still leaving sufficient room to be a genuine caring protector and provider for his people, particularly the civilians, in meeting their needs.

The dux reflected on this as a brief afterthought after hearing his wizard advisor's explanation about vaccinating their forces and unleashing a devastating campaign against their adversaries. He appreciated both sides of the scale that he saw through both his advisor and his concubine lover in advising and influencing him to an extent on the decisions he would make. He was aware that both of them had started to develop some degree of mutual content and respect toward each other as both Agaroman and Lucia started to understand each other, to respect their observations and insights to work more in unison, though the dux had resigned himself to let the two work out and solve their own areas of disagreement over time, seeing that they both would likely find common ground in advising Decius as well as influencing him in ways that he did not consider before that would be beneficial in his approach to governance.

When Lucia asked about estimates of the vaccination supply, Agaroman nodded and confirmed that they had produced at least enough for administering five thousand doses in several days prior to deployment for invasion of the Collis regions and ultimately the Nordling forest homelands north of it. The wizard also mentioned that the second reinforcement army would receive a new batch of five thousand doses a week from when the first batch of vaccines was administered. He reported that the dux would have an army of ten thousand soldiers and that the next focus would be to vaccinate the rest of the city of Sanctum Novus along with the various combined goblin and orc settlements, where the various trained goblin shamans would be dispersed to tend to their respective home settlements and supervise the administration of the vaccines.

Again, another slow to moderate series of applause was given after the wizard had announced this last part of their campaign strategy. Understanding such a strategy, Lucia had pleaded for the wizard to ensure that the next to receive the vaccine, after the military and various settlements' controlled population centers, would be the inhabitants of the Nordlings' territory and Swordbane kingdom if and after the latter two surrendered to the dux and recognized his authority and his role as the future divine chosen vessel to make the deities of war and death become one through him.

Agaroman, seeing the potential value of such a plan, acknowledged that Lucia was right and perhaps he would look into it to ensure those who survived among the afflicted were given a chance if possible to change their fealty from Swordbane to the dux.

As the meeting drew near to a close, Agaroman raised another matter after reading verbatim of a report from one of the city guards that the goblins and orcs residing in the city in makeshift tents were being educated to read through a literacy initiative that the dux's own financial treasurer, Lucia, had started. Nearly all of the council were startled, with the exception of Lucia, the dux, the goblin shaman, and the orc war chief who seemed unfazed. While noticing the other faces present in the council having bewilderment from the report, Lucia simply shrugged and confessed in her own form of apology that it would be beneficial for the orcs and goblins to become literate. When her own father, Senator Diem, asked why, the same thought Agaroman also shared, Lucia sharply retorted that it was necessary for the good of the Remnant to have more literate soldiers in their forces, including orcs and goblins, in order to be effective in transmitting and dispatching detailed written orders and correspondence, including across the field of battle. She also pointed out that this initiative she started helped foster better relationships between the Citadellan citizens of Sanctum Novus with their relatively newfound orc and goblin allies as the former would interact with and teach the latter.

Though unorthodox in her approach, the members present who were at first in utter shock quickly saw the pragmatism of her approach and agreed with it being mutually beneficial for their desert city. Following one random member of the council standing and applauding, several others did the same while commending the dux's appointed treasurer and unofficial concubine. Even her father as well as Agaroman, though somewhat dumbfounded by her action, changed their expressions to being impressed and steadily clapped to acknowledge her cunning. As the claps persisted for a few more moments, Agaroman standing next to Senator Diem said quietly though audibly for the senator to still hear him admitting that though he would prefer the dux to not be in love with anyone, the senator's daughter truly was becoming in his eyes perhaps worthy after all to be the concubine and eventual wife of the dux, with a remarkable degree of shrewdness despite her caring nature. The senator, somewhat proud of such a compliment, nodded and replied that he was grateful and honored to have Lucia as his daughter.

After the applause ended, Senator Diem admitted in humility the foresight of his daughter surpassed his own and acknowledged before the council that he and perhaps the older members, despite their seniority and experience, needed to admit and step down in deference to the younger generation, including the dux and his daughter Lucia to lead Sanctum Novus (as they were already doing anyway) to a new age. He recognized that the reforms and actions taken by both the dux and his daughter ultimately were pragmatic and necessary for the desert city to adapt and thrive in a new age that was becoming more unfamiliar than the one that he and perhaps even Agaroman were accustomed to as older council members, of an earlier generation. Agaroman nodded his head in confirmation, though he had no intention to permanently step down from his duties. Regardless of the drastic changes, the wizard had sworn a personal vow before the dux to advise him and help him pursue his quest to become the chosen vessel to make the deity spirits of war and death become one. For Agaroman to do this still, he had to ensure that Decius would stay on the path and not stray from this quest, while paving the way and sowing the seeds of war and death as much as was required to attain that divinely dark and sacred goal.

Seeing that it was a long morning, Decius adjourned the council after announcing the final part of his briefing, when he would assemble the forces in Sanctum Novus to march north to the Collis high-basin region and eventually to the barbarian lands of the Nordlings in the deep wooded mountains of the interior. He decided to leave both Senator Diem and Lucia in charge as acting consuls for Sanctum Novus until the dux's return. The dux reminded the council that before his arrival in the Collis regions, both Dirty Dale and the Dreadful Knight would launch another wave of raids and razing buildings against any settlements that still resisted the dux's authority over them.

Though the council would object to a woman being installed as acting consul as it went against Citadellan tradition, no one at this point objected. For them, the actions of Lucia demonstrated at this point her decisiveness in her office as well as the admission of her father, virtually everyone in the hallway room agreed that some old ways had to change and some new ways had to be made for Sanctum Novus to prosper.

Senator Diem, putting aside his personal reservations, conceded the decision that the dux issued and acknowledged sharing joint temporary leadership of the city with his daughter. Diem was content to admit quietly to Agaroman that at least he had a new elevated position despite the unusual circumstances and he was at least in company to share that leadership with someone he was familiar with.

Lucia, pleased by the promotion to acting consul, thanked her lover Decius after the meeting, while the dux told her that putting his feelings aside for her, she had earned the position to be shared with her father. He reminded her that this elevated position would require both her ambition and cunning to be prepared for a possible attack by Swordbane if they saw a moment of opportunity as the dux would assemble his army to campaign in the Nordling lands. He told her that he would march with his initial forces from the city on the next day's sunrise.

Chapter Twenty-Three

Sowing and Reaping War and Death

The next day, the dux's plan was enacted. Both Dirty Dale and the Dreadful Knight, after departing the council meeting, rode forthwith north to the Collis regions to resume their duties of raiding and destroying to pave the path of destruction upon Decius's arrival. On the fourth day after, early in the morning, Dirty Dale and the Dreadful Knight arrived with their small raiding company of several dozen goblins mounted on dire wolves. They rendezvoused with an already deployed small contingent of horse-mounted Citadellan knights along with a few goblins and a very large troll that happened to wield a very large blunted makeshift club that it had fashioned from an oak tree.

The morning countryside from the vantage point of one town on the southern stretch of the Collis region had a small rural village of dozens of hut-like houses with sheep roaming about the hilly countryside of a sea of grass with mountains and gorges seen from the distance behind a river known as Serpent's River. It was like any other idyllic day for this village, except it was not. From a distance, drawing closer like an approaching storm, the raiding party of Dirty Dale and the Dreadful Knight charged at full gallop toward the village Brynn Faoi Ghrian (which the local Collis or Hulliz peoples referred to as Hill Under the Sun).

Loud shouts of fear erupted from the village as the raiding party went about to slaughter, burn, and loot. It was one of a number of villages that had refused the call to swear fealty to the dux as their sovereign several weeks ago when Decius gave orders for several dispatched messengers on horseback to declare the rule of his Remnant and for those notified settlements north of Uruk Kazaht in the Collis region to formally recognize his domain in their region. Like many of the other villages that had rejected the dux's call for fealty and allegiance to him, it was subject to be attacked without mercy.

By the time the raiding party had finished its assault on the settlement, roughly half of the settlement's populace was slain, while only a handful had escaped on horseback. Much of the surviving population would now be considered forced serfs under the vassalage of the Dreadful Knight, whom the dux had promised to have reign over the Collis region on behalf of the dux's sovereignty. Upon encircling the surviving village and getting the villagers to stand down, the Dreadful Knight had given the same proclamation as he did with the other villages that he and Dirty Dale raided before their departure and return from Sanctum Novus. The villagers, being serfs, were expected to produce a stipulated quota to provide as tribute in exchange for their survival and "protection" by the Dreadful Knight and the other forces of the Remnant. Failing to do so would give the Dreadful Knight and his accomplices the authority to punish the village even more severely, including taking some of its population to sell off for slavery, which could include harsh possibilities of working in the scattered mines in the high desert north of Sanctum Novus, fighting in the gladiator arena of Sanctum Novus, or even being slaves in one of the orc-goblin camps such as Uruk Kazaht or farther east.

This tactic of inducing fear and demoralization had worked for the Remnant in subjugating the settlement along with dozens of other Collis settlements that dotted the high-basin prairie land. In due time, which was only a matter of days, the region would be subjugated sufficiently in not only providing the quota of resource tribute that Sanctum Novus had imposed, which included half of a given town's wheat grain production as well as half of the livestock (mainly sheep and goat in that region). In addition, the caravan wagons that had passed would pay toll road taxation in using the dirt path and partially stone-paved roads that went between the various settlements in the Collis region as well as other parts, including south toward Sanctum Novus and west toward eventually the forest bordering north of the Swordbane coastal mountains and even farther toward the western coastal settlements of Swordbane.

After the village was considered pacified by the dux's raiding forces, both Dirty Dale and the Dreadful Knight split their forces, with the former taking his war band of goblins and his troll to scout and lie in wait behind any possible obstructions near the paved road that would hide their presence and provide suitable vantage points for spotting and setting up ambushes against unsuspecting merchant caravan wagons that would pass along the way, where they would be forced to pay a fixed toll according to the goods they were carrying or risk losing all their carried goods and as well as possibly their lives if the given leading caravan merchant resisted. It had proved successful for a few days until the dux would arrive to give new orders for both Dirty Dale's gang of goblins and the Dreadful Knight's retinue of mounted knights.

In the meantime, one late afternoon during dusk, Dale's band of goblins had called it a day from being on guard for maintaining a full manned presence while charging tolls and only a token handful of goblins rotated during watch shifts in stopping any wagons passing by. The goblin war band camped in groups and had their early supper of the local cuisine of cooked sheep and whole-wheat grains (the latter of which the Sanctum Novus Citadellan knights in the Dreadful Knight's retinue called farrumo). Both the goblins and Dirty Dale took pleasure in this meal along with a Citadellan knight dispatched from Baldwin's retinue that occupied the raided village to deliver the food provisions to Dale's raiding party, including both the locally produced Collis lager beer and red Citadellan wine from oblong glass bottles wrapped with blanched straw that the raiders carried along with them to drink with their meal.

Sharing the company of the immediate group that Dale shared his meal with, the dispatched Citadellan knight that delivered the food provisions found the conversation ironically light though amusing, and he stayed for a time as a welcomed guest of company to share the meal with since he and Dale were the only humans at that point. The knight observed and did his best to maintain his composure, though internally he was in laughter from Dale's conversation with his two ranking goblin raiding party lieutenants, Ravager Many Bloody Rings and Scarred Ears. These two goblins' names were attributed to their appearance, with the first having many red bloodstone-looking rings on both his fingers as well as ear piercings, while the other goblin had light mutilated scar cuts on his ears that were self-inflicted to give a more intimidating appearance to his foes. Supposedly each count for both the rings and ear cuts represented the number of kills that each warrior had attained before being recognized with distinction and being given a higher station in rank as well as an ascribed name from their dark deeds in their war raiding parties.

While the goblins' appearance intrigued the knight, perhaps more intriguing were the conversations that they shared with each other along with Dale and their domesticated troll, which they called Blunt Kill for the troll's preference in using his fashioned makeshift oak-tree club as a weapon to kill any opposition with deadly blunt force. Dale made a quick introduction of the knight with the three of his most esteemed in the raiding party. The subtle and quick salutations eventually drifted into streams of thoughtful conversations with the two goblin lieutenants making bets on how many more towns they believed would be pillaged as was the case with Brynn Faoi Ghrian before the dux had arrived as well as after his arrival, to speculating with a sadistic delight on what forms of destruction the dux would unleash upon the Nordling barbarians in the forests and mountains north of the Collis high-basin prairie land. Eventually, the goblins, noticing the knight present, hoped to impress him as devoted followers of the dux by praising how well the dux had approached and embraced his role as the prophesied dark lord to make war and death become one as the chosen vessel.

The knight, though seeing some common cause with the goblins in having mutual loyalty toward the dux, nodded his head while feeling somewhat awkward. He was noticeably less enthusiastic about the diabolical course of the goblins' conversation despite having to agree in a mutual sense of obligation of loyalty toward the dux, though for different reasons.

Hopping to another subject, the knight asked both goblins as well as Dirty Dale how they ended up together. Apparently, the responses made the knight feel as awkward as before, with Dirty Dale stating he was just a bandit who made his way, or totem, of being distinguished among the goblin totems in Uruk Kazaht. Meanwhile, Ravager Many Bloody Rings and Scarred Ears told the knight the same thing, though again segueing back to the dux, stating their sadistic pleasure in looking forward to doing more "honest goblin raiders' work," including looting and killing. They expressed their gratitude in finally feeling appreciated and having self-worth for finding the dux as a worthy enough dark lord to enable them to engage in such vile acts.

By this point, the knight, though finding some degree of appreciation in the Citadellan value of devotion and piety that the goblins seemed to express, was even further lost in thought and words for how to respond, other than nodding and stating that he too (for a different reason) was happy to serve the dux and Sanctum Novus in bringing back the Remnant as an emulation of the former great Lupercalian Empire.

Dale, seeing that the conversation was going awkwardly as much as the knight tried to be cordial in fostering good relations with Dale's company, recognized the knight's attempts as well as his intentions and told the knight directly and somewhat awkwardly that he was just glad they all had their reasons to serve the dux and find their place in this new era, whether it would be a standard knight and soldiers upholding order in their own way side by side with former enemies, including human bandits and beastly races like goblins while being under the same banner of the dark lord himself, Dux Decius. The knight, recognizing Dale's reconciliation efforts, nodded and agreed. In another moment, the knight bade Dale a temporary farewell evening before departing to the Dreadful Knight's camp for any updated orders or messages to relay as the courier between Baldwin and Dale. Not knowing what the next day had in store, Dale and his immediate companions consumed more wine and beer until they passed out from being inebriated. The remainder of the evening was fairly quiet with no road wagon traffic and overall uneventful. It would stay that way until the following morning or so.

CHAPTER TWENTY-FOUR

The Dark Lord's Arrival

On the second next morning, the town of Brynn Faoi Ghrian was dead quiet, though the villagers still went about their duties under fear of the consequences that the Dreadful Knight had proclaimed should he find any of the villages derelict in their labor. They had buried their fallen loved ones on the previous day, the day after the raid. They had hastily conducted memorial services under the gaze of the knights from Sanctum Novus, who were now appointed as the new town guard under the now-proclaimed Lord of Regnum Collis (or simply put, the Collis region), Edwin Baldwin, the Dreadful Knight. No one in the village objected under the risk of pain and/or death by this new self-proclaimed feudal lord. The town was tightly in control in an atmosphere filled with fear.

However, as the second morning following the raid became nearly as depressing and solemn as the previous one, a small but increasingly noticeable sound of howls and shouts began to erupt from the distance. A large swath of mounted figures glistened while being more recognizable as they came ever closer to the town village center. A large blast from the trumpet of one of Baldwin's knights sounded the arrival of the dux himself.

Baldwin, ever eager to gain attention and praise for his violent raid of havoc and the capitulation of the town itself, called for the immediate town villagers to come before the town square and kneel before their supreme overlord, Dux Decius. The villagers, scared and in utter shock to make sense of what was happening other than to be in a state of compliance in order to survive, obeyed their regional lord's command.

The dux, mounted on a large dire wolf, unleashed a huge wolflike howl while drawing his sword from his scabbard and raising it high into the air to signal his power and authority being before all others. His dire-wolf mount along with the hundreds of other dire-wolf mounts and riderless dire-wolves responded in their own howl, recognizing their dark lord as their pack leader. The goblins and lightweight orcs as well as several appointed lightweight and lightly armored Citadellan soldiers and knights responded by unleashing similar but different sounds, distinctive war cries or chants of praise and veneration while circling the perimeter of the village's outermost hut building. Then the dux mounted on his dire wolf approached hauntingly fast and suddenly toward the Dreadful Knight as the latter had submitted himself and kneeled before the dux. Upon seeing the dux come to an abrupt halt with his wolf snarling and growling, Baldwin startled while showing some degree of hesitancy and fear, shivered, and eventually gave his salutation to his dark lord. Decius responded with the motion of his hand and verbally for the Dreadful Knight to rise and report on his takeover of the settlement. Baldwin did so while commenting that he and Dirty Dale's small contingents had suffered very few casualties from the town offering almost no effective resistance.

The dux was pleased, and he grinned while congratulating his subordinate vassal. In another moment, the dux commanded the villagers to all rise, which they did. Decius gave the sizable crowd of villagers a fairly brief but powerful speech in which he told them that they had one of two choices: to serve faithfully and be rewarded with a meager living while not suffering further death and destruction, or if they either became derelict and or rebelled against their new conquerors, the dux would personally see to it that the town would be destroyed and the surviving inhabitants sold into slavery to work in very harsh conditions. The villagers stood quietly though they had visible expressions of fear. From their eyes gazing at him, they could tell the dux meant it, and Decius for his part wanted to make it that obvious for them to tell without any doubts.

The dux, shifting the focus of the conversation, reminded the villagers that they would have their production quotas to meet and give the stipulated portion of their grain harvest and livestock to Lord Baldwin and, by extension, ultimately to the dux and his Remnant army. The villagers silently nodded without any signs of dissension. Upon seeing their fear and confirmation of compliance, the dux dismissed the villagers to start their daily labor, including tending the wheat fields, overseeing the sheep grazing the fields opposite the many acres of cultivated wheat fields. Meanwhile, both the dux's forces and Baldwin's monitored the villagers tending to their daily tasks.

Decius turned to Baldwin to talk in private while the dux's personal dire wolf followed closely behind, acting as a personal bodyguard for the dux. The two of them were joined by Agaroman, who acted not only as chief mage and advisor to the dux, but also oversaw management of logistics for the dux's invading army. As the three assembled, the fourth leading figure, Dirty Dale approached while riding a stolen horse and quickly dismounted in an uncouth manner. The dux had dispatched one of his mounted dire wolf riders to call upon Dale and escort the bandit leader during the same time. Dale was fairly fleet in both responding and traveling to pay his homage to the dux while being briefed on the next phase of the dux's plan for domination.

Finding a suitable place in the village, the dux had two of his Citadellan knights along with some orcs and goblins take a table and chairs from several of the village huts to be brought out near the center of the town next to an awkward set of three large oblong stones that were essentially a shrine to the mythical nature spirit deities that the Collis (or Hulliz) inhabitants worshiped. The regional Collis inhabitants themselves were considered by the dux as well as many Citadellans and even some elves as being semibarbaric or semicivilized at best when compared to the Nordlings (of the mountains and forests) in the former's efforts to build more-permanent buildings though not very sophisticated nor artistic and to engage to some degree of the activities that the Citadellans measured as being marginal progress to what they considered true civilization including engaging in agriculture on a more regular basis as well as consumable animal domestication both on a more regular basis compared to the traditional Nordlings who engaged far more in hunting, foraging, and looting the cultivated foods produced by others, including the Collis inhabitants.

As the meeting was about to commence, Dale, not having any sense of etiquette or decency to respect the local religion, simply urinated next to one of the large stone objects before taking a seat on one of the makeshift arranged chairs next to the table. Baldwin could not hold back the expression of his face in finding the bandit raider's habits as being perhaps beneath not only him and the dux's presence, but also in being a cause of withheld resentment by Baldwin's recently claimed village subjects of his fiefdom. The goblins from the nearby vicinity could not help but laugh and give some commentary praise on the bandit leader's behavior in reaching a new level of desecration and indecency. Agaroman did not care, though his facial expressions did not seem to give much attention to Dale's behavior regardless of the offense it caused the town's inhabitants, with some who swore under their breaths with the predictable anger that Dale's gesture had aroused. Decius was also indifferent, though he took some pleasure in seeing one of his chief subordinates acting on his own initiative while representing the dux to let the local inhabitants know that even their most sacred and holiest places were not above the dux's authority, even in the manner that Dale had displayed, which Decius himself would not personally resort to, instead simply taking his great long sword and striking down the religious objects. Regardless, the dux was happy to feel the town's anger and resentment while knowing they would do nothing out of fear for their own survival. This was exactly what the dux wanted to impose upon his enemies in order to let them know their place of subordination and submission before his authority as well as his newly established Remnant, which would restore the legacy of the Lupercalian Empire.

Calling the meeting to order as the dux stayed seated, he opened up briefly in a religious incantation offering the brief conflict as well as the death and destruction in the village as a gift to the deity spirits of Laran and Calu. Agaroman seconded the prayer along with the goblin shaman and the orc war chief, who both came to attend the meeting just prior to it starting.

Following the recited prayer of the dux's war and death offering, Decius next discussed with his war council the next stage of their operations. Baldwin and Dale would work together in the same fashion as they had done before to pave their wave of destructive raids and settlement pillaging and destruction west across the southern half of the Collis region and eventually continue farther westward through the passes north of the Swordbane coastal mountains and into the forest interior of Colonia Mons Salvinia before mounting a large enough force to assault Salvinia Parf Edhellen. The dux was hell-bent on putting a sudden but decisive incursion of raiding and assaulting lightly defended villages and towns outside the above-mentioned in the hopes of dampening the morale of Swordbane, as the kingdom would be struggling to ready itself for another war.

Additionally, the dux had hoped that this pressure would also enable the deadly affliction to continue to spread more over time still while the populace from the small villages and hamlets outside the main cities would flood and overwhelm the stressed urban centers to their limits in supporting new refugees who very well could be blamed haphazardly by the urban residents for transmitting the very affliction that they were suffering. It was such a diabolical plot that Dale alongside the goblin chief shaman and the orc war captain had impromptu clapped and expressed their admiration for the dux's cunning and devious plan.

Meanwhile, Decius turned his attention to the main part of his plan that he would set out to accomplish: the conquering and subjugation of the Nordlings on the north mountain and forest interior, just north of the Collis region. He informed his council that he and the goblin shaman would set out with hundreds of dire wolves and dire wolf riders to travel northeast at full haste during the cover of night, toward the main Nordling interior settlement of Barbarum Aries. The dux had planned this time to catch the Nordlings more so than the last time he traveled to the place. It was a place that forever etched the start of what would be his resentment toward his former lord and king, with the passing of his former comrades not being truly avenged as the dux would make sure this time around to attack the Nordlings using a far more devastating cause of surprise, fear, and destruction. The council were all pleased one way or another with the exuding confidence the dux had in professing to ensure the conquest of the Nordlings. Even Dale, the goblin shaman, and the orc war chief's speculations in their minds that could not be distinguished from the looks on their faces were of so much spilled blood and war lust they would inflict on their enemies.

In truth, the dux did inform the council that the next phase of his plan would be to do the same with the Nordlings as they had done with the Collis locals by offering to spare the lives of the surviving enemy if they would contribute to the cause of the dux and his Remnant. This would be only after the dux would unleash a token portion of his hellish destruction upon the barbarians of the given settlement in order to cow them into submission. In particular, the dux again pointed out to his impromptu council members the potential advantage of incorporating the barbarian warriors from the Nordlings would help strengthen their coalition's army to be used eventually and more devastatingly against the Kingdom of Swordbane when the dux would later determine the right timing for it.

While Decius and the goblin shaman would lead their dire-wolf cavalry against the Nordlings, the last part of the dux's plan would entail the orc war chief to assemble more goblins, orcs, and even trolls to join their new dark lord in launching an invasion against the western coastal cities of Swordbane. The army that marched with the dux had ten thousand soldiers and would be expected to swell to possibly double or triple that number when they had allotted enough time for various beastly races and their settlements to muster forces and answer the dux's call to rally en masse and ultimately invade Swordbane's coastal heartland.

CHAPTER TWENTY-FIVE

Raising Hell on Dire-Wolfback

Riding with full haste through the high-basin prairie of the Collis region and into the forest line that would lead deep into the mountains of the main Nordling settlement, Barbarum Aries, the large company of dire-wolf riders held torches in hand while being led by the dux and the goblin shaman, who both knew the terrain well from their prior encounter with the Nordlings of that region. They counted up to five hundred strong wolf riders mounted on five hundred dire wolves with insatiable war lust while another five hundred somewhat smaller-stature wolves equally hungry for war followed along riderless. The remaining army of the dux followed closely behind, staying just outside the forest line and left a gap between their position and the forest entrance to stand by for receiving any possible instructions from a courier of the dux to reinforce the initial assault.

However, Decius had planned to do everything possible to ensure a swift and brutal unsurprised assault would be dealt to the Nordlings to the point that they would surrender with no prolonged fighting to require reinforcements. This time, the dux planned to hit the same areas he knew before, harder and with more devastation that would spread like an unstoppable and overwhelming wildfire.

Decius had given a brief but inspiring speech, at least by goblin and orc standards, to remind his soldiers that they had a destiny to fulfill that required their utmost determination without error, to raise as much hell as possible by literally razing barbarian buildings by torch fire and slaughtering the Nordling inhabitants without mercy while on dire-wolfback. This would be done in order to quell any desire they might have to fight back and to demoralize them as much as possible by the time they realized what had transpired from the initial shock.

The dux let his soldiers know that if they wanted to be the feared and powerful dark army led by a dark lord, then war and destruction was theirs to take without any hesitation or error. The mounted riders, many of them goblins and small orcs though some also Citadellan humans, all unleashed war cries and war shouts of their sort. They were instilled with a hunger for war like a predator searching for prey, only they sought to conquer and destroy their enemies until the latter would surrender and admit the dominance of the former.

This would be the next major crucial phase in the dux's much larger quest for attaining his divine vesselhood as well as the next stepping stone in his campaign to be directed toward the Kingdom of Swordbane in conquering the western coastal cities. His planned assault that was impending had two objectives: to serve as a message striking fear in the hearts of any enemies of the Remnant, including ones that were unaware, and to gain the submission of his soon-to-be surviving conquered subjects to essentially serve the role of clients. In doing so, they would be expected to provide their own barbarian warriors to muster and send off to join the Remnant forces to fight against Swordbane.

Barbarum Aries would be challenging to conquer as it required a good distance for the dux's dire-wolf cavalry to traverse the densely covered forest at breaking-pace speed without any actual rest until after they reached and conquered the Nordling settlement that was at the base of the mountains covered in snow. As formidable as it would be to traverse the full distance from dusk to nightfall before arriving at the settlement by dawn, both the dux and the goblin shaman surmised that it was an achievable objective in order to have the greatest chance of catching the unsuspecting Nordlings off guard and facing little, if any, resistance while anticipating much of the settlement's populace to be still asleep if the dux's cavalry contingent could strike in time.

The cavalry indeed made much progress riding hard at full pace through the forest and eventually to the other side of the forest, where there was a clearing of trees next to the base of the mountains and the settlement itself. Before passing the interior forest line and into the somewhat open land next to the mountain base, the dux signaled for his army to come to a halt. They had traversed the distance in record-breaking time, and it was still dark before dawn would set in. The cavalry contingent that had followed the dux and goblin shaman in single file had spread out and grouped themselves in smaller regiments of about twenty soldiers each. They waited until the dux signaled for them to attack.

Decius, staring across the barbarian main settlement, looked for a moment and reflected on his memories from when he last raided it about five years prior. He had held back from being as destructive as he possibly could have been and regretted not being as destructive as he intended to be in the present. This time it was different. This time he would burn every standing structure in the settlement and strike along with his troops without any hesitancy toward any barbarian settler that picked up a weapon and resisted. He would neither stop nor give his soldiers the orders to stop until someone of authority in that settlement gave the order to surrender.

After reflecting, Decius looked down at his own wolf mount and gave it a brief pet stroke while remembering that this moment had come just as the last one had in massacring Ascentius's army. Decius would not let this moment slip by. He would take with full embrace his reputation of being the dark lord commanding a thousand wolves and five-hundred-strong soldiers also on dire-wolfback to raise hell on the settlement until it would bend its knees and surrender. Decius quickly raised his sword up high in the air after taking it out from its scabbard. He then unleashed a loud, terrifying, and surreal wolflike howl that reverberated against the mountainside behind the barbarian settlement in the distance.

Immediately like a choir, the other wolves in the dux's company unleashed their own howls while the mounted riders unleashed once more their own war cries and shouts of war before riding off into battle. Just as Decius had planned, the Nordling settlement had few that had awakened, and the ones that did hear from a distance gave loud screams and calls alerting the settlement guards to be–at arms against the invading force. Like a rising throng, more and more voices and screams of both fright and anguish erupted as the ensuing charge from the dux's dire-wolf cavalry pounced upon the Nordlings. The attack became a complete chaotic slaughter with several hundred Nordlings, mainly male warriors, falling from the blade, spear, wolf bite, and even arrow of the dux's forces. Very few of the dire-wolf riders fell against the defending Nordlings, who tried to put up a good fight of resistance, but to no avail.

Seeing that the settlement's defenses were useless, the barbarian king, the younger brother and the successor to Ulfner, the one Decius had slain years prior, called upon the attackers and demanded that he settle this attack one on one in a duel against their leader. Seeing this opportunity, Decius capitalized on it and dismounted from his dire wolf to steadily walk toward the barbarian chieftain king. The barbarian king unleashed a loud but brief guttural war cry while steadily but quickly charging toward the dux. Decius, anticipating the warrior king's attack, strafed and dodged while in one quick fluid motion, he swung his long-bladed sword toward the barbarian king's neck, severing his head from his body.

The sight of such sudden and efficient ferocity by the dux taking down their leader was noted among the many shocked and fearful former Nordling subjects of the king. They were in awe and had realized that their greatest warrior and leader had been laid low by this deadly Citadellan figure of authority who clearly exhibited uncanny martial abilities.

The dux, for his part, shrugged after striking the barbarian king. Decius, after a brief pause, bent down and picked up the barbarian king's head by the hair and announced to the rest of the settlement's surviving populace that they were effectively defeated and to surrender lest they suffer the same fate as their late king. The crowd of the surviving Nordlings was still dumbfounded and indecisive on what to do, until two tall and muscular Nordlings dressed in notable status, presumably high nobility, walked out in front of the crowd. The two Nordlings announced themselves as being the younger brothers of the now-deceased barbarian king, and in a surprising gesture, the two of them unsheathed their swords to carry across their hands on both ends while kneeling before Decius. They jointly announced the settlement's surrender while acknowledging the dux as their new sovereign overlord.

Pleased and somewhat surprised at the outcome that unfolded since the dux did not expect the brothers of the slain king to acknowledge their defeat and swear fealty in such a short time, the dux commanded both brothers of the late king to rise and re-sheathe their swords while Decius accepted their sign of fealty. The two brothers complied and rose up while sheathing their swords.

Immediately thereafter, the surviving Nordlings of the settlement, looking down and demoralized, accepted their humiliating defeat while being caught off guard. At the same time, the large multitude of the dux's invading dire-wolf cavalry unleashed a wave of war cries while raising their weapons high in the air and chanting in their own language, either hailing him as the dux if they were Citadellan or hailing him in the recognized role as dark lord, as the goblins and orcs called him in their own tongues. The wolves also unleashed howls in celebration of their victory. For the first time in the history of the western lands, the Citadellans along with their beastly allies had beaten, defeated, and outright conquered an entire major Nordling tribal settlement. Even Agaroman could not hold back to mention subtly to the dux of his rare achievement.

Decius, taking the moment to raise his sword in acknowledgment and to savor the victory he led before his army and his newly conquered subjects, replied in a quiet tone to his wizard advisor if the timing along with the amount of warfare, death, and destruction was sufficient, to enact the next part of their quest: to call upon both Calu and Laran to receive his candidacy to be their chosen vessel in merging the two deity spirits' power into him. Agaroman grinned but then made a straight face while replying that the dux was close but had not yet sowed enough death and destruction to reap the vesselhood of divinely bestowed powers. The wizard, after another pause, smiled again and told his dark lord that soon his time would come and Agaroman had another plan to carry out the dux's quest in order to satisfy both Calu and Laran so they would make him their chosen vessel.

Throughout the rest of the morning, the town, though devastated and demoralized just as Decius anticipated, effectively surrendered and the dux negotiated with a strong hand and position in which to establish terms of servitude with the settlement's barbarians as his clients. In exchange for expanded trade and mutual protection, the dux had the region's two most prominent de facto leaders agree to that while also providing both soldier conscripts and tribute in the form of a small proportion of its produced resources for the Remnant within these controlled territories of the Nordlings. It was a strict treaty of exacting terms; however, the two surviving brothers of the late barbarian king had only deep resentment for their older sibling, who treated them as inferior, and they had ambitions of their own, so they saw the benefits to gain future power and possible higher stations of future ruling in recognizing the dux's authority as a supreme overlord.

Internally, many of the town settlement's populace considered the barbarian princes' surrender and oath of submission as a possible betrayal, while others might see it as a pragmatic response for self-preservation, given the circumstances. The Nordlings, however, had no other foreseeable choice in their situation but to accept the fate that their new foreign Citadellan conqueror imposed upon them: tribute and conscription for future wars in exchange for their lives and livelihoods, or at least what was left of it for the ones that had survived.

The dux, realizing the proclivity for resentment and anger they would have toward a foreign ruler, decided without hesitation he had to convince the Nordlings that he was worthy to be seen and accepted as their ruler whom they would not only fear but also, in time, respect. In keeping with Citadellan customs and tradition, the dux saw his newly conquered subjects just like the natives of the Collis region as well as the beastly races such as goblins and orcs, as all being not only his subjects to rule over but also his clients, to whom he had the role of master patron. It was his responsibility to ensure that as much as he expected out of his clients, he also delivered to them as their patron, including being an effective and efficient leader.

With that said and kept in mind, Decius held a small council after a few days. During this time, the dux shuffled and reorganized his army to include a retinue of different Nordling contingents, including archers and throwing-ax men along with melee infantry consisting of spearmen with long pine wood shafts and a varied assortment of short-weapon melee infantry who wielded small swords, maces, and axes. Additionally, the dux posted a small contingent of goblins, orcs, and two Citadellan soldiers to serve as commanders in the barbarian settlement, monitoring and ensuring the Nordlings would be loyal indefinitely while under the dux's command. The children of the nobility would also be sent to Sanctum Novus to be raised in what Decius considered a proper and civilized Citadellan upbringing so that when they were old enough, they would return to their homes and convert what the dux saw as inferior barbarian culture, or lack of it, into something more civilized and Citadellan. In the long run, he hoped this would further cement loyalty of the Nordlings and their settlement to Sanctum Novus. He had no qualms in being this brutal or repressive, as some might consider it. In his mind, it was a matter of survival of the fittest, and he intended to pacify all opposition. After all, he thought to himself, why should he not return the favor to these brute invaders for their historical invasions that brought down the golden age of his Citadellan ancestors when they ruled alongside their Lupercalian overlords?

Eventually at the meeting, which was held outside the doors of the town chieftain's wooden cabin, the dux had a makeshift table brought out along with chairs to seat himself, Agaroman, the goblin shaman, the orc war chieftain, and the two surrendering Nordling princes who had acted as the de facto leaders of the settlement in surrendering to Decius. The dux thought it prudent to include these two princes as clients of equal and respectable standing in his small council meetings in order to demonstrate a token form of respect and enfranchisement so the Nordlings' leading representatives had a stake in the future campaigning.

In reality however, the dux had no personal respect or attachment to the Nordlings. The beastly races of goblins, orcs, and even trolls he found at least honorable when it came to building a sense of hierarchy and expectations for coexistence, unlike the Nordlings, whom he found much more challenging in breaking their sense of autonomy and defiance toward organized hierarchical authority. He thought of the Nordling barbarian tribes as nothing more than uncivilized and brutish humans that had yet to be as civilized as their Nordling brethren of the western coastlands of Swordbane. To him, the latter had at least assimilated and learned the more civilized way of living despite being part of a legacy that the dux found reprehensible in their earlier Nordling ancestors invading and settling in lands that once belonged to the Lupercalian Empire and would eventually be part of his new Remnant.   Additionally, the dux also held their people collectively accountable for the death of his parents, whom a group of Nordlings had raided and killed, along with much of the Citadellan pilgrimage caravan during his infancy. To him, the only way to correct them on their uncivilized behavior of raiding civilized peoples was to do it by force, at the point of a blade and to make sure the barbarians knew their place in not ever thinking they would do the same thing toward his people again. He had no qualms about displaying the same behavior of raiding others, for in his mind, there was justification for it, either as retribution or in giving fair warning toward those he saw as abetting the enemy.

Upon commencing the makeshift council meeting, the dux had Agaroman report the casualties for both his forces and the earlier defeated Nordlings. Decius was unsurprised that his own observational estimate matched the one reported, as Agaroman stated that their forces lost a few dozen while the Nordlings incurred higher casualties in the hundreds, mainly adult males of fighting age. The dux nodded solemnly while asking for the two Nordling princes to report their own head count of how many survivors remained, along with those who were males of fighting age. One of the princes stated (with the other nodding along to confirm) that they had seven thousand and five hundred surviving Nordlings in their settlement with roughly a third of them, or about twenty-five hundred, being of age to be mustered by the princes to serve as auxiliary conscripts for the dux's Remnant coalition army. The dux was pleased to hear it and nodded while asking the princes how many in the nearby surrounding smaller settlements would be loyal to Barbarum Aries to follow suit and swear servitude to the dux while providing more conscripts to serve in the dux's army. The princes replied and confirmed as an estimate, at least another thousand in sum from all the villages surrounding Barbarum Aries. The dux was once again pleased while inquiring next with Agaroman if that would be sufficient to focus next on their efforts to wage war against Swordbane.

The wizard pondered with a somewhat uncertain expression and responded that it might be sufficient, though before taking the war directly to the kingdom's coastal stronghold cities it would be more prudent to use these additional barbarian soldiers to wage an internal civil war among the other major Nordling tribal settlements that lay farther west toward the northwest coast and in the coastal forests west of Barbarum Aries. Decius, realizing the merit of his wizard advisor's plan, acknowledged and praised Agaroman while agreeing to it. It was pragmatic and ingenious in some respects as the other major barbarian tribal settlements perceived as somewhat weaker than Barbarum Aries, as such would be easier to conquer and in turn to do the same in exacting both tribute and more barbarian-warrior conscripts into the dux's army to later use in sufficient number to conquer Swordbane's coastal city strongholds as well as hopefully be enough for the dux to satisfy and summon Calu and Laran for the blessing to be their vessel to merge their powers.

Decius inquired, while turning toward the Nordling princes again, about the strength of the two northwest barbarian settlements, Barbarum Aegir-Hafn on the coast and Barbarum Tribus Wald, which lay deep in the inland coast forest. Both princes responded that while formidable, the two settlements would be no match against Barbarum Aries, not to mention that they would be even more able to conquer the former with the combined force of the dux's army while taking far fewer casualties. The dux nodded and, before dismissing the council, informed everyone present to make preparations for marching west toward the two other major Nordling settlements. It would be a brutal campaign perhaps, but sufficient in the dux's mind to inflict enough death and destruction to merit the attention of his beloved two deity spirits to accept him as their chosen vessel while again the soon to be conquered would add their surviving warriors to his army in order to usher a sufficient invading force to wreak havoc on the Kingdom of Swordbane.

Within the next two days, the dux's army, except for the ones posted to stay behind, marched forthwith to attack northwestern barbarian settlements. It would be a long march, but the dux had planned to make sure he would fill his war lust along with his forces for any Nordling tribes that would resist his authority. He would make sure that throughout all the barbarian tribes, his name and his title as dark lord would be feared and respected even if he and his army would raise hell upon the various Nordling settlements while they traversed both on foot and riding on dire-wolfback.

CHAPTER TWENTY-SIX

Honor Among Raiders and Looters

Meanwhile, hundreds of miles away to the southwest from Barbarum Aries, in the lands between Colonia Mons Salvinia and Barbarum Hulliz (or Colonia Collis), a clear sky glossed over an otherwise serene environment of forest and thickets of trees that dotted an emerald landscape of grass cut beautifully with a striking river and a paved road that led between the two settlements. Hiding among the shade and cover of the thickets lie in wait three figures whose piercing eyes gazed from a distance toward the paved stone road that was a few hundred yards away. The three figures talked among one another while waiting patiently. Eventually a moment later, one of the figures pointed to indicate to the other two what they had seen.

From the distance, a lone elf ran at full speed, charging toward the covered thicket. One of the figures that hid indicated to the other two in confirmation that it was him and could tell from the elf's frantic expression that he had earned the attention of more than he bargained for. Following a distance behind the elf approached a large, giant troll visibly upset and roaring loudly while searching for his pursued prey. Eventually, following the scent of the elf, the troll saw a thicket from a distance, and between the troll and the thicket lay a still figure that was inanimate yet covered in rusty armor, including a helmet.

The troll contemplated in astonishment who that figure could be, but only briefly before resolving toward its lack of temperament to charge at the object and destroy it whether it was an actual foe or not. The elf figure by this point had already hid with the other three figures in the shade and cover of the thicket of trees. Waiting for the right moment for the troll to be close enough to the inanimate scarecrow-like armored knight, the elf, none other than Linitus, drew back the bowstring of his exquisite gold-like bow, and let loose one of his special arrow sabot barrage containers, which quickly dispersed over a dozen arrows all hurling toward the troll and the inanimate object. In another sudden moment, the arrows striking both the troll and the inanimate scarecrow-like object, which had served as both a decoy and a trap, exploded in a ball of fiery flame. In another moment when the blast had cleared the troll, or what was left of it, it lay motionless. The other three figures that had watched cheered on the elf ranger for his achievement of outsmarting and outhunting the large deadly troll. Emerging from the shade, the figures were the elf ranger's comrades: Marin, Peat, and Wyatt. The three of them approached behind Linitus to observe the mortal and destructive blow that he had caused. However, hearing a loud noise from the distance which Linitus could sense from the slight ground vibrations, the four comrades decided to fall back again into the tree thickets while Wyatt, casting a spell, summoned by teleportation from his skyship in the distance a lone wagon that, although not drawn by horses or steered by a driver, was able nonetheless to move by the power of the young halfling wizard's own spell-casting.

Linitus waited patiently along with the other three. Eventually, a war band of goblins catching up to the troll that had pursued ahead of them wanted to find the same elf ranger to hunt down. Much to their surprise and reaction, they found instead a lone wagon moving along the road. The gang of goblins both on foot and some mounted on dire wolves frantically chased after the wagon, saying even loudly and openly that it was bound to have much gold to be worth their attention for filling their personal coffers as well as a portion that they would reserve for the coffers of their dark lord, Dux Decius.

As the first of the goblins approached the wagon to prepare to board it and eliminate any of its occupants, their expressions quickly turned into utter shock, seeing no driver and no occupants inside, save only four explosive oil barrels mounted in the small cabin of the wagon. They quickly shrieked and despaired that the danger they had sought to bring would ironically come back to return the favor unto them.

In another moment, Linitus fired again another sabot cylinder assembly that again dispersed another dozen or so arrows, with some striking the goblin marauders while at least two struck the explosive containers with enough force to trigger an explosion. Again as before, the calculated strike by Linitus resulted in another tumultuous explosion. The effect wiped out a couple of goblins in the vicinity of the wagon decoy.

Meanwhile, observing from a distance on the same side as the goblin marauders, a lone human figure who had scruffy unkempt hair and wore a combination of fur and sheepskin clothing approached slowly to assess the situation. It was grim, to say the least, losing not only a small portion of his goblin army but also his gigantic pet troll, but how he lost that portion of his army upset him even more. Nobody was expected to outwit Dirty Dale in playing his game of tricking and tripping the opposition, even when it came to using ambushing tactics. Yet this time, the outcome dealt such a major setback for the human bandit leader that he could not hold back his mixed expression of perplexity and anger. Frustrated and not caring that he showed it, Dale unleashed a loud-enough shout of expletives to express his dissatisfaction with his raiding bands while swearing he would find the clever upstarts to teach them a lesson in playing against the bandit at his own game.

Dale's outbursts had no effect to deter the hero companions in dismantling the bandit's own operations as well as enjoying the frustration of their nemesis. In another moment after shooting three arrows simultaneously and taking down three more goblins, Linitus shouted loudly while ordering his companions to charge at the remaining smaller but still formidable raiding war party of goblins. Out of the thicket the team of four somewhat-unlikely heroes charged at full speed to engage the surviving goblin raiding party.

Together on opposing groups, Linitus along with the other members of the Comradery and Dale's remaining marauding group engaged each other fiercely. Prior to engaging in hand-to-hand combat, the elf ranger managed to slay with his bow and arrows half a dozen goblin warriors at least before engaging them with his curved elven long sword, much as his three companions were doing. Marin and Peat swung with fierce force to send a chilling message demoralizing the goblins into retreating. Meanwhile, Wyatt cast several lightning-bolt and fireball spells to hurl at the goblins that went after him as well as Linitus.

However, as the team of heroes began to give chase for the ones that were not fighting and were retreating from the field of battle, Linitus and Marin both noticed from a distance a small but loudly growling noise coming out. The sound of heavy horse hooves stomped the ground while at full gallop. In another moment, Linitus and Marin both observed that it was a figure they had not seen for several weeks. It was none other than Edwin Baldwin, the Dreadful Knight. Edwin had decided during Dirty Dale's raiding campaign against Swordbane and its sympathizers that the Dreadful Knight himself would have a role and he was needed to tag along and ensure that the Remnant would not have any setbacks from any raids staged by the goblins. But this time, the goblin raid failed in pillaging this lot of potential victims, with a large portion of the goblins from this raiding party dying from this most recent pursuit.

Just as the heroes had spotted the Dreadful Knight, only a short moment later did the latter spot them as well. However, he did not ride alone. Following behind him were six Citadellan knights of the Order of the Black Wolf. They stood out like a blanket of black-armored knights on the flanks of the Dreadful Knight, who stood out in his bright-red plate-mail armor while raising his flaming long sword. The Dreadful Knight and his small bodyguard company charged at full gallop toward Linitus and his company. Linitus reacted by calling out to his comrades to alert them of the impending danger. Marin was already aware. Peat and Wyatt turned briefly and paused to look in the direction from which Linitus had called to them. The halfling wizard and dwarf guardian braced for the oncoming charge as much as the Princess Knight and the elf ranger stood at the ready.

As the heroes waited to counterattack the enemy knights that came charging closer to trample them, Linitus quickly unloaded several shots of arrows, striking one knight who fell along with his steed, tripping two other mounted knights on the Dreadful Knight's right flank. Meanwhile, the Dreadful Knight and three other Black Wolf knights on the left flank came closer to charging the heroes. Wyatt quickly cast forth a fireball that struck one of the knights off his horse's back, while the riderless horse became uncontrollably frightened and collided with one of the other mounted knights.

Marin took apart a sleek weighted hairpin about seven inches long attached to her hair. She revealed it to be a sharp plumelike dart, or plumbata as the Citadellans called it, except this one was finely weighted and balanced while being shorter than the standard military-issued plumbata. The Princess Knight, being only less than a dozen yards away from the Dreadful Knight and his sole remaining bodyguard, decided to hold back and hurl the dart closely in their direction. It struck the Dreadful

Knight but had no effect because of the protection of his armor, though it was enough to startle his steed into coming to an abrupt halt with such force that the Dreadful Knight lost his grip on the horse's reins and was ejected forward, hurtling toward the grassy ground. Meanwhile, Peat took one of his explosive oil barrels and rolled it toward the other mounted knight. A sudden moment later, the dwarf guardian called to Linitus. The elf responded and drew quickly a magical arrow that would spark a fire upon impact. The elf ranger let loose the arrow from his bow and quickly the arrow connected to strike the explosive barrel that Peat rolled toward the mounted knight only a few yards away. Upon impact with the arrow, the explosive barrel detonated and unleashed a loud explosion with the force of it being enough (with the mounted knight and his horse being as close as they were to the barrel) to force the knight into the air and land with a violent impact on the ground. Afterward, as the downed knight slowly moved and regained consciousness, Peat with a large war hammer walked up to him and unceremoniously struck him mortally with one fell swoop.

All that remained in the fight was the Dreadful Knight, who quickly rose up after being thrown forward from his horse. Baldwin, adjusting his crimson- and gold-laced helmet, cursed at the heroes while openly challenging any one of them to a duel. The traitorous knight did not care which of them he killed as long as he would eventually kill them all one at a time.

Linitus was prepared to answer the challenge and stepped forward, but as soon as he did, Marin also stepped forward and held out her arm by his chest. She pleaded with him to let her challenge Baldwin since he betrayed her original knightly order, the Order of the Eternal Flame. For her, it was personal and she perceived this challenge as an opportunity to settle the score, to deal out punishment for his betrayal to not only her original knightly order, but also to her father as king, and for betraying the Kingdom of Swordbane as a whole. Linitus acquiesced while nodding subtly to allow her to answer the challenge by the Dreadful Knight, but the elf ranger also cautioned her to not give in to her anger to the point that she would be off balance in her concentration and fighting prowess. Instead, he implored her to fight with calmness in the pursuit of seeking justice. Marin shook her head briefly and made several more steps forward, toward the Dreadful Knight.

With their flaming blades unsheathed and shields at the ready, both knights stared intently at each other while strafing and circling. Marin and Edwin Baldwin both stared intently at each other and sized each other up. Suddenly, the Dreadful Knight initiated a taunting laugh to try to draw Marin into anger and possibly losing her composure. It failed, and Marin mocked his efforts. Consequently, her response provoked her adversary into anger instead of her, and he charged at her while raising his flaming sword and poised to strike at the last moment so that she would potentially react too early and expose herself in committing a misstep.

Instead, Marin, catching the Dreadful Knight off guard, simply moved her arm holding her small round shield and pivoted to hurl it at Baldwin's helmet. It succeeded in temporarily knocking his head back in a quick jerk-like motion while he briefly lost composure. It was long enough for Marin to quickly pick up the shield in midair while it ricocheted toward her. She quickly then used the shield while holding it in both hands to charge and bash Baldwin with it. He lost his footing and collapsed with the weight of the Princess Knight falling down toward him. With her knees landing on his armor breastplate, she continued to strike and drive her shield at his helmet until the Dreadful Knight showed no resistance and was stunned. She then yanked his helm off and bashed him with it before regaining her composure and pressing the sharp end of her flaming blade close to his throat and telling him to yield and that his fight was over.

Coming to his senses, Baldwin realized that death was imminent and, valuing his life, yielded with reluctance. Marin then took a pair of iron shackles that Linitus tossed in her direction and bound the Dreadful Knight. She then forced him up and told him that he would be taken prisoner to the king, the one true king of Swordbane, to stand judgment for his part in the betrayal against the king and the kingdom.

Baldwin, enraged and feeling he was above the king and judgment, rebuked Marin and, catching her off guard, used his two cuffed hands along with the iron shackle to knock her down to the ground. He then fell upon her instead as she wrestled against him on the ground. At the first instant Baldwin raised his clasped hands to pummel her, a sudden hiss and whistle-like noise sounded, and the Dreadful Knight froze. He quickly gasped blood that came out while an arrow pierced through his exposed neck. He lay motionless on the ground, painfully choking his own blood while Marin turned and looked back, seeing Linitus holding his bow at the ready. She knew at this point that he had shot her treacherous adversary with one of his own arrows. She sighed and nodded while expressing both gratitude and a sense of relief. She told him that she owed him one, though she could have probably beat Baldwin again. Linitus responded by stating that she did well initially when she fought and defeated Baldwin today before letting her guard down afterward. Frustrated at hearing his critique, she showed anger in her expression, though she quickly realized and accepted the fact that he was right. She nodded again while knowing and admitting that she had been complacent and Baldwin took advantage of it when she least expected it.

Seeing her head lowered in humility from conceding and acknowledging her error, Linitus approached Marin and lifted her head softly with his hand while stroking the side of her face. They locked gazes with each other, and he told her that despite what could have been a setback, at least she was starting to learn and understand her enemies better, even after the moment of her enemies seemingly being defeated. Marin took his hand and held it firmly with both of her hands down toward their waists. She captured his attention while passionately admitting that she was blessed to have someone as patient and wise as him to be not only her lover but also her mentor in martial combat. She told him she hoped that in due time, she could find a way in their relationship for him also to draw upon and gain something of intrinsic value as well as extrinsic. Linitus, showing a touched but calm expression, replied that he already had. He found someone that made him feel completed. He found her as his soul mate in sharing the joy of how he viewed the world, the surrounding nature around them, and the marvels they would encounter together as they traveled. He had always seemed to be at peace and to have attained an inner sense of calmness and joy, but as he told Marin, he never had someone with as much passion as him to share it with intimately until he saw her, first when they were children and now as adults.

Marin, feeling equally touched, stared at him, and without caring what went on in the world around them, whether Peat and Wyatt noticed, or even if Dirty Dale and his top two goblin henchmen noticed after being apprehended by their companions, she locked her lips onto his and shared a deep kiss. Linitus in return accepted and embraced her while returning the kiss at the same time. Their world was between them, and everything else outside was, to them, frozen in time, though time did go on.

Seeing what had transpired, Peat and Wyatt were awestruck, and so were the prisoners that they had shackled and tied to a makeshift post. Dirty Dale and his two goblins, though somewhat shocked and in dismay from the Dreadful Knight falling from combat, were far more dumbstruck seeing two of their protagonist captors engage in a blissful moment of love. Dale regained his composure and cursed at having to be in a position to see this. It was debilitating enough that he himself never found love with a lady, while having the most outlandish rumors cast upon him and his love life, most notably involving sheep, since it was the most common object of his raiding activities.

Meanwhile, the two ranking goblin henchmen surprisingly shared a very different sidebar conversation of their delight at how beautiful though ironic that two of their protagonist adversaries would share such an intimate moment in a situation like this. Wyatt and Peat looked at each other still dumbstruck, with the dwarf guardian confiding that the elf ranger should be counting his blessings that of all the people who could be a possible suitor to the daughter of the most powerful king in the western lands, it had to be him.

Still, while exchanging conversation with Wyatt about the awkwardness of making sense of the affectionate display between two of his hero comrades, Peat could not help but admit that it was perhaps mutual and Marin the Princess Knight had finally found someone that had a strong connection with her and was a good influence for her to learn from and be better. Despite the elf seeming perfect and inadvertently being seen as having better standing in his abilities over a wide range, Peat no longer felt the need to challenge Linitus for some time. The elf ranger was no longer the mysterious newcomer that possibly had questionable intentions that needed to be investigated as he got closer to the king's circle. Linitus's natural behavior and intentions were truly the most genuine that Peat had ever seen of anyone.

By this point, Peat, relinquishing any shred of displayed hostility and apprehension, admitted that the elf ranger even in a still somewhat short period of time had been able to rise above his own station to answer insurmountable challenges in order to serve both the king and Swordbane, so his trust was fully earned by that point. The dwarf guardian decided also that it was perhaps time to no longer look at Marin as the little girl and adolescent he once knew and feel obligated as a former mentor to be as overly protective as he once was. He could now accept and be at peace that Marin had grown up, and while still learning the ways of combat as well as being a future monarch in training, she had become her own adult and she was capable of fighting relatively well on her own while being under watch by someone who cared for her just as much, though deeply in many aspects.

Regaining their composure, Peat told Wyatt it was time for them to return to their mission at hand. Wyatt nodded and the two of them forced their three prisoners into a single-file rank. They would teleport along with the prisoners back to the skyship and return to Citadella Neapola for the king to have his royal guards interrogate the prisoners and uncover what they knew as well as find out what plots the dux had in store for Swordbane.

However, abruptly after having a moment of brief intimacy with Marin, Linitus called out to Wyatt and Peat. The elf told them that before departing, they needed to track down any evidence that Dale and his fellow prisoners had on them that might be of use to assess the plans of their enemy. With a plan in mind, Linitus decided that the company of heroes as well as their three prisoners would teleport back to the skyship while they would locate in the terrain below any signs of makeshift encampment that Dale and his bandit gang had.

Following the plan, the company of heroes teleported aboard the skyship in a matter of minutes and set course in the same direction that Dirty Dale's gang of bandits came from prior to their downfall. It was not long before Linitus spotted and pointed down to the terrain below. Only a few hundred yards off the side of the Royal Road and obscured by a small hill along with a large boulder on one side and a large tree thicket on the other lay a small encampment with tents and storage racks as well as other objects, including what appeared to be a large chest in particular.

Within another moment, Wyatt had teleported the company of heroes down to that very spot in the encampment along with him and the captured bandits that they had defeated.

Upon reaching the encampment, Wyatt and Peat both guarded Dale and his two remaining top goblin lieutenants. At the same time, Linitus and Marin both approached the large and now-discovered locked chest. Marin raised her sword and planned to bash the lock and access the contents. However, right before she would swing her blade while raising it high above her head, Linitus caught her hand and motioned to her that it was rigged as a trap. Marin, shocked and disbelieving, questioned how Linitus would know such a thing for certain.

Linitus carefully approached the chest, took out a small satchel bag that had a key ring with a series of lockpicks and skeleton keys and a long extendable pole with a serrated sharp edge. Seeing a trap wire string attached to the keyhole of the chest, the elf ranger meticulously used the extendable pole to cut the wire and trigger the trap. Upon doing so, a sudden moving barrel with a lit fuse catapulted a few feet in front of the chest. Linitus and the other heroes instantly recognized that it was a miniature explosive barrel. Before reacting to take cover, Linitus quickly used the serrated sharp end of the pole again to cut the fuse, successfully preventing the barrel from exploding. Everyone gave a sigh, including Dale and the two goblins taken prisoner. Dale was impressed and congratulated the elf ranger while stating that he had some skill to maybe train with him in becoming a master rogue if Linitus would set Dale and his goblin henchmen free.

Linitus recognized the bandit leader's vain attempt to persuade the elf ranger to let him go, though it was without expected success, with even Peat laughing and telling Dale that he was better off persuading the now-dud oil barrel to explode without a fuse. Dale cursed at the dwarf guardian while telling the hero adventurers that it would be their funeral for keeping him prisoner when the dux of Sanctum Novus found out. Marin replied snarkily that they were counting on it.

Meanwhile, Linitus slowly approached the locked chest and next took his set of skeleton-key picks from his lockpick collection to decide which one would best fit the locked chest and open it. Dale, seeing the elf slowly working to pick the chest's lock, laughed at Linitus and told him that there was no way an elf ranger could unlock a chest as difficult as it seemed. The elf ranger disregarded the bandit's mockery of his attempt to unlock the warded lock. With Marin placing her hand on his shoulder, she praised and encouraged him that he could do it, though she was somewhat amazed that he had possibly the talent to disarm rigged traps and pick locks in addition to his fighting prowess. He truly was, in her mind, a man of many skills that she envied in some respect, and she wanted to learn from him everything at once.

In a moment of checking the width of each of the skeleton-key picks, Linitus selected the widest one possible that would fit through the entry of the keyhole. In another moment, he slid the skeleton-key pick all the way in while feeling around for a springlike actuator where he would stop and turn the skeleton-key pick to unlock the chest while breaking through the warded lock. It had worked after he heard the click, and it was loud enough that Marin could hear and see. Her face lit up with a wide smile and expression of amazement at her lover's skill. She could not believe it and even admitted loudly by raising the same question that their bandit prisoner had, speculating if Linitus actually was a rogue. Linitus gave a subtle smile while nodding and admitting that though he was trained to be a ranger, he had also a separate set of rogue-like skills that he acquired under the tutelage of his mother. She was a rogue expert herself and had trained him in the same manner she had learned as a former maid in service at a locksmith's house in Parf Edhellen before she met Linitus's father, who had also trained Linitus in how to hunt and fight in the forest outside the walls of Parf Edhellen. Overhearing, Peat also complimented Linitus, sharing the same admiration and praise as Marin of the elf ranger's many skills that had been invaluable to their success in both staying alive and working toward foiling any plans Dux Decius had in his attempted takeover of Swordbane.

Dale and the two goblin bandit lieutenants were in utter disbelief. Dale cursed at himself witnessing a group of what he considered would-be heroes or adventurers and the elf ranger in particular had now outdone the bandit leader who had questioned Linitus's ability to be a rogue when he identified himself as a ranger by profession. It was clear that Dale's mocking suspicion of the elf's lockpicking abilities had come to make the bandit leader look even pettier by underestimating Linitus's abilities. Peat added insult to injury while telling Dale that he was hoist by his own petard of an oil barrel. Dale held his tongue and gave a menacing stare of contempt toward the dwarf, telling him that it would not be as bad as when Dale's lord, Dux Decius, would come to exact revenge and hoist them by their own petard for not setting free the human bandit leader along with his goblin henchmen. Peat shrugged it off and still laughed while telling Dale that they would find out in due time.

Opening the chest slowly, Linitus and Marin quickly found an array of ornate items jumbled with many gold and silver coins along with some written correspondence. There was even a container that stood out noticeably, holding a series of vials with an exotic light-purplish liquid. They were unsure what to make of it at first, then they read through one of the correspondence letters hand-signed by both Agaroman and Dux Decius instructing Dale to lead his bandit gang of goblins not only to harass those on the royal roads to exact tolls and fealty of traveling merchants to Dux Decius, but also to keep the vials at hand along with a syringe to administer the vaccine, or cure, for the great plague to any beastly creatures or allies that had yet to be exposed to the great plague in order to lower the chance that these allies of the enemy would fall from such sickness or affliction.

The realization of what the heroes had uncovered and gained possession of was immense. They could not hold back conversing with each other about it and what to do going forward. Wyatt whispered in Linitus's ear, suggesting that the wizard would personally take possession of it in order to study the filled vials and determine how he could emulate and replicate the vaccine to use and adopt so that as many people in Swordbane as possible would be administered the vaccine before it was too late with too many people dying from the plague.

Shortly after, Wyatt cast another teleportation spell to transport the large wooden storage chest to the skyship, followed by the company of heroes and their bandit prisoners. The skyship, moments later, turned southwest, setting a course for its next destination, Colonia Mons Salvinia. They would have the migrant refugees confirm if their prisoners were indeed the bandits that raided the refugees. After compiling their testimony, the company of heroes would next take the prisoners to the kingdom capital, Citadella Neapola, to stand trial before the king and ultimately face their fate for their violent banditry. For the time being, Linitus and Marin once again found time to share intimacy together, this time inside the great cabin, or captain's cabin, on the stern of the skyship. They held each other in an embrace while peering from the cabin windows and gazing at the far-distant horizon, facing northeast, nearly opposite of the sunset yet still able to see the sun's rays faintly shining down on the open beautiful forest and grass-plain landscape with the local river shimmering from the sun's gradual but eventual departing embrace as it reached dusk and later on twilight.

CHAPTER TWENTY-SEVEN

Continuing to Pave the Road of Hell

After nearly a month of travel going west from Barbarum Aries, Dux Decius's army, enlarged by the new barbarian auxiliary conscripts, finally made it to the faraway coastal Nordling barbarian settlement of Aegir-Hafn. Perched high above on a mountain pass that descended to the wooded coastal plain below, Nordling scouts of the dux's army pointed and gestured to the dux and his advisor Agaroman the precise location of Aegir-Hafn. Though small to sight from a distance, compared to larger walled Citadellan settlements, it was still a noticeable sight to see. It had many large, elongated wooden houses with roofs that appeared to some to have the shape of the upside-down keel of a Nordling longboat, while other longhouses appeared to have a folded rectangular shape for the roof that crossed diagonally and met across a solid single beam. Several wooden docks also extended from the shoreline, and over a dozen wooden Nordling longboats.

Interestingly enough, there were also a few vessels that were of different make. No doubt in the dux's mind they were most likely merchant boats belonging to Citadellan merchants from the mediterranean and temperate Swordbane coastal heartland due south. However, there was one interesting boat of exotic design that was sleek, and it was neither Citadellan nor Nordling. The dux and Agaroman consulted between themselves, pondering the identity of the vessel until the dux recalled making out the design of the exotic boat from a distance. Surprisingly, it was a vessel of Marjawani design. It amazed the dux as well as his wizard consul that to see such a vessel had come from so far away as Marjawan's domain, which had only one notable seaport that lay in the great southern desert gulf from which the Great Desert River flowed out to form the mouth of the river that coalesced with the adjacent sea.

The dux had ordered that just as before, he would lead his dire-wolf cavalry to charge and viciously attack the settlement by surprise, with little or no time for them to react, while the remaining forces would attack while transitioning from a quick march to a double march as they neared the borders of the settlement, to support the dux's cavalry in attacking the coastal barbarian settlement to the point of making their unsuspecting enemy surrender.

With his army ready, the attack run commenced. In less than two hours, the coastal Nordling settlement would suffer and fall in a fate somewhat similar to the previous major one, Barbarum Aries. However, the Nordlings from this settlement were better prepared even when caught off guard. As the dux's cavalry came within visible distance, the settlement's bell had been sounded to warn the locals of the attack. Many came to arms and attempted to stave off the attack using sword, spear, and bow and arrow. To no avail, however, did they fight the overwhelming momentum that the dux's cavalry had gained in pouncing forward and decimating the ranks of the town's local military guard as well as the defending common villagers. The dire-wolf riders sustained casualties of several dozen, but it paled in comparison to the hundreds of the local Nordlings that fell. Much to the dux's regret, however, several Nordling soldiers, including one exquisitely dressed female warrior had boarded two of the moored longboats that were docked at the wooden pier. In a short amount of time, the two large, elongated boats sailed off west before changing course, heading due south. The dux and Agaroman both theorized that most likely, these two boats were fleeing with the surviving local monarchy. The dux did not know where they were heading and surmised that they could very well make their way far enough south to reach one of the Swordbane kingdom's settlements to warn of the impending danger while possibly seeking aid against a common enemy.

The dux had no intention to let these vessel-bound Nordlings disclose his army's location, but decided to address that matter later, focusing on tearing apart the morale of the remaining population of the local settlement. Eventually, he and his army would do just that until one of the prominent figures of the locals called out loudly enough to command the rest of the Nordlings to put down their weapons and offer surrender. Neither the dux nor anyone in his ranks had any clue who this local prominent figure was, but they were all the more content to let a prominent Nordling barbarian persuade his fellow villagers, including kinsmen, to recognize the futility of their efforts to fight off the invaders and pursue peace even if that meant surrender.

When the armed villagers and local guard finally gave in and recognized the authority of the prominent Nordling, they put their weapons down while kneeling in submission. Upon seeing the displayed gesture, Decius raised his sword high above the air, calling loudly for his army to halt, and he announced that they had secured their victory and domination over the settlement. Throngs of cheers and howls were emitted from the dux's cavalry. The conquering army celebrated loudly while chanting to render salutations hailing Decius as either the dux or as the one true dark lord.

Just as Decius had done before with Barbarum Aries, he also imposed the same terms with the now-conquered Barbarum Aegir-Hafn. The now conquered barbarian settlement would be subjected to paying a certain amount of tribute in the form of a proportion of their principal local commodities, including Hafn salmon, huckleberries that Sanctum Novus would use to produce an exotic wine, and timber from Hafn fir trees as well as Aldion red cedar, the latter of which has its range as far north as the coastal barbarian lands such as Aegir-Hafn. Just like Barbarum Aries, Aegir-Hafn's settlement would also be subject to the dux or those appointed under him to conscript a proportion of male fighting adults into the Remnant's military to serve as auxiliary.

However, unlike Barbarum Aries, Decius decided to bestow the title of lordship in Aegir-Hafn to the oldest prince sibling of Aries in exchange for letting the younger sibling have sole control of Aries with another bestowed title of lordship, provided both of them would maintain their sworn fealty to the dux. Both of them pondered when the dux initiated this proposition, and both of them, to the relief of the dux, agreed without fighting each other over it. If they did fight each other, it would not have surprised the dux as he would expect the barbarian princes possibly to resort to such violent means of gaining more power and control over the other.

Lastly, with both of the barbarian princes still in his presence, the dux imposed two other stipulations upon them: the first, both of them would allow Citadellan merchants under the banner of the Remnant's fealty to travel and engage in commerce freely, without any taxation while in Nordling lands; second, the Citadellans would be able to move freely and establish one neighboring settlement in each major Nordling tribal region under the princes' control for both Aries and Aegir Hafn while allowing the native Nordlings to exercise the option to live freely and mingle with the Citadellans. Though the two princes had no issue with the first of the two final stipulations, they were clearly and visibly angry at the last one. They saw it as a competitive threat not only to their localities' immediate control of nearby natural resources but also to their distinct Nordling identity. The older prince raised his initial objection, citing that even if they were to agree to that, the clan elders of their people might object as they believed in not intermixing and having relations with those outside their Nordling race. The younger prince tried to support that claim by indicating that the Nordlings that had conquered the south over a thousand years ago to establish the Swordbane kingdom were no longer recognizable by custom and traditions (even if so by appearance) to the Nordling way of life.

Decius, keeping a straight face and keeping a calm disposition while not caring about their concerns over what he considered their uncivilized manner of livelihoods and identity, told them as consolation that the Norldings would not be forced to move in or intermarry with the Citadellans if they did not want to. The two princes looked at each other with some reluctance but nodded in mutual agreement to each other and to the dux, knowing that they had little say in the matter and refusing to do so would likely come at the expense of their own lives.

Having the conditions settled, the dux called forth one of the chefs of his army to prepare a meal by fetching a portion of the defeated settlement's supply of salmon to cook while also provisioning red Citadellan wine in various goblets. Despite the apprehension that the Nordling princes had initially in perceiving the threat of their society and culture being reduced to eventual rubble, the dux had at least temporarily absolved them and occupied them with what he considered the rewards of their inclusion in the desert Citadellan-led Remnant coalition. Like other Nordlings, their desire and lust for Citadellan red wine was insidious and lucrative enough to attract their attention and make them look the other way, dispelling their earlier concerns about their way of life being affected by the dux's future plans of Citadellan colonization in their lands.

As nightfall loomed, the barbarians of the settlement finished gathering their dead that they would bury on the next day. Standing in the dux's makeshift tent next to a firepit, Agaroman looked at it then turned toward Decius. Decius looked back at him and already knew while responding that close as he was to meriting the opportunity to court the deity spirits of Calu and Laran, he was still not quite ready. Agaroman, telling from the dux's face, acknowledged and confided to the dux that he had grown powerful enough in his abilities to not only command and rule, but he was now able to sense and feel the destruction and death that could be measured upon by himself. It would be enough for him to know his own power and standing among the deity spirits when he would truly be ready to summon Calu and Laran's presence at the appointed time. The dux grinned slightly while responding. He told his close advisor that he indeed knew that this would make him even more fearsome and powerful among both his allies and foes. He would not squander the opportunity against his future foes and targets to build his new empire.

Looking also at the burning firepit, the dux contemplated it while asking his wizard advisor for what he would suggest they do next now that they conquered the two most powerful Nordling barbarian settlements. Agaroman reflected deeply and cautiously before heaving a brief sigh and displaying a sign of resolution to the dux's question. The wizard advisor suggested for the dux to head south to besiege the next major barbarian settlement that lay between Aegir-Hafn and Aldion before they would ultimately strike at Aldion. The dux pondered why they would attack and take over Aldion; it would be too costly for later campaigning against the Swordbane kingdom's capital. Agaroman responded while looking up that they would attack not to take over Aldion, but to take something from there to level the playing field later on and give the Remnant a superior advantage to eventually defeat the kingdom.

Decius pondered again for a moment how they would seize skyships that were based in the city's hangar holdings or possibly deployed high in the sky above. Agaroman slightly nodded, indicating that the dux was of similar mind to his advisor's intentions, but it would not just be the skyships that they would steal, if at all. Their true focus would be the design blueprints or detailed mappings of the skyships and their components, which they would take and swap a fabricated false manuscript in its place to cover their tracks from Swordbane finding out what they had taken. In doing so, the wizard suggested that they could make their intentions and plans more inconspicuous from being discovered by the kingdom while they would escape out of Aldion to take the skyship building manual or blueprints along with prototype-related objects back to Sanctum Novus to construct their own flying armada of skyships to dominate the skies in the war against Swordbane. The Dux grinned again and nodded in approval of his advisor's cunning plan. Over the next few days, the dux would ride out once again. This time, he and his army were going south to continue his campaign of conflict, death, destruction, and conquest.

CHAPTER TWENTY-EIGHT

Discord, Division, and the Pursuit of Unity

Three months had passed since the Siege of Marjawan came to an end. Nearly two and half months had passed since the betrayal of Dux Decius and Sanctum Novus against the throne of Swordbane, and roughly a week had passed since Linitus and his company of heroes returned to Citadella Neapola after both putting an end at least temporarily to the raids outside Colonia Mons Salvinia and unexpectedly finding a cure, or more appropriately, a vaccine, from the storage cache of the goblin raiders' former encampment just east of Mons Salvinia. Wyatt had been fortunate in studying and replicating the vaccine, thanks in part to the recipe list of ingredients that he and Peat later found in the storage chest that they had taken with them on board the skyship after defeating the raiders.

With the vaccine replication assured, Wyatt quickly made several copies of the list of ingredients and distributed them to several priests, wizards, and other scholars at Citadella Neapola to accelerate the production of the same vaccine in larger volumes for later use in mass distribution and administration among the general city populace. The city itself had already lost nearly a tenth of its population and likely would have expected to lose more if the great affliction continued to spread without the discovered vaccine being distributed as quickly as it could.

Already public animosity, distrust, and discord fomented among the various races blaming one another for the spread of the affliction, including human against dwarf, dwarf against elf, some elves even against halflings and gnomes, and even going so far as different humans, including Citadellans, Nordlings who had assimilated to Citadellan urban culture, and the offspring of the two (who normally were considered half Citadellans by some, though they typically preferred to identify as Citadellans as a general practice of preference for their Citadellan customs and heritage over Nordling identity) such as in the case of Marin.

Walking through the streets to survey the city and help the local city guard patrol ensure public safety as well as law and order, Marin being in company with Linitus was not immune from receiving the random sporadic xenophobic calls of condemnation for their respective races, depending on what district or quarter of the city they were in, as well as generally being called out with derogatory words as scorn and rebuke for their public display of being together side by side. One district in particular, the assimilated Nordling quarter of veterans, knights, blacksmiths, masons, and some other professional guilds, was inhospitable as the two heroes passed by with an armed contingent of the king's guard to help escort a small mixed entourage of individual families from various races to return to their own dwellings after receiving vaccination from the clerics of one of the main local temples. From some of the windows, the unsuspected provocateurs of the local district not only shouted toward the crowd but also threw random objects, including small utensils and rotten food, as projectiles toward the crowd.

Marin, reacting quickly, called the city guard to form a perimeter and shield the civilian entourage, while planning to investigate and apprehend the offending perpetrators. Showing unchecked anger and rage as well as disappointment at what the city had devolved into, she resolved to stamp out any xenophobia and other forms of malice displayed within the city. To her, it was not the same Citadella Neapola she had known. Despite the small but frequent rounds or isolated incidents as signs that individuals in the city might have friction between races, it had never reached this point. It had changed drastically since the onset of the great affliction spreading throughout the capital city as well as the surrounding countryside.

As soon as she unsheathed her flaming blade to address the matter at hand, a firm hand was placed against her shoulder to hold her back. Further enraged, Marin turned and prepared to attack whoever would get between her and the perpetrators. However, her face still holding anger eventually froze as she came to realize it was her lover. Linitus calmly told her that though he felt the same as her and knew this was not the city she had come to know or the will that she envisioned sharing with him, her manner of resolving the issue was not for the better.

Somewhat speechless and defiant, Marin questioned Linitus on going against her approach, asking why. He told her that if they did, it would risk further provoking the city or at least that section of it into a frenzy that could easily escalate into a full drawn-out riot. It would further put at risk the lives of the ones they were escorting and protecting to and from their homes, with the potential backlash that might be sparked by them responding with more force against a cowardly but otherwise anonymous perpetrator since they had not clearly seen who had hurled insults and objects at them.

Instead, Linitus suggested that they continue walking as quickly as possible, with the king's guard forming a shield perimeter to their series of destinations in escorting the different civilians back to their homes. Marin, contemplating with effort, agreed with Linitus and acknowledged that despite the retribution she would like to deliver upon the offenders, the conditions were not right as he had pointed out and he was correct in their duty, especially hers as a knight, to prioritize defending the vulnerable, including civilians, over challenging would-be offenders at the expense of abandoning the ones they were sworn to defend, as well as possibly putting their safety further at risk if a riot did erupt from her possible retaliatory actions.

Linitus grasped one of her gauntlet hands and embraced it firmly with both of his hands, telling her that there would be a day when they would make this right, to end the discord in the city and bring its different people together, united after this troubling time with the great affliction had passed. Marin nodded once more. They resumed their current route to escort one civilian family at a time until they were done, before returning to the next major temple in transit and repeating the process over again.

As the time eventually passed, Marin and Linitus came across a large and prominently decorated amphitheater in the distance straight ahead of them. It was the capital's main amphitheater, and it stood over many of the other buildings of the city like a majestic towering jewel. The two of them stopped to look and take in the awe-inspiring view. Marin reminded Linitus that the tournament would be in three days. She recounted that as of tradition during the time of the Lupercalian Empire, the winning champion would be granted their freedom if that champion was a slave or granted a wife if the champion was a freedman. Since those times, she further went on, it had been tradition for a king to ask the champion for one request or gift of bestowment that a king would provide, whether it was a powerful enchanted weapon, an elegant set of armor, a rare decorative type of royal jewelry possibly of magical power, or some other materialistic object. The elf shook his head while letting her know that he was familiar with this lore. She responded to him, telling him that though she had won the tournament once, she was determined to do so again. Though these sorts of tournaments were considered uninteresting public performances of vanity that Linitus was reluctant to embrace fully, he did ponder the prospect and implications of becoming a tournament champion in a given year. Reflecting even further in light of the city's discord while also thinking about the triumph they shared in celebration of their victory against Marjawan over a few months ago, she confided that the gladiator tournament was perhaps one of the few forms of public ceremony that still brought people together even during challenging times.

Pondering for a moment, Linitus turned to her and asked as an audible afterthought, had there ever been an elf champion, let alone an elf competitor? She looked at him somewhat amazed while somewhat dumbfounded, thinking back on all the annals of recorded history she had studied to learn about Citadellan history and culture, including the gladiator tournaments. Never had there been an elf champion, let alone an elf participant in the capital tournament despite the elves having their own gladiator competition at their city of Salvinia Parf Edhellen.

She looked at him and could not hold back from asking what he was thinking, though she would not put it past him to enter the tournament since he had the skill to be a champion. But his motive she was unsure about. He had no interest to compete for the sake of getting the public's adoration to fulfill his own sense of pride or being. The last thing he was interested in would be that, knowing him as intimately as she had, even for a few months. He told her he would do it as much as he hated to perform in front of the public to appease their appetite for again what he considered a vanity display of combat. However, if that was what it took for the general public to find a common ground of respect for someone different from them, to still appreciate and respect that participant regardless of his background, he would do it. He admitted it might not fully heal the tensions and division of the city capital and, by extension, parts of the kingdom that had signs of race discord. Regardless, it was perhaps a hopeful opportunity for him to show his talent for gaining the respect of races other than his own to accept him and, by extension, others who were different. Marin agreed but admitted she would have a hard time holding back to fight him. She had become too close to him to be able to compose herself and challenge him as she did before. Holding her hand again and acknowledging the inward conflict, Linitus told her she had to try and find a way to do it if it would work. If not only the perception of him by the various possible spectators but also the perception of her as a woman with mixed Nordling and Citadellan heritage, then she must find a way to show her martial talent as best as she could muster, even to fight him if it would cause people of other races to admire her in mutual unity and respect, not for her background, not for her title, but for her sheer determination and ability to challenge herself to face any adversity in order to overcome and prevail as much as she could. He reminded her that she had done it once as a champion and it would be no different this time if she set herself the task of doing so again. Marin looked down and then at him while nodding intently. He was right as so many times he had been, as much as she hated to admit it. At least his voice was one that she understood from a place of both reason and esteemed genuineness that appealed to her with a tender care in relating to her concerns and understanding her point of view.

Chapter Twenty-Nine

Tournament and Coming Full Circle

Three months and three days later, after the end of the siege against Marjawan, well over two and a half months after the betrayal at Sanctum Novus, the annual tournament at the capital city of Citadella Neapola was set to commence. It would be a rare one-match all-day tournament (if it lasted all day) set to commence at sunrise and end with the last prevailing tournament participant. The match would be broken down into individuals or teams of two if the participants had agreed to it informally and impromptu or planned ahead of time by mutual consensus. There were three dozen combatant participants for the tournament, hailing from various parts of the kingdom. Nearly all of them were male knights and either of Citadellan or Nordling human background. Only four unusual participants stood among them: an elf ranger in unison with his teammate, a young halfling wizard, and a female knight standing close by the side of a dwarf guardian combatant teammate.

Despite a few occasional offensive comments, the crowd in the amphitheater was ecstatic for the tournament to commence. The combatants, upon being introduced, walked in procession before the king, who watched from his royal box placed prominently in the amphitheater before the other seating placements. King Ascentius rose and acknowledged all the combatants while showing a minor though personal gesture of fondness separately for his daughter, who was the only prior tournament champion that was mentioned with that distinction. The king, however, displayed a similar minor but profound gesture of respect in acknowledging

Linitus when his name was called as one of the new-entry combatants. For Ascentius, regardless of the outcome, he held the elf in high regard and esteem for what he had done so far to preserve not only the king's life, but also his daughter's, the lives of his surviving soldiers, and the subjects of his kingdom. He was truly and internally indebted to the elf ranger, which those close enough to him that observed could tell. For the general public, the subtle gestures seemed to minutely distinguish how the king would acknowledge the other competing participants.

After each of the announced combatants gave their salutations to the king while receiving the king's gesture in kind, a quiet empty air hovered about the arena. The combatants spaced each other at various distances while seemingly sizing each other up, trying to anticipate what each potential adversary might do. Perhaps the two that stood out the most among the combatants were Linitus and Wyatt in how they displayed their stance in anticipation before the tournament. Linitus had sat down and folded his legs in a prayerlike, meditative stance while lowering his head and closing his eyes. The crowd took notice, and some jeered, mocking the elf as likely being the first one to fall in combat. Meanwhile, Wyatt had taken a defensive stance by illuminating a bright shieldlike globe around him that emanated from his silver wand. This shield globe caught the attention of some among the crowd of spectators, who were in awe, while others laughed and considered the wizard simply a specialist of nothing more than cheap illusionary magic tricks.

Only a moment later, loud sounds erupted from the trumpets of the arena being played by trumpeters that helped officiate the tournament. Immediately following, the arena combatants quickly selected and engaged each other in combat, with the bulk of the fighting taking place at the center of the arena. Marin and Peat worked in unison, both charging like a wrecking ball and chain feeding off each other in causing mayhem and havoc toward their opponents. Marin charged first toward one of the combatant knights, using her shield to knock down her adversary, and Peat followed up by darting toward her shield, which the Princess Knight would use as extra support to propel the small dwarf guardian in the air, darting headfirst toward one of the other knights, puncturing the foe with the dwarf's sharp spiked, horned helmet. In only another moment, Peat pulled his spiked helmet out of his fallen foe. Another knight quickly tried to seize the advantage by charging toward the briefly unsuspecting dwarf only when Marin called out for her comrade to take cover. Peat did so, rolling to the side as the Princess Knight took a spear from one of the combatants she defeated and hurled it toward the dwarf guardian's new assailing adversary, catching the latter off guard. The adversary fell quickly upon the impact from the blow. Peat turned around and nodded while praising Marin for her quick reflexes and instincts.

Marin, meanwhile, recomposed herself and took a moment to survey what else transpired as the tournament unfolded. Unsurprisingly to both her and Peat, they caught sight of Wyatt from the other side of the arena spell-casting fireballs and lightning-bolt projectiles toward several of his competitors, some of whom had fallen rather quickly if they did not use their shields to block the incoming projectiles.

In another corner of the arena, they caught sight of Linitus still seated with his legs crossed and in the same meditation-like posture. Peat questioned the approach that the elf ranger had taken as being utterly suicidal and possibly a display of insanity. Marin, however, countered to her dwarf comrade that just as before, Linitus would not fall and he would do what others would not suspect. She was right. As soon as one of the first combatants took notice of the elf ranger as being in a vulnerable state and essentially almost asking to be slain, the given knight adversary charged headfirst, lifting his blade up high and poised to strike with his full force upon the seemingly unsuspecting ranger. However, just as the knight's blade began to descend, swinging downward to strike the elf ranger, Linitus had quickly swiveled with elegance in his stance, doing a half turn while unsheathing almost simultaneously his slightly curved elven long blade ever so gracefully toward one of the few exposed parts of the knight adversary not fully protected by the latter's respected plate-mail armor. In another sudden moment, the two competitors in their nearly solid motionless stances began to break hold, with the elf in a fully risen position, standing on his feet while the stricken knight fell downward on his knees with the full brute force of his armor before finally falling forward again, face and helm first against the ground.

The crowd, being both amazed and impressed beyond expectation, echoed in audible awe before erupting in sudden cheers that began to feel ecstatic, wanting to see what else the elf ranger was able to do. As the other competitors noticed the sudden rising popularity that Linitus had instantly commanded, nearly a dozen of them charged toward the elf ranger. Linitus dropped his transition camouflage cloak while on the ground that covered a round barrel-like object. He quickly unpacked a cylindrical canister receptacle that stored multiple mounted arrows. Drawing the string of his bow using the pinch-draw method, he quickly let loose the projectile cylinder sabot assembly, which then suddenly deployed multiple silver-tipped armor-piercing arrows striking all the charging attackers that went toward the elf ranger. Only one knight challenger got through; however, as that remaining knight still charged unnervingly toward Linitus, the clever elf ranger quickly kneeled on the ground to grab a wired pull string that sparked a flame near the camouflage-covered barrel-like object. Only a moment later, a large explosion was emitted, with the charging knight now being thrown back in the other direction by the force of the blast of what was apparently a well-placed and disguised fire-and-oil barrel bomb.

All that remained with the carnage that ensued were four combatants, all four members of the Order of Comradery. Three of them were in awe from observing what the remaining other one had done in disposing of the opposition with such efficiency and a large display of impressiveness that their jaws had dropped, and even they clapped as much as the crowd if only for a brief moment. Even Ascentius, the king himself, as impressed as he was by the teamwork of his daughter as an elite knight and the dwarf guardian that served as the king's royal guard captain, gave his most visible and audible expression of amazement as well as highest esteem and praise to Linitus and his display of martial prowess. Even many of the crowd spectators and the royal guards closest to the king noticed His Highness's amazement and wonder at Linitus's uncanny ability to fight with skills, wits, and cunning to take down even the most intimidating of knights throughout the kingdom.

Now, Linitus turned to look about and was also in awe, not by his skill and display in combat, but by the response he had drawn and evoked in the crowd applauding and acknowledging his display. Never had the elf ranger seen so many people from various races in such a large public gathering, let alone a public spectacle in particular, acknowledge and praise him. To him, it was both surreal and intimidating. He was shocked and somewhat uneasy with how to react to such widespread support of his fighting prowess. He took it in stride as best as he could while recollecting himself and reorienting his attention to the situation at hand. He realized while gazing about that only he and his three fellow comrades made it this far in the tournament. While the other three might have been surprised by the outcome, given how challenging the competitors were, perhaps not individually but as a large sum to make it where all four members of the

Comradery prevailed with a measurable degree of effort and skill in their own right.

It now came down to the four of them, and they knew only one would be declared champion of the tournament. Linitus, Marin, Peat, and Wyatt spaced each other out while pacing around in a circular counterclockwise pattern before alternating the other direction and going back to a counterclockwise motion. They each sized each other up while thinking and gazing intently to ponder and anticipate how they would engage each other. It was a unique outcome for the final bout of the tournament in which stood a versatile ranger, a heavily armor-clad and determined female knight, a somewhat rowdy and rambunctious dwarf guardian with a penchant for chaotic violence, and a seemingly harmless but cleverly underestimated wizard.

The combatants who were companion-in-arms to each other now put aside their comradery and were each determined to beat the other in order to claim the title of tournament champion for the current year. Again, only Marin had claimed that title, with the other three having yet to do the same.

As the combatants stood circling each other while still poised in sizing each other up and anticipating their next move, suddenly and nearly all at the same time, all four of them charged at each other, unleashing their own forms of shouts or war cries.

As they charged, in a flurry they each unleashed their own ferocious form of a quick and nearly unsuspected attack. Peat unmounted his barrel bomb, which he stowed in a pole-mount-shaped bracket assembly attached to his back supported by a torso and waist band. The dwarf guardian quickly lit and lobbed the barrel bomb toward Wyatt. Wyatt quickly threw a fireball in anticipation but only at the right time, when the impact of the explosion would hurl Peat from the blast rather than kill him. Marin used the weight of her shield while charging and suddenly in mid-motion used her sword to take a wide arc horizontal swing in the hopes of possibly catching Linitus off guard. Linitus shot off a series of arrows aimed at her feet. These arrows were unique in that they were not conventional sharp-tipped arrows but rather specialized with round sticky bulbs of a rare elven silk web that would adhere to the surface and trap an unsuspecting foe caught in it. It had worked as the elf ranger dodged to the side and evaded by leaping backward while shooting the arrows in midair toward the feet of the Princess Knight. Marin's momentum suddenly slowed and came to a halt before she lost balance and fell with the unbalanced force of her weight hard to the ground.

Her fall had knocked the wind out of her, and it gave enough time for Linitus to sigh and catch his breath before deciding his next move in defeating her. However, as this was happening, Wyatt with his small elegant silver wand decided to cast a lightning bolt toward the Princess Knight in the hopes of laying claim to defeating her (without killing his comrade, of course) before Linitus could. As the halfling dark-robed wizard cast his bright static projectile that soared several meters through the air, Marin turned and instinctively reacted by picking up her small round shield and using it to block the jolting projectile. Immediately after she did so, the lightning bolt upon striking the shield of the Princess Knight, it bounced directly back in the opposite direct in a ricochet-like manner and went hurtling back at Wyatt, who was totally in shock and in disbelief that his spell had been skillfully and cleverly deflected at him by someone who, though knowledgeable in combat, was not a wizard like to him master the spell-casting craft to use magic against him. The halfling wizard found out the extent that he was wrong, when Marin had used his own magic against him and the impact of the lightning bolt knocked the wizard out, stunned and down on the ground. Peat crawled up to Wyatt while ascertaining both his wounds and his fellow defeated combatant. The dwarf gave a half shrug while turning toward both Marin and Linitus, both of whom were concerned. The dwarf guardian retorted to both of them that both he and the halfling would live to fight another day, granted they were out for the remainder of today. Peat and Wyatt both gave slightly painful grunts of their expressed weakened state. Linitus and Marin both laughed, relieved that their companions were okay, while taking a moment to enjoy the comedy and irony that their other two companions were defeated from the use of their own means of fighting.

After sharing their brief moment of laughter, Linitus and Marin, both being the remaining two combatants, quickly returned to the tournament at hand, with each determined and focused to put on a good show of not only seeing who would prevail as the tournament champion for the year but also keeping in mind their original and larger intent to put on a good performance and earn the respect of the spectators to see that regardless of their background, they could each command an appreciation for their prowess that the audience would not hold against them because of their background. Ultimately, Marin and Linitus hoped it would translate for the diverse masses of spectators to see each other in sharing that mutual appreciation in harmony together in a fraternal manner while putting aside their racial differences and tensions. For the moment, it had worked. Linitus pointed out to Marin while calling upon her to take a moment and observe. The crowds of spectators in fact cheered and rooted for both of them and were ecstatic to still see Linitus and Marin compete to give their all to see who would be the better combatant.

The two of them stared intently at each other, and though each felt some initial reluctance to attack the other as they were lovers, they both felt even from looking at each other's facial expressions that they were capable of choreographing each other's moves and prowess to make it entertaining not only to the crowd but also to each other. Linitus wanted to see since besting Marin from their previous bouts of practice fighting if she had come far enough to possibly best him in combat and if not, to at least see how much she had improved in holding her own against him. Marin was just as eager, and their expressions toward each other showed that they could reach each other and know that it was mutual in their thoughts about the matter.

In a sudden moment after Marin had broken free her greaves and boots from the last of the sticky ball of silk-webbed arrows planted into the ground, she moved about circling while Linitus counter-circled from her. They both were again sizing each other up and poised to make their best guess on what each other's next move would be in anticipation as well as how to counteract it.

In another moment, Marin, unleashing a war cry akin to the war maidens of her Nordling heritage, strafed forward in a diagonal back-and-forth series of movements. Her tactic made it hard for Linitus to strike and get her stuck again with another of his sticky silk-web bulb arrows. She then whirled both her shield and flaming sword toward the elf ranger. Linitus ducked down toward the ground and, suddenly in a quick manner, withdrew another one of his sabot arrow-cluster projectiles. On the ground, he quickly fired it up in the air vertically without much force while rolling away from Marin, who tried to pin him on the ground and missed. Another quick moment, Linitus grabbed the decorative concealed hairpins holding Marin's hair together, which served as improvised weighted sharp darts. It caught Marin off guard with such a daring and nearly suicidal maneuver. Regardless, she quickly swung in another ferocious arc toward Linitus, knowing he would evade, which he did by ducking and rolling away.

What she did not anticipate, however, was that as Linitus rolled away, he quickly threw one of the two hairpin darts high in the air at the sabot capsule, which altered the direction from the position that it was facing and now was aimed downward toward Marin. She could not believe how her elf companion and lover, who was at this moment her opponent, had quickly outwitted her beyond anything she would have anticipated. He was good, and she could not hold back her shocked expression. However, it gave Marin enough time to quickly use her shield and raise it to cover her as the sabot capsule holding the cluster receptacle of silk-bulbed arrows disbanded and fell downward like heavy pelting rain.

As soon as Marin heard the last arrow drop with a pause, she rose up and lowered her shield, only to find that Linitus was nowhere to be seen. However, the elf ranger had used his camouflage cloak and merely went around her while she was covering from the hail of his cluster arrows. Though she could not see him, she could hear his footsteps, which he counted on in order to give her some way to detect and fight back. As she turned and struck in a diagonal top-to-bottom arc, her flaming sword struck and suddenly collided against a revealing long elven blade that emerged from the shroud of Linitus's camouflage cloak. Linitus's cloak, though initially effective, could not hide him indefinitely when it became noticeable in blocking Marin's attack. His shroud from the cloak, which was like an invisible shadow, no longer could hide him during sudden offensive and defensive movements that he made. As their blades locked, Linitus remarked that Marin had learned well in being attuned to both her instinct and senses. Marin gushed, smiled back while retorting that perhaps Linitus had finally met his match. The elf ranger remarked that while she was skilled with her hand movement in using her blade, she had still some learning about being as skilled with her footwork. Marin looked surprised and wondered what he meant but no sooner than she did, Linitus tripped her while sweeping and using his right foot to trip Marin also by her right foot. It worked, and Marin lost her balance, falling hard again to the arena floor. She lost control of her flaming sword briefly, and as she rolled on the ground to pick it up, she was again met by Linitus, who had pinned her body and held his sword sideways in one hand at an angle in which Marin's flaming sword blocked it vertically a few inches from her face. They were blade-locked, and it was, as it appeared to Marin, a draw. She pointed that out and noted that it looked like they were tied. Linitus, looking at her, moved his eye toward his other hand that did not carry his long sword but instead had in its possession her other improvised hairpin dart, which was pointed at her neck, at one of her carotid arteries. Marin, upon realizing that Linitus had the final advantage in besting her, sighed and dropped her blade in one hand while tapping hard on the arena dirt floor with her other hand. She announced audibly that she yielded.

It was hard for her to swallow her pride in being bested in front of the crowded audience that filled the amphitheater by the tens of thousands, but to her, it was an acceptable consolation to have one of the best sparring duels in her life and she was content in the sight of losing to at least be barely beaten in the way that she did against her soul mate.

Linitus had gotten off her and helped her up, which Marin had accepted. Though he bested her, he told her quietly enough for her to hear him say that she had also bested him. Marin looked confused and asked how so, to which Linitus told her that she had taken down more opponents than him even if he was the final remaining combatant to be victorious. Marin smiled back and told him that perhaps in next year's tournament, they might trade places in that regard. Linitus smiled back also and agreed of the possibility happening in a year from now.

Meanwhile, as they both stood up, the crowds in the amphitheater erupted in a final burst of ecstatic jovial celebration in chanting for Linitus's victory. Even Ascentius, impressed as he was in seeing all the fighting unfold as well as seeing how formidable his daughter was in a way that he had not seen before, stood up to acknowledge both Linitus, the new tournament champion, and his daughter Marin as the runner-up for the current tournament as well as being a past tournament champion.

Within moments, the crowd was silent to hear the king's proclamation of Linitus as winner. Linitus bowed halfway from standing, out of respect for the king, as Marin did so also. Ascentius motioned with his arm to acknowledge the salutation and told both of them to rise. He proclaimed that this tournament was the best he had watched in his entire life and it was possibly the best duel in the annals of tournaments in Swordbane. He commended his daughter for putting up a worthy final duel in this year's tournament while recognizing Linitus with his skills and talent as being the undisputable champion.

Taking another moment for the spectators to clap and celebrate before motioning them to lower their voices again, Ascentius announced, as was tradition for tournament champions, that he as the king would grant and bestow one material possession that he was able to give to the requesting victor. Linitus, taking a moment to pause while thinking intently, responded to the king that there was nothing of material value he wanted, except for a pair of Aritimi necklaces. The masses of spectators in the amphitheater seats were puzzled somewhat by the request that of all the things a newly proclaimed tournament victor could ask, this elf ranger asked for symbolic jewelry of love used for marriage. Typically, victorious champions had been known to ask for some prized crafted weapon of value, an elegant suit of armor, or even a deed and title to a wealthy castle estate or manor. Never had such a request for jewelry been made that alone was symbolic of a future married couple.

Ascentius, somewhat also in shock though for a different reason, knew why Linitus had made a request, but the king had hoped perhaps the elf ranger would find a different time. Ascentius knew that Linitus had fallen in love with his daughter and Marin had been the same way with Linitus. Ascentius did not personally oppose it but feared that such a union between elf and human would not be as welcomed or accepted among his various subjects comprised of several races. At least not yet, he thought. Regardless, knowing the intention for Linitus's love and compassion for his daughter being genuine, Ascentius nodded and conceded.

He probably could have let the matter go away with the crowd still wondering, but Ascentius, in his own daring maneuver, wanted his subjects to come to terms with overcoming their own possible prejudicial reservations. He decided to ask Linitus though it would be granted, to declare his purpose and intention. Linitus took another moment while looking at Marin, who nodded in her own consent. Linitus turned toward the king while addressing him respectfully and kneeling before him. The elf ranger pronounced loudly with confidence and with some humility that he asked for such necklaces so that he might offer to share them symbolically with the one that he loved, His Highness's daughter Marin.

Marin was stirred by Linitus's admission and confession of love toward her. She walked over to Linitus and embraced him before planting her lips on his with a brief solemn kiss. She did not care what anyone in the crowd thought, not even her father (as much as she loved him and held him in high regard).

Not knowing what to expect, they heard an almost-silent gasp only in passing, a subtle but gradually pronounced clap, followed by an increasing wave of thousands of claps that emerged from the spectator audience. The crowd seemed to have admired and been stirred from the passion that

Linitus had displayed not only in combat but also in courage and humility of what seemed to be an appeal for a shared mutual value of his open vulnerability and desire for love that transcended any barriers or signs or preconceptual resentment the crowd from various races might have toward the prospect of an interracial relationship.

Ascentius, nearly in tears, held back from shedding any, but his face was clear for anyone close to him to make out that he had been stirred in his heart of conviction once again by Linitus as well as the positive influence he had on the king's daughter. Waiting for the cheers to die off, the king waved his hand once again and announced that Linitus's wish would be granted if Marin wished it also and they would be granted the king's blessing to get married. Marin nodded and stated loudly and clearly that she wished it so before gazing intently and sharing another (though more deeply intent and romantic) kiss with Linitus. The crowd erupted in cheers once again and staged an impromptu makeshift celebration. Even as Peat and Wyatt started to regain consciousness, they were also both touched by the love their comrades had for each other, and slowly, the dwarf guardian and young halfling wizard got up to stand side by side to clap and celebrate this rare moment.

CHAPTER THIRTY

To Finally Attain Divine Appeasement

Colonia Aldion stood like a watchful protector city looking north beyond the Aldion River and toward the barbarian forestlands of the Nordlings, being the first to safeguard the defense of Swordbane along the northern coastal frontier of the kingdom. The city was more of a military fortification than a simple urbanized settlement. It was walled with stone like the other coastal Citadellan cities and was also fairly well armed, given its much smaller population size compared to the urbanized settlements of Citadella Neapola and Salvinia Parf Edhellen. Colonia Aldion's enclosed layout was cluttered with stucco and concrete buildings covered with red double-field tiles for roofing. Central among the militaristic-looking barracks buildings of the settlement lay the regent governor's urban villa estate. Outside the well-guarded city stood its local municipal amphitheater that, while smaller than the grand amphitheater of Citadella Neapola, could still house well over ten thousand spectators and was a notable site just outside the city walls. The amphitheater was well guarded in addition to the city walls and was purposely utilized in that way to prepare to protect both the priestly and wizardly academies that lay outside the city walls also on the south end of the settlement facing away from the Aldion River, which separated the cleared arable landscape and the city from the great northern coastal forests, which were largely inhabited by the Nordlings.

Both the priestly and wizardly academies were of somewhat average size for Citadellan religious and scholarly sites. However, there were several adjacent buildings that were well guarded and served as museums or knowledge repositories, including libraries. These religious and academic temple complexes housed various volumes of ancient and contemporary knowledge, religious texts, as well as rare exquisite experimental contraptions and rare enchanted items that few had ever laid eyes upon. Among them stood the rare prototype skyship contraption that combined elements of batlike wings along with a prototype rotor with a screw in the shape of a spiraling helix soft woven material mounted to a frame to secure it. These items were devised by a great deceased scholar who had migrated to Aldion many years ago from the kingdom capital. His contraptions though experimental were never fully mastered and demonstrated successfully in practice. Only the wise scholar's contraption of a hot air balloon that induced heat into a special cloth bag to displace and fly high in the air had been successful enough for wizards to alter with the use of their magic while mounting such contraptions onto rigged-hull ships with a caravel or galley design to enable the normally sea-traveling ships to be refurbished for traveling in the sky such as in the case of the one used by Wyatt the Wizard.

Indeed, only a few dozen skyships had been in use, and all of them were commissioned strictly for the service of those under the king's command, including most notably wizards, but also priests and some high-ranking military provincials that ruled various Swordbane settlements on behalf of the king's authority. Typically, only one of these recently adopted and fitted contraptions were allotted for each of the rulers of the settlements except for Sanctum Novus, which was remote and had not yet received such an imposing platform of flight. The exception to that allotment had been in both Aldion and Citadella Neapola, as both were prominent enough to be allotted six each of these flying platforms. Aldion even had these contraptions deployed in the nighttime sky, hovering above the fortified settlement to assist in scouting and patrolling for any possible threats of intrusion and invasion that would be posed outside the fortified settlement's walls and its outer dwellings.

The night was as typical as any, with nothing seeming to stand out as eventful even for the city guards garrisoning small settlement city walls, the outside major dwellings, and the patrolling skyships high in the air. However, that was suddenly about to change.

At nearly the same time, small bright and lit portals began to open with emerging figures stepping out onto the deck of each of the locally garrisoned skyships. A ragtag combination of orcs, goblins, and even both

Nordling barbarians and intimidating armored knights of the Black Wolf order had boarded the ships and quickly attacked the Aldion guard crews on board. The fighting became fearsome, and as soon as the first several defending guards called out, the rest of the settlement reacted with a sudden and loud burst call to arms while sounding the alarm bells and trumpets.

Gradually, more and more of the same attacking forces teleported to board and overwhelm the defending occupants of the multiple skyships. Eventually, the attackers prevailed and had hijacked, or for a comprehensive term of description, skyjacked, all the skyships. As the city garrison of armed guards and local stationed battalion prepared to make sense of what unfolded while responding, the skyships had drifted together away from the city and toward the ocean, which was a relatively short distance from the settlement, which was next to and in which the Aldion River bled out to the ocean to form a small but still sizable delta or river mouth. The Aldion garrison, though large, had only a small sizable complement of three galleys at a dock near the river just north of the militarized settlement.

It was a brutal and ruthless invasion that was carefully planned and devastatingly delivered a painful blow to the local Swordbane settlement. Hiding under the thicket barrier of forest trees north of the river and city walls, Dux Decius stood ready as he waited his turn to teleport to one of the skyships along with his wizard consul, Agaroman. In another moment while flashing before the tree covering, the two of them had boarded one of the skyships that had just been fully overtaken by the dux's initial assault force of the skyship.

The dux quickly proceeded to direct the new commanding crew to make preparations for changing course to a flanking crescent to go around the periphery of the enemy settlement to avoid fire and damage from the local forces below that were armed with mounted flaming siege munitions. In due time, the floating skyship arrived at its intended point of destination, about less than two kilometers away south of the city's wall and looking down above the famous wizard and priest complex outside the city gates.

Decius quickly motioned to Agaroman that he was ready, and within a sudden moment, the wizard and chief advisor had opened a portal to teleport both of them along with a small contingent of Decius's Remnant coalition forces and Decius's personal dire wolf. At a sudden instant, the dux, his chief wizard, and the small contingent arrived on the surface grass fields within several hundred yards away from the closest of the two complex schools, the priest temple academy. With Decius's sword raised high in the air, the dux gave a large howl, and while mounted on his dire wolf, he charged forward with his contingent to follow the dux's destructive path. Rushing violently like a tempest battering a small rowboat, the dux's forces had mercilessly slaughtered the defending complex guards as well as assigned priests of the temple who chose to stand guard while others fled to alert the city garrison of a surprised attack.

After viciously slaughtering and pillaging the temple academy with his small raiding party, the dux quickly rallied and diverted his combined surviving contingent of goblin marauders, Sanctum Novus Citadellan infantry, and Nordling barbarian auxiliary to next charge forth to the adjacent wizard academy.

The wizard academy was fairly well-defended in not only having a small but formidable complement of city guards but also a dozen or so powerful wizards who cast various spells of magic projectiles to fight against the dux's forces. From a distance, Agaroman had cast various bolts of lightning as well as fireballs toward the defending wizards. Some of the defending wizards were felled by Agaroman's spell-casting, while Decius and his forces slaughtered the rest of them. Though triumphant, Decius had sustained losses with only three of his contingent, all Citadellan infantry, surviving in addition to himself and Agaroman by the time that they penetrated the outside of the wizard academy and made their way inside to the museum compound. Once inside, two wizards hid and emerged suddenly to cast projectile spells toward the remaining invaders. They failed, with Agaroman casting a bolt of lightning at one of them while teleporting Decius right behind the other wizard. Decius quickly struck the unsuspecting wizard as the latter suddenly turned and realized with sheer fear and terror that the dux had dealt his fatal blow.

Suddenly, with a weird feeling of satisfaction and out-of-body experience of cryptic voices murmuring in pleasure, Decius turned all around himself, trying to detect who it was and the direction it came from in order to slay any remaining wizards that lied in wait. He could still hear the voices, and while not fully understanding what they claimed, his body and his mind felt a weird sense of completeness as well as a sense of being called upon without knowing who it was.

Agaroman had observed, and he could sense that something was calling to and trying to draw in the dux. It had taken hold of the dux's mind, commanding attention. The other three Citadellan infantry loyal to Decius looked at each other as well as Agaroman while pondering what they were seeing as either erratic behavior of the dux or possibly if the dux had detected another defending foe that they had not yet slain. Agaroman addressed the three of them to tell them that it was time. Dux Decius had finally slaughtered enough of his enemies for the divine spirits of Calu and Laran to call upon him and give him an audience. Both spirits were pleased by the amount of war and death Decius had given them to grant the dux an audience and make his intentions known to them. It would be Decius's opportunity to finally pursue and attain the prophecy of becoming their mutually chosen vessel.

The three Citadellans, who were familiar with their dux's profession of leading them to greatness and vaguely familiar with the prophecy, did not know whether to fully believe in such prophecy as truth or myth, but now after seeing what had taken hold and almost possession of their leader, they were convinced the prophecy that their dux sought to fulfill was indeed true even if they did not fully understand it. All three of Citadellan soldiers knelt before the dux, and Agaroman approached Decius with solemn respect. The wizard placed his arm on the dux's shoulder as Decius turned, still somewhat shocked and trying to make sense of the mysterious voices that he heard. He felt their calling like a compass in which some out–of–body sense directed him to turn slightly southeast. Seeing Agaroman's hand on his shoulder, Decius confided that he could hear voices calling to him. Agaroman nodded and told his lord that he knew that these were the voices of the spirits of both Calu and Laran calling to Decius. It was his time to now go before them and lay claim to fulfilling the prophecy on behalf of both of them. Decius also nodded and told his wizard mentor and advisor that he knew where to go not by map or compass, but by the feeling and calling that took hold of his body. Agaroman nodded again while pointing out that the direction that the dux felt compelled to take and answer that call from the two respective divine spirits while paying homage would likely be the infamous volcano called Mount Inferno. It was a frequently active volcano that lay halfway between Citadella Neapola and the ruined ancient Lupercalian city of Imperia Capitolina. The dux nodded while agreeing.

Another short time later, after securing the historical contraptions of flight displayed from the museum compound of the wizard academy, Decius and his three Citadellan infantrymen teleported along with

Agaroman through a spell-casted portal. On the other side of an opening portal, they returned to the skyship from which they previously departed, while taking in tow the artifact flight prototypes. This was one of the two objectives the wizard had in mind that he would replicate the prototypes to use in the imperial Remnant's future platforms of flight design. The other objective Agaroman had in mind was to convince Decius to select Aldion as the first settlement to bring havoc to the major Swordbane coastal cities to elevate the dux's standing, attaining further favor among the most feared spirit deities of the religious pantheon prior to unleashing their combined powers infused into Decius. Consequently, it now had finally worked, and both Calu and Laran had called mutually to the dux.

As the fortress city of Aldion burned from scattered fires below caused by the Remnant invaders, Agaroman along with a select small group of well-trained goblin shamans began teleporting the surviving forces of the dux while having the stolen skyships change course due north across the river and float high above the dark forest that made its seemingly endless track also going northward. Eventually when the skyships were far away enough not to be visible from the city, they would change course once again and go east before changing course again and going southeast toward Mount Inferno while still staying away from the visibility of the city guard of Aldion. This tactic of changing course was devised by Decius, who wanted to mislead the enemy if they pursued them into Nordling territory to possibly take the risk of being ambushed by Nordlings or if they ventured far enough to possibly find themselves overwhelmed by the dux's forces that were already besieging the settlement of Barbarum Tribus Wald, which lay south of Aegir-Hafn and was considered a way-stop for those brave-enough merchants who sought to do trade about seventy miles inland from the coast on their way up north to Aegir-Hafn. The dux's real, now-revealed destination, Mount Inferno, was one that Decius was determined to pursue without making it noticeable for any would-be foes to follow and oppose him attaining his ultimate calling, to be the chosen vessel receiving the essence of Calu and Laran and ascend to a new and higher position of what many would consider near-godhood.

CHAPTER THIRTY-ONE

Chosen Vessel of War and Death

At sunset a day later, six skyships hovered in the smoky and ash-filled sky high above the infamous active and perpetually slow-flowing volcano, Mount Inferno. Several figures had teleported from one of the skyships above down to the nestled entrance of the terrifying volcanic mountain. An ancient decorated portico in the Lupercalian-Citadellan motif framed the entrance to the inner volcano chasm that was carved long ago with a descending causeway tunnel. The figures made their way through the causeway tunnel to a special large hanging balcony flat-grate platform suspended above the hot magma chamber. In the middle of the balcony stood a small gazebo-like shrine. The shrine itself had a miniature portico-like motif with a table mount, but it was empty.

The figures that entered the balcony platform chamber through the causeway tunnel proceeded to surround the shrine. Among them, Decius and Agaroman came forward before the shrine and, from a beautiful lightly packed chest, took out various items to prepare for the ritual. Among the items were two figures: one an anthropomorphic wolflike figure representing Calu and the second a flaming-sword miniature figure that affixed vertically pointing down to a mounted stand, representing Laran and his sword. Additionally, Decius and Agaroman also withdrew an elegant silver chalice along with a beautiful glass bottle of Citadellan red wine, a beautiful incense burner brazier made of copper and shaped in the Citadellan style of an urn, and finally, twined white sage sticks packed in bundles.

Agaroman supervised while Decius methodically prepared the incense burner by pointing one of the bundles of sage for Agaroman to light the flame with his staff. Decius immediately placed it in the urn along with the other sage bundles that stood at the center of the altar table mount with both the representative symbols of Calu and Laran positioned to each side of the urn with the burning incense.

A moment later, the dux poured from the bottle red wine into the silver chalice while chanting several invocations calling to both Calu and Laran. In another moment, Decius poured the red wine from the chalice intermittently into the urn with the sage sticks used for incense already burning. Each time, a puff of rising smoke would rise from the intermittent pouring. After the tenth time, Decius quickly drank the remaining wine in the chalice while waiting to see if his invocation calling to Calu and Laran had worked. Agaroman waited anxiously as well, while the two figures that stood behind, none other than the goblin chief shaman and the orcish war chief of Uruk Kazaht stared at each other, wondering if the invocation would work and eager to witness their leader realizing the prophecy to make war and death become one as its chosen vessel.

Moments later, as Decius sighed, still patient and confident that he was worthy to pursue such a divine audience, two bright energy-like globes appeared before the altar. One globe was a black sparkling mist that stood in front of the statue of Calu's image representation. The other globe, a bright flaming pool of crimson like blood stood in front of the image representation of Laran. Both globes of powerful aura spoke in one simultaneous and unified voice. The voice stated acknowledgment that they had been summoned and demanding for the person who had summoned them to stand forth before them and their altar while the respective summoner would state his purpose.

Decius did so and proclaimed that he had received their invitation, their calling of him recognizing the dux's achievement to devote so much war and death in their name that both of the divine spirits would accept the dux's offering of himself to be their chosen vessel and endow the dux with their merged infused powers to make war and death become one with Decius.

After a moment of silence, both globes spoke in unison once again, acknowledging that Decius had indeed done well to honor both divine spirits, war and death, to receive their blessing and conferment in selecting him as their chosen vessel. However, the unison-speaking voice from both divine spirits called upon the dux to make one final sacrifice for each, war and death.

Decius nodded with determination though internally holding some sense of remorse. He turned back toward Agaroman while confirming that his wizard advisor was right. Decius had to make his final two sacrifices and ones worthy to demonstrate his devotion to receive each deity's blessing and conferment of divine power. The dux called upon both the orc war chief and the goblin chief shaman with a voice of firm determination as well as lamentation. Both Decius and Agaroman had planned this possibility and let the orc war chief and goblin chief shaman know ahead of time that their sacrifice given their stature would be necessary if called upon in order for Decius to satisfy the deity spirits and ascend to deity-like status.

They all looked at each other and knew what to do despite the feeling of hesitancy that each had. Waiting for the orc war chief to nod as well as the goblin chief shaman, when they did so, Decius unsheathed his blade instantly and the orc war chief did the same with his weapon just barely to parry the dux's first strike. The two of them engaged in a quick ferocious sword fight. As formidable as the orc war chief was, Decius eventually overtook and bested him while striking one piercing fatal blow to the orc's abdomen. The orc fell down to the ground in a growing pool of black orcish blood while Decius kneeled down and prayed before the dying orc, with the dux saying that he would ensure that the orc's sacrifice would have meaning and the dux would lead his beastly race of orcs along with the goblins, trolls, and the united dark forces of humans to dominate the world and bring a new era of empire. The orc spouted out blood, struggling but managing to say in his own tongue that he knew and believed as such.

After mourning for the loss of one of his best lieutenants, Decius rose and turned facing toward the goblin chief shaman. The holy goblin kneeled, and speaking in its own tongue while looking intently and sadistically proud of the dux, he stated how proud he was to serve alongside the dux, including the first time they encountered each other and fought together for survival against the Nordling barbarians of Barbarum Aries. The goblin went on to say he was proud to have such an honor, to be chosen for a role like this so that the dux would be elevated as chosen vessel for the deity spirits of war and death. Decius nodded while pointing his sword and replying mournfully that he would remember both the goblin shaman and the orc war chief for what they had done, sacrificing their lives for his cause to become the dark lord and chosen vessel. He pleaded in earnest hope for both of his now-slain devoted servants of darkness to find a new position of standing in the dark void to the underworld of the afterlife and awaiting the dux to rule them there in the life to come one day. The goblin shaman once again with sadistic delight nodded and closed his eyes. In another moment, Decius plunged his sword upon the goblin shaman, piercing his heart. The goblin, still on his knees, fell forward and bled in its own dark pool of blood. Decius held on to him afterward until his passing, upon which, the dux rose up and unleashed a harrowing wolflike howl of anger and passion.

He had no qualms killing those he considered his enemy, but it tore him to make such sacrifices among his most devoted followers to appease these deity spirits and receive their approval, blessing, and conferment for him to be their chosen vessel. Seeing a hand upon his shoulder, the dux turned and glanced at Agaroman offering consolation, telling Decius he had done admirably in fulfilling his calling, given the difficulty and circumstances in sacrificing those warriors close to him. Decius nodded solemnly before turning away to face the deity spirits. The dux, looking and still mourning over the slain corpses of his two lieutenants, instructed Agaroman to summon several of the soldiers to retrieve their bodies to prepare for a funeral pyre at Uruk Kazaht on their return trip to Sanctum Novus. Decius would see to it that he would personally give these two slain devout followers of his a full proper funeral ceremony with honors and personally light the torch to their funeral pyres. Agaroman nodded while motioning for several soldiers from the distance to retrieve the slain orc war captain and goblin chief shaman's bodies.

In another moment, the deity spirits spoke again and stated jointly again in a voice of unison that Decius had demonstrated his piety and devotion to be their chosen vessel receiving the merged powers of both Calu and Laran. Instantly, a ray of energy came forth from each globe of the respective divine spirit to touch Decius. Both globes sent forth their auras of mystifying power that encapsulated Decius in a bright flash. So bright was it that Agaroman as well as several dozen of the Remnant soldiers who observed as spectators and witnesses to this divine event had to cover and turn away from the immense luminosity of this deity-like transfiguration (which many on the side of noble good would probably consider as being more demonic).

Emerging from the bright flash stood Decius still wearing his military regalia and armor but drenched in a thick covering of blood and a black mist that emanated from under him. Agaroman and the Remnant soldiers that were present uncovered their eyes, amazed at what they had seen. The globes of the divine spirits had disappeared. Alone stood Decius, who felt the overwhelming power of the effects of the transformation and kneeled down on both his knees. He groaned with some pain that seemed to subside while he took a breath before unleashing a terrifying loud howl. It was one unlike the ones he had given before, including summoning dire wolves to fight by his side. This howl had a frightening demonic echo that made even the volcano of Mount Inferno seem to tremble in fear.

In another moment, a whirling combination of dark shadowlike mist, splashes of blood, and embers of fire shrouded Decius like an encapsulating shield. Immediately taking shape to appear before him, a nearly pitch-black, charred, and jagged gigantic anthropomorphic man-wolf figure burning with an aura of flames around its body appeared. Standing dozens of feet tall, this immense figure moved with the concentrated thoughts that seemed to be communicated through Decius, who was in a deep meditative trancelike state inside this horrifying globe-shaped capsule. This colossal man-wolf, or werewolf, had many of the characteristics described in ancient text, and many of the spectators from Decius's army that witnessed this event could not hold back from speculating if this was possibly the rebirth or return of a Lupercalian from long ago.

The audible voices and whispers among the dux's army came to a screeching halt when they had saw this anthropomorphic hellish dark man-wolf unleash a howl shockingly identical to the one they heard Decius give just before. This hellish werewolf turned around, looking about its surroundings and looking at its own jagged sharp claws before turning to see various figures of the spectators, including a wizard that was closest to this werewolf. The werewolf quickly turned to look back at the spectral globe surrounding the Citadellan warlord, only to be in shock when it realized that this warlord was feeding it his thoughts, his movements, and even his feelings. They were one and the same, with the werewolf being a spectral avatar projection of the warlord and his thoughts translating into commands. This beast howled once again before turning again to look at the multitude of spectators, soldiers loyal to this warlord. Then a voice came out, and it greeted this figure with a handlike gesture and bow being extended before it. This figure was a dark-robed bald wizard. It was his advisor and mentor, Agaroman. He recognized him and nodded, calling out his name.

Agaroman rising from his bow, looked at the hellish werewolf while smiling humbly and with confidence, bidding welcome to his lord, Dux Decius. The wizard congratulated the dux, stating that it had worked. The Dux had now ascended into a walking, living near-deity and prophet-like status in the form of a powerful summoned spectral avatar that assumed a corporeal bodily state and served as the projection of the dux's own mind and will. The werewolf nodded while speaking in a tone like the dux's, though in a somewhat demonic like manner.

Agaroman walked beside it while conversing, and the wizard had asked his lord what the transformation and conferment had felt like. Taking a pause, Decius, speaking in his meditative thoughts through the hellish werewolf, replied that it had felt a state of completeness and utter fulfillment. The wizard grinned while nodding.

The crowd of spectators, all soldiers and followers of the dux, had erupted in cheers and howls of their own. For the first time, they had witnessed the likes of power that they had never seen before, as dark and evil as in the form that it came in. Decius's spectral avatar looked about his followers that spectated in awe while the dux proclaimed with the avatar's voice and tone that finally it was over and the time was now. The prophecy had been fulfilled, and there was no stopping Decius and his army of darkness to conquer Swordbane and bring about a new age, a new empire in resemblance to what the Lupercalian Empire from long ago had once been.

CHAPTER THIRTY-TWO

Following the Tracks of Darkness

Two days had passed since the Remnant's raid on Colonia Aldion. Though the fortress city was sacked and partially razed, it still stood. Many of the Remnant forces pulled out after the raid and withdrew north of the Aldion River either by teleporting to the stolen skyships that sailed away or by the staged boats and small naval ships that entered the river through the mouth of the river that bled out to the ocean. Many of the water-bound vessels were crewed and led by pirates. One of them, the legendary Captain Babok, was recruited by Dux Decius himself who made an alliance with Babok to be hired for conducting the raid in exchange for being entitled to a large portion of the raid loot and be allowed to keep a small retainer of goblin and barbarian Nordlings to stay assigned under the pirate captain's command for future raids along the Aldion River. There were many small settlements south along the river in addition to the main settlement of Colonia Aldion.

During the two days that passed, however, Aldion managed to dispatch a small contingent of couriers with a sealed written message from the settlement's governor and acting provincial regent, requesting aid directly from the king in Citadella Neapola. A series of connected rest stop stage posts were devised every thirty miles between each major settlement along the King's Road and the distance between the major Swordbane settlements was three hundred and sixty miles. With the dispatched couriers switching horses at each rest stop while traveling at roughly twenty-five to thirty miles an hour, it took nearly the first day for King Ascentius to receive the message of the raid at Aldion. The king immediately summoned Linitus and his daughter Marin along with their fellow comrades Peat and Wyatt.

After a briefing of the company of heroes at the king's throne room, the group of heroes with haste made last-minute preparations before departing in Wyatt's skyship. Along with the hero company, the king had deployed a contingent of royal infantry soldiers and knights from the Eternal Flame order along with a small cadre of elven rangers and several priests of healing to tend to the wounded casualties from the raid as well as the departed. The king himself ultimately decided to address this matter directly in order to shore up morale of his subjects, despite considering the advice of both Linitus and Marin to not risk exposing himself to a possible ambush. Marin offered to represent the king in his stead while assisting and providing whatever support they could to Aldion.

Ultimately with the king also departing to Aldion, he summoned additional forces for protection, including another contingent of Eternal Flame knights and a small cadre of his most trusted dwarven guardians. With sizable forces, the king had a separate skyship hastily provisioned and readied for departure along with Wyatt's skyship. By nightfall more than two days after the raid at Aldion, the two skyships had departed, though Wyatt's skyship, being more prepared, had a head start and departed during late dusk.

As Wyatt's skyship departed high above the majestic skyline overlooking the cosmopolitan Citadella Neapola, Marin and Linitus made the most of their circumstances and their next venture to enjoy the view in passing while sharing their intimacy in a stream-of-thought conversation about their views on both the current situation and what their future together would bring. They both confided the uncertainty of the times they lived in while admitting that despite the hardships, they would find a way to prevail. Marin expressed that as the war with Sanctum Novus dragged on and with the various maneuvers that Decius devised along the way, she felt as if they were ultimately following the tracks into darkness. Linitus agreed but assured her that they had made it this far, surviving and being triumphant, and they surely would do so again as long as they held true to their convictions and did not give into despair. Both of them embraced each other for another moment before standing up to recompose themselves while having a briefing from Peat and Wyatt about the skyship's status and operational ability after the dwarf guardian and halfling wizard had supervised and familiarized the new temporary assigned crew of knights and ranger archers about the ship.

By early midday on the second day following the raid on Aldion, both skyships had arrived, hovering above and edging closer to the settlement that loomed below. The sky, though still somewhat smoky, was less so compared to the previous two days following the nighttime raid. Many of the buildings, both inside the fortress city walls and outside, including the complexes of the wizard and priest academies, were ravaged and in need of repair. Roughly half of the city buildings survived in good condition without being affected by the scattered torch fires that Decius's forces had inflicted on the night of the raid.

Linitus imagined how beautiful and serene the city and its surrounding buildings might have looked before and could tell from the expression of sadness on Marin's face and her heartbroken reaction. It truly was a loss (even if partial) that weighed heavily on her. Marin admitted with tears that she had some fond memories of the settlement when she was younger and frequently traveled there with her father. It was a prized place of learning as well as one of the few places that Nordlings from the barbarian tribes had traveled to engage in trade and foster some degree of peaceful relations with the kingdom.

Marin even recalled to her elven lover that this was the place that her father had first laid eyes upon her mother when they negotiated a peace treaty with Aegir-Hafn, the home of Marin's mother. Now, Marin, shaking and saddened, saw it as another symbolic memento that tore into her consciousness and scarred one of the most peaceful places she had treasured from her childhood. It was another reminder of a greater loss that she could never forget: her mother Gretchen.

Linitus held her in his arms to provide comfort while listening calmly. He did not know what to say at that moment, and he resolved with his own sense of empathy that this would be a moment when words were perhaps not needed to soothe the pain of the one that he loved intimately. He held on to her long enough until she was ready to compose herself and let go.

Marin knew it also and, appreciating his sense of compassion, gave him a brief kiss before letting go and thanking him for being the one that she needed in her own times of sorrow, thanking him for being the one that the divine spirits had sent to her. She wanted to let him know and did so, telling him that he was an angel to her that was sent from the divine above and he saved her not only physically from harm, but also emotionally and mentally in supporting her.

He was the only one that she could truly feel comfortable and open up to about her feelings despite the posture and persona she portrayed in being a stately member of royalty and a knight that was perceived and expected to not give way to expressing any vulnerable sense of emotion. She carried and exhibited that to everyone, even her own father. However, it was not so with Linitus. He was a teacher of life experiences as well as spiritual and emotional outlook, so she was learning to appreciate life in a way that was immersive and pure, from the politics and violence she had become accustomed to. She knew it would never be something that she could fully escape, but with him, life was less lonely and she could draw from appreciating the innocence that he saw and shared with the natural surroundings. It was truly rewarding.

CHAPTER THIRTY-THREE

Hoisted by His Own Lust for Loot

After teleporting to the surface below, King Ascentius and the company of heroes were briefed by the provincial governor of Aldion about what transpired since the night of the raid. The dispatched forces of the two skyships assisted the city in various ways, including clearing some of the rubble from the buildings that gave way and collapsed from the fires as well as the deployed priests who assisted the populace of Aldion by providing various forms of medical assistance, including remedies for the wounds that had been inflicted on those from the settlement who had been fortunate enough to survive despite being wounded.

When one of Aldion's local scouts mounted on horseback had returned from surveying the surrounding countryside south of the river, the scout reported to the present company of the settlement's governor, the king, and the heroes of the Order of Comradery that happened to be present about sighting several pirate ships that raided some surrounding Citadellan and Nordling hamlets along both ends of the river going eastward both inland and upstream. The scout was eager to convince the heroes of the Comradery to follow his lead in pursuing the pirates from their last known whereabouts. With the nod from the king giving his approval, the heroes immediately prepared to set off and mounted three of the local provisioned horses. Linitus, seemingly cautious, told Wyatt to stay behind while awkwardly motioning with his eyes in an upward direction toward the skyship. The young halfling wizard nodded and prepared to teleport to the skyship but only after his three hero companions had departed Aldion from its city gates while following the scout who took the lead.

Only a few hours had passed when the scout stopped up ahead at a hamlet of a few Nordling round makeshift hut-like structures that lay ahead. Though the Nordlings typically resided north of the riverbank, a few of barbarian tribal clans that were friendly to the kingdom were permitted to stay on the south side of the bank as was the case with this particular hamlet. The hamlet's huts stood in front of the river's south bank while behind, only several hundred yards, three pirate vessels stood on the riverfront. One of them was of the exotic Marjawani design while the other two appeared to be Citadellan galleys of the commercial type.

The scout motioned for the three heroes, Linitus, Marin, and Peat, to still follow him. Linitus, however, suddenly motioned for his two companions to halt while quickly dismounting and drawing back his bow with an arrow from his quiver pointed straight at the back of the scout. His two companions looked at him with utter shock, wondering what he was doing. The elf ranger quickly called out loudly and inquisitively to the scout, asking who paid him and how much he had been paid to deliver the heroes to the pirates. The scout, looking back with a shocked, amazed, and dumbfounded facial expression, could not believe that the elf ranger had realized the ruse. Linitus pointed out the makeshift huts of the hamlet had no occupants or any signs of prior ambush, including damage to the hamlet or slain bodies. He knew that something was out of place and the scout had possibly misled them and that these makeshift huts were possibly made by the ambushing party themselves. The scout's reaction quickly turned to anger and resentment while replying that he had been paid well and treated far better in the service of Dux Decius and the Remnant than the meager station he had in being a loyal subject to the crown. Marin and Peat, still in shock, quickly composed themselves and dismounted while equipping their respective weapons and now were poised to support their fellow hero companion, Linitus, against their would-be attackers.

Linitus called out again to the scout that it was his move first. The scout, still mounted on horseback and wielding a spear in hand, pressed forward with his steed to charge at the heroes and was prepared to hurl the spear at them, but Linitus had let loose his bow and arrow to strike down the traitor. Immediately following, several Nordling warriors from the Barbarum Aries tribe lying in wait quickly darted out of their makeshift huts and charged at the heroes while unleashing their own frantic war cries. As they were doing so, the pirate ships' crew with ship-mounted siege weapons fired toward the heroes. Linitus aimed high in the air and let loose a flashing arrow that sparked bright in the sky. This was his cue to Wyatt, who was on board the skyship floating high above from a distance to come to their aid in fighting the ambushers below. The wizard teleported immediately down to the surface right in front of his comrades and quickly cast a spell with his wand to emit a large-enough bubble-like shield to protect himself and his companions from the oncoming projectiles. Meanwhile, Linitus had told Wyatt to transport the company of heroes to the main pirate vessel. Wyatt, with the flick of his wand, had done so.

In a sudden flash, the heroes found themselves hundreds of yards away on board the deck of the large Marjawani dhow vessel near the bow of the ship, staring in front a crowd of thirty confused pirate crew members that included a mixture of Marjawani pirates along with some of their newly allied barbarian and goblin soldiers who were assigned by their dark lord dux to serve and assist the Marjawani pirate captain in raiding and pillaging the river settlement and hamlets. The pirate crew's expressions changed from confusion to visible anger, while in another moment, walking before them was a somewhat large and burly Marjawani man wielding a big ornate iron mace and wearing various elaborate pieces of jewelry along his neck and wrists while sporting a flashy vest that left his chest otherwise bare. He also wore black trousers and leather boots along with a noticeable decorative green-and-yellow turban embellished with a large ornate feather and ruby gem on the front of his turban. Though Linitus was unfamiliar, Marin and Peat knew from the tales that this was none other than the legendary Captain Babok, the infamous pirate scourge of three western seas.

Needless to say, Babok had heard of their reputation as much as Marin and Peat knew his. The pirate captain was delighted and haughty while laughing intermittently that he had finally met the heroes of Swordbane whom his new employer and contact, Decius, had warned him about, causing a fair amount of inconvenience to the dux's plans. The pirate captain demanded that the four heroes surrender while laying down their weapons. Babok would consider being merciful enough to take them as prisoners to offer as a gift to the dux. Linitus admitted that he had no idea who Babok was, nor did the elf ranger care, but he would make the same offer to the pirate captain and his crew to surrender freely to stand judgment before the king. Babok laughed and proclaimed loudly that this would be an interesting fight for him to engage in while being pleased to know that he would have an opportunity to find a worthy match to contend against. Marin replied by letting the pirate captain know that he was not in their league to compare and it would be the pirate crew's own funeral if they did not reconsider offering their surrender.

The two opposing forces stood still, eager and waiting for the other side to make the first move while possibly leaving a vulnerability exposed. Babok made the first move while raising his mace to prepare to take full swing in mid-charge toward Linitus. The other pirates followed suit, each picking their own target among the four heroes. Peat quickly dropped a round oil barrel that he withdrew from his back pole-mount bracket. The dwarf guardian kicked it quickly along the deck of the ship while shouting for Wyatt to shoot at it. The wizard did so, causing a small explosion on the deck of the ship that took out at least four of the crew members.

Meanwhile, Linitus had quickly drawn three arrows and shot them with haste toward Babok and two other pirates. Babok narrowly dodged one of the arrows, while two of his other crew members from behind him were not as fortunate and were struck down. Linitus quickly ducked while the pirate captain took another swing at the elf ranger. Immediately while in a low ducking position, the elf ranger dropped his bow, spun, and tripped the pirate captain, while quickly unsheathing his elven long blade. By the time he pointed his blade toward Babok, the pirate captain had already rolled across the deck and quickly picked himself up while a goblin and a large Nordling barbarian with their weapons in hand charged at the elf ranger. Linitus quickly parried their attacks.

As fierce fighting ensued on board Babok's dhow, the heroes, despite facing initial overwhelming odds and resistance, swiftly and effectively took down Babok's pirate crew to the point that only Babok and three of his crew members were the only ones still fighting against the heroes. Wyatt had shifted his focus to spell-casting multiple fireballs toward the other two adjacent pirate vessels before they were able to effectively moor along the port and starboard sides of Babok's ship and replenish their complement of pirates to assist Babok in fighting off the heroes. Instead, the two other ships caught fire, and the pirates on board, filled with panic, leaped overboard the two ships to swim away to the north bank of the river. Two of the pirates each engaged in fighting Linitus and Peat.

Captain Babok, ever known for his trickery and dirty fighting, grabbed one of his pirate crew and swung him toward Marin, briefly catching her off guard. She reacted defensively by bracing for the impact with her shield to rebuff and knock the oncoming pirate down hard with her shield. However, in that brief moment as she had done so, Babok quickly went around her flank and grabbed her while pulling a dagger close against her throat. He held her firmly while standing and turning toward her comrades in arms.

The pirate captain now commanded the other three to put down their weapons. Linitus, however, aimed his bow and arrow carefully toward the pirate captain's skull, which was slightly exposed behind Marin's head. Babok knew this and tried to position himself with the least amount of exposure possible, making Linitus's aim to let loose an arrow to strike the pirate captain nearly impossible. As they each stood poised and posturing toward each other, Marin called out, telling Linitus to take the shot. However, Babok and the elf ranger both knew the overwhelming challenge and risk. The pirate captain mocked Linitus and dared him to take the shot also. Linitus held his posture, still tense and uncertain on how to proceed before devising a hastily improvised solution. He smiled and then asked, looking toward Marin, about how good a catch she was. Marin and even her then-temporary captor looked confused before Marin realized what Linitus was going to do. She replied, smiling back, that her catch was as good as ever. Linitus nodded before aiming low and only faintly pulling back to shoot off one of his arrows. When the arrow soared flimsily across the air while dropping only about less than two and a half feet above the deck of the ship, Marin had caught it in midair and jabbed the arrowpoint straight to the upper right thigh of Babok. The pirate captain lost his grip while giving in to the pain from the arrow that Marin had caught in midair and used to stab her now-former captor. Immediately, Marin turned around and gave a knee-busting action toward the groin of Babok, causing the pirate captain to collapse down on the ground in further pain. While in pain, Babok soon found himself in chain shackles that Wyatt had teleported and cast onto the pirate captain. Peat waited another brief moment before yanking Babok off the deck of his own ship and formally announcing that the pirate captain would face trial by the king for his involvement in recent raiding and ambushing as well as for past piracy and smuggling activities.

Linitus saw Marin in a somewhat shocked state, still coming to terms with how close she was to facing sheer death, at the mercy of a deadly and infamous pirate. They both embraced each other while Linitus assured her that it was over and she had done well on her part to outdo the pirate captain despite his trickery and cleverness in catching her briefly occupied and off guard. Marin shook her head to acknowledge what Linitus had said to her and stated that she knew. The two embraced each other one more time before composing themselves and focusing on the next course of action from the aftermath of defeating the pirate raiders.

Linitus instructed that it was up to them to not only take Babok as prisoner before the king, but also search the pirate captain's ship for any possible valuable information. Just as in the case of the Dreadful Knight's camp having important documents locked in a box like a treasure chest, Babok possessed several large locked treasure chests. Linitus had Wyatt take the locked chests to teleport on board the skyship with their newfound pirate captain prisoner.

Once on board the skyship, the heroes secured Babok in one of the brig prison cells. Linitus took his time with his special set of lockpick key tools to unlock the chests to acquire any valuable information and items that were inside. The contents that Linitus had found included several written letters. Of particular importance was a letter of instructions with the dux's signature, about the orders by the dux for Babok to stay behind to further pillage the nearby countryside south of the Aldion River while the remaining forces would split up and go north to assist in the assault against Barbarum Tribus Wald. Tribus Wald was a well-known barbarian settlement located north of Aldion and serving as roughly the halfway point between Colonia Aldion and Aegir-Hafn, including as a way-stop when it came to travel and commercial trade between these respective settlements.

This news of recent developments and correspondence between the dark lord Dux and one of his chief lackeys startled the heroes as they read the letter. Although they did not consider the Nordling barbarian tribes that lived outside the boundaries of the kingdom as close allies, they now realized that Decius was hell-bent on not only taking over the Kingdom of Swordbane but also the western continental lands of Hesperion as a whole and possibly the known world. Marin confided to Linitus that they had to not only present this news to the king along with taking Babok back as prisoner, but it was imperative that they also urge the king to send his forces to Tribus Wald's aid before Decius would conquer it and possibly force the Nordling barbarians of that settlement to submit to the dux's command.

Still, they wondered what had compelled Decius to raid Colonia Aldion while spreading his forces elsewhere in places like Tribus Wald. The skyships of that settlement that the dux had captured were certainly one reason, though they were still baffled if it was just for that reason alone or not. It was not until they read another written message signed by both Decius and Agaroman for Babok to recite before any standing forces. The message disclosed that whoever stood in the dux's way had a choice to either die or submit before this dark lord who would fulfill the prophecy to make war and death become one. Marin and Linitus were both familiar enough with the religious lore of Swordbane and of the preceding ancient Lupercalian Empire to know what that message meant. They were visibly shocked and terrified, thinking what would happen if Decius ever was able to fulfill such a powerful prophecy of being a chosen vessel.

CHAPTER THIRTY-FOUR

Into the Wilderness of War

Only after reading the notes again and more thoroughly, Linitus and his companions decided that time was of the essence. The siege of Tribus Wald had started, from what was disclosed the letters that the group of heroes had uncovered. They decided to use the skyship to sail back to Colonia Aldion to not only inform the king of this assault while transferring custody of infamous Babok, but also receive as many reinforcements as King Ascentius would provide to come to support the Nordlings of Tribus Wald against the dux's forces. Ascentius sensed the impending direness and implications. If Tribus Wald, the last known major Nordling settlement in the western lands, was to fall to Decius' forces, then not only would Decius remove a potential ally for Swordbane to use against him, but also the Remnant warlord would likely coerce the surviving Nordlings of that settlement to become his vassals or clients while supplying him with their barbarian warriors to add to the strength of his Remnant forces against Swordbane. For Ascentius, it was a shrewd but sensible calculating decision to send at least half of his forces that he arrived with to be assigned to Linitus's command.

Within mere hours, Linitus's skyship had departed Aldion almost as quickly as when the skyship had returned with the captured Captain Babok, who would be transferred under the Aldion governor's custody. During that transfer and briefing between Linitus, Marin, and the king, half of the total complement of the king's original dispatched forces made preparations and boarded the skyship via Wyatt's teleportation spell-casting.

The skyship, as soon as it had fully finished boarding the assigned soldiers and supply provisions, quickly made course due north. It would take about two hundred and seventy miles for the skyship to reach Tribus Wald. If the wind conditions fared well as they had so far, the skyship carrying Linitus, his companions, and the allocated soldiers from the king would make it to the Nordling settlement by midnight and well into nightfall.

Along the way, Linitus and Wyatt took advantage of the time as best as they could, orienting the new crew members to familiarize them with the various features of the ship, including improvised mounted siege weapons that Wyatt had installed at several locations. These siege weapon upgrades on the skyship were made when the skyship arrived at Citadella Neapola after the war against Marjawan and right after Decius's betrayal at Sanctum Novus against the king. It was Linitus and Wyatt's goal to figure out how best the king's soldiers could help in the efforts to provide assistance and relief for Tribus Wald. For them, having the soldiers master the latest siege weapons on the skyship to operate in war seemed the best course of action. While on board, Peat was teaching the soldiers about his smoking habits while also sharing war stories to serve as lessons to use and incorporate in their expected battle against Decius's forces. The dwarf rambled and reminisced a good half hour or so about the hero company's previous adventures and how they triumphed against overwhelming odds with the various skills that he, Linitus, Marin, and Wyatt had used.

Meanwhile, Marin took some other soldiers who were skilled in the use of archery to access stores of arrows that Linitus and Wyatt had stockpiled. Marin, though not skilled in archery herself, still understood and applied what she considered the practical approach of assembling archers in formation on the deck of the skyship to be prepared in releasing volleys of arrows to rain down on Decius's forces below.

After two to three hours, the crew would be broken in two watches so the crew on board (at least half of them) could rest before the impending battle to save Tribus Wald from the Remnant. Once nightfall had set in, Wyatt used only a light from his magic wand at a low-illumination setting so that the skyship would hover high in the air as quietly and visually discreet as possible without giving away their presence easily to any hostile foes below, including any scouts of the Remnant. This plan was successful as the hours passed with the skyship soaring unnoticed high above a bright patch, a series of lit torch flames below. After spotting the settlement of Tribus Wald below, Linitus motioned quietly to the rest of the ship's crew to quietly prepare to wake up their crew members and quietly prepare their arms and go to their assigned combat stations on the skyship.

It was difficult to not get spotted outright, at least not until the skyship was high enough above the likely line of fire from Decius's forces below as well as being close enough for Wyatt to prepare to teleport several crew members at a time below to the besieged Nordling settlement. Though it was too dark to clearly make out the settlement's defenses, it had two layers of palisade stake wall rings that encircled the main settlement building. That building appeared to be a Nordling chieftain's lodge and mead hall. It was large and elongated, being inside the first inner palisade wall ring, while the other settlement buildings were between the inner and outer palisade walls.

As Linitus pointed below, spotting several prominent Nordlings, who pointed back at the skyship, it was clear that they had begun to spot and take notice of the skyship with a feeling of awe and bewilderment. Seeking to relieve their concerns, Linitus had Wyatt teleport him and Marin first before teleporting the rest of the intended soldiers to come to Tribus Wald's aid.

Upon arriving near the center of the settlement and in front of the village chieftain's hold and mead hall, Linitus and Marin were greeted by two prominently dressed Nordlings, one of whom seemed to visibly recognize Marin. That prominently dressed Nordling called out Marin's name in an inquisitive and curious manner. Marin looked back and shared a similar face of shock and visible recognition. She asked if that was her aunt, Helga. The prominently dressed Nordling woman nodded while stating it was indeed her. Marin's face dropped in emotion and a longing of reconciliatory sadness. She had not seen her aunt in roughly twenty years, since the day of her mother's funeral when Helga received correspondence from one of Ascentius's dispatched couriers. Helga departed her then-ruled Nordling kingdom of Aegir-Hafn. Linitus, puzzled, quickly introduced himself to Helga while asking about how Marin knew Helga despite being so far apart. Helga paused and explained their familial connection while reflecting back on her younger years, twenty years ago.

Despite the intricacies of the political relations between the Kingdom of Swordbane and the various Nordling tribes, Aegir-Hafn with Helga as its once ruler maintained strong and well-connected relations with Swordbane. It was in fact her consent as the female chieftain of the settlement who offered her younger sister Gretchen to wed Ascentius (despite Ascentius first laying eyes on Gretchen when she accompanied Helga for a diplomatic meeting with the Swordbane King at Aldion). Upon Ascentius's first formal state visit to Aegir-Hafn, it became the rare occasion with a Swordbane monarch of the likes of Ascentius to break off from tradition and decide to marry a Nordling woman of noble status rather than one of his kingdom's local imperialistic Citadellans.

The wedding and the relationship between Ascentius and Gretchen was not without its own share of controversy then, as much as Linitus and Marin had noticed from the reactions of others in seeing them together. Over nearly a thousand years despite having male Nordling lineage, Ascentius had a stronger affinity as well as a more identifiable association of being Citadellan in nearly all aspects, including much of his mannerisms and appearance as opposed to his direct paternal pedigree line of Nordling ancestry. As such being the case, many among the Nordlings saw him (as well as several generations of his predecessors) as no longer being a worthy claimant of the Nordling royal bloodline that ruled Swordbane for over a thousand years during the fall of the once-great Lupercalian Empire. Instead, many of the Nordlings residing in their traditional lands north of the lush temperate and mediterranean coastal Citadellan settlements saw Ascentius as a claimant in name only, who had to prove his claim as being truly representative in legitimizing his reign among them, as much as he did with the Citadellans and Nordling descendants that had assimilated to Citadellan culture within the confines of the Kingdom of Swordbane, at least west of the coastal mountains that separated it from its former desert holdings, the latter of which were largely now beholden in recognizing Decius as their legitimate leader.

Helga, being the older sister and ruler of Aegir-Hafn while seeing her younger sister Gretchen long for a rulership of her own, decided to offer Gretchen the chance to marry Ascentius upon noticing the two being attracted to each other.

Despite Ascentius's purpose at the time in genuinely wanting to visit for reestablishing formalities and strengthening bonds between Swordbane and the north coastal Nordling settlement, both he and Gretchen caught each other's eye and stared at each other with intent and curiosity back when they first met at Aldion. They were both ambitious, and Ascentius could tell from Gretchen's personality that she had a longing to rule alongside a spouse if she would be proud to be called his queen. It was not long after the evening reception at the chieftain's mead hall that Gretchen found a reason to approach Ascentius in a somewhat curious and modest manner of her own perspective to personally offer the Swordbane monarch a chalice of mead and she would break into asking to join his company at the table. Ascentius accepted the offer, and the rest, many would say, was history and cemented in the two of them spending a long time socializing during the mead hall festivities to the point that they both became comfortable enough to come to an understanding that they wanted to be together one day at a time. Gretchen would find any reason for each day during Ascentius's visit at Aegir-Hafn to be close to him. Helga and nearly everyone else in the settlement clearly knew Gretchen's attraction to Ascentius, who (despite being of minute Nordling ancestry) was very much foreign and intriguing with his predominantly Citadellan background to captivate Gretchen to want to be part of his world to share it with him.

The first time she had Citadellan wine and olives while learning from Ascentius how to play the Citadellan board game of scapegoat when she visited his ship prior to his departure was enough for her to want to escape Aegir-Hafn and explore with Ascentius the many sights, smells, and enchantments that she had never seen outside the Nordling coastlands and forests. With her humble plea while confiding personally to her sister, Helga had granted Gretchen permission for Helga to make a formal request of betrothal between Ascentius and her younger sister. Ascentius, having a genuine attraction and personal interest in Gretchen, agreed while also realizing that it was a rare political opportunity to cement stronger relations between his kingdom and the Nordlings, at least the ones in Aegir-Hafn and along the western seaboard.

Only within two years of marriage did Ascentius and Gretchen have Marin as their first and only child. Upon hearing news of Marin's birth, Helga made haste personal preparations to see her younger sister and newborn niece while being received formally by Ascentius at Citadella Neapola. It was the first time that Helga had not only seen Marin but also the capital of the southern western coastal kingdom, Citadella Neapola. The second would be over five years later under less promising circumstances when Marin was a child standing alongside her father, the king, receiving various foreign and provincial officials who paid their respects at the funeral of Gretchen.

Paul Joseph Santoro Emerick

Now holding back her tears while recalling this brief story of Helga's relation to Marin, Helga, the former Nordling queen or chieftainess, returned to the present in explaining her current predicament. She had recently lost her chiefdom of Aegir-Hafn from a combined force that she thought was unfathomable: Citadellans from the Black Wolf order of knights, Nordlings from other tribes in the northern interior, and even more troubling, beastly creatures including goblins, orcs, and trolls. She went on to describe to both Linitus and Marin that she, members of her house, and several among Aegir Hafn's nobility and various warriors among Aegir-Hafn's clans had escaped on the chieftainess's longboat south to the delta and riverway leading to the nearest major friendly settlement, Tribus Wald.

Looking at the outer perimeter of the settlement with many lit torches surrounding Tribus Wald, Helga now informed Marin and Linitus that she once again was being attacked, or more properly, besieged along with the local Nordlings and the settlement's leader, Chief King Voksen, who hosted her in granting temporary refuge. Helga next introduced the local barbarian chieftain. Voksen stood tall, displaying a prominent ornate goatee along with flowing blond hair and had a muscular body disposition. He held down to the ground vertically upside down a great two-handed double-bladed war ax, though he looked as if he could easily pick it up and carry it in one hand, which he did while having it slung against his shoulder.

Linitus and Marin quickly introduced themselves to the local Nordling chieftain. The two comrades explained to both him and Helga not only their reason for being there to provide aid against the siege of Decius's combined forces, but also to explain in greater context Decius's betrayal and his pursuit of conquering and expanding his control of the western lands. Linitus explained to both Helga and Voksen that it was now more important than ever for them to work together and fight back, for not only the Kingdom of Swordbane, but also the other western lands of Hesperion to not fall into the darkness of Decius's planned new world order.

Helga and Voksen looked at each other. They both agreed while nodding. Helga, however, from having prior experience seeing how quickly with sheer dominating force the enemy forces won, cautioned to let Linitus and Marin know that in her assessment, there was no way they could permanently hold back Decius's forces from eventually overtaking the Nordling settlement in which the enemy outnumbered them roughly five

250

to one. Marin sighed from frustration, asking reflectively if there was no way to stop Decius. Linitus, putting his hand on her shoulder for comfort, told her that as long as they were still alive and fighting, there was always hope. Marin sighed more positively while nodding and placing her hand on his. She admitted he was right, while deferring to Linitus's judgment about what possible formulated plan of cunning the elf ranger had in mind.

As the elf ranger and Princess Knight interacted, both Helga and Voksen could not help but stare and be somewhat amazed at the openness and visible attraction that Linitus and Marin seemed to have for each other. Voksen, in particular, could not help but ask openly if they happened to be in love and married. Helga, somewhat shocked and feeling embarrassed by her fellow chieftain counterpart bringing up such speculation in a dire time, asked if that needed to be brought up, given the circumstances. Voksen shrugged while stating that he found it admirable though somewhat awkward and unheard of for a human, much less of partial Nordling ancestry, to be in love with an elf. He admitted it was unheard of, but such openness should be welcomed. Linitus and Marin felt awkward with Marin somewhat blushing toward the end while looking back at Linitus. Linitus, finding an opportunity to defuse the topic while shifting back to the situation at hand, briefly mentioned that the love between two can overcome many obstacles and differences when the couple is committed to a common cause in being together while letting Voksen know that just as Helga had mentioned between Gretchen and Ascentius in being attracted to each other despite being so different while finding common bonds, Marin and Linitus himself were much the same.

Helga nodded and agreed. She admitted that she herself and many Nordlings north of Swordbane in their upbringing were not accustomed to having relations with non-Nordlings, but her sister Gretchen and her brother-in-law Ascentius had made her rethink what identity means between those who are so different. A part may share a deeper appreciation of common values than they would with anyone else they may have more in common with, including same group identity. Linitus nodded while telling Helga that despite not knowing much about Nordling culture, he found many aspects of it that may have resonated with Marin and her personality, which he had come to appreciate despite their differences. Marin nodded while admitting all the same was true with respect to Linitus and his elven heritage, but more importantly, she was drawn to who he was as a person individually, more than his heritage as an elf and perhaps she was coming to understand while hearing Helga's story, a deeper aspect of how much love her mother had for her father, in a way that she never thought of before and being able to now make sense of it cathartically in her present relationship with Linitus.

While taking this moment in sharing together, there was not much time left as Tribus Wald began to shake with large flame-lit pots and stone projectiles hammering away at the ringed palisades as well as the cabin buildings of the settlement. Already, Decius's Remnant forces were using catapults to hurl and pelt at the Nordling settlement with the goal to wear down and weaken the defenses before amassing in large numbers to make a rush assault in various directions to penetrate and overrun various portions of the settlement's palisades. Linitus was quick to observe this and point it out with Helga and Voksen nodding. Unfortunately, knowing time was short, Linitus proposed that rather than making a final stand and likely falling from the large force of foes, instead the defending forces would make haste to break out from the palisades at the weakest besieged point closest to the most covered portions of the surrounding forest so that it would be difficult for the Remnant forces to easily spot and pursue while the skyship would provide cover fire from above and drift away from the forest to move out of range from any siege weapons that might divert their attacks to the skyship.

Voksen nodded while indicating he would gather the elders, women, and children along with several Nordling warriors to guard them with the bulk of their warriors to flee last and hold down the settlement from the other directions of attack. Marin followed up the impromptu devised plan by suggesting that Wyatt would teleport both Helga and Voksen and as many of the elders, women, and children as the skyship could carry. The two chieftains looked to each other and nodded, but Voksen stated he would make his stand before falling back. To him and his ascribed beliefs in Nordling custom, it was not fitting to retreat from a battle rather than make his final stand and die with what he considered a Nordling sense of honor. Helga again nodded and understood while Marin was somewhat conflicted but also understood. Linitus, seeing differently and not sharing that same aspect of Nordling culture, questioned it by raising the possibility that it would be better for Voksen to remain alive and fight another day even if it meant losing at present. Voksen shook his head in calm disapproval while stating that he was a Nordling king and male chieftain and if his settlement fell, he was expected to fight until the very end even if he went down with his settlement. He would look forward to songs possibly praising his last heroic stand against such an insurmountable force. Linitus still did not agree or fully understand, but he was resigned to accept the Nordling's decision while holding his arm in a respectful embrace to wish him luck. Voksen nodded and told Linitus that while Helga was also a chieftain, she should not lay her life so freely in battle before the enemy. Instead, Voksen asked both Linitus and Marin to guard Helga with their lives to lead the rest of the fleeing Nordlings to safety and start a new settlement when the time was right. Linitus and Marin both nodded and swore the vow they were asked.

Moments later, the siege assault unleashed again with another salvo of the Remnant's catapults, which gave way for pause and steady streams of the combined Remnant forces storming the various segments of the outer palisade wall ring that had now fallen. Linitus had quietly placed painful bearlike snare traps as well as tripwire barrel bomb traps that he had set up near the front outer palisade gateway as well as the inner palisade gateway. He stood at the top of the settlement's moat hill next to the chieftain's mead hall. Near his foot standing vertically were several sabot receptacle containers holding clusters of arrows ready to be dispensed. He would help hold back and stem the rising tide of invading forces as much as possible while fighting alongside Voksen before the elf ranger called out for Wyatt to teleport him and any of Voksen's elite berserker barbarians that wished to fall back in safety to the skyship. All of Voksen's chosen warrior bodyguards declined, except for one whom Voksen had appointed as a witness to retreat with Linitus to the skyship at the last possible moment so that this Nordling could share his account of his fellow warriors' last stand in order for songs of praise of their valor to be remembered, told, and retold for future generations. Voksen personally charged Linitus to ensure this chosen warrior, or essentially the village's elder druid priest, would return with the elf ranger to the skyship along with any other fortunate survivors that the skyship could carry. Linitus nodded and agreed.

As this was happening, Marin called upon Wyatt to teleport several Eternal Flame knights that were assigned to the skyship to assist her on the ground in helping the retreating villagers (for the ones who did not yet board the skyship) escape the assault, while they would attempt to repel and make an opening at the southeast end of the settlement's palisade outer walls. Upon arriving and waiting for the initial wave by the Remnant's forces on the southeast to commence their attack, the skyship's armed crew members unleashed volley upon volley of arrows as well as deploying explosive barrels to the surface below that rained havoc and exploded with chaos upon the Remnant forces of the southeast. Within moments, the forces on the southeast end of the settlement were in utter disarray and pulled back in various directions. The plan had worked, and the Nordling settlement's escaping villagers and several friendly barbarian warriors made their way in that direction to escape into the thick covered woods with guarded support under Marin's command.

Meanwhile, the Remnant forces from the other directions began to take notice but still held their focus on hurrying their pace of storming and overrunning the settlement. The local Nordling warriors that stayed behind fought valiantly, holding as much ground as they could while taking out many goblins, orcs, Nordling adversaries from other settlements, as well as several fearsome Citadellan Black Wolf order knights and armed trolls. The fighting became fiercer over time, and eventually, the Nordling defenders of Tribus Wald slowly began to fall one by one.

Linitus, holding the high ground on the moat hill, unleashed volley upon volley of receptacle containers of sabot arrow clusters that dispersed with hails of arrows striking at least a hundred or more of the enemy forces. Voksen was impressed, complimenting Linitus on his ability to decimate the enemy so swiftly from afar in such a short amount of time. However, that would not hold the dark forces of the dux back indefinitely. Linitus knew it, and he knew it was a matter of time before he would have to retreat into the skyship. He had only hoped that staving off this assault and distracting Decius's forces would buy more time for the rest of the Nordlings to escape with their lives.

Sharing the same concern and nearly a mile away, Marin tried to encourage and hurry as many of the villagers as possible to follow her guards in a single column deep into the woods outside Tribus Wald. She, at least two other Eternal Flame knights, and half a dozen Nordling warriors guarded the rear of the fleeing group to ensure that no enemy forces would close in and attack them from behind, at least not without a fight, which would happen in a matter of time. When it did and the fighting broke out, it also became fierce.

Dozens of goblins and orcs caught up and tried to pick off the fleeing crowd of Nordlings along the forest. Although Marin, her few provisioned Eternal Flame knights, and the small defending group of Tribus Wald Nordling warriors did their best to fight back and intercept the pursuing beastly creatures, the latter was able to still inflict wounds and kill some of the fleeing Nordlings.

It was both daunting and frustrating to hold off the swarm of Remnant forces from below as well as from the skyship above. The settlement itself was becoming overrun with enemy forces, had limited visibility of the sight of the forest below with the many trees and their canopies obscuring the view and the path of the escaping allies on the ground. At the last moment, Linitus fired a flare high above to signal to Wyatt to teleport both Linitus and a Nordling shaman that Linitus held on to. Appearing on board the skyship high above, Linitus saw a clearer and suddenly complete picture of the carnage and onslaught that the enemy forces had brought against Tribus Wald. He saw below Voksen hold out and take down several enemy Nordlings from Tribus Aries as well as several large armed orc warriors. Eventually, the local Nordling chieftain king and heroic warrior fell as more and more of the enemy Nordlings and orcs overwhelmed him and his defending bodyguards.

Linitus, consistently calm and methodical in his approach in combat and strategy, could not hold back in shouting an uproar of the emotional swell of anger, sadness, and guilt he felt in knowing that he had survived while mourning for those he fought alongside. Everyone on board the skyship, especially Wyatt and Peat, knew that this was a rare passionate and emotional display from their elf ranger companion. As such, Peat provided comfort, placing his arm on Linitus's shoulder and back. The elf took a moment to turn and look while nodding in appreciation of the dwarf's gesture before composing himself to the matter at hand once again. Linitus ordered Wyatt to quickly divert the skyship above to provide rapid continuous volleys of arrows on both broadsides of the skyship while the elf ranger himself signaled for Peat and his few trained crew members to deploy fire barrels toward the southeast perimeter of the fallen settlement to dispatch as many pursuing enemy forces as possible from catching up and overtaking Marin and the fleeing Nordlings below.

Linitus himself next ordered Wyatt to teleport him to a clearance next to the forest outside the fallen settlement's walls, where the elf ranger would intercept the pursuing enemy forces below. Peat at first objected while telling Linitus that it was too risky. However, Linitus waved his hand to disregard the dwarf guardian's concern. Linitus replied, letting Peat know that he could more than take care of himself while fighting in the forest and it was the best way to ensure saving as many of the fleeing

Nordlings below as possible as well as Marin. Peat still objected, stating that Linitus was mainly doing it because of Marin and that he loved her. Linitus paused and nodded, admitting that Peat was right at least in part, but Linitus still justified he was right also, making his point that he had a better chance of providing cover fire and taking out more of the enemy from below without the forest canopy obstructing his sight. Peat nodded and grunted in acquiescence without saying a word. Wyatt nodded also while casting a teleportation portal for Linitus to walk through that sent him immediately through an opening portal on the surface below.

Quickly making sense of his location while looking above in using the skyship as his bearing, Linitus quickly veiled himself with his ornate camouflage-like cloak while running full speed and withdrawing several arrows from his quiver to use in conjunction with his bow that he held in his other hand. Entering the forest from the small clearance, he quickly spotted two dozen pursuing goblins and orcs that were behind but closing in on Marin and several Nordling warriors. Linitus also noticed several corpses of orcs, goblins, Nordlings, and by his count, two Eternal Flame knights that had fallen along the pathway of the escaping Nordlings of the settlement that still survived. Still running to get closer to Marin and provide supporting fire with his bow and arrows, Linitus quickly let loose several arrows at a time, firing toward any close enough groupings of orcs and goblins that he could take down.

Meanwhile, Marin and three Nordling warriors formed a small loose wall perimeter as a last stand against the pursuing goblins and orcs. They fought fiercely for dear life. Marin, taking the moment of surprise to quickly eliminate multiple goblins, withdrew two of her sharp dart hairpins and threw them quickly at the goblins while charging toward them and ramming any in her path with her shield. She quickly swung in wide ferocious arcs in a feeling of desperate uncontrolled rage, one that Linitus even took a moment to observe. He attributed it to her embrace of her Nordling heritage when fighting in a fierce uncontrolled rage. It may have been unbalanced and (by Linitus's standards of elven martial fighting) undisciplined, but he knew that for Marin, this was instinctive in her own manner to hold on and fight for dear life when she felt there was no other means of resolution. It was fierce and overpowering. She had literally taken out half a dozen goblins. However, a trio of orcs quickly began to notice and close in on her after taking out the three Nordling warriors that fought alongside Marin. These were the last three that Marin turned and noticed were no longer alive to fight beside her. She sweated intently, feeling winded and needing to catch her breath. In part, she knew that it was probably over. As strong as she was, fighting three large berserk-looking orc warriors, by her standards, seemed near impossible in her fatigued condition. She had hoped it was enough at least before she fell alongside the other defending warriors to be a sacrifice not in vain but successful enough for the fleeing Tribus Wald Nordlings to have enough time and escape the pursuing forces.

Mustering her remaining strength and resolve, she quenched her flaming sword while holding it up and raising her shield, she sized up and strafed in imitating patterns about the three orcs who sought to surround her from three different angles. As the orcs gave a loud roaring shout before raising their weapons and making their first moves against what they thought was the last defender and a worthy possible kill to claim as their trophy in combat, a quick and sudden whistling noise screeched through the air. Aching with pain, the three orc warriors looked down at their abdomens as well as Marin, seeing that she was the only one not struck with a piercing arrowhead. The three orc warriors fell down on the ground. Marin turned from the direction in front of her and behind the fallen orcs, looking about. In truth, she knew before even spotting him that it was Linitus. Her presumption was confirmed at the next moment when emerging from the top of one of the trees and dropping down while removing his camouflage cloak indeed was her elven lover. She sighed with relief, as did he. They both walked toward each other, meeting halfway to embrace each other.

If she could share the moment with him longer and rest for the entire day, she would; however, Marin knew as well as Linitus that they both had to recompose themselves and make their way in catching up with the fleeing Nordlings. Without saying a word and looking intently at each other's face, they both turned back in the direction that Marin originally fled with the escaping Nordling villagers to catch up with them. Eventually, the two of them did catch up and led the way, going upstream and eventually finding a path of clearance. Only several hundred villagers and a few dozen allied Nordling warriors had made it alive. Linitus, spotting the skyship in the distance, unleashed another flare arrow high in the sky in order to signal his position to Wyatt and the rest of the crew.

Within minutes of noticing, the skyship had changed course and soared in the direction of the sparkling flare arrow. Looking below, Wyatt spotted several hundred Nordlings along with Linitus and Marin. The two companions below waved and signaled to the young wizard above as dawn began with the sun rising. Setting about in a manner of prioritizing who was most vulnerable and least protected, Linitus ordered for Wyatt to teleport (with the exception of the wizard himself and Peat) all available fighting crew members down to the surface while teleporting back up as many of the elderly, children, and several women that they could take on board from the surface below. They would remain on board the skyship as it followed the same route that Linitus, Marin, the armed soldiers, and the remaining Nordling villagers were headed on the ground due south out of the forest clearing and into some more open land with a few scattered thickets of trees. They had made it, at least so far. It was for a time enough for Marin and Linitus to slow down and catch their breath while still keeping a fair degree of alertness for any pursuing enemies. Sensing the pressing need for leadership and guidance, Linitus asserted his leadership and position of command to announce to the soldiers and escaping villagers that they would continue southward and gradually westward along the coast, with their nearest destination being Aldion. The march would be a long grueling one, with Linitus intending for them to traverse at least ten to twenty miles per day. At that pace, it would take them at least two weeks to a month to reach Aldion. Marin pointed out the direness in orchestrating it that way. However, Linitus shrewdly thought of an alternate adjustment, suggesting that Wyatt and Peat with the young and vulnerable on board make a break to venture ahead of them on the surface to reach Aldion first to notify the king, unload the survivors, and make a round trip with the skyship and possibly Ascentius's other skyship that he could spare to pick up the remaining survivors and soldiers on the ground still en route to Aldion. By doing so, it would be possible for those on the ground marching to be picked up and be brought back to safety in a manner of two to three days. After briefing the soldiers and Wyatt of his plan once more briefly on board the skyship, Linitus teleported back to the surface to lead soldiers below on the long march toward Aldion.

Marin, relieved after all that had transpired, suddenly and unexpectedly stopped while marching with the soldiers. She took Linitus to the side while telling the rest of the soldiers to continue to march. With a slight smile, the Princess Knight nodded while embracing a surprised and unsuspecting Linitus. She confided to him her gratitude while confessing in her heart that he truly was a divine angel sent from one of the benevolent deity spirits with a gifted mind in saving those innocent in their greatest time of need. Linitus, taking it in humbly, embraced Marin back and recomposed himself while prompting her also. For elves, as much as they were affectionate in certain ways, public displays of affection were matters that Linitus ranked in the realm of vanity that he was apprehensive about exhibiting before others, at least publicly. Marin understood that and, for that moment, respected his wishes while they walked beside each other back at the front of the formation line with the rest of the soldiers and Nordling warriors marching behind.

The other soldiers and Nordlings, however, did notice, and while some whispers among them circulated in the awe of seeing a half Nordling and Citadellan human being together with an elf romantically, it mattered little with the direness of the situation from which they were fortunate to emerge alive, at least so far. The rarity and controversy of such unions between different sentient beings also mattered little to them when many of them considered how much genuine love and compassion the two heroes exhibited not only toward each other, but also for the well-being of the Nordling survivors as well as the soldiers that they led and served alongside.

For now, everyone was content at least to still be alive to see another sunrise despite mourning internally for the ones they knew who had fallen and not being able to bury them, at least not right away. It was consolation enough to look at each other and know that they were fortunate to be alive and they could still persevere and live with purpose and meaning to honor and not forget the ones they loved who had fallen from the onslaught. Linitus knew this, and at some point during their retreat, he paused to give those marching pause to rest briefly while reminding them that their lives still had meaning as long as they sought to pursue it.

CHAPTER THIRTY-FIVE

Fortune Favors the Persistent

A day had already passed since the skyship departed. The long march south continued after Linitus led the surviving warriors of the escape from Tribus Wald and after they made a brief makeshift rest camp at midnight. They were at least thirty miles or more away from the fallen Nordling settlement. Already, several of the surviving Nordlings that marched on foot showed fatigue but were still as determined and roused by the words from Linitus earlier: to strive and persevere in finding meaning in their lives to survive. They were determined not to rest with their guard down, at least not until they had found sanctuary in another safe land and settlement.

The Nordlings along with Linitus, Marin, and the surviving dispatched contingent of Swordbane soldiers, knights of the Eternal Flame, and a small group of elven rangers had maintained the same resolve at early dawn to continue their march still due south. The terrain was scattered with open plain land covered with thickets of trees all about and the coastal mountains lying to the east by several miles. This surviving caravan gradually continued southward as well as westward to get closer along the coast. Linitus had told Wyatt and Peat before they departed with the most vulnerable survivors to look for the rest of the marching survivors along the coast in order for it to be easier to spot them when Wyatt and Peat returned with their skyship as well as hopefully King Ascentius's skyship to board the rest of the surviving caravan to fly away to safety toward Aldion.

By midday, Linitus could sense somehow that something was not right. He paused the caravan and faintly was able to detect a movement on the ground that he could hear from far away in the north. It gradually became louder, but still very faint. In his mind, it most likely had to be a dispatched reconnaissance, possibly scouts of Decius's forces mounted either on horseback or even mounted on dire wolves. Assuming the worst that it was indeed the enemy, Linitus quickly with a loud yet calm and commanding voice let the rest of the marching caravan know that they were possibly being pursued. He told all those present to quickly march in relatively close formation at a fast pace, at least as fast as the slowest one in the caravan was able to travel, while staying together. The elf ranger told the caravan as they quickly began to march that he would pick the best place to make a stand if they had to and he would make the place of his picking as ideal as he could with the terrain.

As such, there was one hill covered in a thicket of trees that seemed ideal to both hide in and make it difficult for the enemy to engage against them using cavalry to overrun and/or outflank them. Upon taking position in the forest thicket, Linitus and Marin had the forces organized with Swordbane knights and infantry near the front while posting the small group of elven rangers that came along at the front. The Nordling villagers stayed in the center mass as well as the right and left flanks for their fellow Nordling warriors. They waited patiently until the enemy scouts came, which they eventually did.

Several minutes later, a large pack of two dozen or so dire wolves mounted by goblins and small slender orcs rode forth toward the distance, facing the thicket hill. Within moments, they looked intently toward the direction of Linitus and his traveling caravan of soldiers and Nordling refugees. The enemy could not see them clearly, but they knew that the survivors or at least something of interest was out there. It was noticeable enough for the dire wolves' sense of smell.

In another moment, the dire-wolf riders began pursuing toward the hill thicket. Linitus told the surviving caravan in their maintained formation to hold and not attack until he gave the order, and the small group of elven ranger archers would fire first when the dire-wolf scouts were within range of their arrows. Once they were, Linitus quickly gave the order while also drawing an arrow from his bow and aiming to let loose himself toward one of the mounted wolf riders. As the volley of arrows flew forth, it struck without much reaction the surprised dire wolves and their mounted riders. At least half of them fell, while the other half still charged even quicker toward the thicket. Linitus instructed the infantry, including the Nordlings, to still hold their positions and brace for impact against the dire wolves; however, seeing that there was still more time, Linitus quickly instructed the other elf rangers to prepare one more volley of arrows to fire toward the remaining dire wolves. They did so along with Linitus. It was just in time while the remaining enemy forces fell only a few yards from the front ranks of the survivor caravan's impromptu formation. Only one wolf rider remained alive and began to quickly change course to retreat. However, before he could, Marin hurled a throwing spear at the dire wolf, forcing it to collapse hard on the ground while the lone goblin that mounted it landed face forward. The goblin slowly got up, but before he did so, Marin closed in and decapitated his head from his body in one precise slash of her flaming long sword.

Looking about and at each other, Marin and Linitus realized and shook their heads, confiding that it was over at least for now. The rest of the caravan sighed and cheered. For many of them, it was a miracle as well as a counting of their blessings that they were led by capable and motivating leaders the likes of this one particular elf ranger and the legendary Princess Knight. Only a short time later after recomposing and taking a quick muster count did Linitus call the caravan of survivors to march again southward and slightly westward toward the coastline.

By sunset, they would see the coast below from the cliffside where they stayed along such high ground. Before sunset had ended and become nightfall, one of the soldiers shouted with excitement while pointing in the distance to indicate that there were two skyships across the distance in the sky. Before being the last to teleport to the Wyatt's skyship, Linitus and Marin locked hands together, and they stared toward the western sun as it set its last glimmer of light upon the coast while feeling the soothing breeze of the wind blow against them. Linitus uttered to Marin that each day they shared a sunset or sunrise together was a reminder to him that fortune favors the persistent such as them to strive to live and cherish those moments together. Marin nodded and confided back to him that despite all the sadness and pain she had in seeing innocents being threatened and killed by forces of darkness, she at least felt an exhilaration in being able to adventure and fight back those forces alongside her lover.

Taking one last look, in a flash the two comrades and lovers teleported aboard the skyship. To their surprise, they found King Ascentius on board with Wyatt and Peat while leaving his personal skyship under the command of one of his lieutenants that followed closely behind them. The king embraced Marin at the same time as she embraced her father. Meanwhile, Linitus kneeled and stayed in that position until Ascentius came to him and told the elf ranger to rise. Ascentius instead, in a gesture of humility and deference showing his gratitude and respect, told Linitus that it was he and the rest of his kingdom that should kneel instead for everything the elf ranger had done, including up to this point. As soon as the king bowed before the elf ranger, everyone on board, including Marin, did the same, bowing with gratitude for Linitus's leadership. Linitus nodded with humility while shedding a tear in reflecting on what Ascentius stated. Marin and Ascentius both looked puzzled and asked why the elf ranger was in tears. Linitus looked toward them and then looked in the direction of Tribus Wald while stating humbly that as grateful as he was for the king's gesture as well as everyone else's on board, he did not feel worthy of it. He regretted not being able to save all the Nordlings of the settlement as well as losing some of the lives of the kingdom's soldiers that were at great peril in saving the settlement's remaining population.

Marin placed her hand on his shoulder and told Linitus that while they could not save everyone, his efforts in leading the ones that they could save still mattered. Linitus shook his head while placing Marin's hands on his lips to kiss before nodding and stating that he knew and that she was right. Marin, trying to alleviate his sadness, stated before him and all those present that at least they had each other to mourn together, to provide comfort, and to persevere in finding purpose and maintaining purpose with their lives going forward. Linitus shook his head again before quietly telling her that she had grown and matured in no longer being the same haughty knight he once knew of her. Instead, she was now becoming one who could reflect and share her thoughts together with him while also reminding him of the important lessons in life as much as he reminded her. Marin nodded while confiding that he was a good influence in helping her to find herself beyond being just a knight. Linitus nodded again while embracing her. The king and all those present admired and were captivated by the two. They took a moment before quietly excusing themselves to let the two share their intimacy in each other's arms near the bow of the ship as it drifted gracefully high in the air, above the snow-covered mountains in the distance to the east, above the grass fields with forest thickets all about, and above the darkened blue coastal shores in the west. It sailed gracefully along with its companion skyship to their next destination, Aldion.

CHAPTER THIRTY-SIX

A Love the Famous Will Never Receive

Nearly a week later, after becoming the chosen vessel for Calu and Laran, Decius with Agaroman by his side floated high in the sky, in one of the six captured skyships that the dux's army had seized from the raid at Aldion nearly eight days prior. It was midday, and the dux's acquired skyship fleet floated high above the Great Western High Desert after leaving Orcum Tribus Uruk Kazaht, where the dux himself personally led a funeral pyre ceremony for his most loyal lieutenants that sacrificed themselves in order for him to fully attain chosen vesselhood. Upon finishing a captivating eulogy for the departed orc war captain and goblin chief shaman, Decius vowed he would make their sacrifice count as well as the sacrifices of all his soldiers to bring glory and prosperity to his coalition's emerging empire. As in other cases before, his speech rallied the goblin-and-orc settlement to cheer on their dark lord while being fervent as ever to serve his cause and follow him wherever he commanded them.

Now, after the funeral ceremony at Uruk Kazaht had passed two days prior, the dux's floating forces were less than an hour away from arriving at the Remnant capital of Sanctum Novus and the great high-desert city sparkled like a jewel from the horizon while being surrounded by beautiful red-rock desert mountains in the distance and multiple lots of scattered palm groves and oases at various distances and proximities within the general vicinity of the desert city. Even the spectacular and majestic-looking concrete aqueducts that supplied water to the city from the Great

Desert River dozens of miles away could be seen. It was truly a spectacular view to behold from the sky above the high desert plain.

The new crew on board all six skyships was eager to arrive, with great anticipation. For them, it was a rare defining moment that the dux and a fairly large number of his surviving veteran Citadellan soldiers and Black Wolf knights had awaited to finally stage a triumph in the city that would surpass all triumphs that Sanctum Novus had undertaken before. It would be the first that the local victor and commanding warlord would undertake the parade celebration and festivities while floating high above the city skyline in lieu of the traditional war chariot and foot march down the city's main colonnade street to the central plaza and forum adjacent to the central temple district.

As skyships approached closer to the city below, Decius wore a special dark-crimson stole with black embroidery of his order's sigil totem. He wore the stole slung along his shoulder in a sash style over his military regalia. He also had a makeshift altar arranged on the aftercastle of the skyship, where he would perform an incense-and-libation ceremony to give honor and offerings to both Calu and Laran, represented again by the same statues he had used from the earlier ritual in which he had received their blessing and conferment of chosen vessel in merging their powers, while also being practically deified.

Agaroman observed intently and was pleased by the devotion and transformation of his former mentoree. Now, the wizard thought to himself, the dux had truly surpassed him and all other living beings with respect to the dux's mortality and unnatural and deity-like power. He had truly earned his attainment of the title of dark lord and cemented this achievement with his transformation and near deification.

The soldiers on board the skyships had observed and shared much of the same sentiment as Agaroman, some perhaps more than others. The beastly races on board, including the goblins and orcs, were utterly convinced of Decius being their dark savior, while the Citadellans loyal to the dux saw him as the ultimate worthy leader and warlord to serve under as well as being open to the possibility that Decius was indeed a deity-like chosen vessel of the two most feared and wrathful deity spirits of the Citadellan pantheon.

The barbarians of Tribus Aries, who served recently as subservient auxiliary vassals to the dux, did not think as much in unison of the dux's newfound identity and status nor were they as enthusiastic about it. Some of the Nordlings thought as much as the goblins and Citadellans of Sanctum Novus while other Nordlings simply saw the dux as an acceptable leader without much choice in them having a say of their newfound patron conqueror as well as their perceived place in the bottom-order hierarchy of the Remnant social order. The dux saw the Nordlings as nothing more than uncivilized cannon fodder to be used to fight and die for his cause in exchange for permitting them to live in his new emerging empire in which he valued the goblins and orcs on equal terms in comparison to his fellow Citadellans. Regardless, they all shared one commonality of Decius. He was worthy and rightfully feared for not only his fighting prowess and war strategy, but also his acquisition of newfound infernal powers. He was utterly terrifying, especially the first time that they saw him cast an avatar-like projection of himself in the form of a corporeal gigantic dark jagged werewolf emitting burning flames intermittently on its body. Now, the dux had assumed only what was considered his normal human form without the projection and manifestation of his hellish and beastly form to summon, at least not until he decided it was time to do so.

Floating above the entrance of the south city gate and walls that gave way to the main city road, Decius, Agaroman, and the other forces of the dux on board looked below and watched with awe and amazement the large masses of the populace below filling the colonnade-bordered streets. They could hear their cheers, jubilant shouts, and proclamations of praise toward the dux. Many of the people in the desert city carried palm leaves in hand along with black-and-red shawls (representing the dux's standing colors). Garlands and petals of roses were thrown in the air, flowing ever so delicately to the ground that looked like a sea of red blood.

Another moment as the dux motioned, Agaroman called to several of the armed guards on board to bring out the prisoners. They were captured barbarian nobles who had fallen from resisting the dux's calls for submission even after being bested in battle from various Nordling settlements. A dozen or so barbarian prisoners in all were shackled and chained together. Once out on the deck, Agaroman had teleported them with armed escort guards below. As customary with triumphs, Decius and his wizard advisor saw to it to make an example of their conquered foes while displaying their perceived superiority in beating the Nordlings who resisted, to have the defeated prisoners march in bonds to their humiliation while receiving the ridicule and scorn of the locals below. The Citadellan locals of Sanctum Novus held a deep animus toward the barbarians as they mocked them. Some of the Citadellans even reminded them that this would be their payback for past raids against their merchants and overdue revenge for surviving kin of the few unfortunate merchants that died at their hands from past grievances.

The shackled and chained Nordling noble prisoners kept marching without resisting, knowing that doing so would invite a likely more painful beating that one of them so far already received in reacting and trying to attack the crowd. The Citadellan guards and knights of the Black Wolf order inflicted a sudden and painful series of blows to the one Nordling who did resist in particular, before forcing him to get up and resume marching in pain with his other fellow prisoners.

Another group teleported after the prisoner party display had proceeded. This group was among the most respected and trusted of Decius's Black Wolf knights. They numbered two dozen and marched in a formation of four columns and six rows while keeping ranks. Finally, a third group teleported from one of the skyships. This included an elegant Citadellan war chariot being hauled by six dire wolves carrying Dux Decius as chariot driver holding the reins while Agaroman rode beside Decius, and the wizard held an elaborate silver laurel above the dux's head. The laurel resembled a halo symbolizing and expressing the dux's status of victor as well as his near deification. Decius was also covered in red face paint with a black coal-like marking being hand rubbed upon his forehead. The marking resembled the emblem of a black wolf encircled by laurels.

The parade procession with Decius and Agaroman riding chariot at the rear were flanked and protected by the rear with assembled dire-wolf riders, six in all mounted on their respective dire wolves. Four of the riders were goblins and lightweight orcs (two from each beastly race), while the remaining two dire-wolf riders were among the most lightweight in Decius's Black Wolf knights who were able to ride their wolf mounts while wearing their armor.

As the procession made its way to the plaza center and forum, Decius dismounted from his chariot along with Agaroman. The dux handed over the reins to one of his knights that had followed along on foot during the procession. Decius and Agaroman walked up to the local city's rostra, or a large elevated platform, where Decius saw standing before a series of elegant chairs his beloved Lucia along with her father, Senator Diem, standing next to her. Diem rendered a stately Citadellan salute by placing his right hand to clench as a fist against his chest before extending it toward Decius. Decius returned the same gesture while quickly holding Lucia's hands and lifting them up to kiss. Lucia returned the same gesture and held back as much as she wanted to embrace him, out of respect for exhibiting the stately, dignified appearance of an engaged woman and future spouse of the one of the most powerful men in the continent.

As the triumph procession came near its end, Decius had Agaroman arrange a makeshift altar and shrine on the rostra platform before the local populace and Remnant soldiers. The dux offered an incense offering and wine libation in another ceremony dedicated once again to both Calu and Laran. The associated representative symbols of each of the two deities were placed adjacent to the lit incense brazier while the ceremony was conducted.

As the dux recited several prayers and gave a speech to recount to the locals about his campaigning since his last departure from the city, Lucia stood by his side, watching passionately and intently. Agaroman had taken several steps back behind the dux, observing while aligning himself next to Diem. The Senator looked intently at his daughter while observing the masses and how they exhibited an exalted and celebratory disposition toward both the dux and his daughter. Agaroman mentioned in a low, discreet, and very quiet tone about sharing the same observation with Diem, noticing how the people of the city seemed to place a high value of regard toward the dux and his future consort. Diem nodded with a small streak of tears in his eyes while stating that he knew.

Agaroman went on to continue to acknowledge and praise Diem for his joint management of the city with his daughter, while singling out his daughter as perhaps the ideal exemplar of what a Citadellan wife (especially as a consort) and mother was expected to be in managing the internal matters of both the dux's domestic and political estate. Diem nodded again while shedding tears. He responded to Agaroman, stating that they loved her. The people loved her, even the beastly denizens that recently settled and adjusted to Sanctum Novus. Of course, Decius loved her, from what everyone else could tell. However, nobody would share the same love for her that he had for her as a father. They were close when he had her involved in tending to his personal estate and merchant activity alongside her mother, Diem's wife. Lucia and her father became close and rekindled their bonding as father and daughter even in such a different capacity as adults. It was hard for him to feel like he now had to return her to someone else that she would share her love with, even in different aspects, whether intimate with the dux or political celebration with the general public. Diem still wished that he could go back in time to be in the same constant state in which Lucia would bond with him as they did before as daughter and father. Again however, he knew there was no going back. She still had set aside that space in her life for him as her father, but much of her life would be set aside as Decius's wife and co-ruler as well as future mother to his grandchild when it was time. He was looking forward at least to that prospect of being a future grandparent.

Diem recomposed himself from his thoughts. He abruptly admitted and startled Agaroman to be lost for words while the sorcerer had a sense of newfound respect for the senator in revealing his most honest vulnerability. The senator admitted that while the people loved his daughter dearly as well as the dux (again in another light), the love that he had for his daughter and the near-fatherlike love that Agaroman might have like an adoptive father for Decius were both forms of parental love that both the dux and his future consort would never receive from the people. Even if the masses thought of them as parents, they would not share it as personally as the senator and the wizard advisor had for the ruling couple respectively. As cold and calculating as Agaroman might be, as well as suspicious of those that got close to the dux other than himself, the wizard and chief advisor placed his hand on the shoulder of Diem while nodding and confiding that both Diem and Lucia had earned his full trust and confidence. He would no longer be as suspicious of them as he was before. Diem nodded while reflecting on the current situation and stating that this new war against Swordbane, as brutal as it was and would perhaps be, was necessary in bringing out the best from what each and every one has to offer as much as it possibly could bring out the worst.

By the time Diem pointed that out, with Agaroman nodding, the dux had finished his speech and final closing prayer before the altar. In another moment, he stood meditating and concentrating before the crowd. Thereafter, a dark crimson-and-black smoke aura surrounded the dux like a globe. As this globe took shape, a huge corporeal figure took form while it emanated behind the dux on top of the rostra. It was the avatar of Decius that appeared again, a haunting giant nearly pitch-black werewolf lit with small embers and flames all about its body, unaffected by the heat or burning sensation where others would give in to pain. This avatar of the dux unleashed a loud, near-deafening howl, which triggered various dire wolves in the procession as well as within the city's walls to howl in a terrifying and deafening chorus. Many among the crowd as well as some of the high-ranking senators, oligarchs, and high-ranking military figures shuddered in initial fear before this terrifying product of infernal feats and destruction. Except for those that already witnessed the dux's ascension into being a chosen vessel with the essence of the deity spirits of war and death infused into him, it was a truly frightening sight to behold.

Eventually and at short notice, those who seemed to tremble in fear realized that this was a power that was on their side. The dux's claim of being the chosen vessel had now been validated before everyone. Nearly everyone in the city recomposed themselves to cast various forms of exalted and verbal praise before the dux. He was not a threat to them but rather a newly realized sign of interpreted divine grace now beyond the doubts of what was considered just a dark religious superstition. Even if he was ascribed the title of dark lord, at least in the minds of many Citadellans of Sanctum Novus, he would be both their secular and religiously divine dark lord to lead them into what he had preached would be a future and new age of prosperity.

CHAPTER THIRTY-SEVEN

Bride of the Dark Lord

Nearly three months had passed since Decius returned to Sanctum Novus while holding a triumph after campaigning in victory. The dux had held daily council meetings just as he did before he left on his last campaign in the north against the resisting towns of the Collis region and the various Nordling barbarian tribes. He had fulfilled his vow, at least as he saw it, and with Agaroman's confirmation of approval to no longer be bound in resorting to an ancient tradition of common-law marriage. Instead with Agaroman's cunning idea, Decius decided to coincide and propose to Lucia with Diem's approval to wed his daughter in a formal Citadellan marriage ceremony on the very same day that Lucia would attain the general recognized status of marriage by common law through cohabitation in the dux's house for a year. That day would mark the anniversary of when Decius and Lucia first met.

Lucia was in high spirits and could not hold back in mutually exchanging a kiss with her future husband as he proposed before her while inviting her father Senator Diem and the rest of her family to a small-gathering dinner at the dux's estate palace. Diem as the father of the bride could ask or negotiate anything he wanted that was reasonable for Decius to set aside as dowry for marrying the senator's daughter, but Diem had only one personal request, which Decius granted before hearing what Diem mentioned afterward. The senator took a subtle half bow while stating what his request was: to have Decius and Lucia's firstborn to raise as his own son at least only when the dux was away to campaign and when a fatherly figure was needed to be present in the life of the dux's son, presuming one of the dux's future children with Lucia as consort would be a son.

Agaroman, having his own future plans in the matter of the dux's offspring's upbringing, had objected when was present with the dux, his consort Lucia, and her family. Decius raised his hand to command silence. Everyone complied and listened to what he had to say. The dux agreed to a compromise on behalf of Diem in which the senator would be able to have custody and supervision of his future son during his absence in matters that the dux would attend such as campaigning. However, the dux, appeasing his mentor advisor, let Diem know that Agaroman was in charge of instructing his future heir when it came to military matters and warfare. Diem, knowing that this was perhaps his best compromise to make with the dux, nodded and agreed, while Agaroman did the same. Decius, taking a quick moment in pondering, asked Diem why he made such a request though everyone at the table seemed to already know. The concept of family even by extension was held in high regard by Citadellans and Diem admitted that he never had a son. The future male heir to Decius and Lucia would be the closest he would be able to cherish a sense of near fathering, though the senator admitted that the child would still be the dux's son. He admitted that he would be a very delighted grandfather if the deity spirits granted that. Diem raised a wine glass while proclaiming salutations for family, with everyone following.

Another month passed before Lucia announced with testimony from a local priestly doctor that she was pregnant. Decius, as well as others close to Lucia, were delighted. She and the dux hoped that it would be a boy. Her carrying to term for the pregnancy, however, felt different even with the temple priests taking note of its progression taking a faster and seemingly turbulent pace. Something in her womb was different, and even Decius as well as Agaroman sensed it. The child would possibly be delivered to term in a span of six months. It would be close, but after the planned coronation date of the dux's wedding with Lucia as his consort.

On the day of the wedding and the anniversary when Lucia first met Decius, preparations were made to hold the wedding at Sanctum Novus' titular Temple of Laran before an altar and shrine devoted to both Laran and Calu. It was an elaborate processional wedding, and part of it would be held inside the temple while part of it would involve a processional transit under armed escort, which the dux arranged, between the entrance of the dux's palace estate and the Temple of Laran. Decius would ride with his closest Black Wolf knights to serve as matrimonial witnesses to attest to the dux's wedding and as the dux's armed escort. All of them proceeded to the temple while mounted on dire wolves. Six of the knights went along with Decius, each carrying a symbolic bundle of grape vine or olive wood sticks wrapped together, mounted on a sharp pointed obsidian spearhead as a symbolic Citadellan (and even before, originally Lupercalian) gesture and tradition of displaying the dux's power and unity that he brought to his new emerging empire.

Lucia was following behind in an elegant horse-drawn carriage that was also holding her parents, Senator Diem and his wife. The carriage was armed with over a dozen mounted Black Wolf Knights on horseback. Upon arriving near the portico entrance of the temple, Lucia and her parents exited the carriage and made their way inside the temple entrance. The crowd, upon seeing Lucia, was in utter shock at her beauty. Her skin shone brightly while having a beautiful olive-cinnamon hue. Her beauty was further complemented by her dress for the occasion. She wore a red dress with laced embroidery of various floral designs fitted to accommodate her stage of pregnancy. Her hair was covered in a wreath with a veil as well as having a gold hairnet inside it.

Decius, who had his eye fixed on her upon seeing her enter the temple and approach the altar, caught her attention just as much. The dux had donned a sleek red cape with a black emblem of his chosen wolf sigil with a sword pointed upward. He was covered in his stately military governing attire having a black breastplate with the same sigil, only smaller, and segmented shoulder armor plates along with an ornate black belt with hanging leather strips followed by an undercovering of a black-and-red tunic and black Citadellan trousers called braccae that went down to the dux's ankles though it partially overlapped with the black-painted steel greaves or leg guards that Decius wore above his ornate sandals. The dux also had on the same red stole that he wore on the day of his triumphant return to Sanctum Novus after receiving his chosen vesselhood and after his successful campaign against the Nordlings.

With the soon-to-be-wedded couple present and standing next to each other, both Decius and Lucia were anxious to announce their vows but also excited to celebrate this occasion. Lucia had already resolved months ago that their marriage would be established by only common law, until both Decius and his advisor Agaroman found a compromise to satisfy that condition concurrently to reconcile on the same day that Lucia and Decius would be married both satisfying the common-law tradition and still being able to hold the formal Citadellan wedding ceremony, which was now considered justified by Agaroman since Decius had already attained his status of chosen vesselhood.

As the ceremony began to proceed, Agaroman invoked the deity spirits and recited the formal words for holding the wedding ceremony. Lucia took out a knitted doll-like figure and cast it into the burning brazier that stood on the altar. This symbolic gesture was done to signify in part her ascension to womanhood and being of age to pursue marriage while discarding any symbolic objects that would allude to her still being a child. Upon doing so while she and Decius recited their initial vows and waited, Lucia's parents both came forward as witnesses while taking Lucia's hand and placing it over Decius's to symbolize that they had given consent, transferring the authority that they had over their daughter to Decius as both her husband and the leading head and alpha male of their future family. Decius next removed Lucia's wreath and unveiled her before the attendees at the wedding temple. Her beauty stood out among the attendees with further chatters in the background, expressing their amazement. The dux also exchanged his vows with her, and the two exchanged pieces of bread made from a sacred recipe that Lucia's mother had made. The couple next exchanged glasses of wine and offered these to each other after they each made an offering before the altar to Calu and Laran. Finally, Decius and Lucia gave each other a kiss before the audience, and they shared one chalice filled with wine to offer in the burning brazier as a final offering and pleading for the ultimate blessing of their marriage by the divine spirits. Agaroman concluded the ceremony while extinguishing the flame from the burning incense inside the brazier.

This last act concluded with the announcement by Agaroman affirming the status of husband and wife for both Dux Decius and Lady Lucia as his official consort and newly proclaimed ducissa, or more commonly known as duchess. She would be recognized as the second most powerful leader and alpha female for the Remnant as well as her own household. She knew it as well as her own parents. Her mother was proud of her elevation of station in life as well as her father, though he held back this time shedding any tears from his reminiscing memories of how close he was to her. It was time to move on, and Diem recognized as well as accepted it. Though Decius would be the head of his family and dynasty,

Lucia would be the center, in managing and taking care of matters on the dux's behalf internally for both the dux's household as well as for Sanctum Novus by extension for political domestic matters. She had met and exceeded not only Decius's expectations, but also those of his soldiers that stayed behind in the city as well as the common citizenry and even the likes of Agaroman and the representative heads of the beastly races of orcs and goblins. She was perceived as exactly what she wanted and sought to attain, the highest status that a Citadellan woman was able to attain in her society, the perceived Domina Matria, or lady mother in the Citadellan tongue. Her processional walk while holding hands with her wedded Decius was validated with this title as many among the crowd of the masses called out to her as much as the dux. Decius took notice, and while he could have held a degree of jealousy, he did not. He knew what she had done in acting as patron (or more properly, matron) and benefactor to the common masses of citizenry including those most marginalized such as the orphans of the city. She was exactly the woman he sought in his life to balance out his disposition that, while being very charismatic among his subjects, was also widely feared and did not hold back in building his reputation by such perceptions. To him, it was business and prophecy. He had to be the dark lord and chosen vessel that would bring chaos and order to an otherwise corrupt western continent that had decayed too long with what he considered inept and tone-deaf leadership on the throne even before Ascentius. Multiple agents of the crown's authority and influence would take advantage, furthering the already compromised legitimate authority to assert in the western lands of Hesperion. Decius would have none of it after treading carefully in plotting and pursuing with his mentor Agaroman to attain the path of righteous usurper as well as dark warlord and chosen vessel.

To Decius, this role he assumed was morally relative. If he had committed the most horrible acts toward his enemies and those guilty of corruption, it was in part because of necessary redress and balance against what he considered an already corrupt order and status quo that would only understand and yield to change in a language that it understood. It was a language of fear and destruction that he would exact until order, his order, was met to bring back the western lands under a new prosperous era of revival as it once was during the ancient times of the Lupercalian Empire.

He reflected and thought about such things after the night of his wedding while cherishing Lucia for being accepting of him. He still did not know how or why she had accepted him other than genuine attraction they had for each other and sharing mutual raw ambitions in attaining a higher station in life, in pursuing the Citadellan cultural concept called cursus honorum (the course of honors). Despite their differences in behavior, attitude, and approach, they had come to a deep level of understanding each other and seeing how they respected each other's values in a militaristic approach to empire building on one hand while asserting a role and space of compassionate patron (or matron) to promote harmony of society within.

Decius, already retired to his estate following the wedding night with Lucia, now officially his wife, reflected on their path together with a sense of contentment and appreciation of their paths in coming together. He wrapped and held his arms around her as she was deep asleep at night while they were in bed after the wedding. He broke his stream of thought about their future and ambitions, when realizing he felt her womb bulging. She was expecting their first child, and it seemed she was very close to delivering. Softly and slowly, he caressed Lucia's bosom while pondering the future they would share together as parents with their expected child.

CHAPTER THIRTY-EIGHT

Birth of a New Omen

Less than three weeks after their formal wedding ceremony, Lucia was in labor and expecting to deliver. She was tended to by midwife servants of the dux's estate along with a local priest who had working knowledge in the arts of medicine and healing.

Decius at the immediate time was away from his estate and observing the progress that Agaroman had undertaken in a deeply guarded siege workshop adjacent to Sanctum Novus urban military barracks. Agaroman had worked for several months in constructing a new skyship design that was vastly different from the traditional floating caravel and galley hull designs used before in conjunction with an attached assembly to hold the inflatable balloon apparatus. The dark sorcerer had studied and adopted into the construction plans for his new skyship designs the prototype models of flight that Decius and he took from the scholarly museums of Aldion during the night of their infamous raid from ten months past.

Decius stood at a distance and could not help but admire the imposing as well as terrifying design of the flying contraption. The large helix screws were carefully placed horizontally and attached toward the rear fantail of this sleek and terrifying beastly-looking skyship that resembled a combination of a bat and a wolf. The wings from the glider or flap-model prototype that they had also taken from Aldion were replicated with a light yet durable metal material that was placed on the sides of the main hull frame of this elaborate skyship. Decius, being impressed, could not hold back his astonishment and pleasure with Agaroman's progress.

Agaroman, for his part, nodded humbly and explained how this contraption was different from the other skyships as well as how it worked during warfare situations, surpassing the capabilities of common fielded skyships. This flying contraption was intended to be a fast and deadly moving aerial platform that would use its aerodynamic design to outmaneuver, outrun, and consequently even outram other skyships, including that of the Kingdom of Swordbane.

Decius stood and touched part of the metal frame of the sleek beastly-looking designed flying contraption. It was smooth yet sharp at the edge. The frame of the contraption itself was supported in the air by a series of suspended scaffolds and wire rope, which also held the contraption together until it was completed.

Curious about the progress of the contraption, Decius asked his wizard advisor how long it would take before it was done. Agaroman replied two more months as his best estimation. Decius was pleased and was also surprised when Agaroman followed up by stating that there were two additional models starting to be made in addition to this one. In total, they would have all three models ready, including the more recent two in three months' time. Decius could not hold back his grin. If these contraptions were indeed as deadly as his mentor wizard advisor claimed, then the dux's forces would be able to launch a new offensive against Swordbane in a way that Ascentius would least expect. Decius had many images in mind as possibilities of how they would use these new flying warships for his future planned designs.

As the dux pondered his future plans, a knight of the Black Wolf order appeared, saluted the dux, and informed Decius of his wife's prognosis of going into labor. Lucia was poised to give birth to a future heir who would inherit the dux's throne perhaps one day when Decius found a way to travel and conquer other planes beyond the mortal earthly world of Terrunaemara in which he currently resided.

Concerned and eager, Decius excused himself while Agaroman decided to follow him to witness the expected birth of the dux's first child and heir. They both made their way inside the dux's estate and into the dux's master bedroom, where they saw Lucia struggling as she went into labor. Eventually she did push hard enough in intermittent rhythmic cycles with the assistance and supervision of the midwives along with a local temple priest who possessed sufficient medical knowledge to ensure the delivery of the dux's first child. Decius held Lucia's hand as she struggled in having contractions while pushing. The feel of her lover's hand was promising and renewed her confidence to still persevere through her contractions while pushing. Eventually, a head popped out that was hard to fully discern as Lucia's amniotic fluid was nearly pitch black and had also come out and covered the newborn child. The newborn gave small, faint shrieks almost like miniature imitations of howling, and with the exception of Decius and Agaroman, nearly all those present in the dux's master bedroom for the delivery were shocked upon using a towel to clean off the amniotic fluid from the newborn. The newborn had arms and legs like any other child; however, the face of the newborn was that of a newborn wolf pup with pointed ears like a wolf. The newborn child also possessed black furry hair. It was ironically similar in anthropomorphic disposition to the iconic mural art and statue depictions of Calu, where the deity spirit in physical form represented an anthropomorphic werewolf-looking beast. Despite the shudders of initial fear and shock, the priestly doctor and the midwives still maintained their composure. They wrapped the human-wolf hybrid-looking newborn in a towel as they proclaimed before the dux and his wife that the child was a male and possibly a werewolf given the appearance. Lucia held this wolfling or young werewolf-like pup in her arms alongside Decius. Both of them did not care, and Lucia looked at Decius as well as those around her to proclaim that her child was not a curse but a blessing. Her child became the symbol of the birth of a new omen that validated Decius's claim of not only the title of dark lord but also his newly assumed divine vesselhood in being chosen by both Laran and Calu, who again was depicted as anthropomorphic in a way comparable to his and Lucia's new son. They were both pleased, and even Agaroman shook his head while pointing out that Decius's powers apparently allowed him to be the new progenitor for recreating (or procreating) a new future generation of Lupercalians that had not been known to walk the western continent, let alone anywhere else on the planet, for over a millennium. Agaroman noticed this from observing Decius when he glowed with a certain pitch-black mark near his forehead that displayed a symbol of a wolf's head in the foreground with a sword pointing upward in the background surrounded by a laurel in an enamoring fashion. This glow became noticeable whenever Decius was in close proximity to his newborn son. Many in the continent of Hesperion would expect to hear this anomaly being mentioned to better legitimize the dux in his adopted role of fulfilling prophecies, with a darker role to still later play against the kingdom.

Decius held his baby alongside Lucia. A moment later, upon hearing the news, Senator Diem along with his wife came to the dux's estate and went on to congratulate his daughter as well as Decius, his son-in-law, for having such determination to bestow a blessing that they did for one. Lucia and Decius acknowledged their parents and parents-in-law's compliments while offering the opportunity for the senator and his wife to hold their beloved newly born grandson. The two new parents were not sure what to expect in reaction but hoped that Lucia's father and mother would be as accepting as Decius and Lucia both were about their newborn child. Diem and his wife assured their daughter and son-in-law as such. Decius then took his son from Diem and invoked Citadellan custom by holding up his son while proclaiming and accepting the child formally as his.

CHAPTER THIRTY-NINE

New Revelation/Mark of the Dark Lord

Only a week after the birth of his wolfling-like heir, Decius had decided upon a name for his son. He confided to Agaroman while the dux inspected his wizard advisor's progress in building the new flying skybeast prototype model. Decius had decided upon naming his son Lucianus Canus, in likeness to the masculine form of his wife's name and in likeness to his heir's features as part of the name Canus, in reference the Citadellan word meaning doglike or wolflike. While proclaiming his son's full name, Decius told Agaroman it would be Lucianus Canus Decius Diem, with the dux using his first name as his heir's first surname while also including his wife's family name as the second last name, which was customary for Citadellan culture.

Agaroman, keeping a straight yet somewhat sullen face, let the dux know that while the name seemed appropriate, he wanted to share with him important information concerning his origins based on rare correspondence letters that Agaroman had received from a small raiding party of goblins and orcs that had managed to steal what they thought was initially chests of loot from the king's royal archives that were stored in Aldion (in addition to the capital of Citadella Neapola). The chests, once opened, turned out to be confidential letters Ascentius wrote to each of the regional governors (including the governor from Aldion) for rare standing orders.

Decius inquired now with the sense of curiosity that his advisor had roused in the dux. Agaroman shook his head and summoned one of his servants to bring the pile of letters stored in a now-unsealed chest container.

Bringing the container, Agaroman quickly sorted through the pile to take a particular letter that he identified and let Decius know that it was one that the wizard would read aloud that happened to be signed by Ascentius himself more than twenty-eight years ago.

Decius listened intently as Agaroman read, and the dux gradually became stirred with visible anger. Agaroman beforehand had informed Decius also that the wizard advisor had read the letter along with the other ones from the pile in the container, all personnel letters of correspondence that Ascentius had with various important public officials, which Agaroman made sure to verify.

However, this letter that Agaroman picked and selectively began to read had revealed that the king was aware of an impending Nordling barbarian raid beforehand over twenty-eight years ago along one of the roads near the ancient pilgrimage site and ruins of Imperia Capitolina. The content of the letter revealed that this group of barbarians was eager for spoils including from pillaging off devoted pilgrims, which included Decius's parents. The king tried to prevent the raid from being carried out but was apparently too late. After the raid, the letter revealed, only a few notable survivors managed to stay alive, including a wizard named Agaroman and a young male infant that the wizard had found, tended to, and was nursed by a pack of wolves along the roadside near the ancient city ruins. This young child had no identifiable connection to any of the parties when he was found, except that one female, a Citadellan lady noble from the house of Anicia, also known as the Anicii, had carried swaddling clothes when she had fallen. The letter went on to indicate that this couple were none other than the esteemed couple Lucius and Juliana Anicii, who dressed inconspicuously like commoners and made a clandestine pilgrimage with the company of other followers of a controversial cult, the cult of Calu, to Imperia Capitolina.

Already, Decius was filled with a range of emotions. He was excited to finally know the names of his parents but, at the same time, startled with a sense of misunderstanding and further curiosity. He directed his reaction with both shock and further questions in seeking clarification. He pressed for Agaroman to explain how he was there but was not able to identify the bodies of fallen pilgrims including his parents, who were evidently nobles. The dux also wanted to know why Ascentius never told Decius of this and how his fate became sealed that day after the pilgrimage raid.

The wizard advisor told the dux that he had no way of knowing who these members of the Anicii family were since they were dressed inconspicuously well like peasants and the only indication he could have was denied to him when he later found out from the letters that the king identified the Anicii by their signet family rings and necklaces, which they still wore concealed despite posing as meager pilgrims. Ascentius had the rings and necklaces removed to conceal the identities of the Anicii couple without disclosing his reasoning in the letters. Still furious while having more questions, Decius continued to press for more explanation. Agaroman responded patiently and told Decius that his answers would be further revealed as he finished reading. The dux nodded painfully with a straight angry face while clenching his fists.

Agaroman continued to read and stated that Ascentius's soldiers had apparently caught up to the barbarian raiding party and defeated them while taking no survivors except for one Marjawani who was among the company of the barbarian raiders at the time the Swordbane soldiers intercepted them. The lone Marjawani individual male was a contractor and merchant. Upon seizing the merchant and his possessions, the king's men had found a written letter with a bounty offering a generous amount of gold for the Nordlings to attack, which they initially did. Now that the Marjawani merchant was the only survivor and viable witness of the raid, he was brought before the king to explain his role in the raid. In fear for his life by this point, the Marjawani admitted what the contents of his captured letter revealed: the Kingdom (or Sharjdom) of Marjawan was seeking common enemies to occupy and keep Swordbane at bay from benefiting from its ever-growing expansion and trade influence that Marjawan feared would grow unchecked if not challenged even by subterfuge. There was apparently another involved party which the letter indicated that King Ascentius explicitly ordered not to be recorded nor mentioned at his court. The king, after finding out about the plot, wrote to this particular regional governor of Aldion that the discussion of the matter as well as the letter mentioning who was involved, such as the Anicii couple, was to be sealed and not discussed under pain of death, for the good of the kingdom in order to avoid war with Marjawan.

It was a clear cover-up. The only question that remained was why? After Agaroman read the last line, Decius was still stunned and still going through a flurry of emotions from outright anger, sadness, and a deeper feeling of anxiousness in not knowing something that directly influenced the path of his own upbringing. He asked Agaroman plainly about why

Ascentius, the king of Swordbane, the most powerful ruler of the most powerful kingdom, would resort to covering this up simply to avoid a war that ironically did occur later against Marjawan. Why cover up a major diplomatic offense and unsanctioned assassination against subjects of the crown, including a noble ancient Citadellan family that happened to be the parents of Decius? There were still more perplexing questions than answers for the dux.

He turned to Agaroman and asked the same thing, thinking that his mentor advisor had held back or possibly deceived the dux. Agaroman sensed it: Decius's feeling of anger and questioning of trust after what the wizard disclosed about what he had read and his limited role in that event.

Agaroman responded solemnly while reaffirming what he had stated earlier that all he knew was what he saw: a raid by barbarians against a traveling group of pilgrims including Agaroman himself, and he and Decius, who was temporarily cared for by wolves, were the few survivors of that raid outside the ancient ruined city. The wizard restated that he had no idea that members of the once-prominent and rare Anicii family were among the cult followers of Calu that undertook the pilgrimage, and there was no way the wizard could know, with their identities being concealed along with Ascentius preventing the only noticeable way for them to be identified, by having their signet rings and necklaces removed.

In another moment, however, Agaroman did mention to Decius that the wizard himself was told directly from King Ascentius at that time (being a direct witness of the raid) that the wizard was ordered by the monarch, under pain of death, not to tell anyone of what happened during that particular raid, though Agaroman did risk telling it to Decius when he was a boy old enough to understand, out of remorse and a sense of wanting to help raise Decius even as his own son and as a mentor to help lead the dux in fulfilling the prophecy of chosen vesselhood at least in part to exact revenge against both the barbarians and Ascentius, along with anyone that stood in their way, including the subjects of the king who were either undyingly loyal to the king or were corrupt officials of the crown. Decius knew that much about Agaroman and his genuineness toward the dux.

Decius apologized to Agaroman after feeling convinced that he possibly acted harshly in his line of interrogating Agaroman about his role and knowledge of that event. Agaroman understood and dismissed Decius's sense of guilt as being understandable from what he had been presented as a grave amount of information to absorb, with such an impact on the dux's life in growing up.

Bringing closure on his part, Agaroman stated in reference to the letter that this was the point of the incident when the king ordered him to remain silent: to avoid a costly war against Marjawan. As such, the wizard knew that Marjawan would be the ideal and ironic catalyst, with its retainer of assassins to not only possibly remove Ascentius from power in order for a more suitable candidate, the likes of Decius to take Ascentius's place as king. But Agaroman's plan did not work exactly as he had anticipated, with Ascentius and his daughter Marin surviving that fateful attempt on their lives at Grimaz-Kadrinbad over twenty-one years ago. Instead, it led up to a long painful war that would still see the potential of a different leader to rise up in the ranks of the Swordbane kingdom and challenge the legitimacy of Ascentius. That rival, as Agaroman pointed out, would not allow any revealed parties of factions to go unpunished from subterfuge and bribery of barbarians to attack subjects of the crown even if they engaged in secretive pilgrimages as part of Calu's cult. It was something that Ascentius had done even if his reasons were different and now revealed that Marjawan had apparently engineered such a devious trap using one of the migrating groups of barbarians as a false-flag plot to implicate the barbarians as scapegoats without Marjawan or the other unmentioned party being traced and held liable for orchestrating such a daring and brutal raid.

Decius now not only saw the barbarians before his takeover as being responsible, but now the dux had further reason to hold deeper animosity toward Marjawan and its involvement in the raid that led to the death of his now-revealed parents. Ultimately however, Decius held his deepest anger and resentment that further stoked his hate and justification of what he considered another pretext of reciprocal betrayal toward his former king, Ascentius. Decius held Ascentius most liable for being complacent and derelict in not declaring war against Marjawan earlier and instead the king decided to only do so a few years later when the perceived personal attack was directed squarely against Ascentius himself and his family at the desert dwarven border fortress of Grimaz-Kadrinbad by Marjawani Kalashi assassins.

This now made the dux have further reason to build up his hatred toward Ascentius and to strive to remove Ascentius from the Swordbane throne once and for all. This former king of the dux had, in Decius's mind, sold out the chivalric responsibility of exacting justice against all foes and while putting aside the dignity of his own vassals' lives, particularly nobles, for the sake of avoiding a war that would come several years later, only when it affected the king and his family more personally as the intended target. He resented how the king would not prioritize his subjects to take the same comparable action that he did when it also affected his family comparably in being attacked even if it meant war.

Decius took a moment to pause and reflect. He proceeded to thank Agaroman for all those years of serving as the former's mentor, while hugging Agaroman. He told the wizard advisor that he was right about deposing Ascentius and bringing an end to what was considered a corrupt kingdom. The dux was made aware later in his adult life after confiding to Agaroman about his first sign of resentment against the king for treating his fellow soldiers and knights as an expendable sacrifice, that Agaroman had also confided his secret plot to remove the king after the pilgrimage raid. The wizard concealed his identity and traveled to Marjawan over twenty years ago to persuade the Sharj to stage an assassination attempt against Ascentius and his royal court as ironic revenge for the king's disregard to exact retribution against Marjawan for its role in the pilgrimage raid.

Ending the conversation, Decius turned to look again at the skybeast prototype vessel and asked Agaroman about what weapons the skyship would be potentially outfitted and armed with, such as various siege engines including possibly catapults, ballistas, and scorpion launchers. Agaroman for his part went on to share the paper diagrams of his prototype flying craft in order to assure to the dux that there would be fixed mounted weapons (or at least some of them) on these prototype flying contraptions. Decius smiled while nodding and told his wizard advisor to maximize whatever siege weapons they could mount on the skybeasts as well as the skyships that his imperial Remnant forces had captured at Aldion. The dux told Agaroman that he would make sure Ascentius and those loyal to him would suffer and pay dearly at the next battle.

CHAPTER FORTY

The Promised Reckoning

After two months of strategic planning and a large buildup of sky naval forces, including completion of the three skybeast vessel prototypes along with dozens of skyships, Decius had assembled the largest known sky naval armada poised to set sail in the skies above. He had assembled in formation inside Sanctum Novus as well as outside the city walls a large diverse army composed of three thousand Citadellan soldiers, including hundreds of knights of the Black Wolf order; seven thousand goblins and orcs, including several hundred that were light enough of weight to be assigned as cavalry mounted on their dire wolves; two dozen large armored trolls; and over a thousand Nordling barbarians from the Aries tribal clan settlement.

Additionally, Agaroman had personally configured to equip the skyships with at least one or two teams of siege engineers along with siege equipment and well-trained goblin shamans capable in using magic at least half as good as Agaroman himself while at least being capable of teleporting allied soldiers to and from the skyships.

Assembled before the main street colonnade leading up to the central plaza and forum, Decius's army stood rank and file facing the central plaza and listening intently as their dark lord, their dux, appeared before them on the city rostra platform. Before speaking, Decius alongside his wife Lucia, as well as next to Senator Diem and Agaroman, had performed the wine libation and incense-offering ritual as a way to appease the deity spirits. The ritual offering was devoted in particular to Decius's adopted deity patrons, Calu and Laran. Upon giving the offerings and seemingly appeasing the deity spirits, the dux turned toward the tight formation of his army as well as many of the local citizen onlookers. The dux addressed them all. He told them that this would be the day that Sanctum Novus and the rest of the Remnant forces would assemble to board the skyships and sail forth in the sky to bring havoc to their enemies in Citadella Neapola along with the other aligned cities of the Swordbane kingdom. The crowd, ecstatic and motivated by their leader's impeccable ability to command and deliver, cheered loudly before quieting again to listen once more to their charismatic and ambitious dux.

Decius continued, stating that for too long, Sanctum Novus suffered under political neglect and was relegated to an insignificant provincial role at the expense of corrupt politicians, merchants, and clergy that the dux had personally dealt with over one year ago. The crowd of citizens as well as soldiers once more cheered before listening again.

Decius resumed again, stating that over a year ago, Sanctum Novus had sent a message to the rest of the provinces in the kingdom that the Citadellans of the desert would no longer submit before the yoke of corruption and the royal crown that turned to look the other way. Decius reminded the audience that it was Sanctum Novus forces along with their beastly allies: goblins, orcs, and trolls, which had put aside their differences with the desert city to bring a new age under the dux's leadership in which there would be order and prosperity not known since the long-forgotten times of the Lupercalian Empire. This order would continue to seek to resurrect that once-great empire in a new form and spirit. Decius motioned for his wife Lucia holding their swaddled wolfling son, Lucianus Canus, in her arms to step forward. She nodded and went forward while handing their son over to Decius. The dux unswaddled their son and raised him in the air before the citizen crowd and before his army, proclaiming as he did on the day of Lucianus's birth that this child was his son as well as his heir and the symbol of a new return of the Lupercalians.

The crowd as a whole was astonished, while the soldiers (at least the Nordlings and some of the Citadellan city guard) were equally astonished, for those that had not seen the dux's son before in person. With the exception of the dux's summoned gargantuan werewolf, never had they seen before with their eyes until now the sight of an actual werewolf-looking species granted in its infant stage. The crowd that spectated and were unfamiliar could not hold back sighing in shock and disbelief. For some, it was hard to bear, adjusting to seeing what they had long relegated as fairy tales from times long ago; now they had actually seen it. They had seen a Lupercalian offspring returning to a world that had not seen such a species in over a thousand years.

Eventually in comprehending and processing what they have seen, the crowd did gradually in unison chant the name that they called this prophetic son to be born from what they considered the living vessel of Calu and Laran. They chanted the name Son of War and Death. Most excited and jubilant among those looking on were the beastly races, goblins and orcs along with some of the trolls that were able to comprehend enough of what they were witnessing.

Finally, Decius gently and fluidly transferred his son back to his duchess consort, Lady Lucia. The dux resumed his speech telling all before him with his army as his witnesses that he would lead them as their dark lord, their warlord, to the promised reckoning that they would deliver upon the Kingdom of Swordbane and its king, Ascentius. It would be from the ashes of ruins of that kingdom that they would show the rest of the realms in the western lands of Hesperion to fear and pay respect before this new empire in which Sanctum Novus along with its partners would no longer be neglected as a backwater, but rather as a new center of civilization. It would be today, according to Decius, that would mark the first day among many in which he would lead the combined forces as their dark lord to pave the path of a deeper hell that their enemies, including Swordbane, would not be able to imagine. The crowd cheered again a final time before the dux signaled and gave a final goodbye to the city's populace in letting them know that he along with the army were departing soon in their pursuit to pave hell upon Swordbane. Decius kissed and embraced Lucia while also rubbing his head gently toward a playful Lucianus Canus, who was still too young to make sense of what was unfolding. This would be the rare and uncertain moment for Decius to embrace Lucia before departing. They did so one more time while Lucia gave their son to his grandfather Diem to be held. If she could, she would hold Decius forever and be held by him forever in his arms. They knew they could not indefinitely and she relented after a moment of embracing him. She gave him a quick kiss and then told him to not hold back in his ambition and purpose while remembering what he had come to set out to do. She would wait for him.

Decius nodded and told her he would do everything possible to come back to her and that as much humanity as he would lose in being the prophetic dark lord that he believed in being destined to be, she would always be there to remind him that he was still human. That he still had someone he genuinely cared for along with those that served under his command and the general citizenry that he represented in Sanctum Novus as their leader. Lucia nodded in stating that she knew so also.

Turning to Agaroman, Decius signaled it was time to depart. With the quick motion of his wizard staff, Agaroman teleported both himself and Decius to one of the skybeast vessels floating high in the air side by side with the other two skybeast vessels and scattered loosely in a sea of dozens of skyships that floated high above Sanctum Novus. Wave after wave, Agaroman along with the dozens of goblin shamans teleported groups of soldiers eventually totaling in the thousands from below, within the city and outside its walls. Once all were aboard, the skybeasts, led by Decius at the helm of one of those terrifying vessels, guided the way for the other dozens of fully crewed regular sailing skyships to set course northwest. The sky sailing fleet maintained a wide checker-pattern formation. In due time, the skyships would reach and soar over the Western Coastal mountains before reaching their ultimate destination, Citadella Neapola.

CHAPTER FORTY-ONE

Bracing the Reckoning

Citadella Neapola, the largest coastal metropolis in the western lands overlooking the great bay of Swordbane. The city, like many other days, enjoyed the glistening sun sparkling over it like a light fixed toward a crystal diamond. Looking below the city skyline and at the southeast center of the metropolis stood the Grand Circus. It was a large stadium seated spectacle that had an elongated oblong semicircular shape used for hosting horse-chariot races. Dry dirt filled the track surrounded by hundreds of thousands of spectators at the periphery of the track in various gradual elevated positions of seats. The grand majestic sporting complex was considered among the wonders of Citadella Neapola's many ancient and still standing buildings that were still in use. Additionally, it was also considered among the ten wonders of the western continent, sharing that title additionally with three other wonders in the city: the Great Temple Basilica of Sol Invictus, with its beautiful colossal statue of a blue dragon that was considered the totem symbol of the respective deity spirit; the Great Amphitheater of Swordbane; and the Royal Crown Palace, with its soaring thirty-story-tall cylindrical citadel tower with an observation view encompassing the entire Great Bay of Swordbane and the land surrounding the bay.

On this particular summer day, many months had passed from the king's return along with the four heroes from the Order of Comradery, who were about to receive a newly bestowed title by the king himself. Before commencing the annual ceremony of chariot race games, King Ascentius, rising from a throne seat in his royal box seating area before a crowd of over 250,000 spectators, had announced that this game would be held in honor of the four members of the Order of Comradery in receiving the title as Legends of Swordbane, in recognition of their past heroism as well as their most recent display in rescuing the Nordling survivors of Tribus Wald, including the king's sister-in-law, Helga, refugee queen of Aegir-Hafn. Helga stood beside Ascentius while nodding at his proclamation and also acknowledging the crowd.

A moment later after pausing, Ascentius had also announced formally that he had bestowed a marriage ceremony between his daughter princess and Linitus to be held at the next annual horse-chariot race tournament. Ascentius motioned for Linitus and Marin to stand as they previously were seated behind the king. They did gracefully while nodding as the crowd erupted in cheers while still standing also.

Ascentius paused and looked at the engaged couple, telling them both of how proud he was and that this kingdom would be inherited in good stewardship by the both of them. Linitus and Marin nodded while Marin held her elven companion's hand. She could feel his tension. He did not want to be a king and rule behind the confines of a palace. He would rather spend the rest of his days adventuring in the various lands that he had not seen. Marin felt the same, though she was more acquainted with the royal life, which she had been privileged to live in. She turned and whispered in his ear that it was not so bad, considering she had been a knight. As royals, even when inheriting, they could still travel to the far corners of the kingdom and beyond, only that they would be more heavily guarded and perhaps wearing more fancy attire. Linitus, understanding his lover's intentions in soothing him, nodded while whispering back that he would find a way to adapt as he always had. Marin replied quickly that she knew him well enough to presume just as much before surprising the elf and kissing him. Linitus, though caught off guard, kissed her intently back.

The crowd, still elated, cheered on along with Ascentius, Helga, and the couple's other adventuring companions: Peat and Wyatt, who stood on each side of the hero couple. A brief moment later, Linitus and Marin broke off their kiss before taking one final bow before the crowd and before Ascentius. Ascentius nodded.

In another moment, everyone remained seated after Ascentius had motioned to do so. Then rising up again, Ascentius called forth for both Linitus and Marin to take the wreath of garlands from one of the king's servants who had held it before Ascentius. The hero couple did so while standing at the edge of the box seat, looking below at the various chariot drivers who stood poised to start while holding the reins attached to their horses, which numbered four per chariot. As the two of them stood, they waited while sounding out a count of three before dropping the wreath toward the dirt-track ground. As soon as the wreath hit the dirt floor of the track, the chariot drivers with their respective horse chariots quickly took off. The race was designed to end after ten laps. However, before the first lap had even been completed, a loud horn noise sounded off.

Looking about and immensely alerted, Ascentius along with Helga, the king's guards, and even Linitus, Marin, and their fellow companions, Peat and Wyatt, all rose up quickly. Though this was a formal royal event, Linitus and his fellow comrades had refused to change into more regal attire than what they normally wore in combat. The elf's reasoning was to always be prepared and expect fighting even when it was least expected. This time, his reasoning had been validated more so than ever. He and his hero companions quickly unsheathed their weapons while more of Ascentius's guards surrounded both him and Helga.

Meanwhile, the crowd, bewildered and frightened, shouted with anxiety, wondering what had happened. Some knew and shouted that it was the horn to alert the city it was being attacked. More and more of the crowd quickly broke off and stampeded in various directions where multiple exits lay about the Grand Circus. Some of the crowd still stayed, surveying as much as the heroes of the Comradery and the royal guards, who looked all about, wondering where the attack was and assuming that it had to be outside the city walls.

Looking up in the sky, Linitus pointed above in the distance, a large swarm of skyships. He also spotted a few small awkwardly sleek and jagged-looking objects in the distance that emerged from the swarm of skyships and were fast approaching. These objects were difficult to make out and had haunting jagged-looking wings along with a forward jagged gnarled protruding ram head in the shape of a demonic-looking wolf. It was Decius's army, Linitus knew it.

The elf ranger quickly called forth, alerting and identifying before the king and his guards that the dux and his army were attacking from the sky. The elf ranger told the royal guards to escort the king and Nordling chieftainess Helga away from the Grand Circus and to find safety in the king's Royal Crown Palace. Linitus motioned to his company, including

Marin, that they would get to the skyship as quickly as possible after they followed the king's guard in retreating to the palace. However, as they began to make their way to retreat, the frightening hybrid-looking wolf and batlike skyship, or more properly known to the enemy as a skybeast, quickly hurtled downward toward the Grand Circus.

Emitting outward from the descending flying beast-like contraption were multiple large spherical rounded flaming projectiles launched from catapult and ballista mounted launchers along with large arrow-like bolts hurled forward from large crossbow-like launchers known as scorpion launchers. These projectiles pelted down upon the large masses of crowds of both civilians and the king's royal guards while the respective skybeast vessel made a searing and screeching pass crossing high above the Grand Circus. The deadly flying contraption turned around and, this time, hovered around in a wide circular motion while unleashing another volley of siege weapons down upon the occupants of the chariot spectacle complex. This flying contraption was high enough and moving fast, which made it difficult for Linitus to get a clean shot to fire one of his special explosive miniature oil-barrel arrow projectiles. When the elf ranger did fire one such arrow projectile while anticipating the movement of the floating beast-like vessel, the projectile struck and exploded without any noticeable damaging effect. He turned to Marin, Peat, and Wyatt while looking in awe. He motioned that they needed to take that flying vessel down some way, somehow even if it meant boarding it. Wyatt shook his head but also pointed out with his hands that the ship was moving too fast for him to focus and teleport the hero companions to it. Linitus acknowledged while asking the halfling wizard if he could more easily teleport them if he could get to their skyship to be at a more elevated level in teleporting the other companions to the top-deck roof of the floating beast. Wyatt nodded while Linitus told him to hurry and teleport Ascentius, Helga, and several of the king's closest guards to the Royal Crown Palace while returning with Wyatt's skyship (which was docked within the royal palace grounds and would need time to be ready for deployment in battle) to enact their impromptu plan. Wyatt nodded again and did so.

Just as the halfling teleported the king, Chieftainess Helga, and some of the king's closest royal guards alongside himself to the Royal Crown Palace, at various places around the chariot-racing complex, including the dirt track itself, dozens of armed orcs, goblins, Nordling barbarians, and darkly armored Citadellan warriors teleported down to the surface in steady intervals every couple of seconds. These newly arrived enemy warriors quickly made haste and attacked anyone they could reach, whether it be ordinary civilians or members of the royal guard. The invading forces struck and killed indiscriminately and without mercy.

Reacting to the sudden onslaught, Linitus rallied the remaining royal guards at the sporting complex to ready arms and fight back. Marin and Peat led the group of guards that had remained at the king's royal box seating area to relocate onto the dirt track to fight back the growing wave of Decius's enemy army. Meanwhile, Linitus decided to quickly shoot his regular arrows in clusters of three. He did not want to risk using his more powerful arrows to strike down his foes while his companions would possibly be at risk from friendly fire in engaging the enemy at close combat.

As the battle heightened, it not only took place in the Grand Circus, but all around the capital city. The swarm of Decius's regular skyships began to envelop various locations of Citadella Neapola. These skyships along with two of the other skybeasts hurled volley after volley of various siege equipment munitions down toward various congested populated areas, bombarding any and all unfortunate persons, whether soldier or civilian, that were on the receiving direction. From the ramparts and towers of the capital city, the king's royal guards and other soldiers unleashed their own volleys of arrows and siege equipment that were mounted at fixed locations along the ramparts. It had little effect in only felling a few enemy soldiers at best, for the skyships that were low enough in elevation and the ramparts and towers that were high enough for the king's forces to be able to strike back.

As the fighting took place fiercely high above and below, the city's half-dozen or so skyships were deployed and exchanged mutual volleys of munition fire in the sky against the Remnant's sky armada. In a matter of minutes, the overwhelming force of Decius's skyships and skybeasts tore and shredded apart the kingdom's few defending skyships, which were only able to take down two of the invading enemy's skyships.

Meanwhile, just as in the Grand Circus, dozens and dozens of Remnant forces still continued to teleport down to fight the king's defending forces for control of key strategic points of the city including mainly the wall ramparts, towers, and gateposts. The fighting became equally fierce in the various contested locations of the capital city just as much as it had been at the Grand Circus. Gradually Decius's forces began to overwhelm and overtake the royal guards of the city as more and more of the imperial Remnant still continued to teleport at quick intervals.

Most intimidating were the armored war trolls, which wielded large pikelike two-handed war hammers that swatted the defending royal guards and other defending forces of the king.

Next also came groups of dire-wolf cavalry that, upon arriving on the surface of the city streets, charged and pounced upon any fleeing civilian that lay in sight or any defending soldiers that stood in their path to challenge them.

The city burned at various locations while voices all about screamed in terror and agony until suddenly some were silenced, while other voices continued to still scream. It was utter chaos and looking from the inside bridge cockpit of one of the skyships, Decius turned to Agaroman, both pleased by the scale of death and destruction that they and their army had caused. Agaroman commended the dux as he also did to his advisor for anticipating the victory that they had ultimately sought in bringing down the kingdom at its very core. All the dux's army aboard his skybeast erupted in howls, war chants, and war cries in relishing the carnage they had done and were planning to still do.

Looking below as the skybeast hovered around the Grand Circus complex, Decius and then Agaroman saw what the dux considered the one blight to his promised day of reckoning. Below they had seen the last hope of resistance that stood in all defiance, even against the odds, to the dux's forces. A lone elf ranger rapidly firing arrows from his ornate bow, a female half-Nordling and half-Citadellan human knight in ornate purple-azure armor with a flaming sword, along with a small old dwarf wearing a spiked horned helmet while wielding a large imposing war hammer, and a few couple of still standing royal guards. The dux sighed and scoffed with disappointment in his forces not being able to overtake them from the dirt racetrack below. He muttered to Agaroman, overhearing that Decius would deal with them himself personally.

Concentrating in a meditative and seated form, Decius closed his eyes while uttering words and calling upon his powers and inward being to project outward. A moment later, a burning portal was emitted at the ground surface. Crawling up from the portal emerged a large, gargantuan werewolf-like beast. It was Decius's summoned avatar beast, a towering wolflike beast that had the body build of a human and the face as well as distinguished features of a wolf. It emitted throughout its darkened black body sparkling flames. All the occupants from the skyship who watched both the dux in his meditative form and in his summoned avatar-like beast were in awe. Once again, they unleashed a chorus of howls, war chants, and war cries, while Agaroman proclaimed that Decius, the dark lord of death and destruction, had brought forth his ultimate tool of reckoning.

On the surface below, the sight was equally filled with awe as well as terror. The dux's forces broke off their attack in fighting the defending forces of the king. The enemy soldiers were enveloped behind the gargantuan wolflike beast while also chanting and howling at its power. Linitus unleashed various arrows at the gargantuan beast with no effect. Frustrated, he knew he had to call the remaining defenders to fall back and retreat. Marin and Peat did not want to, with Marin indicating that they could not afford to let the enemy take the city and Peat saying that dwarves like him only knew death in the face of fighting an enemy. Linitus snapped without hesitation, telling them that there was no choice. The city would fall either way, he told them, and there was more meaning to retreat in defeat while living and fighting back another day than to die with no one else left to fight. Marin nodded while subtly agreeing and looking toward her dwarven companion Peat to tell him that Linitus was right. They had to fall back and find another way to fight back even if it meant losing the king's own capital city.

They started pulling back but not before the summoned towering beast swatted several royal guards. Marin luckily dodged to the side while Peat tumbled below from one swat by Decius's summoned spectral werewolf. Linitus fired several explosive arrows to catch the beast's attention before firing a large smoke-emitting arrow. Shockingly, this particular arrow contraption did work in distracting and disorienting the beast from finding the remaining defenders while they pulled back and scaled the wall toward the king's royal box seating area. Linitus helped Marin and Peat get back up to the royal box seat area before Marin motioned which direction to follow her in retreating. Only two royal guards survived along with them as they exited the racing complex and made their way along the winding streets toward the Royal Crown Palace.

Along the way, buildings burned, which they could see while fighting broke out in various pockets. Voices of civilians screamed in various directions. Wherever Linitus could let loose his arrows to strike any of Decius's attacking forces, he would do so to save any bystanders that he was able to spot. However, he could not save them all. Marin knew it and saw the frustration on his face, and he showed it inwardly as much as he could see her frustration from wanting to fight what he considered an unbeatable adversary. Marin placed her hand before his shoulder while standing on top of a fixed grate that led to the entrance of one of the sewers of the capital city below. She told him while motioning to follow her and Peat down below as Peat demolished the gutter fixture with his hammer for them to fit below at the entrance to the sewers. Linitus nodded and followed her, Peat, and the surviving two royal guards that were with them.

Marin knew the way. She had snuck out from the Royal Crown Palace and played around the sewer system of the city when she was younger. It was her way of being mischievous, wanting to venture out away from the palace when she felt too isolated and alone with her father the king and his royal estate household. Eventually, she was caught by Peat himself, but the dwarf made her a deal in the interests of her safety and well-being in which Peat would follow her, provided she remained close to him when venturing under and outside the royal palace complex.

Now, years later, Marin and Peat, ironically enough, were trying to escape the carnage of the city below and find their way back to the Royal Crown Palace. Marin still knew the way. For now, they knew they were safe at least for the time being.

Chapter Forty-Two

Dark Passage to Hope

Making improvised torches with the burning oil Peat had carried along with individual shafts of sticky silk-bulb arrows Linitus provided from his quiver, Marin and the two of them along with the two fortunate royal guardsmen that survived the onslaught on the surface above now all treaded carefully in navigating the dark and dank sewers below the capital city. The Princess Knight took point lead in traversing through a series of tunnel passages and several junction chambers slowly and methodically within the sewer system network. Along the way, Marin stopped at one particular junction.

Being still but showing some signs of uncertainty, Marin had paused to think deeply and recall the different tunnels and where they would lead. She looked at particular markings along the way. These were markings she made during her youth that served as short-form references of locations between where each tunnel led. At the junction, the tunnel they were previously in had opened up to an intersection terminal of four different tunnels. As Marin studied about, she could not hold back recalling, the brief pauses in the stream of thought about her childhood, the days when she wished she returned to what she considered her better days of life, with less responsibility and with less sense of worry than she was now faced with. It pained her to remember and look back at those days with all the times she wanted to explore and pop up somewhere randomly on the surface anywhere in the city far away from the place she once called home, the Royal Crown Palace, which she once considered a prison. Shedding a few tears while dwelling upon the memories, she could not hold back her expression from the one now closest to her, Linitus.

Searching for and drawing upon empathy, the elf ranger asked with a degree of presumption if Marin was looking back upon her memories. Marin shook her head though somewhat shivering and in a low tearful voice replied, affirming. Linitus, feeling saddened for her, placed his hand on her shoulder and then drew her back close to his chest while embracing her. He could have said anything else at that moment, but he decided not to. In his mind the best thing he could do was hold her, be passive, and let her express herself or take in as much of the swirling of emotion and pain she felt, to transfer how she felt to him in a way. Marin knew it and realized it in another moment while taking his hand from her shoulder and kissing it.

Observing quietly, Peat took the other two soldiers to keep a distance and stood watch briefly while letting his two fellow hero comrades have their moment together and somewhat alone. Once the two of them broke off their embrace and assumed a posture resuming their current business, the dwarf guardian called upon the other two guards to break their stance and return, following behind Linitus and Marin.

However, suddenly as the small escaping company began to resume their course to find the tunnel that led to the palace, a large clutching snap-like noise sounded, along with a long harrowing screech and gnarl. Linitus turned and knew instantly what it was, while Marin had sensed it also, by her reaction. Peat and the two other guards wondered what had happened and were completely unsure of the possible source of noise. The elf ranger stated they were not alone but rather being followed, presumably from the reaction, by goblins. The rest of the company still wondered what was going on and how the elf ranger was certain, though Marin knew Linitus well enough to trust his instincts and still shared the same suspicions.

Linitus showed from his carrying bag next to his quiver, two foot bear traps. He mentioned he had deployed one already and had two more ready to use. Wasting no time, he set one of them upon the tunnel that they came from that opened into the tunnel junction while saving another to put in the passage that he and his company would next take when Marin became certain where to proceed and led the group to follow behind her again. This time, they accelerated their pace. A moment later followed by another moment in which time passed, both of the last two foot bear traps had sprung with a similar eerie sound of two goblins screeching in pain and agony. There had to have been three goblins still already in pursuit and Linitus could hear faint splashing from a distance.

The pursuing goblins were closing in on them. Still having two more sets of arrow sabot capsule racks wielding multiple arrows, Linitus used one of the projectile assemblies to deploy upon pulling back his bowstring and letting loose at the first moment he could sense the enemy was close enough to be within range of his deployable weapon. Immediately upon shooting, the separation and impact of the cluster of arrows succeeded in taking out presumably several goblins, though it was not bright enough to know how many exactly.

Hearing more shrieks, Linitus and the rest of the surviving group were able to make out that more goblins had come into the sewer. The company of heroes along with the two royal knights continued to run the current course that Marin led. They were close to reaching the shaft that led to the royal underground catacombs and cellar. Marin was certain of that. She guided them finally to the shaft that led upward, while indicating.

However, the swarm of goblins was able to close in on the company of heroes to force them to stand their ground and fight off the enemy. Though unable to get an exact count, Linitus estimated there were at least a dozen and a half of them, perhaps two dozen. The small green wildly pointed ears and jagged jawline and teeth along with sharp noses made the goblins stand out in addition to their relatively short height, being no taller than Peat, and possibly slightly smaller.

Linitus quickly fired three to four shots before switching from using his bow to unsheathing his slightly curved elven blade to strike down quickly and gracefully the other remaining goblins that lunged toward him to engage in melee combat. Marin did the same, slashing any goblins within reach with her flaming sword while bashing several with her small round shield. Peat, meanwhile, whirled circularly to the nearest goblin he could find before hurling sideways his large ornate war hammer at the remaining goblin that stood before him and was mortally struck by the blow of the hammerhead. The two soldiers bore arms but did not do anything other than to watch in amazement while waiting for any goblins that had survived the blows delivered to them and managed to cross the path of the two guards. They never had the chance as the three heroes dispatched the remaining goblins in a very efficient manner.

As soon as they had dispatched the goblins, they caught their breath momentarily before resuming the next course of their destination. Scaling a series of vertical metal steps, Marin led the group up into the shaft, which was sealed by a special hatch that had to be turned with a special wheel in order for them to proceed to the next destination, the royal catacombs and eventually the cellar to the royal guard palace. Upon opening the hatch, Marin scaled the last metal step of the shaft through the hatch port, which led to the surface of the catacombs. She helped Linitus along with the rest of the group to pull themselves up from the sewer shaft onto the surface of the catacomb floor before closing the hatch. Seeing that one of the soldiers carried an ax as well as a spear, Marin quickly took the ax from the soldier and used it to lodge the turn wheel of the hatch from the surface end. Linitus quickly borrowed one Peat's oil barrels and also made an improvised trap that would set the fuse to light off the barrel using a trip-wire snare that was attached to the hatch turn wheel. Peat as well as the two still-fortunate surviving guards watched on with amazement at the quick and cunning thinking that they had seen from both the Princess Knight and the elf ranger. They worked in one sense separately but in unison found a complementary way to deal with any remaining pursuing goblins or other foes if they managed to try to follow their group this far into the entrance of the catacombs. After a short moment, Marin quickly motioned the group to still follow her as she still served as de facto guide in leading them from this dark passage to eventual hope in reaching the main-floor level of the castle.

As moments passed, they managed to make it more than halfway through the catacombs, where Marin motioned and spoke in a low voice that on the other side of the catacomb passageway within in sight was the stairway that led to the cellar of the royal palace. However, soon quickly even from a distance, the group could hear a hard struggling and wrangling sound. Another wave of goblins had tracked the path that led to their fellow dark minions' death. The noise from the hatch became louder until something loud shouted with an audible monstrous noise and then a loud boom explosion sound was emitted. Linitus's improvised explosive trap clearly seemed to have worked at least for the time being, with no immediate sound being made right after the explosion.

Wasting no time, the group led by Marin quickly composed themselves and continued to make their way from the catacombs, up through the stairs, into the cellar. The entrance from the catacombs to the cellar, however, was locked. Marin pointed this out as she tried to open the passageway door. Linitus quickly tapped her shoulder and signaled for her to let him try to unlock the door. However, Marin reminded him that this door was different and that it had a crossbar lock on the other side. Peat next decided it was his turn to take action and told the rest of the group to move back as he swung heavily with his mighty war hammer toward the center of the door, hoping to break through it to the other side. Sure enough, after several stroke attempts with his war hammer, the door along with the crossbar lock gave in and broke apart.

Linitus pointed out that while it was a relief that they had broken through to reach the cellar, it was also a concern as it became one less barrier to keep the pursuing enemy from following them and possibly overtaking the castle, should the enemy numbers swarm through this same route. Taking another moment and borrowing another oil barrel from Peat, only this time smaller, Linitus set up another trip-wire trap near the doorway and close to what was left of the broken door, for any unsuspecting enemies to risk blowing themselves up and/or setting themselves on fire if they still decided to pursue Linitus and his fellow comrades by this point.

After setting the trip-wire oil barrel trap, Linitus and the rest of the group continued to follow Marin's lead. They still hurried with their improvised lit torches through the dark cellar that housed many vintages of Citadellan alcohol as well as various novelties from various races over the years that Marin's family line collected through the centuries.

After several minutes, the group made their way to another set of stairs blocked by another door with again another wooden crossbar that had the door locked in place. Marin tried knocking twice. As she was about to knock a third time, Peat swore he would break this door again, just as he did the last one. However, the dwarf guardian was interrupted as he was about to finish his statement when the door slit slid open, showing two piercing and inquisitive eyes looking at them and asking who they were. Marin, speaking with authority, informed the apparent guardsmen that it was she, the Princess Knight, along with her companions who had retreated from the onslaught from both the surface and the ground below against many goblins. The guard looked at her and studied briefly before closing the eye slit and deciding to let them in before shutting the door and barring it back in place. As they came in from the other side, the group of heroes sighed with relief that they had made it, at least this far.

CHAPTER FORTY-THREE

To Lose a City or Not
Fight Another Day

Upon exiting the cellar and entering the first floor of the Royal Crown Palace, Linitus and the other members of the party were still feeling relieved from the hasty and harrowing retreat they successfully made from the chariot racing complex. They made their way to the king's throne room, expecting him to likely be there to discuss the next course of action in dealing with the Remnant's assault on the capital. The group quickly went up one flight of stairs after another while observing anxious royal guards either moving about to shore up the defenses of the palace and standing their post in anticipation of holding their ground if Decius's forces were to cross paths with them. Marin stopped one of the guards to ask about the king's present whereabouts and the direness in needing to meet with him. The guard informed her that he was in the chamber on the fifth floor.

The party of heroes, along with the two accompanying soldiers that escaped with them from the sewers had reached the fifth floor, where the king was in one of his chambers for a briefing with several important dignitaries and high-ranking members of the kingdom's army. They were in the middle of discussing which last-minute plan was the best, either making a certain stand to hold their ground and eventually make a counterattack, or ordering the remaining forces to retreat away from the city to either Aldion or Salvinia Parf Edhellen. Upon the Comradery's hasty entrance, nearly everyone in the room was astonished to see the members and their present company. Ascentius was both relieved and in awe after seeing even from the palace window outside the chaos and havoc that Decius's forces were causing all about the capital. For a moment, he had confided to himself, pondering if his daughter, Linitus, or Peat had fallen to the dark lord's forces. He was comforted to see them and know that such was not their fate.

Seeing her father, Marin, not caring anymore about proper salutations even as a knight, simply rushed and embraced him. While any of the high-ranking military officers could have complained that such a display was not appropriate in her capacity as a knight with respect to the king, even if he was her father, none of them did. They each understood the gravity of this situation and that it very well could be Marin's last moment or the king's to embrace each other as daughter and father.

Taking a pause, Marin turned to Linitus with a visible expression of deferment to his expertise and leadership prowess to advise her father, the king, on what should be done. Linitus instinctively, without wasting any time, told the king that the city would fall no matter what, given the overwhelming force of the opposition, and if they stood their ground to try to stop the Remnant, then they likely would fall along with the city. Their only choice, Linitus concluded, was to pack up and take as many people as the king could to escape and head eastward toward Salvinia Parf Edhellen to find refuge among Linitus's elven people, who were still fiercely loyal to support the king. Eventually, the king could call for aid from the various other settlements within the kingdom to help him amass enough forces to make the elven settlement an ideal future staging point to launch a counterassault to later retake the city.

Ascentius took a moment and paused while looking again at the room window and observing from a distance the smoke, the fire, the rubble, the screams, and the corpses of his loyal subjects. Sighing in disappointment and reluctance, the king nodded his head in agreement with Linitus's plan. It seemed there would be no other way to prevail without making a strategic withdrawal in which they would devise and implement a later plan to retake the city when they were ready. Still, the manner in which Decius launched his daring assault and deployed an overwhelming number of soldiers loyal to his side was unexpected even to the king. He never thought, despite being as cunning as Decius was, that he would have such audacity and leadership skill to succeed in the way that he had set out to.

Ascentius had underestimated his former vassal and ex-regional governor for what he hoped would be the final time.

After receiving the king's support, Linitus quickly made plans to survey and help prepare the two remaining skyships, which were grounded for the time being but would be used to deploy and flee quickly from the soon-to-be-fallen city. Before exiting the room door with Marin and Peat by his side, Linitus turned and asked the king about Wyatt's present whereabouts. Ascentius quickly responded that he assigned Wyatt to be in charge of making last-minute preparations for both his personal royal skyship as well as the Comradery's skyship for deploying.

Linitus, along with Marin and Peat, nodded while giving a salute toward the king. The three companions made their way through the hallway toward the royal palace back patio bailey that held a large hangar bay enclosure. The king's royal skyship was docked inside while adjacent and outside the hangar stood also the Comradery's skyship. Upon exiting the back side of the Royal Crown Palace, Linitus and his two companions rushed through the open area of the bailey courtyard to approach Wyatt. The wizard was intent on overseeing the king's servants and available soldiers to make preparations as quickly as possible in loading the skyships with supply provisions and weapon munitions prior to deployment. However, the young halfling wizard was well attuned to hear from a distance the approaching sound of footsteps, so he turned. He was elated and relieved to see his three fellow hero comrades make it safely back for them to be able to reunite.

Peat being the first to embrace, gave Wyatt a strong bear hug, making the wizard show his visible reaction of feeling compressed while absorbing the emotional and physical shock. Eventually, Peat let go while surprising Wyatt yet again by being rambunctious, holding the wizard in a headlock and rubbing his head while laughing quickly and then letting go.

Marin and Linitus could not help but laugh in a low tone while staring at each other, seeing how they shared the same impression of the unexpected silliness and yet fond attachment that Peat had shown even to such an extent to Wyatt when they had previously butted heads on more than one occasion, even over trivial and frivolous disputes. Linitus commented on seeing that as a good omen of how much the dwarf guardian and young halfling wizard had grown in working together and being an effective team. Marin, looking back at him while staring in admiration, commented that it was in large part due to having a great leader to guide them. She took his hand and, in a reverse form of chivalry, kissed him while letting him know that she was thankful to be with him every day to fight side by side and explore whatever challenges came their way. Linitus, feeling humbled, blushed, took Marin's hand, and kissed it back. He vowed to her that if she did follow him wherever he led, they would not go astray on the path of righteousness. Marin, taking his other hand and kissing it, replied that she knew while affirming he was the best influence, the best person that had come to her life. He was her angel sent from the divine, and she would be guided to him like a star that was always constant.

Their moment seemed as if it could last forever, and they both wished it did. Linitus was the first, however, to recompose himself after kissing her other hand and letting go. He helped Wyatt direct the cargo being loaded onto the skyships while personally checking on the various forms of munition that were making their way on board Wyatt's skyship. Looking back after seeing provisions of oil barrels being loaded, Linitus turned to Peat and came across a resounding thought in his mind. He approached Peat along with Wyatt and Marin to let them know he had an improvised idea on how they would escape. After sharing his plan, Linitus and his fellow comrades quickly redirected the oil barrel munitions that were loaded onto Wyatt's skyship to be stored on board the king's royal skyship. Wyatt had also used his magic to teleport the oil barrel munitions between the two skyships. After several minutes of hastily made preparations, fighting had made its way and ensued at the front inner walls of the royal palace complex. The four heroes of the Comradery could tell that there was no more time left to spare. They had to make do with the provisions they had already transferred between the two skyships. Linitus sent two of the royal guards that still were present with him since the circus and sewer escape to be dispatched as messengers to alert the king that it was now time to leave at once and board the skyships. As Ascentius with a contingent of his most trusted royal bodyguards left the royal palace to make their way to the back bailey courtyard, Linitus briefed the king of their plan. The king nodded while he and his bodyguards proceeded to board Wyatt's skyship and switched places for Linitus and his hero companions to board the royal skyship. Within moments and just in time, both skyships launched into the air, and gradually with increasing speed, the two skyships drifted high above the royal palace complex.

Looking below, all the occupants that accompanied both skyships saw the carnage and onslaught that still ensued. Several armored trolls battered at the palace's outer wall that secluded it from the rest of the capital city. These trolls along with a makeshift ram broke through the outer palace complex defenses and swatted away multiple royal guards and other soldiers of the king's army that swore to hold the enemy off as long as possible in order to ensure that the king and his selected accompanying soldiers and knights would escape, which they did.

Within another moment while still watching from above and looking below, Ascentius lamented while noticing that the few armored trolls that prevailed over the defenses gave way to more of Decius's forces storming in. This included packs of mounted dire-wolf riders and goblins that hurried along on foot, followed by Nordling auxiliary forces loyal to Decius, and ultimately several contingents of Sanctum Novus Citadellan soldiers and Black Wolf knights loyal to the dux. Perhaps what was most terrifying that approached farther in the distance was a giant, gargantuan half-wolf/half-man beast that took large slow steps toward the palace. It stopped and looked back to observe from a distance. It saw and realized that not all the king's forces had fallen. It peered from the distance to realize that two skyships had taken off from the palace complex and were departing away from the city. This colossal beast unleashed a large howl that was perceived to be a summoning of sorts or a call of alarm to action. Within another moment, a skybeast ship soaring in the air from a distance had turned around in the sky, appearing to have heard the call, and was poised to answer.

On board the king's royal skyship, Linitus motioned for the other skyship that held the king and the bulk of the passengers to continue to press forward to its destination, Parf Edhellen. One of the crew from the other skyship held a spyglass and communicated to the king the signal and cue that was made by Linitus in executing the next part of his plan. The other skyship continued to maintain course while Linitus and the hero companions on board the royal skyship changed their course to diagonally shadow and follow behind the other skyship while keeping part of a portion of either the starboard or port side exposed. This was done as the respective skyship made diagonal strafes to periodically change course while facing the skybeast vessel that was rapidly pursuing to intercept.

It seemed that whoever was commanding and steering the enemy skybeast vessel clearly had their sights focused on the royal skyship while ignoring the other one as that skybeast tried to imitate the patterns of the royal skyship with the enemy's presumption that the king was on board when in fact he was not, but on board the other ship. Peat and Marin, surprised and elated, shouted ecstatically that the decoy trick was working and that this horrid vessel was pursuing them, thinking the king was on board. Linitus nodded and stated that he had counted on this decoy trick to work.

Quickly without wasting too much time, Linitus told Marin to light the fuse that led some distance to the center main mast, where dozens of oil barrels were stacked in a mound. Meanwhile, as Marin prepared to do so, Linitus asked Wyatt if the wizard would be ready to teleport the four of them to the other skyship right before the moment of collision impact with the skybeast or detonation of the royal skyship, whichever came first. The young halfling wizard nodded his head. Next, Wyatt instructed Peat to man one of the scorpion launchers that was configured with a large grappling hook. Peat acknowledged and had ready on the port side one of the scorpion projectile launchers to be prepared to fire an attached chain-link harpoon-like grappling hook. Waiting for the skybeast vessel to come within range, Linitus told Peat to hold back from firing until the elf ranger gave the command to do so. Once the skybeast vessel was within range, Linitus quickly ordered the dwarf guardian to fire, which Peat promptly did. With a sharp swooping noise, the grapple chain hook harpoon projectile soared through the air and struck the skybeast vessel. Without any luck, it was not effective in latching on to tow the enemy vessel. Instead, the large projectile object caused enough force to have the flying enemy vessel temporarily lose control before it maintained stability in flight again. Making another pass, the skybeast vessel sought to ram the royal skyship from the other side, starboard side. Knowing this, Linitus quickly ran to the starboard side ballista launcher to ready it while also modifying the chain-linked projectile by taking out from his satchel a jar of sticky silk material that he had used from time to time on his arrows. The material was fairly strong when coated to an arrow tip, but Linitus decided to take a glob of it and apply it to the front tip of the scorpion chain connected harpoon hook by dumping the substance from the bottle tilted downward. Upon doing so, the elf ranger next manned the ballista launcher on the starboard side. Taking steady breaths and aiming carefully, Linitus at a sudden moment fired off a chain-linked harpoon hook and was able to connect to the skybeast vessel with the adhesive from the harpoon hook latching on strong enough to hold the skybeast vessel in place with as much slack as Linitus and his companions on the royal skyship would allow.

Linitus next signaled that it had worked and that they, at least for the time being, had secured the enemy skybeast vessel to the other end of the chain-hook harpoon. The skybeast vessel tried to maneuver frantically with limited available while Linitus used the connected chain to pull in the enemy skybeast. The enemy ship would not give up so easily, and it still frantically tried to outmaneuver and break free from the attached chain while it was gradually reeled in.

Seizing the moment, Linitus now instructed Marin to light the fuse that led to the stacked barrels on the center mast of the ship. Marin nodded while smiling and indicating her pleasure. Upon doing so, Linitus instructed his companions to be ready for the next phase, in which they would teleport away. Linitus next motioned to Wyatt to enact the next stage of their plan, to which Wyatt nodded.

As the skybeast vessel still wrangled to break free from the harpoon and chain-link grapple while being only a few hundred yards away from it, Wyatt began to concentrate, with his companions circling close around him. The young halfling wizard peered across the distance at the other friendly skyship. He focused his thoughts on the location where he wanted to teleport himself and his companions. Within moments, a dimensional portal opened that sent streaks of lightning about them. The portal had enveloped them, and in another sudden moment, it appeared again, this time, from the far distance on board the deck of the friendly skyship. Another few moments while the skybeast ship made a final pass heading toward the royal skyship to take it down while still being towed by the latter's chain harpoon hook, a sudden burst of explosions erupted with a loud boom. The force of the explosions knocked the skybeast vessel into an uncontrollable spiral. Meanwhile, the remnants of the royal ship along with the chain hook still attached to the ballista assembly dropped straight downward from the sky. The wrecked royal skyship still had enough weight to take down along with it the still-attached skybeast vessel, which plummeted in a vertical snap-like motion. Both flying hulks made their way to an impending crash in the southeastern part of the capital city.

Ascentius and his soldiers on board the other skyship had watched. The soldiers had all cheered and celebrated, thinking only of the victory and damage that their most celebrated hero warriors had inflicted upon a seemingly invincible enemy. Ascentius nodded in a somewhat mixed form of approval but also despair. His thoughts were first and foremost on his only beloved daughter, Marin. He did not see the teleportation portal that emerged in the distance. For a dire moment, he thought he had lost her and she had perished along with her other hero companions whom the king also held in high regard. He could not hold back in looking down in the distance at the site of the crashed wreckage that produced a burning and smoking heap that lay on top of now-destroyed stone buildings. He could only imagine how many lives were lost among the people and soldiers that might have been garrisoned in the immediate destroyed buildings. All lives that were lost, he thought, all precious. They died, and he wondered, for what? His throne, his survival, the concept that was somewhat abstract called the kingdom. For a moment, Ascentius paused and thought about his own purpose. He wondered what good was a king to live or be defended so vigorously at the expense of others, especially the common people of his kingdom without making their well-being more meaningful on his part? He knew, or thought in his own heart, he had to do more. He had to make whatever ultimate sacrifice that could be made directly on his own behalf without having others loyal and close to him make any further sacrifices to defend his reign.

As he stood reflecting on such things, Ascentius could not hold back in shedding his tears. Just as much as he felt he had lost at the turn of a moment including his own beloved daughter, suddenly he realized while hearing a familiar voice that he recognized calling out to him from behind. Ascentius turned while still in tears to see that his daughter Marin and the other companions, including Marin's lover, Linitus, had in fact remained alive. The king realized at once that they had teleported in time before the explosion and quickly approached his daughter to embrace her while confiding before all those that could hear how much he worried that he had lost her. Marin returned the embrace and told her father that she knew and that she was sorry for causing him such pain, but it was necessary for her, Linitus, and their other two fellow comrades, Peat and Wyatt, to risk their own lives and that they each knew what was expected of them. They knew what they had to do in order to preserve the kingdom and to defend her father's claim as rightful king and all the lands under his domain.

Ascentius nodded once again in a solemn yet understanding manner. He told her as well as addressing loudly all those present on board Wyatt's skyship that he knew and was well aware of the sacrifice that they and each of their fellow warriors in arms had made for the kingdom and for him still retaining his rightful claim to the crown. He told them that they would regather and get more support from other allied cities and settlements in the kingdom to fight back and retake the city. More importantly, he told them that he would lead them directly to do it and he would not have them sacrifice more than he would have of himself. His words were able to resonate strongly with those on board, with all the present soldiers, knights, the few dwarven guardians, as well as the heroes from the Order of Comradery: Marin, Linitus, Peat, and Wyatt.

Taking another moment looking back as they drifted away from the capital city in the distance, Ascentius told all those on board to look back also and remember what they had lost. He told them to remember that as saddening as it was, they needed to ensure to go on to live and fight another day to take back what was left of the capital and to rebuild from what they had left behind. All the crew on board nodded.

As time went by and Wyatt's skyship continued to sail away farther from the edges of the capital, a group of several skyships had already noticed from the debris of the crashed former royal skyship and the wrecked skybeast vessel that there was possibly a surviving skyship of the king's army that Decius's forces had not disposed of. Approximately five of the pursuing skyships of Decius followed the same course as the lone surviving skyship of the city still in service to the king. Linitus took notice of it and pointed it out. Anticipating as such for this scenario to unfold, Linitus called upon Wyatt and Peat to gather two improvised cask barrels filled with a mixture of sugar and saltpeter. Having the barrels ready, the two companions placed them sideways with improvised mounts to keep the barrels stationary before the top stern deck of the ship, the poop deck. With the fuses facing the stern, Linitus and Marin both each took a torch and lit each of the fuses. Within seconds, the burning fuses had carried the flame into the cavity of both barrels, and within moments, a large plume of gray-white smoke was emitted from each of the barrels. Over time, the plumes dispersed more and more of the smoke, creating a barrier cloud with a potential means to disorient the pursuing ships into being lost in this noxious cloud and risk crashing into each other. Another effect that this contraption would have because of the ingredients was that it could potentially irritate the eyes and lungs of the pursuing enemy with their own crews onboard.

A few short moments later, the pursuing enemy skyships broke course and turned around without risking the chance to cross through the cloud of smoke in further pursuit of the king's lone fleeing skyship. When it became clear to all those on board that they were no longer being pursued, multiple soldiers cheered again, reveling with some form of consolation the small claim of victory that they did see from surviving the onslaught in which many of their other comrades were not so fortunate in being spared such a fate to live on and fight another day after the onslaught that Decius had launched against the kingdom's capital. Eventually, within a few hours and when dusk was due to arrive, all on board the lone kingdom skyship would arrive at their new place of refuge, the elven city of Salvinia Parf Edhellen.

CHAPTER FORTY-FOUR

Dark Victory

Walking through the main street during dusk, one could see dead bodies lying all about, while multiple buildings were in ruins with some still burning. The once-prominent capital of Citadella Neapola was now as close to hell on earth as any place could be. Emerging from the death and destruction that he and his army had caused, Decius now made his way to the Royal Crown Palace to survey the extent of the damage he had caused from the ground while also using the palace as a symbolic staging point to declare what he considered his dark victory before his army and any survivors that they could round up to bear witness to this dark lord's edict.

Decius made his way to the palace after crossing the drawbridge and barbican gateway that separated the palace castle as well as the stormwater drainage moat from the rest of the city. After entering the front bailey palace courtyard, Decius along with Agaroman by his side next proceeded through a stairway that led to one of the palace castle wall battlements. Upon reaching the top of one of the battlements, the dux next walked over the top of the barbican gateway at the front of the castle. From there, Decius looked over along with Agaroman in surveying the damage from a higher view though not as high as what they saw from above while on board one of the skybeast ships. Decius, though now walking freely, still had his mind in two places at once. He found a new way to master his divine spirit powers in summoning and commanding his feral gargantuan werewolf-like hell beast while no longer being stationary and confined inside the exotic supernatural crimson blood sphere. He could move about independently while at the same time controlling his mental thoughts to move his summoned avatar beast also. The summoned gargantuan hellish werewolf walked over in loud strides toward Decius before turning and facing the same direction as the dux away from the palace and toward the rest of the city.

Meanwhile, hundreds of warriors from the dux's Remnant army began to file in. Many were goblins and orcs, while some others were of surviving barbarians allied to the dux along with his own Sanctum Novus Citadellan regular infantry and at least two dozen members of the elite knighthood Order of the Black Wolf. Finally, several more goblins filled in with several captive soldiers of Ascentius's royal army along with various civilians of the city from the different races including human Citadellans, local human Nordling residents of the city, some elves and dwarves, and two halflings. Behind them finally marched in about a dozen trolls who had survived the onslaught battle along with several dozen dire wolf riders. Though not all, a good number of the ones that had assembled were visibly injured even as they were present to listen to Decius's proclamation. Decius could see it well enough to take notice and even he lamented that this was the cost of war at the expense of his own forces, while still accepting that such consequences from his decision to launch the assault were necessary and that if he had to do it over again he would without hesitation.

After waiting another moment from the last remaining soldiers and captives of the city that were able to assemble, Decius finally proclaimed victory of his army over the city. He announced that this would be the beginning of a new day and that a new ruling order led by him taking the role as dark lord and as chosen vessel of the deity spirits of Calu and Laran was necessary in order for the western continental lands of Hesperion to rid the corruption that had spread for so long in the Swordbane Kingdom as well as to maintain order from future would be foreign invaders. Decius asserted that it was necessary for his Remnant army to conquer all those resisting and bring them before their knees to recognize what he considered the rightful place in restoring a new Lupercalian Empire out of inspiration from the legacy of the original one. While the captured soldiers loyal to Ascentius along with those local bystanders who were rounded were quiet in accepting solemn defeat, none of the captured visibly seemed to be convinced nor convicted in their minds by Decius's speech to rationalize and justify the widespread slaughter and destruction his army had caused. All the captured locals could do was stay silent, with some wishing they were dead while others in some state of fear of not knowing what the victorious dark army would do to them next.

Decius, taking a moment of pause and reading the reaction of both the captured locals as well as his own soldiers, next declared that this day that was about to end would mark the start of a new day and a new era in which he along with his dark forces would focus on rebuilding all that was fallen and destroyed in order to repurpose toward his vision in remaking this new inspired version of the Lupercalian Empire.

Finally, looking more intently on each group of his soldiers that were amassed, Decius told them to remember this day and night in which history would acknowledge their dark victory. He reminded them that he along with them had delivered his promise in ushering the promised reckoning that he had sworn right before they departed Sanctum Novus to attack this shell of a once-great prominent capital city that now lay in heaps and ashes. The dux promised them that there would be more great reckonings and that as long as they followed him from life unto death, he would lead them further as their dark lord even unto death. Listening to this, his various surviving soldiers erupted in loud cheerful displays of shrieks, howls, shouts, and war cries. Even the gargantuan hell-wolf beast while still under the control of Decius as its avatar instinctively unleashed a loud howl that was followed up by a chorus of surviving howling dire wolves assembled among the gathered crowd.

Despite claiming victory, more bloodshed and fighting within what was left of the capital still ensued. It would not be until sometime the next day during the morning hours in which the remaining army and knights of the kingdom as well as some patriotic loyal citizens that formed into makeshift militias, gave their last efforts of resistance against Decius's forces until falling one by one to the last fighting man. Afterward, the remaining forces of Decius's army had rounded up more of the local citizenry and had a large number of them, upward of about fifty thousand, fill the seats to the Great Amphitheater. The dux's soldiers stood guard at intermittent spaced intervals between local citizenry that watched, nervous and anxious, out of fear for their own lives as well as their loved ones'. Decius along with Agaroman once again gave another rousing speech toward the general populace, who were forced to listen and to bear witness to Decius declaring once again his forces' victory over the kingdom along with his invested power as the chosen vessel to usher in a new era of empire out of inspiration from the Lupercalian Empire from long ago. Before closing and in gaining a further display of his power to exact fear and respect from the city's survivors that were present in the amphitheater, Decius summoned again his gargantuan avatar hell-wolf or as some among the crowd would perceive more descriptively as a werewolf colossus from hell. The summoned beast under Decius's assumed control once again unleashed a loud terrifying howl followed by a chanting chorus of goblins, orcs, as well as some dire wolf riders that were present with their dire wolves and the surviving armored trolls, the latter two occupying the amphitheater arena pit. By this point, the visible looks from the masses of the crowds were apparent. Not only Decius and Agaroman could sense their collective aura of fear, but also out of it, their consignment to submit from defeat. The people were completely deprived of any will for further bloodshed to resist their new would-be conquerors.

By threat at swordpoint and spearpoint, the general crowd reluctantly chanted on Decius's name in exaltation, though it seemed more like a depressing wailing chant. Clearly and utterly, they were defeated and chose to live under humiliation rather than die resisting for what they considered an utterly hopeless cause at this point.

Decius, standing and raising his sword in victory while sounding one loud howl-like shout, then began to sit down while motioning with his hand for the goblins and dire wolf riders on the arena pit to open the gates. At this point, the dux surprisingly had the forced crowd of spectators watch one of the armored trolls emerge from one of the pit gates to fight in a series of gladiator fights against its opening on the other side of the pit gates. They were several of the captured barbarians from Tribus Wald; apparently, the dux's army had taken some as prisoners. Though the fight would last for a small amount of time, the captured barbarians that were forced to fight in melee combat were inevitably given a death sentence as the fearsome troll made certain to win with utmost ferocity and no sense of remorse or mercy for its opponents, who would get slaughtered eventually one by one.

Meanwhile turning to Agaroman, Decius had the wizard brief him on the latest casualty report from their assault on the city. Agaroman responded with a best estimate that their forces had done well, but still incurred losses that amounted to roughly half of the dux's initial army fighting force for this city assault. They essentially went down from ten thousand combatants to just barely over five thousand. Decius nodded with some displeasure though a degree of understandable resolve to know that such casualties were likely to be expected especially in a strategically challenging attack where the king's forces in the city outnumbered them initially anywhere between five to one or ten to one. The dux's only advantages at the time were the element of surprise as well as initiating a high shock-and-fear value among his enemies, not to mention they had overwhelming sky-fleet dominance in the skies.

Decius then proceeded to instruct Agaroman further to prepare one of the two skybeast vessels for Decius to use to pick up his wife consort as well as their son. Agaroman at first was somewhat perplexed while not being able to hide his reaction. Decius understood but responded that while he intended to still have Sanctum Novus as the capital of their new empire, he intended also to have his family rule alongside him. His wife consort could be depended upon in rebuilding Citadella Neapola with her proficient urban administration skills. The dux reasoned after all that if they were to genuinely attain acceptance by the people of this city as well as the other coastal Citadellan cities, then the responsibility fell squarely on the dux along with the appointed officials and members of the dux's family to gain that acceptance of the conquered people as being legitimate and certainly to exceed the perceived legitimacy that Ascentius had previously established during his control of the coastal metropolis. He wanted to be feared, but in time, he wanted even more so to be respected and loved by the people he conquered so long as they knew not to cross the dark lord and chosen vessel of the western lands.

Drifting away from this stream of thought, the dux looked again to his wizard advisor. Agaroman understood and acknowledged while responding that he would dispatch one of the two remaining skybeasts at once.

CHAPTER FORTY-FIVE

Finding Ascendancy and Divine Blessings

Hovering above the city and skyline of Salvinia Parf Edhellen, the view of dusk soon turned to pitch-black night. Before it did, however, a lone skyship drifted from high above in the air before it announced itself by trumpet and it proceeded to land near the main plaza of the settlement. The local peoples of the elven settlement were all surprised and wondered what occasion it was for a lone skyship to travel and land in the city, but then again, many of the local folks were already familiar in spotting out this skyship from before to recognize that it was the same one that had carried the king then as much as now.

As the lone skyship docked at the plaza, a brow, or ramp-way connected the skyship's portside to the plaza's exotic cobblestone street. Sounding off with a small guard detail and series of blows from two trumpets, Ascentius's arrival was announced while the king proceeded to walk from the brow in a somewhat expedient fashion. The king was greeted by the acting chief captain of the elven city's town watch guard who consulted with Ascentius. The chief captain briefly expressed a visibly shocked and saddened facial expression upon hearing the devastating news of Citadella Neapola falling to Decius's forces of darkness.

The elven chief captain returned to the matter at hand and dispatched an elven sentry guard to alert the city's regional appointed governor along with the town council to convene for an emergency summit with the king. Within less than a half hour, a well-dressed ornate elven figure, the settlement's governor, along with several other ornately dressed elves representing the town council appeared before the king to be briefed in the same manner as had the city's acting chief of the watch guard. Their reaction was no less different, being in the same state of shock, disbelief, and sadness of hearing what had transpired.

Ascentius, though not talking too loudly, talked loud enough from his fairly high state of urgency and gravity of the dire situation to communicate with these most senior elven officials. It was at this point that the king made sure to include Linitus, Marin, Peat, and Wyatt, to be involved with their discussion in what to do next. Ascentius turned over his briefing and full trust over to Linitus to discuss how best to proceed in retaking the capital. Linitus came to the same initial conclusion as he had earlier suggested, that the king dispatch couriers to call upon all the other settlements of the kingdom to send forth all available forces they could each muster to meet up and assemble at this elven city before marching forthwith to retake Citadella Neapola.

The elven local leadership nodded and agreed with the plan while one of them asked how the city fell and what powerful forces made up the strength of Decius's army. Linitus responded by indicating that the enemy's forces numbered in the thousands, possibly tens of thousands, and its most feared contingents were armored trolls, dozens of skyships including at least two of the remaining terrifying skybeast ships, and finally from recalling with great reluctance a powerful summoned colossal beast that was in the form of a werewolf covered in embers and flames.

The elves nodded again though this time with reluctance expressing the concern in their ability to be able to effectively fight back such powerful units in Decius's army. The elven council went on to say in speculation how it was that such power, especially this colossal and hellish beast was able to be controlled by one such as Decius. Ascentius shook his head, stating that he did not know but surmised that Decius had apparently succeeded in invoking the legendary and once long-lost prophecy of becoming the chosen vessel for the powerful spirits of death and war, Calu and Laran. The elven council and regional governor all nodded in unanimous agreement.

Ascentius took a brief pause before bracing with anticipation how he could next propose dealing with Decius and his new deity-like powers. The king told the elven council that they knew as well as he that they had to appeal also to divine spirits in order to receive their blessings and powers to wield against Decius and keep him in check as a counteraction from becoming all-powerful. The elven council members were once again in shock, only this time in hearing the king's extreme proposal before considering whether to agree with it or not.

While contemplating, one elf council member indicated that it was only reasonable to do so in order to preserve natural harmony and balance from what would be considered an otherwise upset order of darkness. The other elf council members agreed unanimously with the elven governor. After consulting the elves in their own native tongue, the governor announced that Ascentius was right and they agreed it was time to conduct a ritual to invoke a rare passage of ascendancy from the plane in which their world, Terrunaemara, resided into a different plane that was very surreal from the one many people of Ascentius's plane would be acquainted with.

Ascentius nodded while asking them to take Linitus and Marin with him as he had trusted the two of them as much as himself to pursue this form of ritual to receive the benevolent divine spirits' blessings and powers of chosen vesselhood to later use against Decius and his forces. The elven governor nodded in agreement to Ascentius's plan while asking the king when he wanted to conduct the ritual.

Ascentius, taking a moment to pause, responded that it was necessary for him and the other two heroes closest to him to conduct the ritual right away and travel to the other higher plane as soon as possible. The elf governor nodded once again while motioning for the king along with Linitus and Marin to follow him and the other elven council members.

Ascentius along with his daughter Marin and her lover Linitus followed the elven officials through the city and just inside the city walls away from the local aqueduct. They eventually made their way up toward a hilly slope that at the summit was surrounded by a grove of rare maple-wood trees with an open clearance of land and structures in the middle of the summit base. These structures were a series of ancient exotic rectangular horizontal stones that were arranged and connected to a pair of exotic vertical standing stones in a circular manner. In the center floor of the peripheral series of standing stones were a series of ornate rocks moving in a circular outboard pattern. The elves carrying torches assembled all around this monument while directing for Ascentius along with Marin and Linitus to assemble on the central decorated floor. The latter three did so while staring all about them in their immediate surroundings. They each were feeling suspicious at first, wondering what these elven dignitaries were up to that might change the outcome of the war against Decius and, by extension, Sanctum Novus.

Soon, however, the high-ranking elves alleviated their concerns by ensuring that where King Ascentius and the two heroes stood would be the exotic teleportation pad that would send them when they were ready to the gateway of the astral plane and abode of the divine spirits, Caelum Praesidium, as it was called. The king nodded while asking promptly if both Linitus and Marin were also ready. The two heroes, somewhat hesitant in not being sure what to expect, looked at each other intently and then nodded before holding hands while standing behind the king.

As they waited, the elven dignitaries chanted several times ancient words in their elvish tongue as a form of divine prayer and called upon the heavens in divine appeal. The mood at the center of the ritual pad became tense for Ascentius, Marin, and Linitus. They each desperately wanted to get it over with and find out if they would be able to make it to the other side in order to appeal to the divine spirits for receiving ascendancy and divine communion in sharing the respective powers that the divine spirit would otherwise determine each of them as being their own chosen vessels to represent their interests and counteract the vesselhood of Decius and his comparatively new acquired powers.

Suddenly, a series of bright light halo rings streaked down toward the marked ritual circle in which Ascentius, Linitus, and Marin were standing. As the rings quickly showered down, they soon filled the circle with an aura of light before suddenly vanishing and taking along the king and the two hero companions. All that stood, left in wonder with amazement, were the elven council members along with the regional governor as well as Peat and Wyatt, the latter two who decided to follow along, being curious and now awestruck by what they just witnessed. The two of them could not help but approach the elf regional governor to ask what had happened and where their fellow comrades and the king had disappeared to. The elven regional governor said solemnly that they had vanished and ascended into a higher plane, one in which the three of them would be visiting the abode of the deity spirits to seek their blessings of power and commune with them if found to be worthy of chosen vesselhood.

The somewhat cryptic and eerie response surprised the two remaining companions, but they accepted it while asking as a follow-up how long it would take before the king and their other two companions returned. Once again, the elf regional governor replied that it would take as long as the deity spirits decided and that time has no meaning to the deity spirits in the way that it does for living beings in this plane of this world.

The two remaining companions, still somewhat speechless, did their best to focus on the task at hand as the elven regional governor reminded them. The dwarf guardian and the young halfling wizard would help to oversee and coordinate in organizing and outfitting the kingdom's forces with the necessary provisions while those forces from various settlements in the kingdom would join them in the coming days to assemble at Parf Edhellen and march with King Ascentius and their fellow hero comrades upon their return from their astral plane pilgrimage to attain chosen vesselhood.

CHAPTER FORTY-SIX

Divine Abode

Caelum Praesidium, an eternal abode that the divine spirits call home, a place of vastness that seems unlimited with the stand-alone exception of a large temple complex at its core. Outside the temple complex boundaries lies the infinite frontier of space, with galaxies and stars all about. Within the temple itself stood a courtyard with a simple circular fountain followed by a stairway leading to a portico that gave way to the entrance of the temple sanctuary itself, which had no wall coverings, save only multiple pillars that covered the perimeter. The material for the building as well as the rest of the complex was a bright sparkling grayish marble hue, or at least that was the most comparable material to equate with from the world that Ascentius, Linitus, and Marin hailed from. In an instant, at the center of the temple sanctuary stood a circular patterned floor made in a similar fashion as the one from Parf Edhellen. Within the circular pattern, a series of bright rings rose up, and with it after a bright flash emerged three figures: Ascentius, Linitus, and Marin.

Upon arrival, the three of them looked all about while being both amazed and perplexed. Linitus and Marin openly asked where they were at and if it was the intended destination that Ascentius had sought. Being familiar and confident since his youthhood about the mythological descriptions of what he read over the years, Ascentius had replied that they had indeed reached their intended destination, Caelum Praesidium, also known as the divine council of the deity spirits.

Still looking all about in amazement, all three saw the surroundings as still surreal for them to fathom, though Ascentius was familiar enough to remember the mythological stories of this place to have a sense of understanding of the locale, though he also could not hold back his amazement that such a majestic and exotic place indeed existed before his eyes. Perhaps what caught him, as well as Linitus and his daughter Marin, by surprise the most was a sudden emergence of spherical entities appearing before them, hovering in the air high above the ritual circle emblem on the floor of the temple sanctuary. The spherical entities came in different colors including green, violet, blue, as well as crimson and black. While still hovering, the distinct orbs of color glowed with energy, with the blue glowing most prominently as a voice called out. It asked in a language somehow translated instantly and intelligibly to the three visitors to understand. The blue glowing orb inquired why the three visitors disturbed the deity spirits in their divine abode.

Nearly flabbergasted at what they had seen, Ascentius held himself firm to concentrate and reply that he as well as his two companions had come to beseech personal divine blessings of power to be conferred upon them as chosen vessels by the divine spirits in order to counteract one who had received divine powers to cause imbalance to his kingdom and his world.

Reacting in a defensive rebuttal, the crimson and black spherical orbs of energy glowed while responding that the one whom King Ascentius had mentioned was bestowed such power because he had demonstrated his worthiness by satisfying the conditions of making perpetual offerings that appeased the nature of the two respective deity spirits, Laran and Calu, to grant him chosen vesselhood.

Shocked even more so than the three guest intruders, the blue, green, and violet orbs of energy radiated with electrical-like energy very intensely. The blue orb responded with a tone of inquisitive anger about why the black and red orbs had done this without consulting the other three, and the blue orb addressed the black and red respectively by name as Calu and Laran. The black orb Calu responded, while addressing the blue orb as Sol Invictus, that it along with Laran the red orb were not obligated to as the rules for their council and bestowing divine favor did not require consultation among their divine peers. The green and violet orbs siding in protest with the blue orb called Sol Invictus, addressed the two other orbs, Calu and Laran, in being deceitful and selfish for their own gain to feed off the energy that they represented death and destruction through war while not affording the same opportunity to select candidates for them to feed off in their respective realms of energy or aspects of life that pertained to the other deity spirits.

Lost for words while observing the feuding that took place, Linitus and Marin both could not hold back asking what this was about. For them, it seemed as if a bigger plot or context was at work. Ascentius, recalling from his knowledge of mythological lore, was able to some extent answer their question by stating that these orbs were none other than the deity spirits themselves, each representing an aura or aspect of sentient life. The blue orb, impressed by the mortal king's sense of understanding, commended Ascentius while acknowledging that he was correct.

Following the deity spirit's announcement, the blue orb decided to introduce itself as Sol Invictus, deity spirit of the sun and his totem being representative of dragons. Sol Invictus next introduced each of the glowing orbs in succession from left to right that stood before the king, Linitus, and Marin, with each orb emanating its respective color upon being called as a way to give its form of greetings. The next to start in being introduced was the green orb, which was Silvanus, deity spirit of the woodlands, forces of nature, and sacred boundaries; followed by the violet orb, which was Aritimi, deity spirit of love and hunting; and the last two orbs, which gave off visible auras and movement gestures that seemed hostile while hovering. These last two orbs, being black and red respectively, were Calu and Laran, the deity spirits of death and war/violence. Linitus and Marin both looked intently with scorn at the last two, seeing them as being part of the larger problem for all the trouble they had caused in empowering Decius with a portion of their essence to be able to take control of the capital. Regardless, Linitus and Marin both knew to keep their anger in check and rely upon the king's lead in beseeching the other deity spirits to empower them as a means to bring balance and counteract Decius and his deity-like powers.

Ascentius briefly explained the situation further about how Decius seized power against him and his holdings in the Swordbane kingdom as the deity spirits of Sol Invictus, Silvanus, and Aritimi listened intently. Calu and Laran, both knowing the circumstances, were dismissive in listening to the recent worldly plane arrivals while urging the council of the other deity spirits to banish back the newcomers from whence they came. Sol Invictus, however, sensed that these newcomers had exhibited themselves as being objects of intrigue and curiosity with a seemingly genuine approach and intent to seek them out. As such being the most powerful of the deity spirits, Sol Invictus, cut off Calu and Laran's attempts to banish the newcomers while stating that he along with Silvanus and Aritimi would like to hear further of the nature of the newcomers' request of them.

Ascentius, recognizing the opportunity, quickly responded that he and his two companions only sought to undergo a divine trial like Decius had in order to attain the blessings and powers that the deity spirits would bestow upon them after they had passed their initiation rituals in the form of trials to prove that they were worthy of such blessings and conferments of power to also be awarded chosen vesselhood. Linitus and Marin nodded while visibly expressing the same intent as Ascentius. The deity spirits of Sol Invictus, Silvanus, and Aritimi turned toward each other while gracefully emanating arcs of visible electrical energy. Within a short moment, Sol Invictus addressed the heroes to confirm that they had agreed with their request. Calu and Laran disappeared in a small shock explosion while feeling threatened by the possible tips of the scales of power that these three newcomers would pose toward their mutual chosen vessel, whom the latter two deity spirits would feed off in growing their energy from the dark warlord's actual ability in sowing war and destruction within the mortal plane he resided in.

Surprised and startled, Ascentius and his companions still turned toward the blue orb deity spirit, Sol Invictus, while indicating they would be ready for the initiation of the trials. Sol Invictus responded that each of them would face separate trials with each of the three remaining deity spirits. Upon successful completion of the trial, the three newcomers would return to the temple complex of Caelum Praesidium, and ultimately, they would be returned to their own worldly plane while receiving their powers of chosen vesselhood. The three newcomers nodded while Ascentius asked Sol Invictus which of the three of them would be assigned to the corresponding present three deity spirits.

Sol Invictus emanated his blue-aura energy while responding that it would be up to three of them to choose which deity spirit that they thought would be best paired up with that most accurately reflected their own personality in order to increase the likelihood of passing their own respective trial.

Taking a moment to ponder and consult, Ascentius along with Linitus and Marin agreed which deity spirit would best suit each of their personalities. Linitus would choose to undergo his trial with Silvanus, given that Linitus best reflected the aspects of appreciating nature and being at peace with it. Marin would choose to be paired in undergoing her trial with Aritimi, given that Marin exhibited the strongest displays of affection and love in various forms, which Aritimi was representative of. Ascentius meanwhile chose to face trial under Sol Invictus, given that Ascentius could identify most strongly with the leadership position that the blue orb deity spirit held in presiding among the other deity spirits. Additionally, Sol Invictus was seen as the deity spirit in dispensing justice as well as having a strong emphasis in valuing justice. This was a trait that Ascentius gravitated heavily toward in pursuing as a monarch head of state.

After the three newcomers to this extraterrestrial astral plane had made their decision, Ascentius came forward to let the deity spirits know they were ready. Sol Invictus, emanating a blue phosphorescent energy, acknowledged and instructed each of the three newcomers to step forward before an altar, where Sol Invictus along with Silvanus and Aritimi each hovered along the periphery of the temple sanctuary. Linitus, Marin, and Ascentius each walked up toward their chosen corresponding deity spirit. Within moments, a series of ring bands dropped down around each of them before flashing brightly and taking along each of them to vanish once again, this time separately to separate planes with their chosen deity spirits to undergo their trials for chosen vesselhood.

CHAPTER FORTY-SEVEN

The Trial of Freedom and Nonattachment

Teleporting through a bright flash of light that was all about him, Linitus saw the effects finally dissipate until there was nothing but a patch of cleared land surrounded by forest trees along with a circular river fed by a cascading series of waterfalls. In the center of the patch of land stood a large majestic shrub bearing bright-red fruit. Around the periphery of the land roamed various creatures at peace with one another including a bear, a squirrel, a fox, a snake, a small woodpecker, and even a wolf. Each creature drank from the water surrounding the central circular periphery of land while also taking turns to pick and eat exotic red fruit that came from the majestic shrub. Seeing the creatures and the beautiful scenery, Linitus contemplated, wanting to partake in the same delights and at first was tempted to do so. However, a part of him opted not to, but rather, feeling at peace, he decided to sit down and take in the ambience around as he crossed his legs and began to meditate. He realized he had all that he needed without wanting anything or having any sense of desired attachment. He truly felt as if he was in harmony with his natural surroundings more than ever.

Suddenly however, before him appeared the deity spirit of Silvanus in his preferred form of a green energy orb. Still deep in his meditation, Linitus could feel the aura in the air, sensing Silvanus just as he did before in the strange temple from the astral plane that he was previously at. The elf ranger maintained his focus as the green orb hovered all about him. It taunted him and tempted him. Rather than give in, Linitus treated it as if it was not there while focusing his thoughts.

Another moment and then a voice called out in his mind; he could hear it. It was Silvanus. Mentally the deity spirit communicated through Linitus's thoughts, daring him to both catch him and summon him while uttering rare spoken words in elvish that Linitus was able to recognize despite not being able to understand the meaning of every word as it was an ancient form of his elvish tongue from long ago. Maintaining his focus, Linitus uttered the same words until slowly a steady force of wind began to emanate before him. The wind began to swirl at an exponential pace that started gradually but became much more rapid in a short amount of time. The wind or whirlwind became strong enough until it pulled in nearly everything around it, except for Linitus, who still remained seated and stationary. Commanding the force of wind, he felt he could control it, its direction, its strength, and its speed. Soon, he began to move the wind around Silvanus until it caught a hold of the deity spirit. Its green orb tried to move, but each time, Linitus strengthened the intensity of the whirlwind until Silvanus had exhausted itself and was no longer free.

Finally in another moment, the orb dropped while Linitus, sensing it had given up, decided to let go of his control of the whirlwind so that it would come to a sharp halt. Exhibiting a slight faintness of its green luminosity, Silvanus conceded that Linitus had prevailed and passed his trial by being able to display nonattachment of having any wants while being able to focus on using the forces of nature, particularly the wind, to free himself of the distractions in life, which Silvanus symbolized in attempting to disturb and distract the elf ranger's attention as much as possible in order to get Linitus to break his concentration. The deity spirit was most impressed and informed the elf that he had attained Silvanus' blessing and gift to receive his essence as a chosen vessel in being able to summon the forces of nature including most notably the power to summon destructive and powerful whirlwinds.

Linitus, standing up, took a moment to thank the deity spirit while asking curiously what else he must do, what else must he learn in order to be ready for what the elf considered the ultimate trial in facing off against Decius and his divine conferred powers from Calu and Laran. Responding, Silvanus told the elf ranger that in due time by trusting himself and relying on the forces of nature, he would find a way to prevail.

Linitus nodded and thanked the deity spirit. Silvanus told Linitus to follow it. Linitus did so as close to the exotic fruit shrub as he could get, as Silvanus floated above it. Quickly, the same series of rings that transported the elf ranger along with Silvanus to this serene realm of nature began to rain down again before flashing and vanishing away both respective sentient beings.

CHAPTER FORTY-EIGHT

The Trial of Pursuit and Passion

Appearing before a different plane at the flash of a series of ringed lights, Marin looked about in a circular motion to ascertain where she was, though she knew she was already uncertain. Unlike Linitus, who found himself in a plane very similar to the natural environment of his native forest dwellings, Marin found herself in a bright white room like a void empty of nearly everything. She was amazed but also frightened in feeling so alone. Her thoughts, however, dwelled upon those that she also cared deeply about including her father the king and her lover, Linitus.

Appearing behind her with a glowing form of energy in the color of violet that emanated from the same color orb, it spoke to her suddenly. The orb commonly ascribed as the feminine deity spirit Aritimi by mortals in Marin's native world of Terrunaemara called out mysteriously while reading her mind. The deity spirit was astonished in its own right by how much Marin had feelings of love in different aspects that resonated so highly even when Marin was alone by herself and not thinking so much about her own predicament.

Marin turned upon hearing the deity spirit's voice and acknowledged in reply that she did indeed have her thoughts and feelings for the ones she loved most. She composed herself, however, and asked where the ones that she thought about were. Where were Ascentius and Linitus? Upon following up, her next question was asking where she was.

Aritimi replied that they were safe and facing their own trial as Marin was currently undertaking with the deity spirit of love and of the theme of hunting. Aritimi next told Marin that surprisingly she was halfway through in passing her trial in seeing how strong her feelings were for others to be worthy of the deity spirit associated with love to acknowledge it and confer to Marin Aritimi's essence of powers for chosen vesselhood.

Marin, still astonished with both what she had found out from Aritimi as well as still processing in understanding her current surroundings, next thought and asked the deity spirit what the next half of the trial involved.

Aritimi, while hovering circularly in front of Marin, told the Princess Knight that she next had to show or unlock her potential of how far she would go to demonstrate that love. Marin would be tested and even taunted, by Aritimi to see the extent of Marin's determination to project her love. The deity spirit informed the Princess Knight that her next challenge was to pull and draw upon herself the potential energy she had to hunt down Aritimi, who, with the latter's glowing orb moving around increasingly faster, began to show separate motioned images of Linitus and Ascentius being teleported but not yet arriving at their destinations. The deity spirit still also mildly taunted both verbally and physically while emanating light sparks that shocked her as Aritimi in her orb form moved about quickly. The deity spirit challenged Marin while still taunting her by asking her what she would do to reach the ones she loved and if she had the resolve to reach the deity spirit to bring the ones she loved to appear before the Princess Knight. At this point, Aritimi was now transitioning the aspect of her representation toward humans as the deity spirit of love to one of hunting as this spirit was essentially calling and challenging Marin overtly to catch it as if it could affect the outcome of Marin's current situation of wanting to be with her father and fellow companion lover or at least know that their well-being was not in danger.

Instinctively, Marin lunged and swiped with her sword toward Aritimi, but the glowing deity spirit orb evaded the Princess Knight's attempts. Marin tried again and again several times before realizing that she had to change her strategy.

Thinking about what her lover Linitus would do if he was by her side, she knew he would tell her to be patient, to concentrate, and focus on seizing the opportunity. Marin thought to herself that if this was indeed a hunt challenge, if she could draw from this plane of light, a heavenly spear long enough and fast enough, she could hurl it with unstoppable force. Such a thought reminded her of past treasured memories of how she cherished her youthhood in participating in royal wild boar hunts alongside her father. Within another moment, she realized that perhaps in using her focus and the feelings from the energies of the plane she was in as well as the bright light above, she could find a way to harness and manipulate that energy, that light, and her thoughts to create such a heavenly and near-corporeal spear of her own to unleash. She stood still while concentrating on her thoughts, the energy of the plane, and the light that shone upon the plane. Using her arm, she extended it outward while praying silently and believing that she could pull in and shape with her hands a bright object that began to materialize and extend itself into a long, narrow shaft with a sharp piercing point.

Seeing this, Aritimi became more impressed while still hovering and giggling as a mild form of still taunting the Princess Knight. However, within another moment, Marin sharpened the shaft, which had now fully taken form as a visible and practically corporeal spear emanating bright light. Marin angled it back while holding it with her right hand and then threw it quickly where it struck Aritimi.

Feeling the impact and shock of the divine-like weapon that Marin called upon and unleashed against it, Aritimi lay near motionless, wounded on the ground with its bright energy starting to dampen. Marin took a moment to process and digest what transpired. She thought to herself that she likely made an uncalled-for mistake and hurt the being when it was unnecessary and unwarranted. She realized with awareness and remorse that her anger and passion had overtaken her for possibly the worst. Marin rushed toward Aritimi on the ground, and the Princess Knight pleaded for forgiveness while asking if the deity spirit was okay.

Aritimi replied directly and somewhat cryptically to tell Marin to heal her. Shocked and not knowing what to do, Marin suddenly told the deity spirit that she did not know how to treat its wounds. Aritimi still challenged the Princess Knight to find a way to do so. The deity spirit told Marin to use the same thoughts and energy again to produce her untapped potential of powers. Marin nodded and thought compassionately about the deity spirit. The Princess Knight tried to imagine the spirit as her mom when thinking who best to reflect upon and challenge her inner aura.

Shedding some tears while thinking how to use the energy from the plane again, Marin moved her hands in a ball-like motion form while reciting a prayer she heard Aritimi faintly utter in Marin's mind in a low voice. It was the same prayer that Marin remembered in her youth when tended by priests of Aritimi that calls for healing. Slowly recalling the prayer again, verbally and concentrating her circular motion movements with her hands, Marin began to create a blue-green ripple wave aura in the shape of a sphere that was the size of a large fist. Still forming and taking control of this small energy-like orb, Marin next used her sphere to cast with the motion of her hands in moving toward Aritimi.

Within moments, Aritimi's deity spirit or orb took in the rare enchanted casted modified healing attributes of this blue-green healing energy ball and the deity spirit orb quickly teleported itself from the ground back to the air several feet away from Marin. The deity spirit abruptly congratulated Marin and told the Princess Knight that she had passed the test in demonstrating herself as a worthy vessel to receive the deity's powers pertaining to love and hunting.

Marin nodded though somewhat confused in trying to process what had happened and the reasoning for the test that Aritimi had her undertake in the way that she did which was strange to Marin. Regardless, Marin still looked back and thought about the present. She could not help herself in asking the same question again. She really wanted to know the fate of her father and her lover.

Taking a moment to acknowledge her thoughts which the deity spirit could detect, Aritimi replied Marin would soon find out. Rising above and moving all about just as freely as before, Aritimi called upon Marin to also rise and follow the deity spirit into the center of the light where it was greatest. Marin complied, and within another moment, a rapid procession of ring bands glowing with light hovered down upon Marin and Aritimi before hovering upward in the reverse direction. Within moments, a flash emanated, and the void of light was now empty of the presence of its recent visitors.

CHAPTER FORTY-NINE

The Trial for Justice and Sacrifice

Flashing before ring bands of light that rained down, Ascentius and the deity spirit of Sol Invictus emanated from the very same spot from which they briefly disappeared. Ascentius looked all about and saw nothing different from what he saw before, being in the inner sanctum of an exotic temple beyond any comprehension that most people from his own world would struggle to fathom in imagining without actually seeing. It was a temple suspended among the cosmos in which nearly every star and galaxy could be seen but beyond the human focus in counting accurately, with the beheld visible object being so vast in number that it was overwhelming in trying to do so.

Looking still all about his surroundings, Ascentius saw Sol Invictus's bluish orb hovering around him. Visible energy emanated from the deity spirit as it spoke to Ascentius. Sol Invictus had informed Ascentius that he was the last of the three mortal visitors to undergo trial in receiving divine blessings and conferment if Ascentius was able to pass the trial and be deemed a worthy host for vesselhood.

Ascentius, facing Sol Invictus, intently told him he understood and was ready for the trial. The deity spirit's orb radiated and emanated with its blue energy once again while acknowledging Ascentius's response. Sol Invictus informed the Swordbane monarch that since the deity spirit is considered the patron for the aspects of judgment, power, light, and is associated with the symbol of a dragon as its totem, it was only fair to expect for Ascentius to exhibit the same aspects in his trial if he is to be deemed worthy.

The deity spirit followed up by telling the king that throughout the history of existence, it was he who presided first and foremost among the other deity spirits, with the exception of Calu, who represented darkness and death and existed at the same time as Sol Invictus. As such, Sol Invictus guided Ascentius through the circular fountain. The deity spirit began talking about its existence briefly along with the other deity spirits as well as their yearning to no longer be alone among themselves, but to create life in which to observe the dynamics of others who are both alone at times while many times are not. Essentially, the deity spirit expressed what he and his other fellow deity spirits described as a manifest replication of their embodied behavioral aspects to be magnified and transmitted from themselves to other forms of life that would reverberate the same aspects to the source deity spirit from which they harnessed: light, darkness, justice, freedom (including nonattachment), love, death, hate, and war being among the most identifiable aspects.

Now looking into the standing water from the ornate fountain, Ascentius had seen it all quickly in moments or flashes before him. Each depiction from the fountain displayed a major historical event in the beginnings of his mortal world of Terrunaemara to its present and even to the near future. Surprisingly as he was viewing this in ways that were beyond normal mortal explanation, Ascentius was somehow able to process it. He had seen from viewing the mortal history of his own world a common and recurring cyclical theme of war and death, the rise and prosperity of civilizations that led eventually to their tragic decline and end of existence, only to give rise to other new civilizations and repeat the same previous cycle over again. Somehow he understood as the deity spirit of Sol Invictus had revealed to him. After seeing the same events repeating again and again, Sol Invictus intervened, asking if Ascentius would like for the deity spirit to stop revealing what he had seen.

Ascentius patiently replied that though he would, it was important if he was to come to a clear decision that he had to see all that was presented before him as evidence of mortals from his world. Sol Invictus was impressed and acknowledged that the mortal king had shown the first sign of being worthy of the deity spirit's powers in reserving judgment until a fully informed pursuit of uncovering information was conducted. However, the visual depictions from history long ago on Terrunaemara had come to an end. The deity spirit next tasked Ascentius to consider what was revealed and give a verdict about mortals in his world.

The Swordbane king being tested and thinking holistically acknowledged that it would be unfair to judge the sins of general society and attribute to individuals inherently but also admitted that mortal nature (albeit human, elf, dwarf, orc, and goblin, or otherwise) was not perfect and had its own set of individual and possibly collective characteristic behavioral flaws. Ultimately, the king, putting aside his personal feelings, admitted that mortal society was guilty in the taking of its own lives and that collectively it was guilty, though not necessarily individually as Ascentius deemed that such judgment largely fell on individual basis.

Astonished and impressed by Ascentius's response, Sol Invictus congratulated Ascentius on his ruling, which represented a broad but effective view of the king's judicial philosophy and interpretation. The deity spirit next asked the king given that he at least found mortal society collectively guilty about what its form of punishment should be.

Ascentius internally wept and, at the same time, marveled at the prospect of himself casting not only a judgment verdict, but also in being delegated as part of his trial to call for an appropriate sentencing verdict toward his own fellow sentient mortals throughout the entire planet he was from. Ascentius pondered and mulled on the decision briefly before responding. When he was ready, he stepped forward before the deity spirit of Sol Invictus and orally gave his verdict that sentient life (humans, elves, dwarves, and even goblins and orcs) since being collectively considered guilty for their various separate actions that holistically piled up as grave sins against life were to be sentenced to death, but he had decided to commute such a sentence with a reprieve. Impressed by such a determination in dispensing the sentence that he did, Sol Invictus inquired to Ascentius about what lesser form of consequence or sacrifice would be made for allowing such a reprieve.

Ascentius took a deep breath before looking about the cosmos in searching both internally and from inspiration of the immense view of the universe externally for a resolution to address the deity spirit's follow-up inquiry. Sighing, he knew that there had to be a tangible form of consequence and sacrifice at the expense of sentient mortals even to substitute for all the sentients mortals on Terrunaemara in being condemned for their sins in order to appease the deity spirits in dispensing their standard and interpretation of justice. Seeking no one else to call upon but himself, Ascentius declared that he as judge would vouch for his own life or humanity as collateral for the sins of Terrunaemara's sentient beings.

Glowing with visible blue energy, Sol Invictus again was in awe and impressed by the mortal vessel candidate's proposition. Ascentius would exchange his own life as part of his trial for vesselhood undertaking. Seeing the contradiction of the trial being led to error, Sol Invictus was now in what he saw as a preposterous dilemma. The candidate would sacrifice his own life for the trial of judging and condemning collective sentient life from his own planet, but individually, Ascentius himself had now passed his own trial and proven worthy as a candidate for receiving vesselhood. Sol Invictus searched in thought for comprehending how to proceed with what otherwise might have seemed an incompatible dilemma and unanticipated paradox. Ascentius could tell the orb of the deity spirit was somewhat unstable and frustrated, from its emission patterns of visible blue energy while searching for a resolution. The Swordbane king knew he had issued his own death warrant, but at the same time, he had to live long enough for receiving vesselhood. Seeking a compromise and what he considered an appropriate feasible resolution, Ascentius offered to Sol Invictus that the human mortal monarch would forfeit his human body even in the form of a physical death, while having his soul transmitted in a new incarnate being that would be infused with the powers of Sol Invictus's conferment of vesselhood.

Pausing and stabilizing his uncontrolled aura of blue emanating glowing energy, Sol Invictus's orb pulsated with a bright steady glow of energy that appeared more at ease while verbally affirming approval of the suggestion from his mortal candidate and now proclaimed vesselhood recipient. The deity spirit told Ascentius that though he would be transported into the body of a different being, his soul would merge with the powers that Sol Invictus would invest to make a worthy corporeal being for vesselhood. Ascentius nodded in solemn approval and nodded again when Sol Invictus inquired if the mortal king was ready to make the sacrifice of his own human mortal life as he proposed. Upon confirming, Sol Invictus discharged arcs of pulsating blue energy, which entered Ascentius's body and quickly exited him. Immediately and invisibly, the aura of his soul was seized by the emanating energy of Sol Invictus. Within a bright flash, the energy from the aura of Sol Invictus swirled and hovered around the aura of Ascentius's soul while a bright glowing light flashed before turning into darkness before flashing once again.

Watching from a distance after emerging victorious from his own respective trial, Linitus had only seen the last moments of the king forfeiting his life and accepting it in a way that perplexed the elven ranger, who did not appear to witness the full duration of Ascentius's trial for vesselhood. Reacting only in the limited context from which he understood, Linitus shouted frantically, distressed by what he saw. Ascentius, his potential father-in-law to be, had now perished. The elf did not know if the king had failed his trial and his life being forfeited was a consequence, or if strangely, the king had succeeded in passing the trial at the expense of his own life.

However, only a moment later with another flash of energy emitted, Ascentius's body had disappeared, and in its place appeared a sight beyond comprehension from what the elf had ever seen before, much less in any other modern sentient life from his world. Lying prone, a half-dragon, half-man anthropomorphic full-size figure appeared in the same position and spot that Ascentius lay when his life was forfeited. This creature had dark-green charcoal-hued skin coloration. It had a spiked tail along with a pair of muscular arm and leg limbs with three sharp claw-hand digits for each of its limbs. This half-man, half-beast dragon creature had a narrow reptilian dragon snout with a cranium that had jagged ridged crests protruding outward and leaning from its skull. Behind its shoulders were what appeared to be attached, curved, and jagged wings adjoining its back. Essentially, this creature was considered by mortals of Linitus's planet to be the mythical winged half-dragons. From his vantage point, it was an anomaly beyond belief and even to process not only what had happened but also seeing the being's very own existence being confirmed.

Taking another moment before directing his attention toward the blue deity spirit orb, Linitus asked almost demandingly what had happened and where Ascentius was. Sol Invictus calmly and assertively replied that this mortal candidate had passed the trial but at the expense of his own human life and body, so Ascentius's soul, through his aura, had to be allocated to a new body host, which the deity spirit had made in the form of an anthropomorphic dragon, or more commonly considered a half-dragon and half–man.

Speechless, Linitus asked for what reason did this have to happen and if there was any way to reverse this, as well as the elf offering to give his life instead.

Sol Invictus, quickly and assertively replied that there was no other alternative unless it had followed through with the king's verdict without giving a reprieve to spare all of sentient kind on their world of Terrunaemara from immediate termination. That was a fate Ascentius wanted to avoid even at the expense of his own life while ruling impartially.

Linitus, in a rare act of feeling both remorseful and resentful, could not hold back his own emotions of outrage at what happened while stating that it should have been him to offer his life and not the king's.

Sol Invictus replied, stating that it was necessary since Ascentius was the selected candidate who indeed had the best likelihood to receive the corresponding powers that Invictus possessed and would dispense to Ascentius. The deity spirit pointed out that while Linitus would have been a worthy candidate by his character and sense of self-sacrifice, Linitus did not have the vast experience and skillset to be able to hear a trial involving the fate of all of sentient life from his world and unlikely be able to objectively render a verdict along with a sentence as Ascentius had. For the elf ranger, it was hard to hear that, but he knew himself well enough to admit he probably would struggle too much on the side of mercy to pass down an even-handed sentence that even the deity spirits would approve as being just and fair.

Looking back at the cosmos all about, Linitus next had his thoughts on Marin and asked the deity spirit about her and when she could expect to come back. He wanted to know if she was alive and well. The deity spirit responded cryptically, stating that Linitus could ask her that himself when she appeared before him.

Beginning to assume consciousness, the half-dragon man creature slowly began to move and slowly picked itself up. Feeling uncertain and also somewhat reluctant by the fearsome, intimidating appearance that this creature bore, Linitus mustered himself to overcome his apprehension and fears by forcing himself to appeal to his own conscience. The elf ranger quickly approached the dragon-man creature and helped the anthropomorphic creature to fully get up.

The creature maintained his balance despite initially struggling and slowly turned to look at his surroundings as well as the one who had helped him. His stare was fierce and intimidating to make even Linitus look like a still statue uncertain how to react. The creature's eyes were a silvery color that contrasted much with its dark-green charcoal-hued scaly skin. Taking a moment, the creature responded by thanking Linitus while addressing him even by his first name. Witnessing this gesture, Linitus was further amazed and speechless. The elf could not help but ask how it knew him.

The creature, giving a brief humorous laugh, told him that he knew him now just as he did before in his last life in a different corporeal body.

Still processing what had transpired, Linitus asked if this was indeed Ascentius, king of Swordbane. The reptilian-like man-beast responded that in large part he was but also that his soul had intertwined and fused with the essence of Sol Invictus. Still amazed and in disbelief somewhat, Linitus turned to the blue orb being with a visible expression without uttering any words if that was true. The deity spirit emanated a steady glow of energy while reading the elf's mind and speaking audibly to confirm that it was indeed true.

Linitus dropped down on his knees in a submissive posture. He had always believed in the deity spirits, but to see what he had witnessed in what would be considered from his frame-of-time reference of less than a day was still all very surreal as well as challenging to process and fathom. He asked rhetorically and loudly in a manner of practical absolute capitulation about what he must do, in the direction of Sol Invictus.

The blue orb deity spirit replied that he knew what had to be done and that if he had such a question, he would not be in this place if he did not know even when asking from seeking comfort. The deity spirit was correct and Linitus knew it. There was nothing else to do otherwise from what the elf ranger, his companion lover, and the now newly incarnate form of Ascentius had originally set out to do. Linitus nodded while responding aloud that he along with Marin and what was now in part the being of Ascentius were there to gain powers and blessings from the divine spirits to be chosen vessels in order to deal with the unstable threat and balance that Decius now posed in receiving prior his vesselhood powers from both Calu and Laran.

Walking over toward Linitus with a large clawlike hand over his shoulder, a voice with a firm sense of understanding and command directed the elf to rise and follow alongside him to fulfill their endeavor. Turning steadily and looking at the dragon-man creature, Linitus acknowledged and got himself back up from the kneeling position to now standing. The elf ranger still kept Marin constantly in the back of his mind and still asked about her whereabouts while asking what he and others should now call this new incarnate form of the former king. The creature responded that he was still the same in many aspects and that he would always be Ascentius by name even under a new form.

Linitus smiled subtly while nodding and letting the dragon-man creature know that out of respect as he had for him then as well as now, the elf would still address this being by his title as king. The creature turned and nodded also. If the elf ranger as well as others who knew him from his private life felt obligated and comfortable to address him as before, he would permit it but also let them know that his new purpose was not so much to rule a kingdom now as much as it is to help save what was left of this kingdom and the various communities that composed this kingdom from the unbalanced chaos created by Decius. Linitus nodded also while feeling at peace. He confided freely to this creature, this being who was still in large part Ascentius, that though it would take some time to get used to, the elf ranger knew deep down that this was still a king who was worthy to be called by such a title out of compassion for his subjects and defending them in a higher position of standing.

As they were finishing their conversation and captivated by each other's words, a series of circular band rings rained down upon the temple sanctum along with a bright flash of light. With the light fading, a lone figure appeared. It was Marin.

Marin saw Linitus as he saw her, and they both ran quickly to each other to embrace each other one more time, not knowing if and when it would be their last time to see each other. While embracing him and looking over his shoulder, Marin noticed this large dragon-man figure and asked her lover Linitus if he knew who that was as well as the whereabouts of her father.

Linitus, uncertain of how to explain while being somewhat lost for words, shook his head lightly with a visibly saddened expression. She could tell and knew that something was not right, that something had happened to her father.

Letting go of her embrace toward her elven lover, Marin walked over toward the dragon-man creature while unsheathing her flame sword and carrying her shield in her other hand. She asked without fear in a confrontational manner if this creature had seen her father or if it had caused any harm upon him. She repeated herself in a more threatening and violent tone. Again no response. Before she could respond again while in a state of uncertain anger in assuming that this creature might have been responsible in some capacity concerning the fate of her father, Linitus broke the tension to be able to muster the words and let her know that this creature, this dragon-like man, was her father, or at least part of him was.

Shocked and dumbfounded just as Linitus was before, Marin turned and asked inquisitively with disbelief to Linitus about what he had said. She pondered if something adversely had happened to her lover, if he had come under some sort of hypnotizing spell or an inexplicable affliction of spectral possession of his mind and body. Linitus shook his head in a manner to deny that such a possibility was the actual case. Marin again turned toward this newly encountered, newly appearing corporeal creature, from whom she would demand once again to know her father's whereabouts. She was in denial that this creature was somehow her father, even in part. She looked at this creature and pressed onward again to boldly demand for it, for him to tell her where her father was and what this creature had done to him.

In response, the creature stepped forward and looked at Marin face to face and stared at her intently. It next declared that the person Marin asked was indeed her father the king, though in the form of a new body of a different corporeal type of being. Marin, still in shock and disbelief, asked how and why.

The creature responded that it was necessary in order for Ascentius to still receive Sol Invictus's blessing while passing his trial for divine conferment of the deity spirit's powers. The creature went on to explain that because of Ascentius's trial in which he himself was being observed and delegated the role of carrying out justice toward sentient life on Terrunaemara being on trial for its history and civility, including charges of collective crimes against various parties of sentient life. The deity spirit had honored the verdict, the sentence, and the altered arrangement of the sentence for Sol Invictus accepting Ascentius's human life as a sacrifice in payment as reprieve for all the sentient life on his world. In doing so, the wise human king, as the deity spirit noted to Marin, had presented Sol Invictus a dilemma to resolve how to honor both the arrangement of the king's self-sacrifice and to bestow Ascentius the divine powers that he had earned in passing his trial.

At that point, Linitus fully realized both the immense intellect and wisdom of Marin's father. He knew this was going to happen, or at least somehow in a manner similar to which it did. The elf could not help but point out his realization aloud, indicating that this outcome had to happen, with the king being given a new body and, in a sense, a new life (after sacrificing his own life with his previous human corporeal body) merged with a part of the essence of Sol Invictus. Linitus, however, did come to ponder in realizing that things would not be the same even from receiving vesselhood.

Still fueled with anger and resentment in accepting that her father had sacrificed himself to be transformed into this unheard-of form of a creature which she could still not yet accept as her father, Marin asked literally her thoughts about why she should believe in this creature to make her accept that he was indeed in part her father even in a different form. The creature replied instinctively by telling her while calling out her mother's first name: Gretchen believed in him when she was alive from when they first met at Aegir-Hafn to their last night together with Marin when Gretchen gave her life for him and Marin at the Great Massacre at Grimaz-Kadrinbad. The creature went on to say that Marin's mother still believed in him in his past life as well as what he now had to become.

Marin, still enraged and yet mystified by the creature's response, asked him how he would know that, how he would even know her mother's name, not to mention having the audacity to bring her name up. The creature replied again, stating that he knew because he missed Marin's mother just as much as Marin did ever since the night Gretchen perished over twenty years ago. Marin dropped on her knees with her sword and shield down. She felt vulnerable and internally convinced by what she had heard and now was ready to accept that, however hard it was to imagine, somehow this creature indeed was her father.

The creature, Ascentius's new form, went over to Marin and placed its outstretched clawed hand gently over her shoulder while she had her head down in tears. As soon as she realized, she got up and looked at this creature, now her father as she came to accept. She wiped her tears with her two of her fingers and then in a mild gesture of acceptance, spread that over to its long jagged snout. Ascentius, in his new form, accepted it while taking his other clawlike hand and gently stroking the backside of it toward her face in return. Appealing to her personally, he told her that if he could spend the rest of his life with her mother in Caelum, the Citadellan concept and word for heaven, he would. However, it was not yet the right time or his calling to do so. Marin nodded and hugged him while catching him by surprise, despite this half-dragon anthropomorphic creature being so big that she could not fully wrap her arms around him. Regardless, she embraced him as his daughter as best as she could.

Watching patiently and quietly as this unfolded, Linitus in his own sense of prudence realized that his approach in being a supportive and quiet observer was perhaps the best course of action he could take. He was glad that he did so while taking comfort and consolation intrinsically in admiring the bond that Marin had restored with her father even under these unimaginable and surreal circumstances.

Keeping that thought in mind now though, Linitus realized the hard part perhaps in deciding how to approach and explain to others upon returning about what had happened to Ascentius and imagining how others might come to accept him in his new form.

Two voices however came in response at the same time, from the glowing orb of Sol Invictus and from Ascentius, who was able to read into Linitus's thoughts. Both voices said the same thing in unison, that Ascentius would not be returning together with Marin and Linitus until the covenant among the deity spirits Calu and Laran along with Decius as their chosen vessel was violated.

Marin slowly broke off and shared the same shocked look on her face as Linitus in both of them asking how and why. Ascentius in his new form responded that he would observe as a watcher in the pantheon temple sanctuary how developments would unfold in Terrunaemara, using the enchanted fountain and its magical reflective depiction of what transpired on the planet below. Since he wielded the power of divine judgment and the power of the energy of light from the sun and other stars, he could not pass judgment even against the forces of darkness until its chosen vessel, Decius, violated the rules of vesselhood that Sol Invictus along with the other deity spirits had agreed upon eons ago. A chosen vessel could only represent his or her patron deity spirit while using only the allotted portion of power given by the deity spirit's essence and only to commit acts within the scope of the chosen vessel's own forces, abilities, and bestowed powers that he or she had received from the deity spirit patron. If the chosen vessel merged the deity spirit's realm to a different dimensional plane, including that where the chosen vessel resided, to further channel its power and/or use resources directly from the deity spirit's plane, then it would create what the other deity spirits considered as a direct challenge to the hierarchy and stability of the pantheon order. Such an action would be perceived as a threat that would not be tolerated by the other deity spirits, as Ascentius sharing the spirit and mind of Sol Invictus went on to say.

After listening intently, Marin said aloud the same question Linitus had thought about. What should they do now to prevent that from happening? Ascentius grimly responded that he could not tell them and that only if and when it did happen, he and the other deity spirits would respond.

Embracing Marin one last time before she went on to kiss him on the side of his dragon-like snout, Ascentius escorted his daughter and Linitus to the center circle of the temple sanctuary. Before departing by teleportation, Ascentius told them again that until the covenant was considered violated, he had to wait as a reactionary watch guard and it was up to the two of them until then to use their powers and lead the forces of light in his stead against Decius and his dark army. Marin and Linitus calmly nodded while sending their last salutation as they vanished in the same series of vertically hovering rings that had transported them earlier. They were now homeward bound.

CHAPTER FIFTY

Returning Home

It was now daytime with the sun shining down upon the ornate and exotic elven city of Salvinia Parf Edhellen. On the hilly slope with a grove of rare maple-wood trees that lay inside the city's wall boundary stood the same megalithic stone array with a center decorated with an elaborate series of stones on the ground making a unique spiral-like circular design. The sky was clear save for a few clouds, and the birds chirped frequently along with other intermittent ambient sounds. Several of the city's guards stood watch at the site along with a rotation between members of the city's council. Peat also stood guard throughout the day and night at intervals when not assisting Wyatt in making the preparations to assemble, arrange, and provision the gathered forces loyal to the king from various parts of the kingdom that answered the calling to form up in Parf Edhellen and attack as one united force to retake the capital.

Aside from the clouds, what stood out even more visibly were the dozens of skyships that each of the major kingdom settlements were able to supply and deploy to Parf Edhellen. Though not as many as Decius' forces, the skyships that the kingdom had assembled so far were at least three dozen strong and only about a dozen or less from Decius's remaining skyships. They were on standby as much as the forces on the ground were also making their preparations for the anticipated second massive battle ahead for control of Citadella Neapola.

However, as those forces were making preparations and amid the quiet and serene ambiance from the hillside maple trees, a loud noise was emitted from the array of megalith ruins near the center circle design on the ground. Within moments, a bright flash appeared, blocking all visible sight toward the center of that stone structure array. Emerging from the flash that diminished stood two lone figures.

Peat squinted before rubbing his eyes and walking closer to peer at what he had seen. It was Linitus and Marin. As soon as Peat realized, he dropped his war hammer and ran quickly to approach his two long-missed companions. Receiving his embrace, Marin and Linitus informed their dwarf companion that they had much to discuss. Peat shook his head to acknowledge but took a look all about the array of ruin structures. He did not see Ascentius anywhere and asked about the king's whereabouts. Marin held back her emotions as best as she could, knowing it was challenging for her to come to terms still with what happened on the other side of that portal. Linitus could tell and mustered his own thoughts as best as he could say in words of what happened while forewarning Peat that even Linitus himself had difficulty taking in and making sense out of what happened in the astral plane that he, Marin, and Ascentius were in. As they walked toward the city, the elven city guard that were within their proximity along with the respective city council members approached Linitus and Marin, all of them sharing nearly the same curiosity as the lone dwarf guardian toward the two returning heroes about what it was like where they had teleported to.

As Linitus and Marin proceeded through the city, they were followed by Peat along with the one elven local council member that was present. The council member and Peat briefed the two returning heroes on the status of the gathering allied forces. Behind them followed a retinue of city guards acting as security watch patrol while the four of them were still making their way through the city. At a noticeable pace, several townsfolk who were aware of the mysterious and miraculous disappearance of Linitus and Marin started gathering in droves, marveling at the sight of their unexpected return as many had considered the possibility of them not returning at all. Still, rumors spread about and audibly for even the main procession of Linitus and Marin to hear speculation about the king's whereabouts and why he was not present with them. By this point, Marin and Linitus were still continuing to walk and exchange quickly with Peat the developments that transpired since their last time being together.

Peat was in awe, pondering though willing to accept what Linitus and Marin had described about King Ascentius's fate. It was difficult to process (especially for the dwarf) Marin's own father passing a trial only to forfeit his own human existence in lieu of a harsher judgment and punishment being issued by the king when he was tested in his impartiality to judge all sentient life on their world. Still, Peat was not surprised and always thought highly of Ascentius being willing to sacrifice his own life for the kingdom if it was called for. This testimony from the king's daughter assured him of his conviction about the king's own heroic nature. Meanwhile, Linitus could not help but inject some light humor and sarcasm by mentioning that Peat would not be the only one, as he and especially Marin struggled in making sense of what happened.

Eventually, like the crowd that pressed the same question, Peat also felt compelled to ask about why the king even in his new dragon-man creature form had not returned with the two hero comrades. Marin choked up slightly, having a hard time knowing how to respond, given that she knew she was not likely going to possibly see her father or a measurable aspect of him in his new form for as long as possibly a lifetime or even beyond that.

Linitus knew from the look on her face and responded quickly to mention to their dwarf comrade that the king would not return until the covenant of vesselhood had been broken by Decius. Peat, unfamiliar with what such a breach of covenant would entail, asked his companions how that would happen or what it would look like if Decius did violate it.

Linitus, sighing with reluctance in thinking about such a possibility, was prepared to address Peat's last question until Marin responded before Linitus could indicate that such a transgression would entail, as an example, Decius calling upon and opening a portal to the plane of Calu and Laran, the two deity spirits being patrons that gave a portion of their essence to this dark lord. If such an event occurred, it would allow the deity spirits to use such an opening to serve as a conduit in using their own powers directly to feed off the aspects of humanity from which their respective aspects of power grew: death and violence.

Now in a state of random curiosity of proposing, Peat asked how they could make that happen, in terms of causing Decius to open a direct portal to those two vile deity spirits. The two other companions looked shocked while sharing that same expression to Peat as much as to each other. How crazy it would be for them, of all people, to cause such an action to be enacted? They could not believe that the dwarf would propose such a suggestion, knowing how dangerous the implications would be. However in a split moment, Linitus realized where Peat was coming from in his proposition. The elf ranger admitted that more than likely if they had enough forces to take back the capital, that alone could very well trigger Decius in being aroused with enough anger to the point that he might get desperate and call upon his patron deity spirits for noticeable amounts of demonic reinforcements.

Marin eventually caught on to what her two companions were thinking, and though she did not like the prospect of potentially endangering the city by putting its local populace in the crossfire of what could spiral into a demonic battle with portal gates to hell opening, not to mention a battle against powerful forces of darkness that were already in control of the city, she also agreed that the sooner Decius was stopped, the better. She believed strongly even if meant for them to force the dux's hand and possible lack of foresight to cause him to open the portals to other deadly planes temporarily, it was worth it versus the long-term prospect of further harm Decius would cause in not attempting this deadly plan. On that account, all three of them did agree to go forward in executing this plan if they could pull it off.

Less than an hour after arriving, now at the main makeshift camp with dozens and dozens of tents filling nearly the entire main plaza, Linitus and Marin were ready to receive further briefings from the other elven council members, as well as Wyatt, once Linitus and Marin were able to locate their small wizard companion, who appeared after catching word of mouth that his two departed hero comrades had finally returned.

Upon seeing Marin and Linitus, Wyatt in his own flashy manner cast a teleportation spell while standing on top of a podium where he had directed and teleported earlier various cargo and war-related supplies to the decks of various skyships. His brief teleportation and disappearance had startled not only all the elven locals of the settlement but also Wyatt's fellow hero companions. However, in a quick second or two, emerging from a flashing portal before Linitus and Marin, the youngling wizard quickly stepped out and embraced them both. Linitus and Marin acknowledged and hugged Wyatt back while the former two realized that despite being considered fellow members of the same recently bestowed elite order as Wyatt, he was still only a boy at ten years old, and gifted and responsible as he was, he still exhibited the same feelings and expressions as a younger child would in reuniting with sorely missed older siblings. Their absence had made an impression on him, and all three of them realized along with Peat that in a sense, they were not only fellow warriors and comrades in arms but also, over time, family to each other. The moment resonated for the four of them to realize this even if it was for a brief time.

After taking their moment to embrace each other and be reacquainted, Marin and Linitus retold to Wyatt much of what they had already mentioned to Peat about what they had seen, the trials they endured, and most difficult to explain, why Ascentius, the king, would not return for some time. Finally, in connecting with that thought of the king's return, Linitus mentioned to Wyatt that it was imperative that they and all those forces loyal to the king still continue to fight and retake the capital for not only the original purpose of freeing the city from a dark lord that ruled out of terror, fear, and respect, but also so that they would demolish Decius's forces enough to utterly enrage him. In doing so, they hoped ironically it would be enough for Decius to unleash unsanctioned portals wherever they came from to Terrunaemara, in order to merit a justified pretext for Ascentius in his new deity-like form to use his powers not only to seal the portals of darkness but also to deliver final judgment on Decius and condemn him to banishment to the worst place of the afterlife, Hadao Infernum, the place of fiery hell in Citadellan tongue.

Hearing of their plan, Wyatt agreed with some caution. Though he thought it might be both reckless and suicidal, it was perhaps the best and only way to remove Decius from power. Decius was too powerful and destructive to pursue an alternate path in dealing with him compared to the one they thought was most viable to implement. The drawback was very costly in generating enough ire from the dux to violate uncontrollably the covenant to open up other portals to hell from which to unleash beasts beyond measure to prey upon more souls on the planet and thus satisfy Decius's patron deity spirits as well as himself. However, they had to make such a dangerous plan work to stand the best chance of finding a way for Ascentius to return in his new form and presumably unleash a reliably sufficient degree of power to neutralize this anointed dark lord as well as possibly his denizens.

Within the next two days, Linitus and Marin helped Wyatt oversee the final provisions of the skyships that had assembled high above the skyline of Parf Edhellen. Toward the end of the second day, the four heroes of the Comradery had completed directing and staging the final preparations for the skyships' assault on Citadella Neapola in the hopes of defeating Decius's army and freeing the capital from the dark lord's control. By sunset, all assigned crew members from the kingdom's assembled armada had finished boarding the skyships to take off and depart the elven city while making their plotted course heading to go southwest and then turning to starboard to go due north. They would attack the forces of Decius at the capital, facing the south portion of the city as they would eventually make their way northward under the cover of night while going at a slow speed. They were planning not to attack until during sunlight in order to have a greater degree of visibility when their forces would engage the Remnant. Linitus considered attacking at night, but thought it would be too risky with the lack of visibility and the potential or many variables that could go wrong for the kingdom's outcome in retaking the capital.

As the skyships made their course changes slowly during travel, Marin and Linitus, not knowing what tomorrow would certainly bring, decided to share one more intimate moment together in each other's arms while looking at the sunset together as they had cherished doing several times before. The two held each other's hands while looking at the clouds and pink-orange dimness from the sunset melting away while the sky was still present in their view. Eventually the sky's coloration gave way to a twilight purple before many stars appeared brightly and scattered everywhere about the nighttime sky. While being held in the arms of her lover, Marin asked Linitus something she knew he would not ever want to do or see himself as. She challenged him starting at sunrise to be a king for a day and to use his knowledge of leading to make the forces believe that even without Ascentius being present, the kingdom's army still had someone worthy to lead them both by command and example. Linitus agreed and promised that, though any other day he would prefer not to do it. At least in terms of outward portrayal, he would do so tomorrow if it bettered the cause to improve soldier morale while fighting. Marin nodded while stating that she knew it would and the forces fighting for the kingdom would also. The two lovers had by this point passed out, retiring for the evening while their floating armada continued its course following the shining star in the north, which essentially took over as the guide for their final intended destination, Citadella Neapola.

CHAPTER FIFTY-ONE

Breaking the Covenant

Over two weeks since capturing Citadella Neapola and the dark forces occupying the once-great ancient city had already adjusted to their control over the metropolis while indulging in what luxury provisions could be had. Many of the local populace were upset but also found themselves in a fragile state of not being able to effectively resist and overthrow their occupiers. Still others reluctantly sought to accept the apparent reality in which they would be ruled by a despotic warlord and one who was considered a traitor to their own former king. Now they had to publicly be silent or risk punishment varying from fines, imprisonment, or even possibly being condemned to death by fighting at the city's legendary amphitheater.

However, despite the harsh rule that Decius imposed over the city, ever since his return from his sudden and abrupt departure to his Remnant capital to pick up his consort wife personally to return with him to Citadella Neapola, much had changed even within the past week. Duchess Lucia, as she was introduced by the dux upon making a grand entrance to the coastal metropolis, appeared before the crowd with her wolfling child, Lucianus Canus, that she shared with Dux Decius.

Since Lucia's arrival, Decius had her along with her aides in charge of overseeing the well-being of the city in order for it to be rebuilt and restored in some shape of what it was once before. Much as she had done using her experience in redeveloping Sanctum Novus, Lucia adopted the same approach with Citadella Neapola. She set up several granary distribution centers to coordinate the distribution of the city's grain while also overseeing critical infrastructure, including sewage and running water from the fountains, to be in working order.

Though there was much to be done that could not be completed in the span of a week, the people of the city had generally changed their disposition of being under the rule of Decius in large part due to his wife's influence in acting as a seeming compassionate matron overseer to address their most pressing needs. The general populace would have preferred that they were still under the rule of Ascentius, but none of them would dare to say that and were barely content at least to know that Decius, however cruelly he presented himself as a dark lord and warlord, at least was pragmatic or cared enough in his role of presiding as an acting ruler over the city he had taken over to appoint someone (even his own wife consort) to adequately provide for them their most essential needs.

Regardless, much of what Decius had rapidly done in changing the nature of the city, somewhat for the better but also somewhat for the worse, was a hollow depressing shadow of its once former pride. Decius, though directly in charge of the city, in time would seek to humble it further by taking much of its wealth and administrative resources to transfer to his own titular city, Sanctum Novus, which he called home in the high desert lands to the east. For now, he wanted to rebuild the conquered city and assess not only what changes were needed to assure a strong-enough loyalty from the local population if and when Ascentius's forces sought to attempt to retake it, but also to prevent any strong enough local rebellions to stir and overthrow his remaining complement of forces that would stay behind in control of the coastal metropolis once the dux decided it was time to return to his home capital city in the desert.

However, for the time being while enjoying the partially sunny but cloudy day, the dux had attended the daily gladiatorial combat games staged in the great amphitheater. It was there at the royal box (or what now the dux rebranded as the imperial box) that he inaugurated the commencement of the day's exhibition while seated next to his wife consort, who held their child swaddled in a blanket. Agaroman sat next to them. There was an empty seat to the other side as a mild gesture to honor Senator Diem in spirit of their company, though Lucia's father was not present in person since Decius decided Diem would be left in charge to oversee and administer the Remnant's capital, Sanctum Novus.

As the games proceeded, the fighters were mainly recently released ex-convicts from the Royal Crown Palace dungeon who opted to fight for entertainment and money against enslaved Nordling barbarians that were caged in the cell holdings below the stage floor of the amphitheater. Slowly, the mass fight had one competitor falling after the other until only a few were standing. While Decius and Lucia drank their chalices of red Citadellan wine, they discussed with each other the present state of affairs, including the logistics and supplied reinforcements that were being allocated temporarily to Citadella Neapola from other parts of Decius's controlled territories. They also talked about current and future projects of redevelopment and the progress Lucia had made in providing the basic needs for the city's population as it adjusted to what was considered a new normalcy. She had envisioned adopting for its redevelopment an urban plan model very much like she had done in Sanctum Novus, including setting up orphanages as well as schools and public feeding kitchens for those most economically vulnerable and starving, which was still on her mind in implementing in the coming weeks.

Decius, though prone to war and having a violent nature, had an open heart in respecting and appreciating his wife's nature and intentions that he saw as a beneficial and necessary counterbalance to his way of ruling. Though he wanted to rule in what he considered an orderly and civilized way that mirrored the imperial depictions of how the once-great Lupercalians ruled, Decius knew his aggressive and harsh nature toward his foes had to be counteracted by a capacity to convert them to passive submission toward the legitimacy of his rule. Not surprisingly, many also did hold Lucia in high regard, including the locals of Citadella Neapola as well as Decius' forces, even Agaroman, who now saw and recognized the valuableness of Lucia and what she had been able to achieve in terms of urban administrative management to further the dux's new forming empire.

However, as the gladiator fight neared its end with its final four combatants as Decius still watched and chatted intermittently with his beloved Lucia, a large horn sounded. Two more bursts of the horn sounded off right afterward. Decius and Agaroman, familiar with the sound as a call to arms, knew that it meant a possible attack was imminent. Lucia, though not familiar with the ways of war and tactics, had learned enough at this point that it was likely a call to war. She knew that much at least from conversing and being educated in the ways of warfare and tactics by Decius himself for nearly the past year whenever they were together.

Upon hearing the sound, Decius stood up from his throne at his imperial box to look around and survey the arena. He looked for anything unusual as well as for the location among his forces that had sounded the war trumpet to inquire why they had done so and expected that reporting person to indicate what form of threat they spotted as well as the direction where it was spotted. Finally, looking up near the top row of seats, the dux saw a sentry guard waving his hand in a steady motion to indicate that he had seen from a distance in the sky to the south very faint, small dots in the sky that became bigger and browner. When Decius had Agaroman teleported him over next to the sentry, the dux was able to confirm it and was somewhat startled but not overwhelmingly surprised. His foes had come to return and exact revenge for the loss of Ascentius's capital. Except this time, there were also skyships appearing and lots more than the king's forces had before, when they were originally in possession of Citadella Neapola. As the dots increased by number in the distance while coming into view, Decius quickly told his forces to prepare for the call to arms. He quickly directed Agaroman to teleport him along with Lucia and their son, Lucianus Canus, to one of the skybeast ships. The dux, though wanting to engage in battle, thought first and foremost for the safety of his consort wife and their child heir. Lucia knew that also but warned him that he had to make sure to be ready to lead his forces with whatever time he could afford. Decius acknowledged while assuring her that he had Agaroman in charge of notifying and deploying as many skyships as possible in formation to engage the enemy. Many of the Remnant's skyships were already deployed, hovering in a loose position in the sky since the first and earlier battle for control of the coastal metropolis roughly two weeks ago. Decius was cautious to anticipate an attack even when least expected, while having as many of his skyships as possible to stay deployed as such for that reason.

Now the city was about to be embroiled in another battle for control, including in the sky, except this time it appeared to be more evenly matched as the Kingdom of Swordbane appeared to have fielded dozens of skyships to possibly match up the remaining number that Decius's forces had. Upon boarding the bridge cockpit of one of the skybeast floating vessels, Decius along with an already well-trained and provisioned crew began to ready the ship for battle by increasing the throttle for it to propel while Decius, initially planning to man the steering controls of the vessel, was interrupted briefly with a hand over his shoulder. Startled and at first having a reaction of visible resentment for whoever would dare intervene, he turned and saw Lucia. She pleaded for the dux to let her operate the steering of the skybeast and encouraged him to engage in his powerful state of summoning the colossal hellish wolf beast to use in fighting against the enemy skyships. Decius, recognizing the wisdom of his lover's advice and the potential it had for the outcome of the battle, agreed to her suggestion. Lucia was already personally trained and capable of operating the skybeast when she accompanied Decius on his return trip to Citadella Neapola and received periodic training several times under the dux's own personal supervision in familiarizing her with the controls, particularly the gear levers, of this deadly flying contraption.

After several minutes of makeshift preparations for combat and defense, Agaroman teleported to the bridge of Decius's skyship. Upon arrival, before engaging in his summoning meditation, Decius instructed Agaroman to use his magic to allow for a series of replica projections of various goblin shamans to appear on the bridge. These projections were distortions in which the goblin shamans also used their magic to project themselves onto the skybeast while displaying the same projections on board the respective skyships where each shaman was physically on board. In turn, they also saw projections of Decius, Agaroman, and their other goblin shaman counterparts. Essentially, it was their way of communicating in a hive-like organized manner to coordinate their sky-fleet movements to prepare to attack the invading sky fleet of the Swordbane kingdom. With Agaroman directing the commands and each goblin shaman acknowledging and relaying to their own respective skyship helmsman, the Remnant's sky fleet began to form and move in an organized coordinated checkerboard pattern with the two skybeast vessels leading at the front of the formation.

From the distance, the Swordbane kingdom's sky fleet had formed a similar pattern in order to make it difficult for Decius's forces to engage in combat with them from being conventionally overtaken, though the dux still held (or so he thought) the decisive advantage of utilizing his two skybeasts to strike quickly and with devastating effect toward the outermost flanks of the kingdom's sky fleet.

Meanwhile on board the bridge of his skyship, Decius had already begun to engage in a deep meditative trance with a dark but still translucent red globe covered with black mist surrounding him. Within moments of his chanting, appearing on the streets below of Citadella Neapola was a monstrously gigantic hellish black werewolf-like beast emanating flames.

It was the same beast that Decius had summoned on various occasions before. Using his mind and concentration to control it, Decius assumed the avatar of the beast and began moving it. It charged furiously in loud thunderous steps on the streets to the direction from which the enemy skyships floated above, straight ahead. The creature still charged furiously while increasing its momentum. The skyships were well over two thousand feet in the air, while the hellish gargantuan beast stood as high as about a hundred feet. No one would think that it could do it, but it had. It leaped high in the air, over a thousand feet in an ascending arc while swiping with its large sharp-clawed hands to grab onto one of the hulls of the skyships. It had secured itself to one of the hulls before scaling over the hull of one of the kingdom's skyships. Upon reaching the deck, it howled frantically while furiously charging and clawing at any and every soldier crew member on board. Though the respective skyship's crew tried to resist, their reaction and movements were not fast enough and paled in comparison to this creature's brute force and ferocity. Within moments, nearly the entire crew was dead, and the beast began tearing apart the skyship to take it down before leaping over to board the next adjacent kingdom skyship to repeat the same process. Slowly, the kingdom's fleet was beginning to lose both morale and formation as the other skyships tried to break off and distance themselves in a looser formation while being only about less than a few miles in engaging with the Remnant's floating fleet head-on.

Meanwhile, as the sky battle between opposing armadas raged on, a large and otherwise insignificant cloud mass formation hovered over and moved fairly quickly through the gap between the two fleets of opposing skyships. It was unnoticed in raising any initial call to alarm. Within this cloud was a concealed lone skyship. Various figures manned the deck of it with one in particular who was able to see the ensuing onslaught by the hellish werewolf colossus from looking below. This figure wore exotically made goggle-like spectacles that allowed the wearer to see through veils of mists, including the thick condensation. This figure pointed and gave directions for the rest of the crew on deck to prepare to deploy ramps that sloped from the deck of the ship outward and protruded beyond the port and starboard bulwark of the ship. With acknowledgement that the oil barrel siege munitions were ready from Marin on the port side and Peat on the starboard side, Linitus (still wearing the magical spectacles) told Wyatt to maintain course while signaling for Marin and Peat to be ready to light the fuses of the explosive-barrel munitions before deploying to roll down the ramps.

Within a few moments from looking below, the lone skyship covered by the cloud mass was now on a diagonal trajectory nearly a thousand feet above the Remnant's front column of fleet skyships. As the shrouded skyship laid an intercept course with the front ranks of the fleet, Linitus quickly called out for Marin and Peat with their munitions team of dwarves and human siege engineers to light the fuses of the barrels and release the latch that held back the barrels from exiting the ramp. Both port and starboard sides of the siege munition teams complied, and within moments, the lit oil-barrel bombs rolled down the ramps and fell downward in a progressive and continuous stream upon the unsuspecting enemy skyships as the Comradery's skyship continued to float above them while traversing. Another moment in passing and loud explosions were emitted that triggered even further cascading explosions. Though no one on the deck of Linitus's skyship could see except for Linitus and Wyatt, the latter of whom also had a pair of shroud mist vision spectacles, the reaction from both of them was celebratory, which the crew could tell and cheer on, knowing that they had at least caused some tangible damage to the floating enemy fleet below.

From the vantage point and perspective below, it was truly a surprise that caught off guard the Remnant fleet of skyships. Over half a dozen or so of the unsuspecting skyships blew up and fell down in pieces to the coastal city's urban landscape below. The local populace looked above and frantically ran for cover either inside the buildings or into the cellars of any buildings that had such facilities. The city was about to witness as much if not more chaos and destruction than it had endured over two weeks prior.

Startled from the sound and looking at the destruction from port side of the fleet's formation, Agaroman noticed the disappearance of the projection of several of the goblin shamans, knowing that they most likely had fallen along with the skyships they sailed in. In the cockpit viewing area of the skybeast, Lucia had placed her son Lucianus Canus in the care of one of the goblins who sat in the side copilot passenger seat while holding the dux's heir. Lucia herself, though somewhat shaken, announced verbally that the sudden bombardment of the fleet's skyships came from the cloud above and that she suspected however it was pulled off, there had to be an enemy vessel of some sort that was hiding in the clouded mist. She announced to Agaroman that she would steer the ship to the apparent source and eliminate it if it was indeed an enemy skyship.

Agaroman, though cautious, thought it was perhaps the better choice, especially noticing the cloud's movements mimicking that of a skyship; it had begun to turn and change course, most likely making another pass to take out more of the imperial Remnant's floating fleet of ships.

As Linitus ordered for Wyatt to turn about, the elf ranger told the munitions teams to prepare another volley of oil-barrel munitions to deploy. As the munitions teams complied and Wyatt began to turn the ship about, Linitus noticed from a distance and approaching fast above in an ascending and menacing manner another horrifying flying skybeast contraption of the like he had not seen in two weeks. This one, however, was different, and he could tell whoever was at the helm of it seemed better trained and more unpredictably deadly while making snakelike strafing movements as it furiously charged toward the cloud. Reacting instinctively and abruptly, the elf ranger quickly called for Peat to ready one of the fuel munitions to load behind the skyship's port-side mounted ballista. Peat, not fully knowing or able to see the impending danger ahead, trusted and, without hesitation, complied with the elf ranger's order. Readying an oil barrel, Linitus waited and then personally lit the fuse before firing it off from the projectile launcher as the skybeast came within less than two thousand yards from ramming toward the lone obscured skyship.

Faintly seeing the lone skyship appearing before the clouds, Lucia contemplated ramming it head-on, but decided not to while assuming it might have been loaded with explosive munitions that could easily set off and cause the skybeast to go down with it. Instead, she quickly told the floating vessel's siege engineers to ready a volley of siege munitions to fire on the port side of the skybeast. Agaroman, overhearing what she said, repeated her order while the wizard still communicated with the projections of the remaining goblin shamans of their respective skyships to maintain formation and prepare to board the kingdom's skyships after exchanging initial volleys of siege-weapon fire. As the skybeast came closer to the lone kingdom skyship, it began to turn to expose its port side of ready siege weapons to deploy.

However, spotting a single fast-moving object that appeared to be a barrel with a bright-looking spark, Lucia quickly realized that it was hurling inbound toward the skybeast. She quickly maneuvered evasively to dodge it but not before it exploded and caught the tail end of the skybeast. It began to spiral almost out of control while nearly everyone on board lost their balance and tumbled across the deck of the beastly flying contraption, except for Lucia and the goblin carrying her child, all three who were secured with fastened straps to the piloting seats of the bridge cockpit. Lucia told the rest on board to hold on as she adjusted the lift lever of the controls to try to stabilize the floating vessel while also trying to maintain balance and control of the steering wheel, or yoke, of the flying contraption. Within moments, the skybeast had regained stability. Though it was damaged and smoke emanated from the tail end of the flying vessel, it was still functional, and miraculously, there were no fatal casualties though a few on board had minor injuries. The sudden disruption, however, made Decius as well as Agaroman lose control. None of the projections of the sky fleet's other goblin shamans remained, nor did the summoned hell-beast werewolf that Decius had summoned, which seemingly vanished in a burst of flames.

Decius and Agaroman began to pick themselves up, both visibly shaken and upset. Decius quickly thought about his consort, Duchess Lucia, and their son, Lucianus Canus. The dux rushed forward to make sure they were okay. Lucia, somewhat shaken though still alert and able to focus, said she was okay while looking on to ensure the goblin carrying her wolfling son was also faring well. Both the goblin and her son the goblin carried were well, though Lucianus Canus began to whimper in a canine manner. Lucia wanted to comfort him and called for the goblin to hand over her child to her.

Decius, furious, with his face being clearly visible, had only now thought about causing whatever manner of hell would be needed to eliminate the threat of the lone skyship as well as the rest of the fleet of the kingdom's skyships. He immediately and instinctively let an underlying force, the combined essences of Calu and Laran, consume his full attention. Though the essences seemed to hesitate and not want for him to tap into what he felt was holding back his full deadly potential, he channeled his anger still while unleashing a large howl that was more beastly and demonic than anyone on board had ever heard.

Within moments, the red translucent globe and visage of black smoke began to enshroud him fast until it became less translucent and became opaque like a ball of red blood with a thicker cloud of burning like ash surrounding it. In another moment, the opaque ball popped out and exploded with blood, one that seemed to feel and smell human. Emerging inside from that exploding ball of blood, stood a large man-sized black werewolf covered in burning flames. It was essentially a smaller human-scale version of the same summoned avatar spirit that Decius had summoned earlier.

Breathing heavily while rising from its knees, the werewolf-looking creature turned and looked about the bridge of the skybeast with all members on board astonished and frightened. Suddenly the beast began to speak, telling them that he or it was okay. The beast-like creature then looked intently at Lucia. While she initially was frightened, she realized as it put its clawed hand gently on her shoulder, that it was not a threat and seemed to comfort her. It spoke out and called her name, assuring her it was still Decius himself, though in a new form. Lucia paused and regained her composure while still trying to adjust to what she had witnessed. She called his name, Decius, asking if it was him. The creature nodded and replied that it was.

Still in disbelief, she asked what had happened. She wanted to know why he had transformed into this creature. Placing his other clawlike hand against her face while she accepted it and kissed it, Decius in his new form told her that it was time. He had to become this beast, in order to protect her and their son. He told her to watch over their son while he placed his hand over his wolfling son's furry forehead. Lucianus Canus, among those on board perhaps the least aware of what happened, given his infant age, stopped whimpering and began to make a happy sound like a bark. Lucia looked at their son's smile before turning to Decius in his new form and embraced him while kissing his clawlike hand. He returned the gesture before telling her that she would take the skybeast and fly it away back to Sanctum Novus, while he would have Agaroman teleport him to the other skybeast. Lucia and Agaroman acknowledged and complied while Decius instructed his wizard advisor to stay on board and tasked him to help ensure the safety of his duchess wife and their heir wolfling son. Agaroman, able to tell that this new form of Decius that he had become would not tolerate any objection, nodded again.

Before teleporting, Lucia asked her lover if he would go follow along with them while commanding the other skybeast. Decius shook his wolflike head and told her he would not be with her, at least not until the battle was over. She asked what he would do to ensure that it would be over and he would return to her. Thinking sternly and with a preemptive thought of only the deepest intention, the dux replied that if need be, he would himself open the gates of hell, or Hadao Infernum, to unleash all forms of death and destruction to attack the kingdom and its fleet in order to save her and rid them of their enemies.

Turning away, he told Agaroman to go prepare to transport him to the other skybeast while commanding his wife to change course to approach it so that he would be within teleportation range of his wizard advisor to transport the dux. Within moments, he was teleported on board the other skybeast vessel and greeted the goblin shaman that communicated with Agaroman. Decius told Agaroman through his projection to relay to Lucia to break off course and send their skybeast vessel to head north by northeast in order to stay away from the other enemy fleet of ships. Upon making that heading and reaching Mount Inferno, Decius instructed them to wait for him there before they would decide whether to return back to Citadella Neapola or retreat to Sanctum Novus, depending on the outcome of this battle.

Agaroman, through his projection, complied, and the damaged but functional skybeast that Lucia piloted changed course and made its course away from the ruined coastal metropolis below while the main engagement of the opposing skyships still took place. Lucia, though feeling apprehensive, trusted the command of her husband and, though rarely vengeful herself, hoped that he would indeed cause whatever manner of destruction and havoc that he had intended against their enemies, even if meant opening the portals or gates of the hellish underworld to unleash its deadly denizens.

The main bulk of the opposing sky fleets began to unleash against each other all forms of siege weapon projectiles, as well as hurled spears and fired arrows in addition to trying to ram and board each other. The crews on the various opposing ships when boarding fought frantically with all forms of weapons. Many lay dead whether on board the vessels that still remained floating or the ones that fell perilously downward through the sky and onto the surface of the coastal city. It was perhaps one of the largest battles in the history of the kingdom and certainly the largest one in the skies. Orcs, goblins, some trolls, humans including both Citadellans and Nordling barbarians as well as those with both mixed backgrounds, dwarves, elves, and even some halflings and gnome small-folk, all known sentient species of the different major races in the west were represented and fought fiercely.

As the fighting endured, a lone skyship sailing higher above broke away from the cover of the dissipating clouds in which it hid by the magic of its gifted wizard, Wyatt Spell-Slinger. This lone skyship made a second pass quickly above the column of enemy ships before deploying another volley of explosive siege-barrel munitions. After depletion of the siege-barrel munitions, Linitus called upon Wyatt to teleport him and Marin to one of the friendly, allied kingdom skyships near the front ranks of the fleet battle below so that he and Marin could provide relief and rally the forces of that vessel from being overtaken by one of the boarding enemy skyships. Wyatt nodded and, within a moment, teleported Linitus and Marin to the deck of the respective allied skyship while leaving Peat and Wyatt in charge of the skyship to direct its crew to use other weapons including bows and arrows to fire upon the other enemy vessels below.

Upon boarding the allied skyship, Linitus and Marin quickly engaged in combat with several orcs, goblins, Sanctum Novus Citadellan infantry, Nordling barbarians from Tribus Barbarum Aries, and even an armored troll that bore a large spiked club. Linitus and Marin worked in tandem moving about choreographically in watching each other's back and flanks while dispatching the various foes and receiving aid from the allied crew members on board, who fought fiercely as well to prevent the enemy boarding party from seizing control of the skyship. Eventually, they shifted the tides of the battle and pushed back enough to actually start boarding the adjacent enemy skyship, which had little left of resistance from being captured. As they succeeded in taking control of the skyship, what turned into immediate celebration fleeted away as Linitus and Marin realized half a dozen or so other front-rank engagements transpired between the opposing sky fleets. All the skyships fiercely tried to board each other's floating vessels or to continue to either ram the opposing side or fire enough siege munitions to down the opposing vessels to fall to impending death.

As these multiple ship-to-ship engagements unfolded, Decius in command of the other skybeast quickly hovered from a distance to encircle before making a pass to ram the topmasts of the enemy skyships to cause them to plummet to their deaths below. After doing so and striking at least three kingdom skyships, the dux in his haunting werewolf-beast form next began to hand over the steering controls of the skybeast to his goblin copilot while instructing it to imitate the same style of attack so that the dux could call upon his powers. The dux walked up the stairs of the skybeast to the canopy deck to observe his forces struggling to gain control of the skies against the kingdom. Filled with absolute anger and rage without caring about any restraints on what he was about to do, Decius engaged in a meditative trance. In a sudden moment, he unleashed a deafening howl that nearly all vessels engaged in combat could hear and they paused briefly to listen. The howl, even to those that served under the dux, was unlike any they heard of before. It even haunted them into being intimidated.

Within moments of howling, Decius, able to project his loud voice, called forth various scattered burning flames of portals that began to emerge from the sky. Soon, various small-winged hellish creatures with jagged features and pointed ears began to emerge from these portals. They were known as flying imps, which were able to spit out small burning balls of fire. They came wave after wave in a swarm while hovering around the skybeast where Decius was on board. After assembling several hundreds, possibly several thousands of them, Decius emerged from the top canopy cover of the skybeast, unleashed another deafening howl while pointing toward the rear mass of the kingdom's fleet of skyships. In his own form, he commanded and sicced the hellish creatures to do his bidding, to fly over and start attacking furiously without hesitation or any mercy against the rearmost arrangement of kingdom skyships. These hellish creatures circled about while making passes to swipe, spit out fire, pick up and drop any of the Swordbane forces on board the vessels that they could tear away at and kill. The soldiers tried to resist and fight back, but had limited success, given the fast-moving speeds of these fearsome, hellish flying creatures.

Marin and Linitus, watching from a distance, began to take notice, and they quickly called on Wyatt, with Linitus shooting a signal flare arrow to be teleported. The wizard complied, and within moments, Linitus and Marin were back on board their own flagship vessel. Peat pointed with his war hammer and indicated that this creature that looked like a werewolf or a miniature form of the gigantic creature that Decius had summoned earlier was now seemingly in command of summoning these flying hellish beasts from the extraplanar portal gates. Marin turned and looked sharply to Linitus while confiding that he was right, it had worked, and apparently Decius had violated the covenant of vesselhood by opening portals from another plane, presumably hell, to unleash denizens from that plane upon the kingdom's forces. They had apparently caused enough anger to get the dux to resort to and fall into his uncontrollable anger to respond in such a drastic way that would be grounds for divine interference to redress what was considered an unsanctioned act by the divine spirits. Now they had to hold on to fight, persevere, and wait until Ascentius in his new incarnate form would take notice and respond by using the divine powers of judgment to put an end of Decius's reign of terror.

As they waited, more and more of the demon-like imp creatures poured out from the portal gates that opened a conduit between Terrunaemara and the hellish realm, Hadao Infernum. More and more of these foul flying beasts swarmed and overwhelmed various skyships and their soldier-based crew. However, at a sudden moment, a streak of lightning pierced through the dark clouded sky, and sunlight seeped through. Emerging from the sky high above, a lone flying dark-green charcoal-hued dragon-man figure carrying a large two-handed silver sword fluttered its wings while unleashing a large audible roar-like shout. Linitus quickly pointed with his non-bow-carrying hand at the creature to indicate that it was Ascentius, or at least the divinely infused form of him. Marin turned, excited to see that she was able to see her father from a distance even in his different body and form. She and Linitus both had known that it had worked, with her confiding to him that they actually had succeeded in getting Decius to break the covenant and generate a response from the benevolent divine spirits to counteract him.

In another quickly passing moment, Ascentius in his new divinely infused form called out loudly and declaratively in the presence of all those in the air and land below to hear. He had announced that Decius as vessel for Calu and Laran had broken the covenant of vesselhood by unleashing the powers from the portal realm of hell beyond using his own powers as chosen vessel by opening and maintaining the portal gates that connected the realm of the fiery hell to Terrunaemara. Proclaiming the power of the authority of supreme judgment from the divine spirit of Sol Invictus, Ascentius next declared that Decius and all those summoned from the portal gates of Hadao Infernum would be banished to that realm indefinitely.

Decius, hearing the proclamation, refused to acknowledge the decree while proclaiming that he never would accept the divine judgment of benevolent deity spirits that he held in lower esteem to his patron deity spirits, Calu and Laran. Immediately however, seeing the battle as being too costly while still thinking in part of a way to unleash more destruction, Decius remembered his plan to rendezvous with Lucia, their son, Agaroman, and the rest of the crew on board the other skybeast. The dark lord ordered his fleet to pull back while also instructing the demon-like imps to continue to occupy and overwhelm the kingdom's skyships. He knew that most likely these dark denizens that he had summoned through opening the hellish portals would fall either by the resistance that the kingdom's skyships and soldiers were still mounting as well as by the apparent arrival of a new powerful adversary that the dux had now surmised that this dragon-like creature was potentially as powerful as it, or he, had projected himself to be.

Still unknown to Decius, this creature was in fact Ascentius himself in a different form, though Decius did not realize or consider that. Decius did not yet fathom that this powerful rival was in fact one who had been selected though impromptu as a vessel by the deity spirits along with Marin and Linitus, the latter of the two who had yet to display their divinely conferred powers in combat.

As the fighting above still persisted, the coastal metropolis below also had multiple pitched battles along distinct important control points as well as along the wall towers and ramparts along the periphery of the city. About a third of Decius's forces were on the ground, and they dealt with a sudden mobilized group of local militia among the civilian population as well as several of the military guard that kept a low profile and embedded themselves in hiding to find the opportune time to strike back at Decius's forces after it had initially captured Citadella Neapola over two weeks prior. Additionally, there were several wizards on board the kingdom's skyships, trained to be able to teleport and used their abilities to transport several contingents of the kingdom's soldiers through such magical means of transportation to arrive instantly at those important control points on the surface that were being fought fiercely and were highly contested.

Meanwhile, on land though only arriving after much of the fighting from the air had ensued, a large coordinated combined force of kingdom human knights as well as dwarven elite guard warriors and elven rangers from Salvinia Parf Edhellen had made a full march from the east to the coastal city's walls. This army quickly deployed ladders, siege towers, as well as several wizards on the ground to teleport soldiers to the ramparts of the castle walls to engage against the now-defending forces of Decius's Remnant. The fighting was also fierce, but gradually and decisively the kingdom's forces began to overtake and rout the Remnant forces.

Decius, still on the canopy deck of the skybeast, focused and summoned once again a colossal form of the werewolf-looking hell beast, while the dux's assigned goblin pilot swooped and made passes with the skybeast's strong durable metal wings to cut the masts of the floating kingdom skyships. At least several fell down devastatingly as a result. As the gargantuan hell-wolf beast Decius summoned emanated, it quickly stood on top of the canopy deck of the skyship and behind Decius. The dark lord used the beast as his avatar to control movements, and it leaped forward during one of the passes the skybeast vessel made to swipe at more kingdom skyships. Upon landing from the air onto the deck of one of the kingdom airships, the hell beast swiped and clawed at both the mast of the ship as well as the crew that put up a defensive resistance to no avail.

Linitus and Marin looked on while the elf ranger directed Wyatt to move their skyship forward to come close enough to the skybeast for the wizard to be able to teleport him and Marin to the canopy deck. Wyatt shook his head but indicated that the terrifying flying contraption was moving too swiftly and unpredictably to be able to teleport them onto the deck without the risk of opening a teleportation portal in midair that would not reliably be timed for them to land with their feet on the deck but possibly fall out of the air. Linitus understood and thought of a second idea while still ordering his wizard companion to take the skyship as close as possible to Decius's flagship. He told Marin, Wyatt, and Peat his plan to use one of the ship-mounted ballistae to attach an empty barrel; the elf ranger would substitute the explosive oil with a glob of silk adhesive web material to attach to a bundle of tied arrow shafts along with a rope line. This would be nearly the same he had used before in combat against the other skyship, except instead of using the explosive barrel to detonate, he and Marin would use the connected ends to zip-line down to Decius's skybeast and use their special divine conferred powers to engage in combat against Decius. It was daring, but all his fellow hero companions agreed it was worth such an attempt.

However, prior to implementing this plan, Linitus saw from the distance more of the chaos being sown by the flying demon-like imps as well as the returning colossal hell-wolf avatar that Decius had once again summoned, both of which still posed an immediate threat to the allied kingdom sky fleet. The elf ranger remembered his bestowed powers that he was able to draw upon during his trial with Silvanus. He had summoned a mighty whirlwind that was powerful enough to temporarily capture the deity spirit in its mist. He decided to tell Marin quickly that they should both use their powers to quickly assist the allied forces before dealing directly with Decius on board his skyship. Marin looked at him halfway, nodding but also pondering without knowing the extent of Linitus's powers and how they would be able to do that. The elf ranger told her to remember her trial and how she focused on using her powers to pass the trial. Marin, though somewhat unsure of herself, nodded and did her best to reflect back on the trial and how she was able to focus on drawing upon the holy powers that she used to defeat the deity spirit of Aritimi. As they began to do so, Linitus told Wyatt to plot a course straight ahead toward the main mass of the swarm of imps that were still overwhelming the kingdom's skyships. Peat considered it a suicidal attempt, thinking the risk from seeing the sudden and devastating carnage caused by the hellacious creatures did not outweigh the benefit of potentially ridding them. The dwarf admitted in part he was unsure of how powerful both his hero companions were that received the status of vesselhood. However, he trusted them while swearing and hoping their instinct was correct.

Within a kilometer or half kilometer away, Linitus's flagship skyship was approaching the main bulk of the swarm of imps still flying erratically. From that distance, Linitus felt that he was close enough to summon the divine powerful whirlwind. He closed his eyes while meditating, chanting, and focusing his thoughts on the enemies ahead of him. The imps began, however, to take notice and veered sharply to turn around and dart toward the skyship. As they did so, however, they felt a strong moving mass of air pulling and dragging as a large powerful swirling motion of wind formed quickly. At first, the imps ignored it while still heading across the sky head-on to charge at the skyship. However, the force began to drag strongly enough to suck the imps in. The desperate hellish creatures soon realized the gravity of their situation while screeching in agony and trying to escape the whirlwind but to no avail. They collided with multiple objects, including themselves and debris from the ground below while being caught in the funnel of the tornado. Channeling his thoughts on this whirlwind tornado that formed, Linitus began to focus and direct it to move its position slowly but gradually toward the other flying imps that did not suspect the powerful tornado. The elf ranger tried to avoid getting too close to the allied skyships while still trying to suck in the imps that were exposed enough to get caught in this magically created calamity.

Meanwhile as the imps were in large numbers getting gradually sucked toward this deadly tornado that Linitus had summoned, Ascentius in his flying dragon-man form began to use his long two-handed heavenly silver greatsword to cast lightning bolts that struck each of the many recently created hell portals from which the demon-like imps came. Each time he did so, a given hell portal would flash and dissipate from the sky. Gradually, it would be the first step in undoing the harm that Decius in his vesselhood form created.

Realizing what was happening, the controlled colossal hell-beast avatar that Decius had summoned made its way toward the flying dragon-man form of Ascentius. Ascentius turned and dodged while flying with his dragon-like wings. He then realized that challenging Decius and his summoned beast would be no easy fight. However, he also saw from the distance, his daughter from his previous human life, Marin, chanting in a near-meditative state while she held out her right arm and seemed to be calling upon divine intervention. Within moments, the Princess Knight had completed her thoughts and quickly had called upon a magical bright, flashing gold-like spear to appear before her hand. She gripped it and looked intently from a distance toward Decius's summoned gargantuan beast. Focusing her sights on it while holding this large spear of bright visible light that burned vehemently, she quickly aimed while adjusting the position of her legs and arms before pulling back her right arm with the heavenly spear in hand. In a sudden moment while unleashing a warlike cry, Marin quickly with all her strength threw forward the flashing spear of light across the sky. It traversed quickly while creating a loud audible whistling sound until the enchanted spear struck its intended target from far away, the colossal hell werewolf. The creature, feeling the impact of the bright flashing spear, howled and shrieked in pain before ripping it from its corporeal-like body. Upon pulling it out, the enchanted weapon disappeared.

From a distance, Decius reacted in the same manner while feeling the same pain as the hell beast in the same corresponding body part, a few inches below its shoulder blade. Within moments, the summoned beast, being a created projection of concentration by the dux, disappeared as Decius was not able to concentrate again to project this gargantuan beast's power. Everyone on board the skyship as well as the other skyships took notice. Ascentius, flying and hovering in the air, turned back to acknowledge and verbally praise Marin's effort in not only aiding him but also in finding a weakness against the dux.

However, seeing an opportunity in which to press the advantage in this turbulent battle, Ascentius pointed out that she and Linitus must hurry and fight Decius directly before he would be able to concentrate and summon the deadly demonic avatar again, while Ascentius himself would continue to use his powers to cast a special form of magical lightning to seal the remaining portal gates that bound their mortal world of Terrunaemara to the hellish realm of Hadao Infernum. Linitus nodded and told Wyatt to reposition the ship so that it would run parallel to the broadside of Decius's skybeast, which hovered in a circular motion not far from the position of Linitus's skyship. Once in position, Linitus quickly ordered Peat to fire the ballista and hold its connected line steady after it had connected with the bundle of sticky adhesive silk arrows toward the hull of Decius's skybeast. Upon doing so while still looking down toward the skybeast, Linitus's skyship gradually ascended high enough for Linitus to secure a grappling hook assembly to the rope line and zip line to the other flying vessel below. Marin, looking at him, held on to him, facing each other while he secured another hook to a waistline belt for her. After being secured, they quickly flung out from the skyship and zipped down the rope line toward Decius's skybeast. The other end of the line was successfully secured to the top starboard canopy deck of the skybeast.

Upon making a hard landing on the charcoal metallic canopy surface of the large batlike flying platform, Linitus and Marin began to see Decius, though wounded, beginning to feel healed. However, both the elf ranger and the Princess Knight began to contemplate whether this was the dux or another summoned creature as this one looked nearly the same as the large, gargantuan one they had defeated, except it was the size of a tall muscular man. As soon as they heard the words and voice of the beast, however, they both knew that it had to be indeed Decius, though now in a hellacious-looking form resembling his avatar. Marin confided in a low voice that she surmised Decius had undertaken an anthropomorphic transformation not too unlike that of her father, though the dux's was certainly more intimidating and menacing-looking. He took the form of a dark, nearly pitch-black angry werewolf that emitted burning flames and embers throughout different parts of its body. This hellish werewolf called to them while cursing them and telling the two heroes that they would die and regret this day, for having the insolence to challenge the power and vision of what he claimed would be his domain. As he continued to be enraged, it took him another moment to look back and realize the flying beast that Marin had saved was none other than her father. Decius admitted he was surprised to see his former king and chief adversary in a different form, much like the anthropomorphic one he recently assumed.

Marin and Linitus looked at this demonic form of what once was a human creature with disdain, while both told him that it was over and he would be defeated whether he chose to surrender or not. Decius, in return, rebuked them while telling them that he could never be stopped in this life or the next.

Seeing that there was nothing left but to fight each other, Linitus and Marin both unsheathed their swords while Marin also raised her shield and prepared to get in a fighting stance along with Linitus. Decius called in an incantation-like manner and had created a black translucent long sword (similar to how Marin was able to use her powers to create her heavenly spear of light). Assuming a steady and aggressive pose, Decius mocked them while trying to elicit fear and break their concentration prior to engaging them in melee combat. After they circled and sized one another up, Decius unleashed a deafening and harrowing howl, quickly charging toward Linitus and Marin, while the two of them assumed a defensive bracing posture a few steps away from each other to prepare to parry the dux's attacks while delivering counterattacks. They held their ground as Decius engaged with them relentlessly on top of the canopy deck of the skybeast. For the time being, Marin and Linitus had at least succeeded in preventing Decius from summoning his colossal beast in imitation of his new werewolf-like form. However, the two heroes knew they were also potentially vulnerable as they would have a hard time also to use their own deity-like powers of vesselhood while being preoccupied engaging vigorously in sword-to-sword combat against this new form of the dux. Though he was different from before, his familiarity and prowess in fighting with a blade was still very much the same and, consequently, very ferocious. Decius would strike hard, fast, and nearly elegantly in finding openings where he could slay his adversaries in a single stroke or two. He would not let them have any quarter for pressing the advantage in being exposed to any counterstrikes, lest they exposed themselves first. It would be a long and intense battle between him, the Princess Knight, and the elf ranger, while against the backdrop, the remaining dozen or so skyships from both the Remnant and the kingdom fought on with the same intensity.

CHAPTER FIFTY-TWO

Battle of the Chosen Vessels

Upon flying above Mount Inferno, which stood more than forty miles away from Citadella Neapola, Agaroman consulted with Lucia on what to do next, going forward. Both of them agreed that it was best for the wizard to use his magic to project an image of himself to communicate to Decius on board the other skybeast ship he was on. Agaroman did so while opening a magical means to communicate with a goblin shaman that was on board the other skybeast. When they both saw image projections of each other from the bridge of each other's skyship, Agaroman prompted the goblin shaman to inform him how the battle still fared and if the dux was on his way to Mount Inferno to rendezvous with the wizard and the dux's wife. The goblin shaman informed the wizard that the skybeast was still in the battle and that the dux was currently engaging in melee combat against two formidable warriors on the side of the kingdom, the Princess Knight and an elven ranger.

Upon hearing that news, Agaroman became alert, knowing how formidable both of those two were by reputation, even against Decius. The dark lord could likely beat either of them in single combat, but to engage both certainly would make it harder for him, though not impossible to prevail especially since having the powers of chosen vesselhood. The wizard also remembered observing how formidable the elf ranger was, presuming it was the same one who had practically single-handedly helped Marin save Ascentius and held his ground throughout much of his initial fighting engagement against Decius outside the walls of Sanctum Novus.

It was certainly a grim circumstance in which Agaroman had no quarrels to take this matter into his own hands, as much as he could. The wizard quickly instructed the goblin shaman to order the pilot currently operating Decius's skybeast to immediately change course to Mount Inferno to rendezvous with the other skybeast. The goblin shaman acknowledged, and while he did so, Agaroman followed up by giving further directions, telling the shaman to send all available forces on Decius's skybeast to assist in defending the ship and providing direct aid to Decius to join the fray in fighting against the two formidable adversaries currently fighting the dux. Once the goblin shaman had done so, the final order Agaroman gave before casting away his image projection was for the goblin shaman to use its magic to create any barriers and protection for the cockpit area around the bridge but mainly around the pilot and the steering/operating controls. The goblin shaman acknowledged and began casting several spells, including a shieldlike globe that protected the goblin pilot and a shieldlike barrier around the helm area of the cockpit bridge. Lastly, the goblin shaman, while still having time, cast a series of spells in which he transported by teleportation spell-casting multiple goblins and orcs, a troll, and a few Citadellan knight warriors from the other remaining skyships. The goblin shaman communicated for recently boarded arrivals that it was imperative they stood guard on the bridge to engage and fight any invading kingdom warriors that sought to attack and take over the bridge. The boarded soldiers nodded in compliance, while the goblin shaman decided to deploy the troll and the Citadellan Black Wolf knight warriors as well as a few goblin warriors to the canopy area of the skybeast that was on top of the bridge. They complied and quickly ran toward the flight of stairs leading to the canopy deck outside. They were prepared to assist the dux and fight any of his foes.

Meanwhile, Decius took turns slashing and parrying back and forth against Marin and Linitus. None of them with their blades had been able to overtake the other in combat. As they fought fiercely on the canopy deck of the skybeast, several of Decius's forces came to assist with a few goblins, a large troll armed with a large makeshift spiked wooden club, and three Black Wolf knight warriors. This token relief force charged at the heroes while shouting in support, proclaiming the name of their dark lord and the Remnant. Decius's wolflike face grinned, before backing away and unleashing a terrifying howl. Marin and Linitus quickly realized they were in trouble and possibly about to be overwhelmed.

However, there was some degree of minor relief as the skybeast quickly turned and changed course, moving east away from the city and away from the remaining fighting between the two skyship fleets. This rapid turn caused everyone to lose balance and hit the deck fairly hard, with the troll unwittingly crushing some of the goblins to death from the force of its weight while toppling down hard to the deck. Decius quickly regained his balance, helped his Black Wolf knights get back up, and inquired what was going on. He wanted to know why they were here and why the skybeast changed course. The knights told him that the goblin shaman on the bridge gave the orders to do so. The dux told the three knights to guard the stairway leading from the canopy deck to the bridge while the dux himself went down to the bridge to inquire what was going on with the goblin shaman to issue such orders that Decius himself did not give.

Upon arriving on the bridge of the skyship, Decius noticed a projected image of Agaroman conversing with the goblin shaman. The dux interrupted their conversation while somehow being several yards away from the goblin shaman. Decius focused and drew upon his dark and near-divine powers to somehow create a projected image of himself in the presence of Agaroman on the bridge of the sister skyship in where the wizard was on board. The dux demanded to know what was going on. Agaroman along with the goblin shaman who caught notice on Decius's skybeast ship were both initially visibly startled seeing what had happened while not expecting the dux's power to have reached that ability of projection. The wizard gave a minor bow and salutation of respect while pleading for the dux to excuse him from seeming to overstep his authority, reminding the dux that they had planned to regroup at Mount Inferno. The wizard advisor told Decius, from conversing with the goblin shaman on the status of the battle, he thought it necessary to have the skybeast vessel pull back and receive support from the other sibling vessel.

Decius, taking a moment to realize and assess the situation, agreed and thought of a better idea: crashing the skybeast into the chasm of the volcanic mountain while teleporting to the other skybeast through Agaroman's magic. The dux surmised that such a daring move would catch Marin and her elf companion off guard, to have no means to escape while they would plummet to their fiery demise. Though it was costly at the expense of losing another skybeast vessel, Agaroman agreed, knowing that these two heroes of the kingdom were perhaps the most formidable and threatening to the Remnant's future expansion and overall state. The wizard told Decius that he would wait for the dux's skybeast to arrive at Mount Inferno before they executed their plan and teleport Decius back to the other skybeast vessel. Before closing their projected image form of communications, Decius wanted to know how his wife and child were faring. Agaroman replied that they were doing well given the conditions and he even was impressed by Lucia's ability to pilot the skybeast that they flew in despite the earlier damage it had incurred from the battle. Decius grinned and was pleased. Before having his wizard advisor close their communication, the dark-lord dux, always considering contingency plans as he learned to do from Agaroman's mentoring, told the wizard that should anything happen to him, whether he perished in this mortal life or was banished to another realm, the wizard, goblin shamans, or anyone else, including his beloved Lucia should invoke the libation ritual using an altar dedicated to both Calu and Laran while calling upon the dark lord's name. Decius, feeling the essence of both Calu and Laran, knew that somehow his powers had a way to transcend his projection and image to communicate to others just as he had now done with Agaroman while not using the conventional means of spell-casting magic in the same way as Agaroman and the goblin shamans had done.

Agaroman, though still somewhat baffled, again knew that Decius's powers as chosen vessel did seem to confirm this so far and agreed that he and Lucia would summon the dux or his spirit should he fall by the kingdom's forces. The wizard knew that Decius would always be ambitious and find a way to persevere even if he faced temporary setbacks. Before ending their conversation through projecting their images with each other's presence, Agaroman wished his dark lord the best of luck while pleading for him and his forces to show the kingdom the hell and fury of the dux's wrath for challenging his reign. Decius nodded while bidding farewell to his wizard advisor and mentor.

As the conversation ended between Decius, the goblin shaman, and Agaroman, the scene outside on Decius's skybeast vessel canopy covered deck was much different. Marin and Linitus fought fiercely to survive and prevail against the overwhelming power and numbers of the dux's last-minute reinforcements. The two heroes of the kingdom moved quickly and fiercely in dodging, striking, and parrying blows against the orcs along with the few surviving goblins that were fortunate to avoid and not die when the troll fell upon their other goblin companions while losing balance from the flying vessel's erratic turning earlier.

Additionally, the same troll made passes while charging at the two heroes. The three Black Wolf Knights following Decius's orders stood and watched while holding the post of making sure both the Princess Knight and the elf ranger would not try to pass through them and down into the bridge of the skybeast. Though the fighting was intense, eventually Linitus and Marin gained the upper hand when Linitus switched from using his slightly curved long sword to using his bows and arrows. He instructed Marin to hold their foes at bay while he kept a distance, letting loose one arrow after the next, striking several goblins and orcs at a time while moving about the canopy deck to further ensure distance from any approaching enemies. Marin meanwhile used her flaming sword and her small round shield as both defensive and offensive weapons, including charging at two of the goblins while deflecting their blows and knocking them down with her shield. She then followed up by using her shield to crush one goblin before proceeding to slash with her sword against the other goblin.

Meanwhile, the lone troll began to charge toward Marin while shouting in its awkward terrifying voice. Linitus called out to warn Marin, and the Princess Knight quickly dodged and rolled out of the way while Linitus fired one of his flaming arrows at the troll. The elf ranger did this purposely, knowing that trolls were sensitive and vulnerable to fire, and as such, the arrow caused the beast great agony. Marin followed up by leaping and severing its head with her flaming sword after slashing several times.

Upon felling the beast, the two heroes caught their breath before realizing that three Black Wolf knights guarded a stairway down to what the two heroes presumed would be the bridge deck of the ship, where Decius was also presumed to be for the time being.

The two heroes walked slowly and almost ceremoniously toward the three enemy knights. Both parties had their blades ready and began to adopt their own fighting stances while sizing each other up and anticipating which side would make the first move. Marin, catching both the three knights off guard as well as her companion lover Linitus, quickly concentrated and used her focus to conjure a bright flashing spear that resembled a lightning bolt, which she hurled toward one of the three knights. This divinely summoned spear made contact and instantly killed the knight while it impaled him. The other two knights, though taken back initially, broke their steady pose and quickly charged at the two heroes. Linitus responded sarcastically with praise, stating that was one way for them to even the odds. Marin smiled back, saying she had learned from the best while looking at him. Blushing mildly, Linitus nodded, and the two quickly raised their blades to evade and engage in combat, each against the remaining two knights. Though the two remaining Black Wolf knights put up an explosive series of strikes toward the two heroes of the Comradery respectively, the latter were able to hold their ground. After several more strikes and parries, Marin and Linitus eventually both overcame and delivered fatal blows respectively to the two foes they fought against.

After doing so, they looked at the stairway steps of the canopy deck area of the skybeast that led down toward the bridge. They quickly proceeded down the stairs, and upon entry to the flying vessel's interior, they noticed that the bridge, like the outside of the contraption, was made of the same black charcoal metallic material. The interior design of the bridge was sleek, jagged, and dark with very dim lighting that was given off from the burning lamps mounted at intervals along the bulkhead wall interior of the vessel. The two heroes also saw several goblins at different parts of the bridge, watching and operating different stations, mainly siege weapons that they would be ready to fire if any enemy vessels were in sight and within range. Decius, in his transformed beastly werewolf-like form, quickly caught the attention of the heroes, who spotted him on the bow section of the bridge on the other far end from where they were. The dux ended his transmission communication to Agaroman while stating that he would be there to rendezvous soon. From the forward bridge viewing area window, noticeable but faint, Mount Inferno stood up ahead along with a small dark speck that became gradually bigger as the skybeast continued its course toward the volcanic mountain. That dark speck from the distance would turn out to be the sister skybeast vessel.

Wasting no time, Decius called forth many of the goblins to cease their operation of the flying vessel and aid him in fighting the two heroes. Marin and Linitus slayed them quickly, while Decius called forth again the same translucent black blade that he had magically emanated earlier to once again emanate and he held it with one of his hands. Posing in an aggressive stance ready to ferociously pounce upon the two heroes, he taunted them that he would slay them one way or the other and get his revenge for losing temporary control of Citadella Neapola. Marin and Linitus responded that he could try and he would either fail or they would try again until he did fail. Decius quickly responded that when he was done slaying them, he would bring the full fury of death and destruction the likes of which the western lands had not seen, for defying his authority as chosen vessel along with bringing a new order and a new Lupercalian Empire.

Once again, Marin and Linitus called out their adversary, stating he would fail since he had already broken the covenant, whether he realized it or not, so the divine spirits would not let him rule this new empire that he sought to create. Linitus went so far as to even tell the dux that the glory days of the ancient imperial past were over and the pursuit of this revisionism had done nothing but lead to a society that was worse off than before. Decius laughed sarcastically while mocking and questioning how that would be the case when society was largely neglected to begin with by a monarchy that could barely govern itself, was occupied in a vengeful war only when it affected the personal and immediate interests of revenge for the crown, while leaving for some faraway lands only to look the other way when corrupt officials and clergy desecrated their office and proper relationship with the deity spirits, only for their own materialistic gains. The dux reasoned that despite all the death and destruction he had caused, at least he stayed true to his own code, his own values, and the society he built along with those close to him was far more orderly and better off in not starving from its various needs.

Linitus rebuked Decius's reasoning, telling this dark lord that replacing an imperfect society (having social ills, neglect, and corruption) with a society governed by tyrannical fear while pursuing death and destruction for territorial expansion and acquisition of resources was not better off. Decius howled and retorted in rejection of the elf's last statement, calling him a fool that only grew up with the lies that the kingdom told him to keep him loyal and subservient to the existing system. Marin broke off, saying that arguing further was pointless; the fate of western lands of Terrunaemara would be decided as it always had been when diplomacy failed, by blade and bloodshed. Decius nodded and howled in agreement for once.

Sizing them up once more while strafing about the bridge, Decius finally decided to break stance and charge frantically toward Marin and Linitus, who stood only a few feet apart. Marin and Linitus each parried back, evaded, and then unleashed their own strikes, to which Decius did the same. The fighting continued to be intense as the pilot at the helm maintained his attention toward arriving soon at the volcanic mountain but could not help turning to look frantically, hoping that his dark lord would prevail. The few surviving goblins on the bridge also shared the same look.

The skybeast at this point was within two to three miles from the base of the volcanic mountain. With the fighting still ensuing furiously, Decius called for the goblin shaman to teleport the few surviving bridge crew out of the ship and onto the other skybeast when within range, with the exception of a goblin pilot operator, whom Decius ordered to position the skybeast above the summit of the volcano and then point it nose downward toward the furious chasm of the volcano's magma chamber. The goblin pilot operator complied while Linitus and Marin, though intently focusing on still fighting the dux in melee combat could overhear and realized that Decius was crazy enough to take out the ship along with them in it. Linitus quickly told Marin that they needed to fall back and retreat to the canopy deck and to find a way to get off the ship if possible. Marin nodded while in mid-battle, parrying one of Decius's hard blows. She asked how. Linitus quickly responded, while evading a blow from Decius's enchanted sword, to leave it to him. The elf pulled back while letting Marin fend against Decius by herself. Linitus quickly took from his quiver several of the sticky silk bulb arrows and quickly let loose the arrows toward the jagged claw feet of Decius. The werewolf dark lord howled upon noticing that the splattered arrows, while not having direct contact in striking his feet, still had the sticky silklike bulbs disperse the adhesive substance across the floor, with it latching on to the claw feet of Decius. It made him temporarily unable to walk. Linitus quickly called Marin to run with him back out to the vessel's canopy deck. They did so while Decius used his sword to slash carefully at the sticky bulb material that glued his claw feet to the floor of the bridge deck.

The goblin pilot, taking notice, was already above the volcano summit but held back until Decius looked and told him to still follow through in plunging the flying contraption into the volcanic magma pool that lay at the bottom of the volcano's cinder cone interior crater after making a pass around it. The goblin acknowledged while giving a final salute to its dark-lord leader, to which Decius returned the same salute before quickly swiping away with his blade and finally breaking free of the sticky material that held his feet to the deck of the bridge. He quickly raced out toward the stairway that led to the canopy exterior deck of the ship. He was hell-bent one way or another to ensure that he would kill his two adversaries.

Meanwhile, Marin and Linitus found themselves outside, staring at the immense view, looking downward at the volcanic summit and cinder-cone crater that loomed below. It was awe-inspiring and terrifying to see such a view; however, Linitus quickly looked about, and pulling another sticky-bulb arrow out from his quiver, he quickly withdrew a spool with rope twine from a utility-like ammo belt he wore along with his leather and elven mail-armor cuirass. The elf ranger quickly tied the end of the twine secured by the spool from the other end to the shaft of the arrowhead. After doing so, he aimed the arrow with his bow toward an awkward-looking ancient crane-like structural assembly that he noticed was suspended and holding an exotic skywalk platform suspended above the bottom of the volcanic lava-lake crater that loomed below. After having a steady aim and finding a secured hard point on the suspended assembly, Linitus let loose his silk-bulbed arrow that hurtled quickly across the air and made contact with the suspended bridge-like anchored tower structure. He quickly called Marin, and she quickly held on to him after securing her shield over her shoulder and sheathing her sword back in her scabbard. Linitus also secured his bow back to his attached slung shoulder strap, and quickly, the two leaped off while Marin still held on tightly to Linitus as he held on to the spool. Leaping off the skyship frantically in the air, they both heard at the last moment a loud screeching howl as Decius in the distance cursed and waved his hands menacingly toward them.

By the time he reached the deck however, Decius was spotted by the other skybeast ship above. Focusing on his powers, instead of having Agaroman teleport him, Decius was able to project an image of himself to the bridge of the other skybeast vessel, which Lucia operated. He asked Lucia and Agaroman the status of the skybeast. They reported again that despite some damage from the battle earlier in which it was emitting a trail of smoke, it was still very much operational. Agaroman was confident that once grounded, he could easily repair its aft tail. However, Lucia pointed out that they were being followed from a distance by more than half a dozen skyships. Though miles away, Agaroman was able to discern the flying vessels' emblems being that of Swordbane. It was clear that Decius's forces had fallen from the efforts of Swordbane to recapture Citadella Neapola and now were in hot pursuit of the remaining two skybeast vessels. Decius knew that likely the trail of smoke that the other skybeast made was giving away its position for the remaining skyships of Swordbane to follow.

Sighing, Decius told Lucia and Agaroman to take the skyship away back to Sanctum Novus for repairs and to make their last stand at this capital of the imperial Remnant should the forces of Swordbane pursue them with a counterattack of their own. He told his wife that he loved her and to watch over their son. Also turning to Agaroman, Decius instructed him to teach his son and mentor him much like he did with Decius himself. The wizard nodded and assured him he would have his son continue his legacy of creating a new empire reminiscent of the ancient Lupercalian one from over a millennium ago. The dux nodded and said finally whether he fell in combat or emerged victorious, his vesselhood was indomitable from being permanently stopped. He reminded both Lucia and Agaroman to conduct the libation ritual before the altar of Calu and Laran to summon his spectral spirit should he fall in this mortal life. Agaroman nodded again while his wife Lucia also nodded while professing her love for Decius and telling him to do everything to come back to her and their son. Decius nodded before saying goodbye one more time and ending his projected image.

The dux next thought quickly of the matter at hand as the skybeast he was on still hovered about. He wondered why the goblin piloting the craft did not crash it yet to the magma chasm below, unless the goblin pilot also saw what Decius had just seen, that Linitus and Marin had already gone overboard and were dangling from a rope line below an anchor tower on one of the ends of the interior cinder cone crater walls. He focused his deity-like powers to imitate Agaroman's ability to project an image of himself and communicate to the goblin pilot. He was able to do so and inquired why the goblin pilot hesitated from his order. The goblin indicated that it was trying to decide what the best course of action was since the two adversaries of the dux had already escaped the skybeast though they were dangling below the volcanic wall tower that held the suspended cables to the bridge platform. Decius, though he ordinarily would have been angry at a simple creature not following his orders, had a noticeable degree of respect for this goblin who at least took a moment to contemplate while knowing the situation had changed. Decius decided to tell this subordinate to change his instructions and instead provide cover to defend the other skybeast vessel while it escaped, but only after Decius departed the vessel. He told the goblin that he would teleport himself down to the bridge platform, and once the goblin saw him below, to immediately veer off course and engage in combat against the other enemy skyships that were in pursuit of the other skybeast. The goblin complied and did so after Decius concentrated on his dark powers to eventually be able to teleport himself to the suspended bridge platform below. Slowly the dux was becoming more deadly and powerful as he began to learn in being able to achieve abilities that he previously was not able to do and would depend on his wizard advisor for support, including teleportation.

Upon arriving at the bridge suspension platform, Decius next concentrated and summoned his gargantuan beast-like avatar of himself. This summoned hellacious colossal wolf-beast emerged from the bridge suspension platform area above the volcanic crater. The bridge suspension platform, just as before, was itself suspended by large metal cable-like chains that connected it from the corner ends of the platform to four diagonal towers mounted on opposite ends of the volcano's cinder-cone crater. Decius, with his summoned colossal beast avatar, was able to spot more closely the position of the two heroes that still eluded him.

Decius regretted the outcome since his adversaries escaped the death he had initially planned for them; regardless, he resolved to finish them off one way or another while they were still within the crater of the volcano. They had nowhere to go unless they confronted him at the suspended platform, which only had one exit that he was blocking.

Linitus and Marin were in a more perilous situation than the one recounted from a moment earlier. Upon leaping into the air from the plummeting skybeast vessel, the two heroes were nearly free-falling until the slack ran out from the rope and a large yank was felt and the two were no longer falling. They were suspended in the air, hanging below one of the towerlike structures that was erected awkwardly against one of the cone-crater walls of the volcano. Linitus looked over to Marin and asked if she was all right. Marin nodded and glanced back while giving him a quick kiss. She thought they might as well share this quick moment of intimacy, and she wanted to let him know as such if this happened to be their last moment together. Linitus told her to hold on while he looked about.

Below from a distance, he saw a platform in the center but more immediately below him, which Marin could see also, lay a lava pool that filled the base of the crater. He was secured at least, but he was not sure for how long as he felt the tension and weight of himself and Marin about to give in. The sticky adhesive material could not hold their weight indefinitely, and they had nowhere to go other than descending to their deaths in the lava below. They could not reach the suspended platform as it was beyond reach from them. Marin realized the situation also and told him to let go of her. Linitus shook his head in total fear of what she was saying. He refused to do it, without hesitancy. Marin looked and knew there was no choice that he could hold on to her without them both eventually falling from the weight being too great for the rope line to not break. She still urged him and told him that even if she fell, he still stood a chance to climb up and find a way to get down to the platform to fight Decius. Linitus once again still refused. Time was running short, and he was still thinking, being resourceful as he typically was for finding creative solutions and considering what options and what clever gadgets and items in his possession he could use to ensure they both escaped. He had nothing left that he could or that was accessible in his suspended position in the air. Knowing this while pondering frustrated him even more. Of all the times when he felt hopeless in not finding any creative way to solve a puzzle like this with a creative solution, this was by far the most pressing and dire. He had nothing left to think of, and Marin could tell. She tried to tug and let go, but he shouted loudly and frantically that if she did, he would let go too and fall with her. He did not want to leave her to die alone. She meant everything to him, and he even confided to her that whatever fate awaited her, he would ensure they would face it together. Marin nodded while speculating, wishing they only had the power and means to find some way to escape.

Suddenly, after hearing those words and thinking to himself, she had given him the one idea he did not think about, using his powers. He responded with a surprised face of resolution, telling her that he had an answer; he had a way that they could still possibly survive. Marin did not know what he meant, but he told her to hold on to him. Using his mind to concentrate while chanting, Linitus quickly focused on his inward power and ability to summon a whirlwind. Although it was risky with the lava bed below, he thought this would be the only choice. He continued to chant his words in activating this power as a swirling motion began to take place. Rather than focusing on creating hot air that already existed on the volcano's crater surface, Linitus focused on the clouds above to swirl and generate the cold air needed to interact with the volcanic hot air generated by the lava magma bed. Over time, a large swirl began to form that drew downward between the clouds above and the hot air with its ambient heat being produced from the extremely hot magma bed of the volcanic crater. The swirl became stronger and stronger until it picked both Linitus and Marin up. They held each other together while Marin, reflecting on her own powers, remembered that she had the ability to heal and generate a globe-like orb that would encapsulate a given object to protect and heal. She quickly began to chant as well while holding on to

Linitus. Eventually, a translucent aquamarine-colored orb began to form and expand to encapsulate them both. This orb protected and shielded them while the tornado that Linitus had summoned became immensely turbulent, enough to draw them and the mystical orb they were in from Marin's summoned powers to float and swirl along with the movement of the wind funnel that carried them upward along a spiral updraft. This tornado was unlike any other as it caught flames of magma and fire as it spun while Linitus still channeled his thoughts to move the tornado whirlwind along to the center of the suspended platform before gradually easing the whirlwind to allow him and Marin with the mystical orb they were in to fall downward in a drift. Eventually with the thoughts that he channeled, it worked.

Decius, at first jeering in hopes that his adversaries would plummet to their death, became cautious on seeing the whirlwind form, and he quickly took cover behind the walls of a tunnel that connected the volcano crater chamber to the exterior entrance that sloped under the top rim of the volcanic crater. He also used his summoned gargantuan beast to follow him.

Eventually, after seeing that the whirlwind had subsided, the dark lord himself emerged back onto the bridge platform to see that Linitus and Marin somehow miraculously were unscathed by the summoned whirlwind while the dux saw the same aquamarine-colored globe emanating around them. Clearly, they had attained vesselhood from the benevolent deity spirits, which he had no doubt of, after seeing them avoid the fate that he had anticipated would await them from the magma-filled pool below. Regardless, it mattered little to Decius; he himself would see to it that they were dealt with by being disposed of one way or another.

As Marin and Linitus let go of each other with the mystical healing-type globe disappearing, they quickly turned and looked about. They found themselves at the center of this suspended bridge-like platform with Decius and his summoned gargantuan hell-wolf avatar standing between them and the entrance to the tunnel that would exit from the volcanic mountain to the other side.

Decius slowly took a few steps forward while applauding in a derisive manner to congratulate them for not yet dying, while telling the two heroes one way or the other, he would see to it that they did die. Marin and Linitus, defiant as ever, told the dark lord that it was over. He could not stand a chance against them both. Decius laughed while acknowledging that perhaps they were right and deciding that it would not just be him alone that would fight them. He concentrated his mind to control his colossus hell wolf. The beast seeking to trample them moved in big heavy steps toward the two heroes as it chased after them. Linitus and Marin evaded and ran in different directions, causing the creature to stop and contemplate which one to go after.

As they confused the creature, a lone voice suddenly called out to them from high above. Flying downward in a spiral, Ascentius in his anthropomorphic dragon-man form called out, telling Decius once again that he could not escape the justice that he was due to face for breaking the covenant and opening up unsanctioned portal gates to allow the denizens of hell to come out and aid him in feeding the powers of his patron deities, namely Calu of the underworld. Decius disregarded what Ascentius stated while rebuking him and telling him that nothing was sanctioned or unsanctioned than the force of those who wield and control what they make of it. Soon channeling the same powers of his absolute hate and anger, Decius again began summoning a large portal gate high in the air above the center of the volcano's crater. He called forth another large swarm of demonic imps and commanded them to attack Linitus, Marin, and Ascentius.

Linitus, thinking about what he had done earlier, called out to Ascentius and told him that he could use his powers to hold back the imps while sending them back to the abyss from where they came from. Ascentius nodded but told the elf ranger he had to generate a large enough one to pull them all in while possibly at the expense of sucking himself and Marin before Ascentius could see the portal connected to hell closed. Linitus nodded while looking at Marin. She nodded also and told her elf lover it was the best option to do as long as they sucked up Decius and his gargantuan beast to go in with it.

Decius utterly rebuked, howled, and yelled no in a large defiant voice while charging from a distance toward Linitus and Marin. However, before he could strike them, a long silvery two-handed sword clashed against his black-blade long sword that went from being translucent to opaque. Decius looked up and saw that he was locked in combat against Ascentius in his new form. They were different from each other and more beast-like, as they both knew while giving menacing stares. Decius in his wolflike form only a foot away howled in rage toward Ascentius, who in return unleashed a loud dragon-sounding roar before closing his jagged teeth and huffing smoke from his elongated dragon-like snout. They were both fierce and did not hold back the weight of their own blades while pressing as much weight as they possibly could in standing from opposite directions. Turning back briefly, Ascentius told Linitus to hurry and commence his whirlwind power while also looking toward Marin and telling her that he still remembered and loved her. He then turned toward Decius, who still tried to overpower him while their blades were locked together. Using his mental power at the same time, Decius had controlled his gargantuan so that it charged and used its clawed hand to swipe at Ascentius, but the half-dragon man quickly used its wings to propel backward and evade.

As the battle transpired, the large number of imps with their flying wings swarmed around the hellish portal gate above. Suddenly however, bolts of lightning emanated from the clouds below. Marin looked and pointed upward while telling Linitus of what she saw. Eventually, something was passing in the sky, away from the center of the crater above but visible to them. Marin pointed again, this time toward a lone skyship with a small wizard-like figure with a dark pointy brimmed hat, stretching his hands and moving a wand to cast more and more lightning bolts that struck the imps one by one. From a distance, this lone wizard figure also shot off two very large and powerful lightning bolts toward a skybeast vessel that had attacked it while making fast passes. Though the skyship could not outrun or outfight the skybeast through conventional ship-to-ship combat means, Wyatt spell-casted more lightning bolts and fireballs with relentless speed and force such that he was able to knock the terrifying flying contraption off course. The skybeast quickly swirled recklessly out of control before eventually descending toward the magma lake at the bottom of the volcano's crater, where it sank and melted gradually.

Marin shouted from below, calling Wyatt's name. Wyatt had spotted her and quickly caught notice of both her and Linitus below with the ever-growing whirlwind that Linitus had summoned spiraling more chaotically. Peat quickly told the wizard that he needed to hurry and teleport both of their companions before it became too late. The youthful wizard nodded while focusing on his powers and cast a portal that emerged from both the surface of the bridge platform below as well as on the deck of the skyship. Within seconds, Marin and Linitus were on board the floating vessel. Marin looked about relieved; meanwhile, she as well as Wyatt and Peat noticed that their elf ranger companion was still caught in a deep meditative trance. Linitus was also shaking profusely in convulsions.

Despite the toll it took on him, he would not break his trance and let go of control over the whirlwind until it had not only sent all the hellish denizens back to whence they came but also sent Decius there.

Ascentius, floating high above, waited for the whirlwind to eventually overpower and capture Decius within and send him to the same hell that he had opened a dimension from. However, the werewolf dark lord resisted while using his gargantuan avatar beast to hold him in place with one hand while holding its other gigantic clawed hand on the bridge platform grating. He was going to resist and try to hold out until the whirlwind died out.

Marin, on board the skyship above, looked down at the dux and his summoned colossal beast still resisting against being pulled in by the whirlwind. The Princess Knight then turned to look down and mourn for the pain that her lover seemed to endure from sustaining the whirlwind. Thinking only of her love for him and channeling her thoughts of anger, she quickly focused on calling upon her deity-like powers and quickly had a flashing bright-looking spear emanate from one of her hands. She aimed and threw the spear with all her might in a downward sloping spiral until it struck both Decius and the beast that held him. Both the dux and his gargantuan avatar unleashed a howling cry of pain, feeling as if their life being joined was passing before them. In doing so, the gargantuan beast let go its grip on both Decius and the platform grating. The whirlwind tornado had finally caught them, or possibly their corpses, in its tunnel and sent them upward to the portal gate of hell that Decius had summoned.

Ascentius looked on and praised Marin as well as Peat and Wyatt. Marin, however, turned again to look at Linitus, who was still in pain from sustaining the tornado with nothing left to suck up and send back to the portal that led to the hellish realm of Hadao Infernum. The Princess Knight quickly called to Ascentius and beseeched him to hurry and close the portal gate with his powers, telling him that Linitus was suffering in pain to sustain the whirlwind tornado to ensure no other creatures would escape. Ascentius, flapping his scythe-shaped green wings, quickly hovered toward the portal and chanted powerful invocations that immediately cast a large bolt like lightning toward the portal gate. The impact caused the large portal to collapse. Upon seeing the collapse, the heroes on board as well as the surviving crew soldiers on the skyship's bridge cheered. They had finally defeated the dark lord, the chosen vessel of death and destruction.

Marin, however, cried while holding Linitus, who still shook in convulsions though not as badly as before. Deep inside, he could sense that there was no longer any resistance from the force of the whirlwind that he created, so he finally let go. Marin, channeling her love, focused on her deity-like healing abilities and created the same aquamarine globe that had earlier emanated between her and Linitus. She was unsure if it would heal him or bring him back to consciousness, but she thought it was worth a try. In a short time, it worked. Linitus awoke, seeing his head on top of Marin's thighs that were used to support his neck along with her hands. Marin broke off her concentration, and the healing globe disappeared. The elf ranger, gaining enough consciousness, spoke as he was thinking his thoughts and asked if it was over. He asked again if they had defeated Decius. Marin nodded her head to acknowledge while shedding some tears and telling her lover they did it. They had finally defeated the dark lord and chosen vessel of the deity spirits of war and death. Linitus smiled while still keeping his head comforted on top of Marin's legs. Marin, surprising him, gave a subtle kiss without caring if they were alone or not to share this intimate moment. She confided that she loved him. Linitus smiled back and told her that he knew and loved her also.

Invigorated with admiration, all on board the skyship cheered on seeing the two lover heroes together, with Linitus being well. To both his surprise and Marin's, the soldiers on board picked him up as well as Marin and cheered them on. Even one young adolescent soldier without modesty in using expletives showered the two with plenty of positive ones to share the verbal praise of what they had done in defeating Decius.

Chapter Fifty-Three

Dark Lord's Second Coming

Soaring fast above and distancing itself by at least three times the speed of a skyship, Lucia piloted the last remaining skybeast in a flurry in the air, darting ever closer toward its destination, the Remnant capital of Sanctum Novus. The Remnant only had two strongholds that she knew to go with: her first preference, Sanctum Novus, which she considered and opted for over relocating to Uruk Kazaht. The duchess knew the defenses of Sanctum Novus nearly as well as her dark-lord spouse Dux Decius knew them. She would take full advantage of holding out in the event of a siege and/or assault by the forces of Swordbane.

The lone skybeast vessel had already traversed past the Great Coastal Mountains and made its way southward, going from the high prairie-like basin east of the mountains to her native environment of the high desert region. She looked frequently beside her lap at her coddled son that her goblin copilot was caring for. She was relieved that Lucianus Canus was asleep for the time being. Agaroman, though normally able even from a distance to sense the life force of Decius, was no longer able to sense it. He feared and perhaps knew that his dark lord had indeed fallen in combat. He would not want to admit it, at least not yet, while realizing still even more the well-placed value and potential that his former dark lord had seen in his chosen consort wife. She might have exhibited stately and socially expected signs of female Citadellan noble patrician-class behavior in being somewhat reserved, but when the situation challenged and called for her to persevere like her former lover, Lucia knew how to act accordingly.

The wizard, sighing slowly, resolved to tell Lucia in due time, perhaps when they arrived at Sanctum Novus, of his suspicions of the dux's fall. He knew she would not take it well, but he would also suggest to her to conduct the dual libation ritual while calling upon her lover's name to confirm if he had fallen and if what the dark lord said in his spectral spirit was true, still being able to respond when called upon. Agaroman would doubt his former mentoree having such powers even when he assumed vesselhood. However, even at Mount Inferno, he became more astonished and impressed to find out that Decius, through his channeling of his divine powers, was able to conduct a remote projection of himself to communicate with his wizard advisor. It was possible that Decius might have even faked his own death, Agaroman supposed. Regardless, he concluded internally to himself that there was no way to know until he and Lucia conducted the dual altar libation ritual and called Decius's name. In doing so, they would possibly find out one way or another.

Within another few hours, the skybeast finally approached the horizon of the desert city, though it was already well into nightfall. If the pursuing fleet of remaining skyships, six or seven that Agaroman had counted, decided to still pursue the skybeast, then they would be facing fierce resistance from the city and its unwavering loyalty to Decius, whether he had fallen or not. Agaroman knew his leadership along with Lucia's would be enough to hold the city and its remaining forces to be loyal to them even if Decius had fallen. Lucia alone had shown a deep-relationship type of bond in acting as a genuine patron, or more properly, matron of the city and seeing all its living populace as her citizens and possibly by extension as close to adoptive children, as one could see it metaphorically.

Upon reaching the city, Lucia made several passes above the urban landscape while descending lower and lower until activating the vessel's landing-gear wheels, and it traveled, though bouncing somewhat roughly, across a makeshift dirt road a few hundred yards outside the city's northern walls. After landing the flying contraption, Lucia and Agaroman along with the goblin copilot carrying Lucia's child walked with a heavy escort consisting of the flying ship's crew that escorted them outside onto the ship's canopy deck. From there, Agaroman teleported them to the city's main plaza, from which they would notify the city guard to make last-minute preparations for possible attack by the enemy skyships. Lucia, learning from Decius's example of training her to command and become more politically savvy, quickly ordered several of the city guards to summon the city's leading local council as well as the senators for an emergency meeting. She would brief them about the current situation and expected a likely assault by air from Swordbane's remaining sky fleet.

Looking at her sense of command and determination, once again, Agaroman admired and saw that Lucia had very much embodied a suitable counterpart to her now-late husband. Taking a moment to interrupt and confide privately, Agaroman reminded Lucia of what her husband said in summoning him should he fall while also solemnly telling her he could no longer sense Decius's life force as Agaroman had before. Lucia, snapping and turning her face to the side, rejected hearing what she had hoped she would not have to hear and told the wizard advisor himself that she did not want to hear that. Not now. Agaroman shook his head but reminded her that if it was true, there was only one way to know, and in doing so, at least she would be reunited with her supposedly departed lover. At least even in death, his summoned spectral spirit offered the chance to advise and help them any way they could. He told her also to think about their son and his fate.

Lucia, taking a brief moment of pause, looked down at the swaddled Lucianus Canus as he was deep asleep. She took a moment to reflect and internally agreed. Despite not wanting to hear the harsh possibility of losing her lover, Agaroman was right. She had to make sure and find out one way or another, the fate of her lover. If they did summon him to have his spectral spirit appear and lead them in his postmortal form, it would benefit Sanctum Novus to do so and not hold back any longer.

After nodding and agreeing, Lucia ordered that the soldiers take the altarpieces that were on board the skybeast to the temple of Laran, where she would set up with Agaroman a dual shrine dedicated to both Laran and Calu. Upon entering the temple, setting up the altar, and conducting the incense burning and libation ritual, Lucia and Agaroman, through his supervision and instruction, called out Decius's name while invoking his titles as dark lord, dux, and chosen vessel of Calu and Laran.

At first, nothing happened while both Lucia and Agaroman sighed, but then a large burst and crackling noise began to be heard while, from a portal that disappeared, a pale ghostly body or spectral form of some near-corporeal type emanated. This figure was anthropomorphic and had the body of a man almost with the shape and distinct characteristics, including the head and tail of a wolf. It was none other than Decius himself in the form of a werewolf as he appeared during the last battle of Citadella Neapola when he no longer was in his previous human form.

The spectral figure looked about and felt different than he did before. He knew this place and the people he turned to. He called out their names: Agaroman, Lucia, and his son Lucianus Canus. He told them he was glad to see them while asking rhetorically what had happened, before thinking the same question intently to himself. Lucia replied that he had perished in his mortal life. Though she was saddened and in near disbelief of what she had seen, she realized and accepted that Agaroman was right. Her lover was back, but he was no longer considered among the living and was now in a different form and, in a sense, living in a different life or afterlife while somehow being able to project his ghost, or the shade of his spirit, to commune with them while being brought back in the presence of the mortal world.

Terrified at first to see his spectral spirit, Lucia now tried to further embrace him by placing her hand toward his cheek; however, his spectral spirit was transparent, being a ghost. Her hand went through him like going through thin air. Decius, wanting the same, tried to embrace her as well and placed his hand toward her cheek, though it did not make any contact. Regardless, Lucia still appreciated the gesture, and though not able to feel him directly, she could still feel his presence with him being there.

Recomposing herself, Lucia asked Decius what had happened. Decius, at first unsure, thought deeply about his last mortal thoughts. It became hard, but eventually he did recall with great anger. He remembered being on the suspended bridge platform that hung above the base of the magma-filled crater. He remembered summoning his gargantuan avatar that resembled a large-scale version of his werewolf form. Lastly, he remembered opening a great portal that flooded hundreds of demonic imps to unleash upon his foes, including Marin, the elf ranger she called Linitus, and Ascentius in his own changed form that resembled a dragon with the body disposition of a man. The dark lord fumed and howled furiously, remembering his last moments as he was caught off guard with the elf summoning somehow through what had to have been his chosen-vessel powers a large whirlwind that Decius himself tried to resist being sucked into and being sent to the very same hell that he opened through a portal. He recalled how he used his avatar control of his large, gargantuan hell-wolf beast to hold himself in place while his summoned imps were not able to resist falling into the trap of the whirlwind that sent them back to their hellish dimension. Lastly, he recalled while resisting from being sucked into the other plane, that the other foe he held much spite for, the Princess Knight Marin, had somehow created or summoned, supposedly with what must have been her vesselhood powers, a divine magical spear that she hurled at him, draining his life away from him as he and his gargantuan beast vanished into hell through the portal he connected with the mortal plain of Terrunaemara. He was dead and now a ghost or specter of his former self. He remembered entering the place that he opened up and was now banished to (excluding the projection of his ghost form when summoned). The spirits of Calu and Laran appeared before him after dying to tell him that he would be condemned to Hadao Infernum forever. Yet these spirits still had a plan for him; they still intended for him to use his spectral form to continue his legacy, which he was determined to. And now here he was as he predicted, from the unlikely event of falling in battle against his sworn enemies.

Now, he was turning and reflecting with both anger and a degree of wanting to use whatever cunning and abilities he had left, even if meant using his summoned presence to advise those that would do his bidding and fulfill his cause to establish a new form of the ancient Lupercalian Empire. Hearing this and regretting not staying behind, Lucia kneeled before the spectral spirit of her departed lover while asking forgiveness for not staying at his side. She truly blamed herself and regretted it even if she did follow his command. If she could go back and fight with him even while dying at his side, she would.

Decius, however, also remembered and knew his actions from his last life and how he commanded his wife to leave while he fought on at Mount Inferno. He told her that there was no need to seek forgiveness. He reflected on his new form of life and, now that he was able to be summoned, considered that perhaps this was meant to be for the better. No one, not even Ascentius in his new powerful dragon-man form or Marin and her elf lover and companion, could stop him permanently whenever he was summoned. He was already dead, but his spirit still lived on. He could appear anywhere at any time so long as someone devoted to his dark cause carried out the same ritual as Lucia and Agaroman had and if he decided to appear before the one that had summoned him from the plane of hell to the mortal plane of Terrunaemara.

Taking a moment for Lucia to rise from her knees, Decius next wanted to know what was going on since she and Agaroman escaped with their crew on board their respective skybeast vessel. He knew they were at the temple of Laran in the capital, Sanctum Novus. Marin and Agaroman took turns to explain that they had managed to escape, but they were expecting at least half a dozen skyships in pursuit of them, and those enemy floating vessels would arrive in less than a day. They informed the dux that they were summoning the most important officials of the city to brief them and devise a plan to repel Swordbane's attacks when they remembered Decius's words to summon him should he perish, which they now revealed they had done so.

Decius, looking solemnly at both Lucia and Agaroman, nodded and told them that he would follow them to the local senate capitol building of the city and let them know that his spirit still lived on and even when dead, he was still able to lead for those that would follow him. Lucia nodded and Agaroman grinned, pleased in his thoughts of knowing that Decius had truly reached a status beyond death that the wizard never thought possible. For the wizard, the dux truly was worthy of the mantle of dark lord.

Within less than an hour, the senators of the desert city assembled while taking their seats in the capitol building's chamber. As they did so and talked among themselves in wonder, speculating what was going on, several guards of the order of the Black Wolf knighthood entered and escorted Lucia, who held her son Lucianus Canus with Agaroman following closely behind her. The political dignitaries speculated among themselves, while some asked aloud where the dux was and suggested that he had fallen. Some gossiped that his legacy was over and perhaps it was time to negotiate a truce or a surrender with the Kingdom of Swordbane. Lucia overheard and responded in a loud defiant and commanding voice that they would never do so and her husband's legacy would not be subject to debate out of pretense for diplomatic compromise. She considered and called out such a suggestion of surrender as being both a sign of cowardice and a lack of fidelity to what the dux fought for. Some senators rebuked what she said and questioned her status, why she was even in the senate chamber among the dominant male body of representatives. Lucia gave a quick grin and replied that she was here because her lord, Dux Decius, bade her so. Still, some senators challenged her authority and asked where the dux was, while others loudly stated that they heard already he was dead. Lucia, signaling several of the guards, called them in to bring several objects along with a makeshift altar table. Just as before, she and Agaroman conducted a dual libation tribute to both Calu and Laran while calling out Decius's name.

Within moments, a ghastly flash appeared before darkening. Emerging from the flash stood a pale, translucent hellish-looking werewolf-like ghost figure. Lucia then told all those present and observing to behold the return of their dark lord, Dux Decius.

All those present except for Lucia and Agaroman were in utter shock. Though different-looking in appearance as both a werewolf and as a transparent ghost from how they knew Decius before in his human mortal form, all those present in the senate council remembered seeing a werewolf-like figure that resembled this one, only that the former was a gigantic avatar summoned by Decius. Now, apparently it was Lucia and the duke's chief wizard advisor who had seemed to summon what they called as being the dux himself. Some among the senators asked who this really was and if this creature really was indeed Decius.

The spectral spirit finally spoke for himself and told those who asked that it was truly him. He assured them that though he was no longer mortal in the same human form he once had, he was still the same dark lord and their dux by title. Many in the senate chambers were both terrified and in awe while recognizing the tone of his voice that appeared comparatively the same as when he was human. They truly believed that whatever happened, this ghost werewolf creature was indeed Decius and his reputation had now been even more cemented legitimately and convincingly as being a chosen vessel who had transcended death to appear before them as an apparition even if he was no longer living.

Several of the senators who had previously doubted the legitimacy of Decius's rule now sought to plead for his pardon and forgiveness in placing such doubts. Decius motioned with his hand and stated that despite their initial doubts, any and all who came before him and swore fealty to him must recognize his title as their dux, their dark lord, his cause in still making the Remnant the true successor to the Lupercalian Empire, and his house, which he proclaimed as the forgotten but now restored Anicii family name. In doing so, they would be forgiven so long as they never betrayed him.

Within different parts of the chamber hall, voices began to chat with more and more joining in unison in hailing Decius as their eternal dux, dark lord, and chosen vessel. Lucia and Agaroman both turned and grinned at each other; they knew without speaking words that Decius in whatever form he now came in had truly been inspirational in making an impression on his legitimacy. Even Lucia's father, Senator Diem, was impressed though cautious in discerning in a somewhat superstitious way what sign or foreboding portent might be entailed with the city devotedly still following Decius after death as much as during his time in life as a mortal. Still, Diem cared for his daughter and knew that she was loyal to the very end and would follow Decius even into the next life, which possibly concerned him. He did not want to lose her.

Ultimately, the senator resigned to trust his daughter to decide by her own free will the path she would follow and that fate which would await her while relying on her own initiative. He was resolved to still find time while living the present half of his life to spend with his daughter as family while also cherishing her son and his grandson. Though taken aback by his grandson's unusual feral and wolflike appearance, Diem accepted that perhaps fate had alluded and revealed to a degree of truth about his now former son-in-law being a chosen vessel and passing the effects of it to Lucianus Canus. The most apparent sign of his appearance was associated with the wolf, the representative totem for a large portion of Citadellan society. It was a symbol and totem of the desert city that still persisted and harkened back to the times when Citadellans from Sanctum Novus and the surrounding high desert region were still considered to be unwavering, loyal, and true in upholding the values and traditions of their ancient Lupercalian imperial adopted heritage even while the Citadellans of the coast were considered as straying while falling under the dominance of their assimilated Nordling conquerors during that period from long ago. Granted, the Citadellans were considered the lower-class citizenry at the time, while the Lupercalian canine-like species exerted their status as the dominant upper class. It was still considered a time of contentment and prosperity that the former people of the high desert region wanted to still return to.

To Diem, his perspective in this war seemed to be an underlying historical built-up resentment from the isolated desert-dwelling Citadellans that finally surfaced regardless of the pretexts Decius waited to use to justify drawing a schism between the desert city and its coastal brethren, the latter who became somewhat different over the years by merging to an extent their cultural development as well as social development with the assimilated group of Nordling barbarian invaders from over a thousand years ago. The Citadellans of the coast were no longer sympathetic toward the idea of rebuilding a great empire that they once lived under, nor did they seem to care as much about their affiliation with the traditional totem of the wolf. Instead, upon being part of this kingdom that became known as Swordbane, they adopted the dragon as their sigil and totem, causing a rift between themselves and the eastern desert-dwelling Citadellans. It had finally erupted into war with the built-up hostility and resentment on the part of the latter accusing the former of being too corrupt to lead as being their justified pretext in marking this schism between the two groups of Citadellans.

Diem would have to agree from reflecting on this, not because he thought that the war was beneficial in and of itself, but because he saw the same causes for unaddressed grievances by the crown, and he agreed and shared with Decius the same perspective of this being a continuous abusive and exploitative relationship by the Citadellans of the coastal lands. They would send their representatives or, even worse, their religious officials to embezzle and engage in scandalous corrupt actions that would deprive Sanctum Novus (until the past year or so) of the resources needed to sustain its local population. In return, it left much of the desert city populace impoverished to the point that it would be exploited in the form of local district gangs who would organize to act as patrons in the city to take further advantage of the poor's plight. Decius, once in power, had worked with the local city's senate council to break up such exploitative groups who only existed from conspiring with corrupt local clergy and outside officials that took bribes from these gangs in return for issued writs of indulgences that would pardon the gang leaders and their members from the sins of criminal activities they engaged in, while ordering the local city guards and other government authorities including the dux to cease from arresting them in an alleged crime, or if found guilty, to drop the conviction once the writ was produced by the clergy to forgive that offending gang leader or member. These pardons became considered valid in both the religious and secular public spheres of society that allowed an endless perpetual cycle for these gangs to continue to find ways to exploit their own local citizenry from any resources they had, in exchange for protection from rival gangs that would otherwise also seek to exploit the same citizen clients. It became bad enough that nearly the rest of the kingdom had developed perceived stereotypes that anyone and everyone from that city was corrupt or associated in some form with the organized criminal gangs that preyed upon the city.

Decius vigorously sought to undo that reputation once put in charge as dux of the city and the surrounding region by Ascentius. He had done well to break apart those gangs over time by replacing the clergy as the benefactor of the local city gangs. He had their gang leaders dissolve their operations while receiving clemency for their past operations in addition to receiving positions of office in government to be part of the local senate ruling class. Though Diem was already an established statesman and prosperous merchant and landowner, he understood the dux's attempt to reform and enfranchise these former gang leaders as part of the ruling class to have a more direct means of effecting change while being in a ruling and legislating position to help those among their already existing clientele.

The dux would ensure these newly installed senators would reform from their previous criminal activity while keeping some measure of wealth. If they refused or crossed the dux in returning to their old ways while seeking to receive writs of indulgences from the already corrupt priests, Decius would make good his word to take away not only their standing and wealth, but also their very own lives. Some saw it as breeding a new form of corruption in and of itself with such an approach, but it had worked during the dux's reign in establishing order throughout the city. Very little crime existed compared to before. Much of the wealth resided back within the city itself, save only the high taxation that the city rendered unto the king's coffers until Decius had also changed that when he rebelled and redistributed it among both the ruling elite and the common masses with the public projects that he established along with Diem and Lucia. If the city was to return to the control and oversight of Swordbane as it was before Decius came to power as dux, the senator would only suspect the same exploitative cycle repeating itself as it had before. It was one that could not be allowed to happen again.

In reflecting such deep thoughts, Diem realized and waited a moment to speak about those very same things to point out to his senator colleagues when Decius opened up the senate discussion quickly to a forum before moving to the next item of business, briefing the senate on how he would organize the city's defenses. Before closing, Diem admitted while working with his daughter as city administrators they at least made a difference in allocating the resources to provide for the citizenry and build the city to a much more prosperous life than what it experienced prior to Decius's reign as dux. These were resources Diem pointed out that they had to use for themselves without sending it to Swordbane as taxation or without the assigned corrupt clergy from the coastlands to embezzle it. He concluded it was still necessary if the desert city wished to prosper on its own to still fight under the banner of Decius even under the spectral form of his once mortal existence.

Within moments, applause came as well as exultations in agreement to Diem's oration in support of Decius's return and not wanting to return to being under the control of Swordbane again. Decius seized this moment while realizing that though on one hand, his legacy paved many deaths and much destruction especially toward his enemies, he agreed with his former father-in-law that there was consolation in leaving those in charge that could be trusted like Diem and his daughter to develop the city and other parts of the Remnant. The dux pledged that he would do everything to see that the city, which had never fallen even during the Nordling invasions at the decline and fall of the Lupercalian Empire, would still withstand the impending invasion by the remaining kingdom skyships. Once more, applause went out, while Lucia turned toward the ghost of her departed husband. She asked quietly how and what she and the rest of the populace should do to ensure that the city did not fall. Decius turned toward her and quietly told her he would be there with her this time to guide and supervise her on board the skybeast while also conducting through the goblin shamans and Agaroman as intermediaries the direction of their forces' movements should a large land battle ensue. Lucia nodded while quietly pledging that this time, they would do it together and defeat whatever forces came to confront them.

As the emergency senate meeting came to a close with Decius having Agaroman brief the senators in further detail of the kingdom's retaking of Citadella Neapola and their counterattack, the wizard made mention in closing that he had already come up with two new innovations while making the return trip to Sanctum Novus to use for the lone skybeast ship, which was undergoing repairs by goblin and orc engineers as the senate meeting took place.

Asked by one of the senators about what kinds of innovations were going to be used, Agaroman responded that the floating vessel would be modified and fitted with mounted mirrors, which were being donated by Decius's estate, while Agaroman asked the senators to bring to him, as the meeting was over, any mirrors they had in their home. The wizard advisor would teleport those mirrors to also be installed on the skybeast to use as a weapon against Swordbane's remaining deployed skyships in addition to a special contraption that would be mounted on the forward bow of the skybeast. It would consist of a long large copper-metal tube connected to a large bellows that would help blow flames forward that were fueled by a highly incendiary substance. The other senators knew about this while inquiring if Agaroman would be using a long-forgotten weapon that the Lupercalians once used. The wizard nodded and confirmed that he had read the ancient texts and manuals to formulate this ingredient in which he had already tasked several goblin shamans under his lead to start working on. The senators were elated and confident to trust Decius, Agaroman, and their subordinates, so they gave their full pledge and vows to have family members in their houses begin donating the mirrors.

After the senate meeting closed with all other remaining senators leaving, Decius urged his present company not to waste any more time in making preparations. For Lucia, there would be no rest until this battle was over. She made sure that Decius, though apprehensive and protective over her, would grant her request to personally pilot the skybeast again as she had done earlier. She met with her father, Senator Diem, and entrusted her son and his grandson to him while letting him know of what happened back at Citadella Neapola and why she would still see to it she personally commanded the skybeast in defense of the city.

Diem, being cautious and reserved, trusted his daughter's instincts and decided not to talk her out of what she was doing. Still feeling somewhat shaken and uneasy, especially in seeing Decius's specter up close by his daughter and grandson, the senator pleaded privately with Decius regardless of what form he was in to ensure the safety and well-being of his daughter. Decius nodded while telling him that though he failed in not achieving everything he set out to do, he would make sure in his death (while being a specter) that he would watch over the senator's daughter and their son. Diem nodded while departing with Lucianus Canus but not before Diem embraced his daughter Lucia one last time.

Leaving the senate capitol in the desert city, Decius in his spectral form stepped out to follow along with Lucia and Agaroman. It would be a long night and even early morning until the enemy skyships would likely arrive. The three would oversee the skybeast during its last-minute repairs and fitted upgrades that Agaroman devised to ensure it had every fighting capability that could be used against the remaining Swordbane skyships that would assault Sanctum Novus.

CHAPTER FIFTY-FOUR

A Widow's Revenge

It was now late midmorning on the next day. The sun, though not at its peak, was steadily rising over the high desert basin that surrounded the ancient and ornate urban settlement of Sanctum Novus. Looming over the city while hovering in broad circular arcs was the lone skybeast. It had finished much needed repairs by early morning only a few hours earlier, to travel as fast as it had before, roughly a hundred and twenty miles per hour. It was now well stocked and replenished with munition stockpiles of various siege platforms. These platforms would deploy munitions from the port and starboard side of its exposed canopy deck in addition to the siege weapon ports from the port and starboard side of the bridge where interior port coverings were removed for the siege weapons, including ballistae and scorpion launchers could fire out of though with extremely limited arcs or cutouts compared to the canopy deck siege weapon platforms.

Secured against the port and starboard bulwark sides of the floating vessel were fixed-position mirrors taken from Decius's estate as well as those from the local nobility that had donated toward the cause. Though these mirrors were expensive, especially the adult-size ones, it was considered a necessity if it gave the city that much more of a chance to withstand against Swordbane's remaining six or so floating vessels. Additionally, there were a few mirrors toward the aft canopy deck of the skybeast that were mounted to standing rotation pivots, which the designated crew member could operate and point against the glare of the sun if positioned correctly to aim at a certain arc toward any enemy skyships, which were made from wood and susceptible to possibly burning from the intensity of the heat, or at least Agaroman theorized, with the rest of the Remnant forces hoping as much. Additionally, the mirrors would help serve as a distraction by causing a bright glare possibly toward the opposing ships; it would make it difficult for the enemy to focus and engage against the skybeast.

Finally, though it was nearly completed, Agaroman worked with a small group of goblins to finish installing the meticulous and carefully constructed copper pipe assembly, which connected to a combustible chemical tank and a large bellows would be used to emit a highly incendiary type of fire that could burn any enemy skyship to a cinder. It would be their greatest and deadliest weapon in the battle to come.

Upon completing the installation and instructing the goblin crew members on how to operate this device with the bellows, Agaroman, while still on the bridge, walked toward Lucia only a few yards away. He briefed her that all preparations were ready and just in time before the enemy ships arrived. Lucia sighed while holding the steering control or flight yoke to the skybeast. She looked at the spectral form of Decius for advice on what to do next, while Decius had already supervised and placed four goblin shamans in charge of siege weapons munitions teams, one for both port and starboard sides of the floating vessel for both the bridge and the canopy deck above. The goblin shamans were well trained in magic and in understanding the common Citadellan tongue to communicate with Decius as well as Marin and Agaroman. Agaroman would be in charge of both supervising the special weapons team for the incendiary fixed hosepipe weapon and using any of his magic spell-casting to aid the floating ship. Meanwhile, the dux stood near his beloved Lucia, confident in what she was doing to be able to prevail against the six or so remaining ships, though he had hoped that the same adventurers he stalled from their lone skyship would not be present during the battle as he advised Lucia to be very cautious in fighting them. Lucia, though not able to hold his clawed ghostlike hand, still reached out toward it, imagining as if she did. The gesture meant enough to her where Decius pretended to do the same if it gave her any sense of comfort in feeling as if he was by her side in the corporeal sense, though he only was in the spectral sense.

Only less than an hour passed when a trumpet on board the floating vessel sounded. It was the call to prepare for an attack. Decius let Lucia know that while she acknowledged sitting on the pilot seat, she had surmised as much. Quickly, while shifting a lever for acceleration and turning somewhat sharply with the steering yoke, Lucia told the crew to hold on. From the air, the skybeast accelerated quickly while making unpredictable snakelike patterns of movement. The thrill of operating such a flying contraption had exhilarated Lucia to the point where Decius told her to use caution when calculating the movements and anticipating the maneuvers and attacks of the skyships when they engaged. Lucia shook her head to acknowledge while still flying in such a masterful yet daring way that no sky-vessel operator, not even Decius himself, had handled the skybeast as skillfully. Lucia wanted to get a feel of its utmost capabilities in handling, and she actually felt that she could understand it as much as riding a horse or dire wolf.

From the horizon northwest of the desert city, six skyships sailed over in a loose chevron-like formation going southeast toward Sanctum Novus. The banners had the sigil of Swordbane's silver dragon with a blue background shield or coat of arms cover. It was clear to both Lucia and Decius that these ships were dead set on finishing the last flying vessel of the Remnant's fleet as well as making the desert city capitulate in surrender and bringing an end to the war.

Turning about, Lucia steered the vessel northeast to approach the enemy sky fleet head-on. She had hoped that the vessel would catch their attention to divert away from the city. Upon making a pass, though out of firing range by a mile or two, the skybeast overtook the left front rank of the formation to be able to turn and make a pass to outflank the kingdom's skyships. Lucia had succeeded in catching the attention of the enemy skyships, but in a surprise, she pivoted the vessel sharply upward in the sky to climb above the altitude of the enemy ship formation. Upon reaching a noticeable height of a few thousand feet, Lucia told the crew to hold on while instructing Agaroman to be ready to deploy the incendiary copper-hose weapon that many called the fire-breather. Had the skybeast not been fitted with fixed seating for the goblin and Citadellan crew to be secured to with straps, including on the canopy deck and adjacent to the siege weapon mounts, it would have been certain that nearly half of the crew would have fallen overboard from the duchess's daring maneuvers of the skyship.

Pointing the skyship downward in the air, Lucia went into a high-acceleration maneuver aiming to ram one of the enemy skyships by plunging the skybeast with its haunting demonic-looking wolf-head-sculpted ram at the bow to impale through the center deck area of one of the kingdom's skyships. This maneuver was daring, and it caught the entire enemy fleet off guard. In a matter of moments, the sheer impact had torn the respective kingdom floating vessel in half while debris and soldiers both alive and dead alike plummeted to the ground. Fortunately for the skybeast, the wrecked vessel had no explosive munitions that possibly would have caused some noticeable damage to the attacking vessel.

Lucia next used the yoke and gear levers for acceleration to pull up the flying vessel and stabilize while being a few hundred feet under the other five skyships. She quickly made a pass before turning about and, this time, pointed the skybeast upward with full acceleration to ram the next kingdom floating vessel. Though not as fast as the traction that the skybeast gained in taking out the first enemy skyship, it was deadly enough to leave a large puncture through one of the vessels that was on the starboard flank of the remaining four vessels. Several enemy soldiers fell out, as well as debris. The enemy floating vessel became attached to the skybeast's ram, which was lodged deep in the hull. Decius was impressed but quickly suggested to his lover that she would use the incendiary weapon. Lucia nodded and called out to Agaroman to order his incendiary siege operator to deploy the incendiary fire weapon emitted through the copper metal hose outward, facing the broadside of the enemy vessel that it was lodged into. Agaroman complied, and within moments of pushing multiple times hard against the blowing bellows, it had unleashed the flaming incendiary weapon that quickly spouted out high levels of flame to burn apart the hull of the enemy vessel that the skybeast was lodged into but not for much longer. The enemy ship quickly burned into ashes with some of the enemy soldiers not able to withstand the effects screaming in agony, with some even leaping to their deaths in going overboard before the burning vessel eventually collapsed and fell apart while still burning.

Upon breaking free, the other four enemy vessels quickly moved about and were on heightened alert by the sudden destruction that was befalling them. The remaining Swordbane skyships formed a boxlike perimeter formation while multiple archers readied their bows and arrows and began shooting through the smoke on the other side under the presumption that the skybeast was still there.

However, Lucia once again at the bridge steered the skybeast under the four vessels while ordering the port and starboard-side siege-weapon teams for both the bridge and canopy deck to ready their weapons to fire at the enemy ships. Upon doing so, Lucia next steered the skybeast to level upward into the gap where the four ships had left some distance in their boxlike formation. The four ships were all surprised and still heightened while preparing to fire their own siege weapons. However, with Lucia relaying Decius's order to fire at will, the port and starboard siege-weapon operators on the skybeast for both the bridge and canopy deck area quickly fired their weapons. This happened as Lucia made a strafing pass to attack one skyship on the farthest left corner of the formation with the port side siege weapons firing everything. At the helm, Lucia turned the skybeast, about to make a pass with siege weapons firing from the starboard side. It caused enough damage that the enemy vessel was not able to effectively fire back more than two projectiles, which were not able to strike and hit the skybeast but, rather, soared through empty air. Consequently, the vessel, though not falling apart immediately to its death, was immobilized and in no condition to pose any further resistance against the skybeast while it drifted in the air hopelessly.

Setting sights on the next Swordbane vessel that was positioned up ahead from the first one Lucia immobilized with the skybeast, she aimed her vessel straight ahead to ram itself on the enemy vessel's aft stern. Though it was not an advisable way to ram a ship even when floating, Lucia intended to do as she did with the second ship she took out by weakening it even if lodged and then having the incendiary fire deployed from the metal-pipe assembly that was secured and protruding from the bow of the skybeast. Just as she predicted, the same outcome occurred, with the ship being severely damaged and the skybeast having its ram lodged into the enemy ship until the incendiary weapon would weaken the enemy hull to dislodge the skybeast. The enemy vessel, with much of its crew, burned to a charred crisp, and the few that survived descended to their death along with what debris was left of the skyship that had plummeted.

Now there were two more enemy skyships to go. Both reacted as quickly as they could while the skybeast was lodged temporarily in part of the remaining hull from the last skyship it took apart. The two vessels turned aside to fire a volley at both the starboard and port sides of the skybeast. Lucia, in her most daring tactic while frantically trying to maneuver, called to Agaroman to use his magic to defend the ship. She did not have enough acceleration to maneuver and evade. She, Decius, and even Agaroman knew that. Thinking creatively and remembering that Agaroman had the power to teleport, Lucia suddenly thought of an idea that was considered nearly unthinkable but worth the risk if it meant surviving. She asked the wizard if he could use all his magic and focus to teleport the entire skybeast out of the line of fire between the two enemy vessels that were fast approaching. Agaroman, shocked at hearing the suggestion, was doubtful if he could, but agreed that he would try with all his concentration.

Waiting a few moments as the enemy kingdom ships came about to unleash their broadside volleys of projectile weapons while Lucia tried to accelerate and not be overtaken, Agaroman took his time and focused on where the skybeast was positioned while focusing his mind on a single point or location where he could cast his magic. When Decius observed, he came up with a different and more feasible idea that the wizard could use his abilities to instead cast a spell that would essentially camouflage or disguise the ship into appearing invisible while focusing on using his magic to alter the spectral color of the skybeast to that which would match the landscape. The wizard thought deeply and considered while grinning in agreement, seeing the potential of such a suggestion.

The skybeast, despite the mounted mirrors, was primarily of only one color, a charcoal jet-black of metal. The wizard could easily transfer the color of the light to disguise as another color, in which case he did by causing it to appear the same sky-blue color after Agaroman quickly ran up to the deck canopy of the skybeast. Within moments as the two remaining enemy skyships approached, the skybeast, while still going forward to evade, suddenly appeared to disappear before the eyes of the enemy crew from the other ships. They could not believe what they saw, as if it had vanished.

Meanwhile, taking advantage of this optical-illusion trick, Lucia had the skybeast come to a slow speed while the other two enemy ships overtook the vessel's course to now be ahead of it. Still maintaining the same course, the crew of the enemy vessels did not know what else to do and chose to turn about in retreat while keeping a lookout for the skybeast. However, it was too late when suddenly one of the vessels felt a large shattering rip across its hull from port to starboard. The single cut weakened and caused the floating vessel to split apart with multiple pieces of debris and crewed soldiers trying to hold while many fell suddenly to their deaths. Emerging from this optical illusion, it was evident the skybeast had angled itself to use its large metal-frame wing to shear the second-last vessel in half while hanging loosely on its hot-air balloon assembly.

Lucia had only one enemy skyship left (excluding the other vessel that was disabled from earlier) to contend with as she turned the skybeast about. The enemy crew, out of desperation, fired everything within sight toward the skybeast. Most of the projectiles did not strike the flying contraption, and the few that did bounced off the thick metal hull without causing any damage. Now Lucia quickly began to accelerate and make a pass before aiming the skybeast at the broadside of the enemy ship after it had fired its first volley of siege weapons. She knew she had to ram it and take it out before the siege handlers on the other vessel would have time to fire another volley. She quickly went full throttle on the skybeast to accelerate while ordering Agaroman to cast multiple thunderbolt magic projectiles toward the last remaining ship.

Agaroman, standing on the front bow section of the skybeast canopy, acknowledged and aimed his hands to shoot one thunderbolt of lightning after another toward the last remaining skyship. Finally, he aimed for the center mast that held the skyship's balloon together. After breaking the mast and realizing that other ends of the skyship secured the hot inflatable balloon, the wizard next decided to fire multiple lightning bolts and fireballs toward the hot-air balloon. Eventually, his persistence paid off while striking a deadly attack to blow apart the hot-air balloon, which exploded and suddenly caused the suspended vessel to plummet. Lucia quickly veered the skybeast to the starboard side, now realizing that it was no longer needed to ram the enemy ship. As she veered the skybeast, she instead rammed it into one of the earlier enemy vessels that still floated and was disabled. That vessel eventually fell in cinders once Agaroman used a flammable substance one last time from the skybeast's incendiary weapon. It was the last enemy ship to fall from the battle.

Watching it fall down, the crew on board the skybeast, mainly goblins with a few orcs and Citadellan soldiers celebrated loudly. Even Decius, though not expressing it in the same manner, grinned and looked at his beloved Lucia to acknowledge her achievement. Though he could lead in spirit, it was she who physically took command with the aid of her crew and her exceptionally skilled piloting abilities of the skybeast that delivered the major killing blow to the enemy. He told her that despite losing the second battle at Citadella Neapola, they had won perhaps the last battle in the war with her leadership and command at the controls of the skybeast.

For Lucia, though she smiled, it was a painful victory since she could no longer embrace her lover the same way as she had before. He was there but not in the same way. She held back her thoughts, or at least tried, but Decius could tell from her expression and replied to her that someday when it was destined, they would be together even in the next life. For now, she had to take his place at least physically to lead until their son, Lucianus

Canus, would be old enough to assert the claim to be the next dux, the next leader of Sanctum Novus and what was left of the Remnant's territorial holdings that did not recede from the kingdom's counterattack.

Lucia, still shedding tears, took a moment and tried to smile, acknowledging what she considered the wisdom and pragmatic advice of her departed husband, whom she saw as not just a shade of himself. He was right, she thought, and they both shared the same value of piety for her to feel obligated to fulfill his legacy. She vowed to him that she would make sure their son would be the next leader of Sanctum Novus and the Remnant no matter who would stand in their way. Suddenly, however, Decius's spectral shade was fading. He was only able to maintain it for so long before the next time he was summoned. Lucia began to tremble and worry as she noticed and asked for him to come back. Decius told her before completely vanishing that he would when she next summoned him as she did before. Lucia nodded while telling him that she would always love him in this life and the next. Fading with his words, Decius told her he knew so.

As his ghost finally departed the mortal plane, Lucia stood up to look at the ambience of the victory. Her crew unleashed various shouts of celebratory words as well as war cries, with even some goblins and a few Citadellan soldiers emulating their former dux by howling. They turned however to hail her, Lady Lucia, Duchess of Sanctum Novus, as they gave their salutations. They would also call her their mother, as they saw her metaphorically as their stately mother who cared for them and led them, aside from deferring to Dux Decius's authority when she did do so. It took her by surprise, and she did not know fully how to accept the gratitude and praise other than she simply did. She had the heart for those most marginalized in her society to found public services, including food kitchens and orphanages. Now she realized that they saw her in the same light as Decius, a leader with an ability to command and wage war while gaining their respect, even if she was a woman, which in Citadellan society had a mixed aspect of value, where women were revered as mothers and ladies of authority in their own family house, but not in politics or the field of battle. Lucia had changed that for the first time in known Citadellan history to rival Marin, the Princess Knight.

Taking back the controls from a goblin copilot, Lucia began to land the skybeast but not before making a pass at full speed above the desert city she called home. It was her way to let her people know that the battle was over and, perhaps, the war, with the city spared and victorious.

CHAPTER FIFTY-FIVE

To Mourn a Broken Victory

A lone Swordbane skyship approached a few moments later after the recent battle had ended. Burning pieces of debris floated from a distance high in the sky with much more covering the surface below and outside the gates of Sanctum Novus. Charred and mangled bodies covered the barren landscape along with hulking pieces of debris, much of it also charred. They were too late, and the sight they saw made Linitus and his fellow warriors agonize while trying to hold themselves together. Some could not hold back and vomited overboard from the skyship. What seemed a moment of joyous celebration of ultimate triumph over darkness and evil after defeating Decius the day prior was fleeting to what seemed a broken and sorrowful victory at best.

Linitus was the first to spot and realize this from afar while using one of Wyatt's contraptions called a spyglass, which let the viewer holding the optical pipe instrument be able to see up close faraway objects. When he did see and Marin took notice of his reaction, it remained filled with horrid realization. The Princess Knight asked him what he saw. He held back a moment before telling her that it was over. All six of the other remaining allied skyships that went ahead had all perished. Marin gently asked and took the spyglass from her elf ranger lover to verify herself while still in a shocked state of denial and disbelief. Sure enough, he was right. All six vessels, or presumably all six from the damage being seen, had fallen, save only a few pieces of floating debris. All it took was one skybeast vessel and still she looked all about, wondering where it was. Perhaps she thought, before perishing, the last ship managed to also take that flying contraption from hell back where it belonged.

The lone skyship still traveled on its course southeast to Sanctum Novus with the desert city landscape becoming viewable from a distance. Just outside the city walls, a skybeast had begun to descend, as it was lowering. However, before coming to a landing, it spotted the lone remaining skyship of Swordbane. Soon, it picked up speed again and ascended into the air. Linitus wished that if they did not arrive earlier to save the other Swordbane forces, at least they might have come later when the flying contraption of the enemy had fully landed and would be less likely to be in a position to pose a threat as it did in the air.

Ascentius on board the skyship pondered a moment with a stern face before deciding to act. Suddenly he ordered Wyatt for the ship to come to a halt. Marin was puzzled and questioned why, when they had to do something to avenge those that fought for the crown.

Ascentius shook his dragon-like head and told her that they would. They would end this war and save more lives from being lost than they had already incurred. Even with Decius gone, the king incarnated in the form of a dragon man realized that the dux's legacy, his influence, had clearly made an impact for those devoted to his cause to pose nearly as much of a threat as the deceased dux himself. In Ascentius's mind, it was over. The kingdom had no standing army left to overpower Sanctum Novus, nor would it have enough time to raise another army before the Remnant would do the same. The war was ready to come to an end if given the chance for whoever succeeded Decius to be open to compromise.

Linitus, though he shared the same anger as Marin, ultimately agreed with Ascentius's reasoning. There were enough lives lost already. How many more had to be sacrificed before the war could come to an end? He held Marin's hand and her shoulder, telling her that as much as she lost, it was time to let go. It was time to give up her vengeance. He pointed out to her that perhaps what they saw now in their eyes to call for revenge was the very same that their enemy felt they had exacted as revenge for their earlier losses. The elf pondered also when thinking for once in the bigger framework of the war itself, who was fighting and who had lost that at this point, perhaps everyone suffered enough and it was time to realize that the suffering had to end. He pondered how many brethren killed each other during this war. How many Citadellans on the side of the Remnant possibly killed their brethren Citadellans fighting for the kingdom? How many of their relatives that had stayed loyal on the side of the crown had been willing to do so if it meant killing a relative on the other side? Despite the vastness of the continent of Hesperion, despite how many miles separated them from their home of the coastlands to their enemy's home of the high desert basin, it was still a small world of suffering in which perhaps the biggest favor they could do for whoever was left in the position of succeeding Decius would be to end the suffering of war and seek a chance for peace.

Even when looking at the immediate physical sense and current situation, there was nothing left to continue this war, the elf ranger pointed out to Marin and Ascentius. They had only one skyship left, and the enemy had one flying vessel of their own as well, though seemingly more destructive. They both took massive losses, and there was no telling if they had the numbers to sustain a war as long as Swordbane had been able to do so in the previous war against Marjawan. He admitted that Decius, despite his perceived evil nature and moral flaws, was smart enough to realize that in deciding to rebel against the crown after it had been weakened from the prolonged war against Marjawan, perhaps there was no more opportune time to do so and he decided to take it. Now, they had seen the culminating result of Decius's gamble, and to some extent, he was right. For the Remnant, it had paid off. They were in a strong enough position to not only still demand their autonomy from the kingdom but also to assert that autonomy.

Ascentius, while listening attentively to Linitus, nodded in agreement. He admitted that despite the wrongs Decius had done, he took action to foment his plans in a time when Ascentius was complacent to recognize the underlying reason for the discontent that led to the kingdom being fragmented. Now coming full circle, Ascentius told those in his presence, it was time to pick up the pieces of what could be salvaged from what was left of the kingdom and move on. Marin in tears seeing and listening to this, wanted to resist and finish the war until there was nothing left of Sanctum Novus, until all the enemy were gone, including the beastly races of goblins, orcs, and trolls, and the barbarian tribe of Aries that had sided with them, but then she realized that her sense of revenge, her sense of anger, or worse, outright hatred, would make her no different than Decius even if she had as much cause in feeling angered, given her circumstances. Clenching her fist, she nodded and held back her anger, agreeing while looking at both Linitus and Ascentius that it was time to seek peace.

Meanwhile, the skybeast swerved about in circles from the distance waiting for the lone skyship to move toward the desert city while its crew, especially its commander and pilot, wondered why the enemy vessel had come to a full stop. Perhaps unlike the first six vessels, it would not be as brash as its fallen counterparts to challenge the skybeast, nor try to attack the desert city by itself. Seeing the lone skyship cautiously as not a threat, it was spared while the skybeast still hovered for a time. If anything, sparing the lone ship perhaps might have been the best message to send to the rest of Swordbane with the lone enemy vessel serving as a surviving messenger in telling the fate of how the desert jewel capital of the Remnant withstood defeat just as it had over a thousand years ago from the Nordling barbarian invasions, unlike its coastal counterparts.

Eventually, the skyship hoisted a white flag to signal its intention to either surrender or have a parley to possibly negotiate and discuss terms. The skybeast still hovering recognized the sign and, while not possessing any flags, had a wizard on board project a flag-like image from his magic to agree to the meeting of parley.

Ascentius with his green dragon wings flew out from the skyship and landed on the canopy deck of the skybeast to see the wizard that had responded. It was Agaroman, though the wizard himself was in awe of the creature, which he saw briefly before, during the retreat from the second battle of Citadella Neapola, asked who he was. The dragon-man creature responded in a harsh almost refuting manner that whether the wizard realized it or not, he knew who he was, or at least during his previous life. The wizard was shocked and in disbelief from hearing the voice. The dragon-man creature was right. It was Ascentius, though the wizard knew not how or what became of him. Agaroman could tell and perceive that Decius was not the only one to have undertaken the trials of vesselhood and received near deity-like powers. Returning to the subject at hand, Ascentius told the wizard that it was time to end this war and enough blood had been spilled for what they fought, for regardless of how or what they thought of each other. Agaroman nodded, saying that perhaps it was right to do so, but Ascentius would have to talk to the dark lord and his lady.

The mere uttering of the words nearly confused and bewildered Ascentius, even in his dragon-man and near-deified form. What did he mean by "the dark lord and his lady"?

Agaroman, now seeing that he had the upper hand from the conversation in getting a startled reaction, told Ascentius that he would find out when they discussed terms for peace tomorrow. For now, the wizard told Ascentius that the Remnant would stand down outside the city walls and allow Ascentius to pick up the remains of the dead as well as possibly any survivors until they met outside the city gates at the south of the city. Ascentius nodded and, before departing, told the wizard he would see to it that any casualties belonging to Sanctum Novus or its allies would receive a proper burial or have the remains returned to them. Agaroman nodded while further startling Ascentius in a somewhat demoralizing way by stating that from this battle, the Remnant had no casualties. But the wizard had asked that the same courtesy would be rendered for the casualties sustained on his side in other parts of the war, including in Citadella Neapola. Ascentius nodded and turned around to depart, while Agaroman watched with some curiosity and amazement still of this new incarnated form of the king in being a dragon-man creature that used his majestic dragon wings to take off.

On his return to the lone skyship, Ascentius briefed Linitus and the rest of the crew about the temporary truce that he made with Agaroman in which they would suspend hostilities until after the end of the next day so that they would consider discussing a peace treaty. Some of the soldier crew members were visibly dissatisfied, but no one dared to question the king, especially in his new dragon-man form.

In the meantime, Ascentius had ordered Wyatt to press on and steer the skyship toward the barely floating debris to rescue any fortunate lives that still hung on to the floating pieces of hull debris that were still attached to the hot inflatable balloons. Eventually, the weight would give in and the stranded soldiers were at risk of falling to their deaths (again for the few fortunate survivors) if they did not have aid right away to deliver them from the perilous situation they were in. One by one, Wyatt teleported the very fortunate small number of survivors, which amounted to no more than a dozen soldiers. After teleporting the soldiers both dead and alive from the floating wreckage, Linitus next ordered Wyatt to teleport him along with a dozen or so of the crew members to the surface to continue to search for survivors. He would find even less in this hellish and unforgiving landscape below.

Walking about the unforgiving dry desert landscape with scattered lots of palm trees, sagebrush shrubs, and Joshua trees, Linitus, Marin, and Ascentius along with a dozen soldiers saw every several hundred or thousands of yards smoking wreckage and debris along with the remains of corpses from their fallen fellow warriors. The sight was ingrained so deeply in Marin's mind that she turned and vomited while Linitus, uneasy also in what he saw, composed himself while acting as support in holding Marin with his hands on her shoulders. Eventually, Marin regained her composure also and continued while nodding her head before her comrades in arms.

Every so often, they would tag and collect the soldiers' remains to be later buried outside the city walls several miles away. Hours later as the day neared sunset, carrying a white flag for parley, a lone slender figure wearing a black split-joint half-sleeve jumpsuit along with a red cape cloak embroidered in black lace with the insignia of Decius's sigil and totem, the wolf, appeared while riding a chariot being towed by dire wolves escorted by a dozen orcs, goblins, and lightweight Citadellan Black Wolf knights who also rode mounted on dire wolves. As the leading figure came a few hundred yards, the pace of the gallop slowed until just a few yards away while still riding in her dire-wolf chariot. The figure, after removing the hood of her cloak, unveiled herself while dismounting from her chariot. She was a slender olive-skinned woman of relatively medium height for a Citadellan, with wavy black hair. Raising her hand in the air while still motioning the flag of parley, Ascentius motioned for his company of warriors to lower their weapons while also walking up to approach that figure. Before he even spoke, she initiated the conversation in an assertive manner by stating that she would send several dozen of her warriors to help them cremate their dead outside the city while giving a proper burial pyre if the forces of Swordbane would consent. She disguised her facial expression though possibly inwardly showing some degree of fear and awe at talking and dictating in front of Ascentius in his dragon-man form. In suppressing her feelings, she reminded herself that she had to emulate her late husband, the one whom she held as holding the highest caliber in conquering fear, and she used that train of thought to stay calm and assertive.

Ascentius, though not knowing for certain who the figure was exactly, was able to presume with a good degree of logical assumption. He knew that out of all the women that would be allowed to speak in a city such as Sanctum Novus that clung to traditional Citadellan patriarchal values, she likely had to be of prominence to be Decius's widow, Duchess Lucia of house Diem. It was she that Ascentius and others in Swordbane had heard about, while they were not sure if the rumors were true. Before Decius's rebellion, Ascentius always considered the dux to be fairly reserved and observant in staying celibate as a Black Wolf knight, the standard which was not rigorously enforced. Ascentius's suspicions, however, were removed when he asked who she was and what position of authority did she assume, while pointing out that it was not common tradition for the women of Sanctum Novus to speak as if holding a position of office to negotiate terms to their enemy after a battle.

Sure enough, the woman, with a sense of rebuke and command of authority, identified herself as Lady Lucia, Duchess of Sanctum Novus as well as the widow of Dux Decius. She stated that she was granted by both written decree and popular consent of both the citizens and the military forces of Sanctum Novus as well as the Remnant as a whole to act as regent and intermediary for Dux Decius until his heir would be of age to succeed him. Knowing that he had an heir was even more of a surprise to Ascentius as well as his present company, including Linitus and Marin. They had never known or suspected that the dux did in fact have an heir apparent and future successor until this recent revelation. Their expression of surprise could not be withheld.

Still curious about Lucia, Ascentius asked why she was dressed in such a manner while being still somewhat suspicious and pointing out that it was not tradition for Citadellan women, even of nobility, to be wearing clothes such as jumpsuit pants or leggings as opposed to the traditional tunic dress and stola. Lucia replied that she wore it for practical reasons for it was she who piloted the skybeast, and pride in her tone indicated taking responsibility for her role in destroying all six of the attacking ships from Swordbane.

Filled with rage, Marin interrupted by cursing the duchess and telling her that she deserved to experience the same fate as her fallen comrades and Marin herself would gladly challenge Lucia to open combat at the peril of their own lives. Lucia smiled while waving down her guards as they raised their weapons and were about to position themselves before their duchess to defend her if called to do so. Ascentius held his hand toward his daughter to signal and scold her not to let her emotions get in the way of their purpose in pursuing peace. Lucia grinned at what she saw as her adversary's own internal lack of a show of unity while the duchess responded by telling the Princess Knight that strong and formidable though she was, she lacked the same cunning and ingenuity to do what Lucia did in felling hundreds of troops on board the armed six floating vessels in a matter of minutes. Marin kept her calm while replying that it paled in comparison to her slaying the dux herself with one of her enchanted summoned spears, along with her lover Linitus sending Decius, his summoned avatar, and hundreds of demons back into the portal to hell from which the latter came and where the dux belonged.

Immediately showing a reaction of utter hate and disgust, Lucia told the Princess Knight and her companions, almost daring her, to give her one reason, any reason, to summon the rest of the city's military garrison along with the skybeast to slay them where they stood. Ascentius replied immediately (in order to defuse the situation between the two contending ladies) that it was in neither side's interest to continue this war further. He stated enough bloodshed had occurred; neither side would ultimately be able to mount a strong-enough force to retake the kingdom's capital, nor could the kingdom launch a strong-enough assault to capture Sanctum Novus. The war, as he pointed out, had reached a stalemate that was futile to continue, with no one side being able seemingly to have anything left to gain in further fighting.

Lucia turned and thought for a moment while nodding. She stated that she would think it over while consulting with her advisors tomorrow and that she would cede the ultimate decision to her dux. Ascentius, Linitus, and Marin, all looked at Lucia, mortified and shocked. Ascentius was still confused as Agaroman had alluded to the same thing despite the dragon-man king witnessing the dark lord's death at Mount Inferno. The rest of the king's present company did not know what Lucia meant by that, as she could tell from their looks. Giving a wider grin, she then told them that at noon tomorrow, they would convene here at the same place outside the desert city walls to submit terms for a ceasefire and an end to hostilities. Ascentius agreed, while Duchess Lucia turned back toward her dire-wolf chariot to ride back out and return to the desert city along with her warrior escort mounted on dire wolves.

Moments later, true to her word, Lucia had dispatched several dozen warriors composed of goblins, Citadellan soldiers, and orcs, along with two trolls to scout and retrieve the remains of various fallen kingdom soldiers from the wreckage of the battle. The remains were spread out next to the site where the first pyre was erected, and several more were constructed to accommodate the many dozens of recovered remains. By nightfall, Ascentius, Marin, and Linitus held torches to light the pyres and set them ablaze, with the prepared bodies being rested on top of the pyres. Ascentius uttered prayers in remembrance of the soldiers that fought for the kingdom and gave their lives. He vowed that going forward, even in his new form, he would do what he could to make sure that those who fought under him and in the name of the kingdom would not die in vain and that their lives would have meaning for the sacrifice they gave in building a new path and a new future for the kingdom. Before his present company, the king admitted the hard lesson he realized that some wars were not winnable or sustainable, and compromise while rebuilding and starting anew was the best way going forward, to honor their sacrifice.

Marin, hearing her father's vow while searching herself for inward conviction, quietly placed her hand over her father's dragon-scale shoulder while confessing and confiding that she would strive to do better just as much as he sought to do so. She admitted that they were human or at least sentient (given her realized consideration of her father's new change of appearance) and that no one can live a life without some fault in which to seek to better oneself.

Linitus, who overheard, tried to reflect to find what honest fault he could improve on. He found only one, accepting that he lost his fellow warriors in arms; he could not save all of them, and he could not save everyone, no matter how hard he tried and wished he could. Marin looked at him while placing her hand on his face and knew from his expression that he tried to find fault that would be reasonable to improve upon when he heard Ascentius's eulogy as well as Marin's reflection. Upon capturing his attention and looking directly at him when he turned without him saying any words, she told him not to. She told him that she was thankful for what she learned from him in not only fighting prowess but also in developing a bigger sense of her own morality and selflessness to serve others beyond her own ego as a knight, and to appreciate life when looking at the beauty of nature in the way that he had. She told him that his only fault (he nodded before she kissed him) was that he sought to blame himself for the actions and outcomes that happened to others beyond his control. It was time for him to move on to accept self-forgiveness as much as he had always accepted taking ownership and responsibility for his own actions and station in life. He ultimately had to concede in not blaming himself for the faults of others or the outcomes in which those that fought with him or under him died when he did everything that he could in his capacity. She was right and he knew it.

Linitus, shedding a tear, nodded and took the hand that Marin placed to his cheek to kiss it before embracing her. The two would hold onto each other for another minute before recomposing themselves. Though their display of affection was noticeable, none of the soldiers or Ascentius objected to it. They all knew by this point that the two respective heroes and adventurers loved each other, and those watching admired their raw and genuine display of it as well as how they consoled and comforted each other. Eventually, Ascentius interjected and told them that after the negotiations to end the war, it would be past due for the two of them to finally be wedded as husband and wife. He was ready to abdicate and appoint the two as king and queen of Swordbane.

Linitus gave a small nod though he really did not want to be a king, and though he learned to grow with a seemingly natural, innate talent for commanding and leading, he really did not want to lead, at least not a group larger than those he considered his closest friends and fellow companions: Marin, his soul mate and the love of his life; Peat; and Wyatt. Marin showed a similar expression, and while she did not mind being a ruling monarch, she shared the same passion as her elven lover and companion, of wanting to see more of the world by adventuring in the hinterlands beyond the walls of Citadella Neapola and even beyond the borders of the kingdom as a whole.

Ascentius could read and understand their expressions. Strangely, though he could live in his new form of life perhaps thousands of years, he wanted both Linitus and Marin to still rule and succeed him, both in position and in character. He saw them as the better fit to lead and represent the crown. However, he also thought that perhaps it was best to let his daughter choose her own fate and for her lover to do the same rather than inherit a role that was traditionally expected for one such as her to accept as royal blood even if it was not of her own choosing. Ascentius dwelled upon these thoughts while they were already on board the skyship just before midnight.

CHAPTER FIFTY-SIX

Farewell to War and New Welcome to Peace

Less than an hour before high noon when they were due to meet outside the walls on the south end of Sanctum Novus, Duchess Lucia had arranged for Agaroman along with several goblin shamans to pick up the holy relics and a makeshift altar that would be used during the incense offering and libation ceremonies to be transported to the location of the negotiations. Additionally, the duchess had arranged for several local porters and the city guard to erect two canopy tents. One would be providing shade at a table with chairs for her, Agaroman, and Ascentius along with his closest council to engage in negotiations. Meanwhile, the other tent canopy would be used to cover the makeshift altar and shrine while Lucia along with Agaroman would repeat the same ritual in giving offerings to both Calu and Laran as they invoked Decius's name. They would do this, however, only a few moments before Ascentius and his escort company arrived by teleporting back down to the surface from the lone skyship.

Upon arriving on the surface, Ascentius, Linitus, Marin, Peat, and Wyatt were surprised and instinctively reacted by raising their weapons defensively to bear arms when they saw what they considered the most frightening and threatening sight to behold: a translucent shadowy figure that had the features of a wolf with the basic physical anatomy of the parts of a man. Soon their faces dropped when they realized who it was, especially after hearing the figure speak. It was none other than Dux

Decius himself, or some apparition of him, they thought to themselves. Decius motioned calmly with his eerie translucent clawed hand while speaking, telling them that there was no point since he was already dead and they could do no direct harm to each other.

Marin first responded by asking how, while recalling that it was she who personally delivered what she thought was a mortal blow with her divine enchanted spear against Decius and his gargantuan werewolf avatar and ultimately sent him to the hellhole of Hadao Infernum. Decius responded awkwardly that he was indeed dead (while being slain cowardly, he added from his point of view) and he was indeed banished to hell. Linitus responded next, instinctively asking that if that was the case, then why was he here at the meeting to cease hostilities instead of being at the place of infernal torment? Why was he not in hell?

Decius took a moment while laughing. He then replied that because of his deity-like vesselhood powers and his ability and determination to overcome all obstacles, he made sure with his influence and powers while coming to an understanding with Calu and Laran that he was still worthy as their chosen vessel to keep his status both in the hell he was condemned to and in his newly summoned spectral form when called upon. He also mentioned that when summoned as a ghost, spirit, or shade, he would be able to commune and converse with those who followed the rituals of both Calu and Laran while calling upon and invoking his name. Upon finishing his explanation, the werewolf spectral spirit jeered in enjoying the reaction of his rivals even when he was dead, knowing with his own satisfaction for them to feel that they had been beaten and now had no way to stop him from spreading his influence even after his mortal passing.

Ascentius, giving a dragon-like shout and roar, condemned what he called the treachery of Calu and Laran to allow them to do this. But he was not completely surprised since Decius perhaps was the ideal candidate to still exert influence among his followers and future followers to continue his legacy in sowing death and destruction to appease the vile deity spirits. Regardless, after condemning what he saw as a divine injustice with Ascentius being a vessel for the divine spirit of justice, Sol Invictus, the dragon-man king knew that the peace had to go forward in order to save lives and harmony in Terrunaemara had essentially been restored with Decius no longer walking as a mortal and opening up portal gates to unleash hell in causing an excessive appeasement for Calu and Laran to grow in power to possibly overtake Sol Invictus as the chief deity in the pantheon hierarchy. For that, Ascentius was relieved. Still, he saw Decius's existence even after life, in the form of a spectral ghost, as being concerning, for this dark lord could very well possibly find other ways to violate the stability of the mortal world by using his personal influence as a returning ghost each time he was summoned, to sway others to commit horrid deeds on behalf of him and his cause.

Regardless, Decius interrupted while gesturing his hand toward the negotiation table. He walked with Lucia while she took her seat at one end of the table and motioned for Ascentius to stay on the other end and to be seated. Ascentius walked to the other end but declined to sit at the table versus standing. He did not fully trust Lucia or the two vilest figures that she was associated with, Dux Decius and the former royal wizard of the crown, Agaroman. Seeing their response, Lucia accepted it as their preference, while then moving from the head of the table to surrender her place to Decius.

It was hard for Ascentius to accept, let alone for him to convince those that served under him to negotiate a cessation of hostilities against the Remnant with Lucia, the sole figure who had been responsible for so many deaths at the last battle outside the city, leading the negotiations. But now to add additional insult, she was making an attempt to have Decius, or the apparition of him, take over in leading the negotiations on the Remnant's side.

Decius and Lucia, however, did not seem to care, save only to get an angry reaction out of them to know the dux, in one form or another, still had not been defeated permanently.

Ascentius, though not saying anything, gave a deathly cold stare to Decius while seeing the dux in his spectral form act as he would in his human form by going about the business of his office to engage in political affairs as if nothing had happened. Decius soon called the meeting to order while laying out a draft of the terms he wanted in addition to reviewing the ones from the list Ascentius gave one of his escorts to provide to Lucia. She would bring the draft terms of the treaty over and review with Decius. The terms of the drafted treaty itself were considered by both parties as being direct, straightforward, and while somewhat difficult, it would still be plausible to satisfy both parties. Both sides agreed that the Citadellan coastal lands, woodlands, and the grass-plain borderlands west of the Great Coastal Mountains would still be retained by the Swordbane kingdom as well as the dwarven fortress settlements just east of the north-south coastal mountains. The Remnant meanwhile would retain their de facto control of the high and low desert basins ten miles east of the dwarven fortress settlements and retain control all the way to the eastern borders that Swordbane shared with Marjawan to the south and east. Additionally, Decius was assertive in maintaining his faction's claim that they had control by de facto of the regions north of Sanctum Novus, including the Collis region and the Nordling barbarian settlements further north.

Being keen of the dux's ambitions even after his death while being a specter, Ascentius tacitly claimed that he could not dispute or give those regions for the dux to control since the kingdom's jurisdiction and sovereign rule ended at the borders of the barbarian regions of the Nordlings while acquiescing for the dux to lay claim to the Collis hilly and prairie basin region north of Sanctum Novus. Decius accepted while knowing that the only control that he likely could assert among the Nordling barbarian settlements would be solely Barbarum Aries (also known as Barbarian Place of the Ram). The other Nordling settlements that fell to Decius's forces that lay farther west toward the north coastal region of the western lands of Hesperion were likely to rebel and overthrow the dux's forces. By this point, Decius knew that the best course of action would be to allocate and reconsolidate his forces and possible fortifications to secure control for both the Collis region and Barbarum Aries.

Being calculating and displaying the facade of compromising, the dux offered that he would let Swordbane have the option to exercise suzerainty, or overlordship oversight, of the Nordling northwestern coastal settlements, including most notably Aegir-Hafn and what was left for Tribus Wald to be resettled and rebuilt by the surviving refugees from when it originally fell. Secretly, Decius thought that doing so opened the possible invitation for the Nordlings of the coast to rebel and possibly stalemate Swordbane into another occupied conflict with which the Remnant would not have to deal with. This included possible expected difficulties in maintaining control and possibly finding later opportunities to exploit such a possible future rebellion to its advantage should Swordbane be weakened as it was when the dux rebelled and campaigned against Ascentius after the weary twenty-year-long war against Marjawan.

Seeing through this possible design, Ascentius was again tacit by stating he would ensure to restore stable and prosperous relations with the Nordlings along the north coast to assert their own autonomy while helping them rebuild their settlements and reinstate his former sister-in-law to having de facto control of Aegir-Hafn as its rightful queen. Decius shrugged while stating that it was his choice and possibly Ascentius's loss for future expansion. Ascentius did not bother to reply or give any indication to react and respond to satisfy the dux's reaction of prompting his anger. Instead, Ascentius continued to lay out the next set of terms with respect to trade and the flow of commodities and people.

Both sides ended up amicable in wanting the same resources that they had each depended on each other from opposite sides of the coastal mountains. Decius wanted the many mediterranean and temperate-grown crops that Swordbane had produced to provide a steadier and larger diverse food supply for its citizens. Ascentius still sought the continued trade of commodities that would flow from east to west along the desert trade roads to pass through Marjawan's borders going over to the Remnant's border and eventually crossing over to Swordbane if the dux maintained the same flow of trade as was before his rebellion and intermittently since that time. Decius agreed provided there would be no taxation of the trade between both factions, after consulting briefly with his Duchess Lucia about the trade aspects of the negotiation. Ascentius was also in agreement.

Eventually, Decius turned over the other matters and details of trade over to his consort duchess. Lucia would handle it directly, given that she was deemed very astute in managing economic policies that involved the Remnant, especially Sanctum Novus. Upon finishing trade negotiations, Lucia had agreed to trade the palm date products as well as the exotic desert spices and plants used for incense, which Swordbane would procure to use for its own consumption and for its religious practices that both factions still shared in common with respect to observing the traditional Citadellan religious pantheon and ceremonies. Additionally, Lucia agreed that merchants from the kingdom would be able to trade in all parts of the Remnant's control, including the fertile and relatively productive wheat farmlands and livestock-grazing lands of the Collis region.

Lastly, nearing the end of negotiations, both sides agreed after Lucia brought up the families of many of their soldiers serving and fighting on both sides, to find a way to reconcile with each other despite residing and being on opposite sides of the two warring factions. The duchess was genuine, which Ascentius and all those present could tell about her proposal that the citizens of Sanctum Novus and the subjects of the crown under Ascentius be allowed to cross over to see their relatives on either side of their soon-to-be demarcated borders. Additionally, upon hearing her request and rationale, Ascentius and Linitus were fairly impressed, seeing that despite being their enemy, the duchess had shown a reasonable degree of compassion in her heart, at least seemingly, to the extent that Ascentius pointed it out and complimented the duchess on her display of being considerate for her citizens as well as their relatives that might have remained subjects of the Swordbane crown. Lucia replied that she did so only for the interests and concern of her subjects and that her heart rested solely upon them and her family dynasty founded by the dux.

After nearing the completion of negotiations and almost forgetting, Ascentius raised the issue of the beast sentient races of goblins, orcs, and trolls. Decius responded that just like with the Nordlings, it would be up to his discretion to still negotiate and define territorial status with the beast races, while clearly having no such intention to discard the allegiance he secured from them at Uruk-Kazaht that lay between Sanctum Novus and the Collis region as well as the goblin, orc, and troll settlements that lay east of Sanctum Novus and north of Marjawan's control. Decius planned to continue to rally all the beast races and their settlements under his banner and control and would not relinquish his authority and reign over them. He was, after all, still considered to be the dark lord to lead them, wielding full and unchallenged command among the beast races.

Upon finishing the negotiations, both parties signed two copies of the treaty for each side to keep a copy for their own records. Before departing with Lucia as he began to turn away, Decius suddenly heard a voice, Ascentius again, who decided before going separate ways to ask Decius what they had never talked about as profoundly before, the duke's reason for betrayal.

When prompted, Decius took a moment and told Ascentius exactly as the dux saw it in justifying. He held Ascentius responsible for the corruption that had been left unaddressed by the king when multiple cases of corrupt officials, including clergy, moved into the desert city from the coastlands, only to enrich themselves and engage in multiple instances of bribery, extortion, and illegal acts of indecency, not to mention the writs of indulgences. Decius explained to Ascentius that essentially Sanctum Novus was economically neglected and socially disenfranchised from enjoying many of the benefits that the coastal Citadellan cities had enjoyed.

The dux continued to elaborate further while recalling from the past of Ascentius's lack of regard for his own soldiers while the dux cited the past case of his soldiers getting slaughtered in friendly fire by multiple arrows that came in volleys before his betrayal, when he personally fought on behalf of Ascentius's orders. All these past grievances fomented into the pretext that Decius saw as a just war to rebel against Ascentius and forge a new path, a new beginning, and a new government that would be emulation in the image of the Lupercalian Empire of the ancient times long ago. Decius admitted it was revisionism in part, but one that resonated more as ideal and worth pursuing than the corruption, neglect, and malaise that existed in neglected parts of the kingdom such as Sanctum Novus previously.

Ascentius was resigned to accept Decius's reasons as simply lessons to learn from and move on, but while walking away from the tent to prepare to fly to the skyship, Decius made one final accusation as a pretext for Ascentius's unjust rule. The dux blamed the king for his lack of taking action to make meaningful amends and to pursue vigorous active justice not only for the corruption of Sanctum Novus, but also for a small religious caravan of Citadellan pilgrims that were ambushed while taking a pilgrimage outside the ancient Lupercalian capital of Imperia Capitolina. Ascentius, whipping his reptilian tail while unleashing a roar-like shout, knew what the dux was referring to. It was an event more than twenty years ago when the dux was found by Agaroman as one of the lone survivors of an elaborate plot in which agents of Marjawan hired Nordling barbarian mercenaries to raid the pilgrimage caravan. However, there was an important detail that Decius and Agaroman did not know. Decius mocked the king about his irony to prevent a war against foreign foes who had attacked subjects of the crown, including the most prominent of nobility, only to postpone and engage in it when it affected him and his family was personally affected. Ascentius completely blindsided everyone, including Decius, by correcting him and telling him that the real irony was not that he had postponed an external war by trying to save lives and prevent destruction, but that he was not able to stop a civil war from happening on his kingdom's doorstep but instead had postponed that also.

Decius, confused and dumbfounded, asked what he was talking about. The king told the dux that it was not just Marjawan that plotted to kill the pilgrims from the caravan by hiring barbarian mercenaries to be used as the main culprits, but it was Ascentius's own father, the former monarch, who had arranged the massacre by conspiring with emissaries from Marjawan to his court so they would both gain by killing the Anicii family, who were found to be embedded within the pilgrimage. Still shocked and even before

Decius could ask, Linitus himself had asked the same question everyone else wanted to know. Why?

Ascentius, knowing that it was time to finally confess the plot that even Agaroman did not know in such depth, assured all those present that he did not know about it until after his father's passing, when the former monarch left a letter for him to read in which the previous king confessed that he had conspired with Marjawan in order to secure the throne for his son, Ascentius, while eliminating any potential influential and prosperous adversaries that would challenge Ascentius's ascendancy and legitimacy to reign. The Swordbane kingdom, from time to time throughout its history, had noble houses among the Citadellans challenge the legitimacy of its rulers, believing that it was more suitable for them to rotate in sharing the throne among the nobility rather than pass the line of succession through one house and one male bloodline of succession. Despite their efforts, the most that the Citadellan nobility could settle for were periodic rotations of the Swordbane ruling bloodline to intermarry with a bride from a different house of the nobility for each succeeding generation. Some Citadellan families of the nobility, including the Anicii, however, had found ways to make the monarchy line jealous of them, including in being prosperous in commerce and attaining great wealth, even more so than the monarchy itself. By the time Ascentius was ready to be king and his father was near his deathbed, the former monarch conceived and implemented a plot to rid each of the Citadellan houses of nobility, starting with the most prosperous, the Anicii. Ascentius only found out when he received the letter of his father's will upon passing that included for Ascentius to inherit each of the most prosperous Citadellan houses of nobility's assets after a series of plots were exacted to kill the members of those houses, starting with the Anicii.

When Ascentius read the letter that was meant for him after the king's death, he admitted that he never forgave him and that he would show no displays of honor to his father after finding out his father's sins that Ascentius would inherit along with the throne. Ascentius was able to secretly prevent the other prosperous houses from being assassinated, but not the Anicii, who were targeted first. Ascentius admitted, however, that he was torn on what to do publicly, for if he revealed what his father had done, it would likely set off a civil war between the crown and the Citadellan houses of nobility, with thousands of lives being lost in a bid for him to keep his throne against the other Citadellan houses of nobility that would see him and his father as one and the same even when he tried to prevent and undo his predecessor's horrible plot. Instead, Ascentius ordered any records of his predecessor's plot to be burned in order to prevent such a foreseeable war from occurring, while admitting that there was no way to exact justice after the passing of his father other than to disown him and not honor his father's name for any event of public attendance. Ironically, his actions in doing so and his interest to build better relations with the Nordlings of the north coastal region, not to mention marrying one of them, put the king in the path of receiving the scorn of the very same Citadellan noble houses that perceived him as abandoning their culture in favor of the Nordlings, whom his male bloodline originally derived from. Despite the mild animosity, Ascentius was able to demonstrate his character as a monarch as best as he could to avoid civil war with the nobility until Decius's rebellion.

Ascentius apologized to Decius, while admitting that perhaps the dux was right about underestimating what he should have done in taking action more directly to address the involvement by Marjawan to hold their government and their agents accountable, versus maintaining a stance of inaction to preserve lives and avoid both external war and internal civil war that was bound to happen regardless. The king now said he recognized his supposed fault of inaction while recognizing the value of taking action when it is called for in a proportional response. He speculated also that perhaps nothing would come to change and that Decius would still set off a civil war perhaps under a different pretext.

Decius replied in turn, saying that Ascentius and he would never know. Only the grievances Decius mentioned were enough for him to justify rebellion. Ascentius admitted that perhaps so, despite his good intentions of what he thought was best at the time. Decius again countered that good intentions are typically used as the pieces to pave even roads to hell. The king admitted that if that was true and they were his good intentions, then it was Decius and Agaroman who had paved his good intentions in leading to a destructive destination. Ascentius's regret as such was not seeing it ahead of time. Decius finally countered that there would be no way for Ascentius to see it if he could not see the corruption and neglect that existed outside of Citadella Neapola to properly realize the severity in which it had to be dealt and in which the dux did so himself. Ascentius nodded while exchanging one last comment to the dux. He claimed that the difference between them both was, unlike Decius, he could learn from his mistakes and be a better person, a better king. He doubted the dux could do the same, nor have anything noteworthy left to offer, other than eternal spite, hatred, and war lust toward his adversaries.

The dux laughed with an awkward half-wolf jeering howl before telling the king in the form of a question of which one is better: the one who always will find something to learn and improve upon what one has already learned or one who knows everything there is to know in order to run things as he saw best and was able to justify by attaining the desired results? The dux essentially wanted to show the measure of contrast between the two of them may not be as clear to determine as Ascentius thought, depending on whose standard would be applied. For now, Decius was content to accept a non-answer, seeing that the king took harder steps before flying off with his dragon-man wings to board the lone skyship.

A few moments later, Linitus and Marin looked on while Marin held on to the peace treaty document. She saw the desert city from a few miles in the distance and realized that things would never be the same. This would be an era in which previous thoughts of what was right and wrong, what was known and not known had to be examined and taken more carefully into account along with meaningful action. Before signaling to depart the skyship, Marin looked several more times back at the jewel city wondering if she would ever see it again. Perhaps, perhaps not.

Upon arriving at the skyship as it was departing from outside Sanctum Novus, with the copy of the treaty in hand after verifying all the soldiers' remains of the last battle were prepared for funeral pyre cremation, Marin stood next to Linitus by her side. They both looked at the desert city from the skyship high in the sky. Linitus told her that no matter what was said, her father was a good man who faced difficult choices in order to save lives and that the elf himself both understood and would not blame her father based on his genuine intention to doing what he thought was right at each given opportunity. If he made mistakes, it was from what he regarded as the best and most moral means while avoiding the worst outcomes, even though he did not have the foresight to always know what those outcomes would be. Marin nodded while telling her lover that she knew. She hoped that her father would find some closure to forgive himself.

CHAPTER FIFTY-SEVEN

Forging New Beginnings

Across the western lands of the continent Hesperion from the centers of power of two rivals that had now shared borders of much of the lands they controlled, with one by recent domination while the other in preserving what was left of its historical domain. Two ruling lines from two separate factions had now begun the patchwork of forging their new postwar beginnings.

In the high desert basin, from the plaza forum of Sanctum Novus, Duchess Lucia and now her most trusted wizard advisor, Agaroman, assembled a large crowd of the local citizenry to observe formally the return of their revered dark lord and once-beloved dux. Lucia and Decius, conducting the same ritual again, summoned into the mortal plane the spectral spirit of Decius while announcing before the people that their dux, dark lord, and chosen vessel had made his return to celebrate his triumph after death. Though some in the crowd were skeptical when Lucia and Agaroman had proclaimed this before conducting the summoning ritual, their mood of skepticism and lack of belief quickly changed to miraculous and devoted conviction. Despite the reluctance among some of the doubters, this was the most pivotal and defining point to them that Decius was indeed the chosen vessel to lead them even upon death. Nearly all those present gave a form of salutation by saluting with their hands banging against their chests, others bending down on one knee, while still others prostrated themselves on both knees while setting their faces on the ground. Eventually, after processing and taking in what they had observed, still others were in disbelief or mesmerized by seeing what Decius had ultimately become, a translucent ghost with the appearance of a werewolf in Citadellan armor. Their conviction also came when after raising his translucent hand to acknowledge and silence the crowd, they had finally heard this apparition speak and knew from his voice, his posture, and use of words with a sense of command and ambition, that it was indeed Decius, the dux and acclaimed dark lord himself.

Decius announced that he indeed had found a way at least partially to conquer death by having his spectral spirit to be summoned to the mortal plane by those who conducted the ritual of offering to Calu and Laran before an altar with a lararium shrine just as his consort Lucia and his trusted advisor Agaroman had done. He would answer the call for those that summoned him if their intention was deemed genuine for his cause and if he thought their call to him merited his attention to appear before the prospective summoner. Again, the citizens and other residents of the desert city were in awe and gave their verbal praise in support of Decius, even in his new afterlife form.

As he prepared to give his first speech, he told the crowd of the treaty that they had signed recently with Swordbane, including with King Ascentius himself. Decius let them know from this pattern of thought of why they now existed as a separate political entity on their own and with a path opened to prosperity and prestige. He had told them that prosperity and prestige often arise when those socially deprived and disenfranchised of it have finally been exploited including economically to the point that the cycle would only end when such a people like theirs would dare to come together to lift off the yoke of Swordbane that had been cast on it since the kingdom's earliest years after the lone high desert city eventually opted to join as part of the kingdom in exchange for support in ending hostilities while seeking aid from other invaders, including hostile Nordlings that had not become part of the kingdom as well as Marjawan. Instead, as Decius pointed out, their city was pillaged from within by the corruption that Swordbane exported from the coastal regions in sending its most corrupt officials and clergy to the city to prey upon it. Decius reminded them that it was he who had ended this cycle of exploitation upon their city, upon them. He told the people that as the cycle to pursue prosperity and prestige continues, with its catalyst being social disenfranchisement and economic exploitation to enrich the other, its cycle would continue when the exploited and disenfranchised decide to end it and become the very same against their former oppressor. They had done so by waging war and taking lands belonging to the kingdom and their other enemies. They would do so to regain as compensation the same wealth that they had perceived themselves as being deprived of. This was retribution Decius alluded to in his justification for wreaking havoc across Swordbane as well as pillaging and occupying much of the semi-barbarian lands of the Collis region's inhabitants as well as against much of the barbarian Nordling tribes. The dux reasoned further that his people of Sanctum Novus would find others to form alliances with in having common ground and shared causes for pursuing the same goal of ending the marginalization by those who imposed it upon them and others. Decius indicated that such was already done in finding solidarity to form an alliance with the beast races of goblins, orcs, and trolls.

Lastly, Decius acknowledged solemnly and with a sense of emotion while turning and motioning toward his wife, Lucia, that the path to prosperity and prestige also depended inwardly for what the society's ruling class itself would do to ensure it constantly enfranchised all its subjects to a state of content and devoid of dissension. Such an achieving state would be one in which great edifices of monumental proportions and volumes would be erected to bring the people together and celebrate their greatness and achievement.

The dux, still looking and pointing to Lucia, announced before all the crowd that she, his wife and duchess consort, would help him lead their people to that path and realize it. The dux briefly went on to cite the duchess's accolades, including her charitable development of the city as well as her willingness and actual ability to lead and take command in prevailing against a larger enemy outside the city walls.

Decius had told them as an analogy while looking to his own past and referring to it toward the crowd. Many in attendance were familiar with hearing it. In hearing that just as the dux himself was once adopted by a pack of wolves that were family and would care and nurture him with their lives, both he and his duchess wife would do the same as the respective alpha male and alpha female of the city and the populace being considered their wolf pack. He told them that for those that were orphans and had no mother, his consort Lucia would care for them genuinely as she had before, to be their spiritual mother. Lucia nodded in showing her support while bowing with a simple nod before her husband. After a pause for a quick silent moment, cheers erupted, with the people giving a standing ovation to hail both the dux and his duchess as their symbolic revered father and mother.

Nodding while taking in the applause, Decius waited another moment before he closed his speech by letting the people of his city know that while he would lead them unto death as much as he would unto life, ultimately his son, Lucianus Canus, would be given the rule of the city and the claim of rulership among all the domains of the Remnant as a whole. Decius would focus on his own new domain to eventually take over. It would be the hellish lands he was banished to upon dying, Hadao Infernum. Though uneasy with his last statement, many of the city folks took it as his way of avoiding conflict with his son to ascend and have an opportunity to lay claim to the title and office of dux upon being of age.

After giving the speech for final applause, the audience departed after Decius gave his farewell in the public eye for now and prepared to retreat to his hellscape of torment, to he was originally banished. Before departing, Lucia had one of her servants come out with the infant wolfling, Lucianus Canus, for Decius to look upon. Though still in a stage of development in processing and understanding his surroundings with the various faces he encountered, the baby wolfling, just under a year old, stared at the specter of Decius and grinned with its baby wolflike teeth being exposed from its grinning mouth. The moment was touching for both Decius and Lucia to see their child content even while not fully knowing that he had lost his father at least in large part from the mortal plane. Decius motioned his hand in a gesture of almost placing his hand on Lucia's face to imagine touching her. Lucia nodded and imagined the same in moving her hand toward him though unable to actually touch as her hand went through the translucent projection or shade of the dux's summoned ghost.

Eventually, he departed while agreeing that aside from presiding over the daily briefs of the council meetings when summoned. More personally, Decius would also appear and spend time with Lucia whenever she called upon him. It was a pleasant departure when he was able to be there in his specter form, to no longer see the torment and fiery landscape of Hadao Infernum, where he became its newest powerful denizen. In time, he would explore it, familiarize himself with it, and find a way to conquer and rule over this new domain while usurping its leader. Decius would presume and come to find out that the current ruling occupant of Hadao Infernum did not embody the ideals of what the dux considered a true chosen vessel and dark lord to rule over such a horrid and evil place that was reviled by even its own denizens of torment and betrayal.

Meanwhile from the other center of power, along the Swordbane coastlands in the Great Bay of Swordbane lay the many crumbled buildings and rubble that covered much of the metropolis landscape of Citadella Neapola, which was once but no longer flourishing as it had before Decius's rebellion against Ascentius. Still, much of the ornate and prominent monument structures remained intact and were able to withstand the onslaught of destruction brought on by both previously warring sides from two occasions of battle.

Now a lone skyship appeared, hovering above the city streets. Within a sudden flash, a portal gate on the surface emerged, with Linitus, Marin, Peat, and Wyatt appearing while Ascentius, using his dragon wings, flew down from the skyship. Several of the victorious soldiers from the last battle for control of the city assessed the overall damage. They had begun working to bring order and collaborate with the few available engineers and carpenters. Ascentius quickly ascertained from one of the acting soldiers in charge of the situation and the city's current state. The soldier in charge replied that much of the city was obviously in need of repair, with starvation being an issue if the city was not provisioned with more food supplies as well as multiple streets being blocked with debris and rubble from the two battles that unfolded in the city.

Taking a moment to survey more of the city in determining a proper course of action, Ascentius allocated what soldiers he had available to help clear the debris and rubble. Linitus suggested to the king that the elf ranger would go on his behalf along with Marin to request food supplies from the nearest two major settlements, Colonia Aldion and Salvinia Parf Edhellen.

The king consented while also providing two brief signed and sealed written notes for each of the major settlements to know of his personal and formal request for supplies along with dispatching any available soldiers, masons, carpenters, and other related building tradesmen to help the long process of rebuilding the city. Ascentius confided to both Linitus and Marin while looking still about the widespread damage and dilapidated state the once-grand metropolis city was in that it would take time, but he would see to it that the city along with the rest of the kingdom would forge a new beginning and find somehow and some way to heal from the damage that was brought upon it by Decius. However, as he left off in indicating it, some part was felt differently by Ascentius, in acknowledging even in front of Linitus and Marin about his acceptance of the criticism for why the kingdom fractured.

Ascentius admitted that Decius was wrong in using the means that he did to attain the end result of an orderly and prosperous society. His purpose and means were in pursuit of imperial revisionism from the Lupercalian Empire days of old, and the dux was willing to destroy all those that opposed him, including bystanders if they still kept their fealty to the king before him. He was cruel and harsh, but at the same time Ascentius realized that Decius was right in explaining how Ascentius's inaction for major transgressions and crimes that happened during his reign festered an environment for someone like Decius to fill in that void even when it was, in Ascentius's mind, a misguided cause for further unnecessary bloodshed. The king had learned that he had to be more directly involved in the affairs of his subjects' everyday lives, especially among the subjects being less well-off to survive on their own means of resources. He admitted again to Linitus and Marin that he as king had neglected his duties, though not wittingly. These were duties that went beyond engaging in wars that he still considered justified and necessary. He admitted that he should have invested more time and more resources with the people in other parts of his kingdom versus simply exacting taxation from them, expecting them to contribute excessively, and leaving them at the hands of assigned jurisdiction with unwavering trust and without himself spending more time to have oversight in the day-to-day affairs outside the capital in places that were marginalized such as Sanctum Novus. He pledged that he would seek to do better and he finally understood what was required for a king to keep his kingdom together.

Marin was holding back after hearing her father's confession to her and Linitus, but eventually she did shed some tears and went to embrace her father in his dragon-man form. Linitus was also moved and told Ascentius that despite his faults he might find with himself, his heart was in the right place with the right intentions, and it was natural for all sentient beings to make mistakes. The importance, however, the elf ranger pointed out, was that one learns from those past mistakes, even the subtle ones, and makes changes so that one does forge a new beginning without making the same mistakes again.

Ascentius nodded and while looking at Linitus for a moment, embraced him. Eventually, Linitus, Marin, Peat, and Wyatt teleported back to the skyship and departed first to Salvinia Parf Edhellen and then later to Colonia Aldion to fulfill their mission in securing supplies and skilled tradesmen to bring back to the capital. Additionally, as a gesture of goodwill in receiving the king's new decree, the Comradery announced that each major settlement would no longer pay taxes to the crown but instead invest the collected revenue to use among their own settlements and address the needs that their people had, for which the collected tax revenue would be the funds to address. The king also noted that he and or members of his house, including Marin and soon-to-be son-in-law Linitus, would make more routine visits to each of the settlements to ensure that their local administration was responding and addressing the needs of the given subjects of each settlement.

As far as the capital, the king, or as his subjects now call him, Dragon King, was making strides in rebuilding the city and bringing back together the different communities that made up the city. The city's subjects began to call him that new title out of respect, gratitude, and pride of Ascentius's newfound vigor to assure him that they saw him for who he still was upon realizing his identity as their king in a new form. They, however, adamantly did not see him as a new replacement of tyranny in place of Decius's brief reign over the city. Ascentius was optimistic and eager to forge what he saw as a new opportunity and a new age for the Citadellan coastlands as well as the rest of the kingdom to prosper.

As the days went by and Marin and Linitus helped Ascentius in rebuilding the capital, the people of the city began to exert a more visible sense of pride and normalcy in going about their business as they had before, though it was difficult at times, given the trauma they still dealt with, including the loss of loved ones and being displaced, at least temporarily. The people began to revere Linitus and Marin, whom they began to call, with their Order of Comradery, including Peat and Wyatt, by a new title of recognition and appreciation, Champions of the Kingdom. The comradery of heroes had accepted the bestowed title with both fond appreciation and some reluctance, as opposed to being called simply by their individual names or as the Comradery, which they still preferred as their primary group name of association.

Eventually, Linitus and Marin did hold a wedding after three months from returning and rebuilding the capital. Though the king had planned a large grandiose wedding fitting for a royal couple, the king acquiesced to the wishes of his soon-to-be son-in-law Linitus that he and Marin would be wedded in a small wedding ceremony that would be held twice, once at the king's Royal Crown Palace and a second time at the elven city of Salvinia Parf Edhellen at the same spot that Marin, Linitus, and Ascentius had been divinely teleported to the cosmos plane at the pantheon of the divine spirits. The audience for both weddings was small and kept a quiet presence, but for both Linitus and Marin, it was more meaningful that way as they had Ascentius presiding along with a priest from one of the main divine spirits, including Sol Invictus and, more fittingly, Aritimi, the patron of love.

Upon finishing their second wedding ceremony, Linitus and Marin spent the next several days touring together and enjoying their company alone while spending it also at times with others, including Linitus's family house at one of the hamlets outside the walls of Parf Edhellen. Eventually, they would venture out further and explore the coastlands between Aldion and Citadella Neapola.

On one occasion, they would stay at a house with a fellow soldier they fought alongside and came to know well as a friend. This fellow soldier had retired to live with his family in a lone cabin house. One of his other guests came in and had traveled very far to see him. The guest was a Citadellan also and was apparently a cousin of the former soldier host. When inquiring and sharing conversation with the cousin, a deep revelation began to unfold more personally than Marin and Linitus had anticipated. This cousin was also a retired soldier who had come to see his cousin from a long distance. When asked by Linitus and Marin, the cousin and visiting soldier replied that he came in peace from Sanctum Novus and that he remembered them at both the first and second battles of Citadella Neapola. He served on board the skyship that Duchess Lucia had piloted in the second battle over Citadella Neapola (which later became known as the Battle of the Chosen Vessels, along with the standoff at Mount Inferno) as well as during the sky battle outside the walls of Sanctum Novus at the end of the civil war (which the Remnant called the Battle of the Dark Lord's Second Coming).

Shocked and dumbfounded, Linitus and Marin's faces were unsure of how else to react while the other figure assured them that the war was of course over and he had no personal ill will against the kingdom nor them, save only that he and other Citadellans from the desert region around Sanctum Novus believed in the dux to lead and guide them away from the corruption that had existed before in Sanctum Novus. He reasoned despite the dux's atrocious behavior, there was meaningful change done for them in which the desert region emerged out of a social malaise and they were optimistic about their future after the dux deposed and banished the many corrupt officials and clergy from the region.

Marin instinctively could not believe it and began to question how this recently retired veteran could ever support an evil monster like Decius over the king, not to mention portraying the dux as a misunderstood savior. However, she already knew, given his answer, and she had heard a similar explanation of reflection from her father for why the kingdom fragmented nearly in half. For her, it was still hard to accept.

Linitus, seeing the tense dialogue unfolding, took the cautious approach to defuse the situation with an open mind to seek further understanding from the soldier's perspective. The elf ranger motioned to his newly wedded wife while interjecting that the veteran soldier and cousin of their host had already explained his reasons in part, and they must find a way to understand and deal with it while sharing the respective veteran's perspective. Marin nodded, sensing that Linitus, her husband, was right and now it was time, as her husband said, to pursue the path of understanding and reconciliation, including with those that fought alongside the dux as former enemies.

After sharing with the soldier their stories and experiences including with the war, the soldier though no less different or changed in his preexisting thoughts about why Sanctum Novus had rebelled, admitted to them that he had wished that this war never had to happen, that if the city was not overlooked as much as he and his fellow Citadellan desert dwellers had felt economically marginalized, there would be no cause for rebellion. He did admit, however, that he had a new respect for not only his cousin that served on the other side of the war, but also Linitus and Marin, whom he knew about and had seen them fight from a distance to acknowledge they were perhaps every bit the legend and heroes of their age and were rightfully viewed by Dux Decius as the greatest foes, whom he told his soldiers to be aware of.

Though somewhat awkward in being complimented in such a way, Linitus and Marin simply nodded while the soldier veteran took a moment to pause and reflect solemnly that he was at least happy this war was over through negotiation and that too many he and his cousin knew on both sides had lost their lives and could no longer return to their families. He knew that whatever reason his cousin had to serve Swordbane, there was a universal sense of piety, respect, and honor that they had, perhaps more so within Citadellan culture, in being dedicated to the government and station in life as soldiers, that they felt a part of which would represent their collective interests and socially enfranchise them. The only difference, he said, was that his cousin's sovereign, the king, had more interest in the affairs of the Citadellan coastlands. Meanwhile, his relatively new risen sovereign, the dux, had been the catalyst to rise to prominence and address the affairs that mattered to the Citadellans of the desert, which the former sovereign failed to do, at least not sufficiently.

Though it was difficult to hear at first, Linitus holding Marin's hand to soothe her possible anger, felt her clenched fist subside into an open palm and knew that after hearing what they had heard, she was at peace as much as he was, at least to understand the war. One part, however, intrigued both of them, and they wanted to know from the soldier. They wanted to know how well he knew and thought personally of Decius as well as his wife, Lady Lucia. Marin had known Decius off and on throughout her adolescence and young adulthood whenever their paths crossed before he received the position of dux by her father. She knew of him as ambitious and pious in his own way, though she did not foresee the dark side of his character until it was unleashed against her father as king and the rest of the kingdom. Linitus had only known of Decius from their encounters and what the elf ranger considered the dux's betrayal and rebellion against the crown. They both wanted to know more of how this soldier saw his leader and what aspects Decius embodied that they themselves were possibly not able to see. Was there something that they could learn from him to go forward to understand and not repeat the same mistake?

The soldier, drinking a cup of water, took a moment before responding. When he did respond, he told them that he and all the other soldiers who had fought for the dux saw him as being one of their own; Decius was soldier, knight, and commander himself as much a regional appointed official. He knew how to relate to those who served under him. The soldier told them that the dux showed himself to be a man of the people: he focused on the locals of his settlement and region and aspired for them to no longer be overlooked but pursue a path of order and prosperity absent of any form of corruption. It was a path he spoke of that they as much as he had longed for since the days of old in the Lupercalian Empire. He was truly an inspirational leader to his people, but again the soldier admitted he would be cruelest and vilest toward his foes while relishing it. He knew how to instill fear as much as he commanded respect.

Finally, the soldier spoke of Lady Lucia when Marin wanted to know also about how she was seen in general by the desert-dwelling Citadellans as much as that soldier's personal view of the duchess. The soldier took a moment and replied perhaps more enthusiastically that the duchess was an impressive lady herself who had done much with being the consort of Decius, even prior to their marriage, as his concubine. The soldier listed several of her reforms and efforts to redevelop the desert city, including setting several food shelters to feed the most marginalized and using the city's revenue to set up orphanages for those children without parents, including possibly ones who had lost their lives in serving in the dux's army. He admitted that she truly was a compassionate person and ambitious. He credited Decius with finding a worthy consort to help forge a new beginning for Sanctum Novus. He also admitted that she in her own way, fought fiercely as much as the dux. He was present on the skybeast that she flew in from both the last battle above Citadella Neapola and the battle outside and above the walls of Sanctum Novus. She was determined and vengeful as Decius to obtain victory while also thinking about the people of her city as much as her revenge for her husband, the dux, in dying from the prior battle.

Finding solitude of understanding from his account, Marin confessed to the soldier that she and Linitus had defeated and slain the dux when he was opening a portal gate to the realm of hell at Mount Inferno. The soldier shook his head without being surprised and admitting he knew as much. He affirmed their revelation when he shared with them a copy of a manuscript that had recently been published. It was a biography of Decius and his life, including his most important moments. He gave them one to read while prompting further surprise of the Princess Knight and the elf ranger. They wondered at this point what their belated nemesis had ultimately become beyond his pale spectral form in the eyes of his subjects and followers. Was he a glorified hero? A dark lord elevated to a new deified status after death by his supposed beloved citizens? A still accepted and anointed chosen vessel? Though they were under the impression of Decius as being perceived as a dark savior from what the Sanctum Novus veteran disclosed, Linitus still pressed to ask him of how his people really saw the dux while asking these questions that came to mind. The veteran replied that Decius was seen as all of those things by the Citadellan people of the desert as well as by the sentient beast races of orcs, goblins, and even the trolls.

Hearing what was said troubled Linitus and even more so Marin, which the veteran could tell, and to bring some consolation to them, he assured them that though he held Decius his dux in high regard when he served under him, he thought it was time to move on and start a new beginning in life while making sense of an ever-changing world. It was one in which he thought some among the Remnant had become too fanatical for even him to tolerate in staying there, while noting that the dux and his family had been elevated to a religious cultlike status of either veneration for some or outright worship and divine status recognition. He admitted that he was not even sure if Decius himself was pleased or could control the tide and stem the flow of his glorified status even after death, while appearing as a specter. This was something that did not surprise Marin and Linitus, both being familiar with his new summoned spectral werewolf form and admitting to the veteran that they saw it firsthand when negotiating the treaty to end the war.

The veteran was amazed at how closely their paths crossed and pointed that out, with Linitus and Marin acknowledging. Linitus admitted they were perhaps destined as chosen vessels of their respective patron deities to cross paths and learn from each other.

Impressed and eager to still find common understanding with them, the veteran still offered further consolation, telling them that he respected them even as leaders on the other side and he believed that they were heroes in their own respects as much as he saw Decius and Lucia. Though still seeing them as evil and enemies even when not in a state of active war, Linitus looked to Marin while still holding her hand and replied that he understood where the veteran was coming from, even if he did not see the dux and his consort as heroes to those whom they led and fought for. The two were benefactors and patrons among their subjects, especially the desert Citadellans and the beast races even if they in Linitus's mind fought for the wrong side and for a cause that was not justified, based on Decius and his followers' actions despite the reasons that understandably existed, should have been addressed, and were used as a pretext for the dux's dark path and ascension.

The elf ranger and the Princess Knight feeling some sense of peace and common understanding with the veteran, decided it was time for them to depart. They bade their fellow warrior and host a farewell along with his veteran cousin that served on the other side. The cousin bade them farewell while reminding them that he still never held any ill will or resentment for them and prayed for them a safe journey and prosperous life that they would share together. Linitus and Marin told him that they felt the same in holding no ill will or resentment toward him while praying that the two cousins would find solace however they could in the new era that they were living in.

On a whim of a spontaneous decision, Linitus and Marin, unsure where to go at first, decided to head back to the capital and rendezvous with their fellow companions and champions, Peat and Wyatt. They would venture forth with the skyship, looking for the next opportunity to explore and adventure. As the western sunset approached, they held hands while walking side by side along the north-south traverse of Royal Road that stood out among the glistening grass and mixture of various trees that dotted the landscape with the mysterious redwood forests looming over from the east. They did not know what the new era would bring, but they knew they would face it together.

CLOSING EPIGRAPHS

Those who stand up and take action to effect change bring the most meaning. Those who sit idle bring the least meaning to effect change.
-Paul Joseph Santoro Emerick

Sometimes in war there are no clear victors, just survivors.
-Paul Joseph Santoro Emerick